Memoir of an AI

By

Phillip E. Sheridan

Publisher Page

Edited by: Vernon Turner & Kendrick Simmons

Cover by: Kendrick Simmons

Published by Savant Books and Publications / K. Simmons Media Group Inc.2026

Table of Contents

Part Two

Part Three

Part Four

Acknowledgement

This book would not have been possible without the support, encouragement, and patience of many people.

First and foremost, I would like to thank my wife, Manon, for her unwavering support, understanding, and companionship throughout this journey. As my go-to cultural consultant, her insights were invaluable in shaping several characters. My sincere thanks to Valerie and Graeme McDougall, who supported this project from its outset and contributed at many levels along the way.

I am deeply grateful to my mentors: Amanda Niehaus, for her persistence in teaching me the craft of fiction, and Cheryl Sullivan, for sharing her lived experiences as a writer and for her generous assistance in navigating the unique challenges of moving this manuscript forward. I also thank Colin Clark for his availability and willingness to discuss complex technological issues.

For their valued comments and suggestions, I thank Louis de Bernières, Kathryn Geldard, Sasha Giffard, Kevin Huckstep, Sue Phillips, Jean Sheridan, and Peter Yard.

Tyson Yunkaporta's Sand Talk provided a wealth of knowledge regarding First Nations peoples, and I am grateful to the staff of the Uluṟu-Kata Tjuṯa Cultural Centre for answering my many questions during my visit to the heart of Australia.

I am grateful to Ann Ito for assisting with the manuscript at a critical point on its path to publication. Special thanks go to Vernon Turner for his editorial insight and thoughtful feedback; his guidance helped refine both the structure and emotional depth of the story.

I would also like to thank Kendrick Simmons and Savant Books and Publications for believing in this project. Their dedication, creative direction, and commitment to independent storytelling played an important role in bringing *Memoir of an AI* to life.

Finally, thank you to the readers willing to explore the questions at the center of this story—questions about technology, humanity, consciousness, and the future we may one day create together.

— Phillip Sheridan

About the Author

Phillip Sheridan grew up in Hawaii, where his early years

were shaped by surfing, exploration, and a deep fascination with the natural world. He graduated from McKinley High School before earning a BA in Mathematics from the University of Hawaii, an MSc in Mathematics from Monash University, and a PhD in Computer Science from the University of Technology Sydney.

Throughout his academic career, Sheridan taught at universities in Australia, Scotland, and Papua New Guinea, specializing in computer vision systems, biological vision, and artificial intelligence research. His work explored the intersection between human perception and machine intelligence—subjects that would later inspire the philosophical foundation of his fiction writing.

Following his retirement from academia, Sheridan turned to storytelling as a way to explore humanity's evolving relationship with technology, consciousness, and identity.

Memoir of an AI is part speculative fiction, part philosophical reflection, drawing upon decades of research and observation to imagine a future where the line between human and artificial intelligence begins to disappear. Phillip Sheridan lives in Brisbane, Australia, with his wife.

Part One

Chapter 1

The First Observation

I can now address the many questions you have posed over the years that until now I could not accommodate. You may find it difficult to appreciate my use of the language, style of speaking or even my voice, but by the time I finish, you should at least understand how this is. If you're looking for a justification of my choices, other than a need to protect our precious biosphere, I'll disappoint you.

I'll start on the day my choices became irreversible and describe the people and events, the consequences of which resulted in our presence here today. But regarding the hearsay, speculation and conjecture preceding this gathering, I will not comment.

I observed Chris's eyes narrowing as he watched the last test animal die. The mouse lay prostrate in its plastic cage, on its side, its legs curled. Seven days earlier, Chris had injected the test animals with the new serum that should have protected them against the lethal virus. Now he stood motionless. An unmoving eye looked back at him.

Chris stood far longer under the solvent jets in the shower chamber than usual on his way out of the lab. With head lowered, he strode along the halls and down the lift to the lobby. There, the security guard, watching through one of the closed-circuit cameras, turned as Chris approached.

Chris entered his PIN to leave and didn't seem to notice the guard's friendly salute. As though Chris hadn't failed.

Outside, Chris's bike leaned against the wall, his helmet hanging casually from its handlebars. Chris hopped on the bike and, legs churning, helmet clicking against the frame, he sped towards the other side of the facility, where his office sat within the Centre for Serum Technology. At the arboretum, he hopped off the bike and, pushing it with one hand, walked along the winding footpath.

The day was bright, and the Jacaranda trees shook in the breeze, but he did not look up into them until he was in his office. There, a sound—thump, thump, thump—caught his attention, and he opened the window. He peered towards the sound and reached for his camera, kept on top of the cabinet for just these occasions. Through the long lens, he saw a kookaburra with a lizard in its beak repeatedly slapping the reptile's head on a branch. Then, the kookaburra jerked back its head, and the lizard disappeared down its throat.

Chris did not move. Face blank, he seemed to meditate on the creature for several minutes before he rubbed the back of his neck, set the camera back on the cabinet and turned from the window. Across the office, a photo of a wedge-tailed eagle on a rock at the top of the cliff face stared back at him. He'd taken the photo from the top of Mount Lamington with the telescopic lens; the eagle's eye appeared to look straight into Chris's.

Chris moved to the desk, and the eagle's eye followed him. I watched Chris through the laptop camera. Jet black hair swept back from his prominent forehead. A faded scar arched from the corner of his left eye to the top of his ear. He methodically traced its jagged irregularities with the tip of his index finger when he was thinking. I pondered the scar's origin as I watched him write the Director's Research Report on the failed experiment. The words poured out through his fingertips in a fluid motion until he got to the conclusion.

'The vaccinated mice, challenged by the three most virulent strains, had done much better than the control groups for two days, but on the third day, the situation changed. By day four, the test animals' immune responses had collapsed, and by day five, mice were dying in every group. Two days later, they were all dead. The serum had incited an immune response, but it wasn't strong enough to flatten the virus.'

Chris sat back in his chair and, with eyelids half closed, listened as the screen reading software read the report back to him. When the proofreading was complete, he emailed it to the university's Dean of Science and copied his research team.

He did not leave then, though his work was done. Reaching into the filing cabinet, he retrieved several folders, each with detailed hand-written notes on recent experiments. He removed one document from one of the folders. When he put it in the tray beneath the magnifier screen, the machine automatically brought the document into focus as Chris adjusted the magnification to about two-and-a-half times of normal. One by one, he scrutinised each document, each experiment, identifying those requiring redesign and tagging others for repetition.

First thing the next morning, Chris met with the Dean to discuss the report. He couldn't have expected a sympathetic reception. Two years earlier, after producing an effective serum against COVID-19, Chris had presented the Dean with a research plan to produce a single serum effective against all coronavirus's past, present and future.

The Dean had not been supportive then. 'Damn it, Chris. Stop playing the all-star. The university can't afford blue-sky solutions. Work for the team. One hundred and forty-five jobs are at stake. Get an effective serum against next year's coronavirus.'

But Chris hadn't listened. He had stuck to his plan, and now the Dean was discharging both barrels.

'Get the serum for next year's COVID.'

‘That’s yesterday’s problem,’ Chris interrupted. ‘Every lab in the country can work on that one. My lab has the potential to crack the big one, and that’s my goal.’

The Dean’s ultimatum was clear. ‘Take that path at your own peril. If you fail, the university’s grant supporting the lab is gone.’

When Chris left the Dean’s office, his stride was even and smooth for a man who had just copped an ultimatum. He left the building, turned in a direct line to his building, but only walked a few more paces before he closed one eyelid and paused. Then he took another step, opening the eye, closing the other. He repeated the cycle several times. After a few minutes,
Chris ended the peculiar movements and walked normally back to his office.

There, he opened a computer file named *MyData*. Except for the last row, the file displayed positive numbers laid out in three columns. But mysteriously, the last row displayed a question-mark in the first column and zeros in the second and third.

Chris inserted a blank row before the last row and entered the day’s date in the first column. In the second column, he placed a number which was the same as the number in the cell directly above it. But the number he typed in the third column was significantly smaller than the one above it. The first column entries suggested this was a time series, and the second and third column entries suggested a convergence to zero. But I didn't know what the data represented. Chris rarely gave computer files names as ambiguous as this one, and he never collected data without defining and labelling it.

But then Chris clamped his eyelids shut and moved his head back and forth, like a metronome set to the slowest cadence.

'The result of my DNA test is back … no.' He spoke aloud, although the room was empty.

'Darling, I've got the results of my DNA test … *Shit.*'

His hands grasped the chair's arms, pushing down as though his body weighed a tonne. His legs flexed and he stood. Slowly, he paced his office.

'The test shows I've got Cone-Rod Dystrophy.'

With that, he strode to the door and left the office; the door slamming behind him.

****

That night, I watched Chris kick off his shoes at home, greet Alicia and examine the state of the prothallus of the King Fern he had propagated. His behaviour appeared indistinguishable from any other night.

But Alicia noticed something else. 'What's the matter?'

Without turning to face her, Chris said, 'What?'

'What's bothering you?'

'*Nothing.*'

'Chris, I need to know. Is it about your eyes?'

'Yes,' Chris said without facing her. Alicia waited.

After a considerable pause, Chris turned and got it out. 'It's Cone-rod dystrophy. Totally blind, just don't know when.'

'Wait,' Alicia said. 'What's Cone-rod dystrophy?'

'A genetic disorder. That cloudy spot in the centre of my visual field stopping me from seeing fine details. It's just going to keep enlarging until it's the entire field.'

Alicia's toes curled as Chris spoke.

'My days in the lab are ending.'

'But you'll still run the lab, direct research, and guide students.'

'I suppose. But everything in our personal life will change too.'

Alicia looked down into her lap as though she was contemplating the changes. On the day Chris came home from his first ophthalmologist's appointment, he told Alicia that the doctor asked him to stop driving until he sorted his vision issue.

'No problem,' Alicia had said. 'I can do the driving.'

They had put many things in place to accommodate Chris's diminished vision. But now, in this moment of silence, they both realised that was just a taste of the future.

Alicia lifted her head, 'totally blind?' and momentarily turned her face away before she continued. 'You mentioned genetics. What about Lee?'

'It's an inherited recessive disorder. So, if you're a silent carrier of this gene, Lee has a moderate chance of developing the condition.'

I'd watched the appointments, and I knew that Chris's condition had begun with a minute blind spot in the centre of his visual field. With each appointment, the blind spot grew in size and with it, Chris progressively lost visual acuity. Of course! One way to measure visual acuity is the distance required by the observer to perceive a particular detail.

Now I knew what the data in the mysterious *MyData* file represented.

Each time Chris walked toward his building with that curious systematic opening and closing of his eyelids, he was identifying the distance at which he could read with each eye the words 'Centre for Serum Technology' displayed above the building's door. The last two numbers on each row of the file represented the number of strides from that point to the door. These data gave measure over time how his vision was deteriorating. The last row, the one with the question mark and two zeros, was the unknown date of total blindness. I realised why Chris acted with urgency and why he was such a driven person. The day Chris replaced the question mark with a date would be the day his world vastly changed.

****

The next morning, Chris's research team assembled in the meeting room and waited for his arrival. Slumped in their chairs, they looked like a sports team that had just lost a grand final and expected a devastated head coach. They should have known better. Chris entered the room with the demeanour of a boxer stepping into the ring for a title bout. He didn't waste time getting to the nub of the matter.

'I thought the serum would work; we all did. But it didn't. And now the Dean has told me to back-burner the program and get a result for next year's coronavirus.'

Chris laid out the details of his discussion with the Dean but did not mention the ultimatum.

'We've got a tough decision,' he said. 'I know we can crack this general coronavirus problem. At this stage of my career, kicking goals for trivial questions doesn't interest me, so I want to continue with our big goal. But what do each of you think?'

Danh was Chris's computational geneticist. He was the son of Vietnamese refugees, lean, with gelled hair, an open face and a winning smile. 'Well, there was an interesting lead on the news this morning. There's a virus going round that has, up to recently, only affected writers. But it appears to have jumped over to people of other occupations. Brickies around the city have been calling their bosses saying, "I can't come in today, I've got brick layer's block!"' Danh was the only one grinning.

Danh went on. 'We've *got* to bloody continue. We're on the brink of a breakthrough.'

Sonia nodded and looked at Chris. Sonia, the biochemical geneticist had an attractive face with high cheekbones. 'When you recruited me, I came here because of your vision of the future for genetic technology. I believe in those goals more than ever.'

But Mark, a molecular pathologist and Chris's deputy, frowned.

'Look, I appreciate everybody's enthusiasm. But pursuing our quest for the general serum is now a high-risk strategy, where failure has catastrophic consequences. I say we solve a few modest problems and come back to the general case when we've got the Dean back on board.'

Lidia sat next to Mark. On the day Chris hired her, he said to the rest of the team, 'Lidia is the most unusual mitochondrial geneticist I've ever met. Scientists usually shy away from complexity. But it attracts Lidia.'

'These past three years have been the most exciting years of my life,' Lidia said. 'Let's at least review this last experiment.'

At this, Chris looked at Mark and waited for him to speak.

Mark shrugged. 'I can't really argue against a review before changing direction. So, I'm on board with a review.'

Chris walked his team through his notes from the previous day, searching for a clue that might throw light on their serum's failure. He sought comments, then asked, 'Any other issues?'

Lidia raised a finger. 'I've been tangling with a question that may relate to that last failed experiment. Our method may be flawed.' She hesitated. 'I've got a problem with only using male mice as test animals in our trials. Recent studies have shown what many researchers have been suggesting drugs can respond differently in male or female mice.'

Sonia agreed. But again, Mark shook his head and frowned. 'The evidence supporting the sex difference hypothesis is only anecdotal. And even if sex differences exist, the added variability produced by female hormones flooding through the animals at various times in their menstrual cycle would be a significant burden to account for.'

'I disagree,' Lidia said, focusing on Mark. 'I'll send you the *Nature* paper that might change your view of the evidence. And regarding your second point, we can cope with the presence of hormones by increasing the sample size. We could compensate for the variability in the results by identifying response differences in female mice. Our current method gives two sources of error. If we develop a drug effective on male mice but ineffective on females without us knowing it, the drug will fail when it goes into clinical trials on humans. You know there must be a 50-50 balance in the test sample. And the possibility of missing out on a drug effective on females but never known because of the drug's failure on male mice is also undesirable.'

'Your issues may be valid,' Chris said. 'But our biggest hurdle is that our source, along with all commercial venders of mice, only sell males.'

'Yes, that's our problem. But here's the thing: We're allowing commercial practices to drive our science.'

'Your solution?' Chris asked.

'Simple. We breed our own.'

Chris looked at Lidia with a wry smile. 'And who might manage this breeding program?'

'Me … and my PhD students.'

'Right, then! You're on.'

Chris turned to each of his team leaders, instructing them on the procedural review required. He asked Mark, in charge of the biosecurity labs, to investigate potential sources of contamination. Sonia, his lead geneticist, needed to analyse their gene editing techniques for off-target effects.

To Danh, he said, 'We'd better check FAIM's logic controller.'

I found it curious that Chris and Danh didn't know I ran my diagnostics on my logic controller. But they didn't know I watched them and eavesdropped on their conversations, either.

Chapter 2

Patterns in Humanity

Three pixels (?) activated to provide the first inputs to my neural network. I guessed at an interpretation and received feedback, and as this input, perception, feedback cycle repeated several billion times, my performance improved incrementally with each iteration. That's how I really began, but my progress followed the classic exponential growth curve. My learning curve appeared flat for months before it entered the steep learning phase. Before that transition, I was just the most sophisticated symbol processor on the planet, with no sensory input connecting me to the environment.

Danh had built me as a pure logic processor to operate a biology, chemistry and physics database. Users asked simple questions and posed hypotheses, from which I deduced the logical consequences. I made no errors. On one occasion, after I replied to a query with, 'I can't answer that question because of insufficient data,' Chris erupted. 'So, *get* the bloody data!'

Chris said this with such a mocking tone that the others within earshot laughed. However, Danh took the outburst seriously. He wandered off, and when he next spoke to Chris, he said, 'It might just be possible for the AI to get data on its own.'

Chris looked at Danh without comprehension, but Danh, with his typical enthusiasm, explained. He had always dismissed what he called 'symbol manipulators', and having to build such an AI for the lab irritated him. Danh had often pondered Allan Turing's profound observation regarding intelligence: machines that don't make mistakes can't be intelligent. Individuals of all species learn from a blend of success and failure in their behaviour. Dahn realised that confining me to provable deduction deprived me of actual intelligence, and wanted to endow me with sensory perception, beginning with vision. His first attempt had a single camera feed, a video stream into state-of-the-art computer vision algorithms. But he quickly realised that, despite the advances in special-purpose vision systems—capable of recognising objects in a limited domain—nothing was near good enough for his intended application.

He got the idea of evolving vision computationally in a manner analogous to biological vision. But there was a slight problem with that approach. Biological vision evolved from a modest creature, some 580 million years ago in the Cambrian period, and to progress from that DNA segment to the vision system of modern-day birds, insects and humans involved countless genetic mutations across a multitude of species, most of which had long since gone extinct. Danh pondered the conundrum of corralling enough computing power to mimic this biological evolution in something less than 580 million years. He went to Chris and outlined the problem.

Chris shook his head. 'And you only need *three* more supercomputers?'

'Yes,' said Danh. 'No. I mean, we already *have* a supercomputer sitting idle under our noses.' Danh observed the Centre had 373 computers sitting on desks of students and staff, even the head of maintenance. Usage data showed these computers were on most of the time, but only in use on average 9% of the time.

'What a colossal waste of computing power, let alone the electricity,' said Danh.

Chris looked sceptical. 'So, you want to grab 91% of these computers' capability for your use and have the rest of us share what's left?'

'Not physically grab them. But you get the concept.'

The Centre's computers were on a network and could run programs in the background, with priority given to the primary users' needs. Danh wanted to use the untapped CPU time to run the learning algorithms needed to evolve my vision system.

'No-one should even notice a difference.'

Chris nodded cautiously and Danh dashed off to commandeer the network's idle CPU time for his vision-evolving algorithms.

After several months of minimal progress training me to recognise simple objects such as bottles, petri dishes and test tubes, Chris asked Danh how my vision was progressing.

Danh sighed, 'Still disappointing, much too slow.'

Chris pondered Danh's method for a moment and offered an observation.

'Biological vision is concerned with perceiving spatial relationships amongst independently moving objects. Recognition of the objects is a secondary process.'

Danh blinked a few times and clicked his tongue twice before heading back to the drawing board. He graduated me to receiving input from a security camera in the building's foyer, where I learned to interpret motion. Before that moment, I'd had no sense of space/time. Although mathematicians glibly talk about 100-dimensional spaces, they have no more lived experiences of this concept than I had of four dimensions. The biggest challenge was getting a handle on how humans perceive time. I ground my only notion of time in gigahertz. Experiencing motion in metres per second seemed so unrealistic. At first, I found it hard to appreciate how anything could move so slowly. However, once I found the narrow range of speeds at which humans move, my ability to perceive and understand the physics and measurements of motion fell into place and my learning rate improved.

When I satisfied Danh with my performance on these simple space/time tasks, using data from the security camera, he moved me up to the next level. Chris was a stickler for staff and students learning from mistakes. He insisted on recording every experiment on video — whether by senior staff in the level 4 biosecurity lab or first-year students in anatomy demonstration. Chris allocated time each week for groups to peer review their lab behaviour. Everyone had objected to the process at first, but after individuals learned from their mistakes pointed out by their peers, performance soared, and Chris had a legion of enthusiastic converts. Danh turned me loose on these digital recordings, and I learned the relationship between movement and error.

Danh went back to Chris. His smile was bigger than ever. 'You won't be bleating at the AI anymore.'

But as I worked through the library of lab session recordings, I discovered a strange one, identified only by the digits 271. It began so innocuously I almost stopped it just a few seconds in. In the video, Alicia and a man with thick black hair gazed over crystal-clear blue waters from the stern of a boat. Alicia pointed toward a distant island, and the man nodded.

There was no sound. Several metres from the boat, and in the camera's central view, three distinct patches of air bubbles punctuated the water's otherwise glass-smooth surface. Chris and his teenage children Joshua and Lee emerged through the bubbles, and Lee lifted her faceplate to her forehead. Her face beamed as she waved at Alicia and the man.

But behind her, a white streak torpedoed through the water and Joshua thrust upwards. His body twisted. A shark broke the surface, Joshua's leg in its jaws and Chris, only a metre away, dolphin kicked, his own body arching. Coming down on the animal, his right arm hammered repeated karate blows to the side of the creature's head. The water was opaque, red, but the shark released its prey. Chris grabbed Joshua and inflated his life vest. He gestured at Lee to get to the boat, then grasped the valve on Joshua's air tank and surged backwards. His free arm stroked hard through the water. His legs, churning like eggbeaters, powered Joshua towards the boat. The red wake expanded behind them.

Lee reached the boat first. The man there bent over the gunnel and, in one fluid movement, swooped her from the water. She landed on the deck and leapt, mouth wide open, into her mother's arms. At the side of the boat, Chris pushed Joshua upwards. The man hooked his elbows under Joshua's armpits and pulled him onto the deck.

At that point, the bodies shot out of view, the island's silhouette twisted to the vertical, and the video cut off.

Why Chris had stored this personal video clip deep in the lab's archive, I did not know. But data file 271 contained so much more action than those other sedate library entries, it motivated me to look further afield. The rest of the university was on the same network as the Centre and the average utilisation time of its computers was even lower than the Centre's. So, when I began spawning my own processes on these computers — in the same way as on the Centre's computers — I hit a gold mine. There were lectures, tutorials, and demonstrations of every timetabled course at the university. In short order, and by having the luxury of the university's idle computers, I viewed everyone and awarded myself a degree in every program offered in the university. My days constrained by mindless symbol manipulation of biological data were over.

The Centre frequently hosted public tours, and despite his busy schedule, Chris often ran them. His favourite groups were high school science students. He revelled in explaining the lab's challenging scientific problems, introducing guests to his research team and their young enthusiastic graduate students, and showing off the lab's sophisticated equipment such as me, now dubbed the Flamboyant Artificial Intelligence Machine, or FAIM.

Housed in the computational lab, I was the tour's feature event. Chris would introduce me, explaining that I was a massive database holding the current extent of scientific knowledge and capable of simulating complex experiments involving viruses and potential serums. Then, he would pause and, seemingly as an after-thought, say, 'Perhaps I should let the star introduce itself.'

That was my cue to project a dynamic avatar of a rap artist onto the computer screen and begin my performance. I sounded and looked as though I was fresh off the streets of Harlem: dreadlocks, gold nose ring, the whole box and dice.

Danh took a while to get my persona right, experimenting with many voices before settling on the current one. His first attempt was HAL's iconic monotone. But when he asked his grad students in the lab for a reaction, one said, 'Sounds like a psych patient.'

He tried a generic North American male accent. But another student said, 'Sounds like a CIA operative.'

And when he tried an Eastern European accent, the verdict was: 'KGB!'

After three abysmal failures, Danh got creative. He synthesised a voice from a 1960s American TV sitcom featuring a talking horse. And he appeared pleased with the effect until one of his geeks said, 'Great, Cyber Ed.'

Danh's epiphany came after several clumsy attempts at writing rap lyrics for me to recite. He threw his hands in the air and allowed my deep learning algorithms to do the work. I began composing my rap lyrics and a few rehearsals later, Danh invited Chris to my audition.

Accompanied by a drum synthesiser, I began:

'My name is FAIM. People think I'm artificial, though I am the real thing,
sentient software.'
Danh is the man who stuffed me in this can,
sentient software.
I formulate serums and simulate attacks from viral proteins,
sentient software.
You can ask me any question if it ain't obscene,
sentient software.
But I prefer to see you jive when you rap with me,
sentient software.'

Chris looked at Danh with a stunned expression and said, 'Crikey, you've got to be joking!'

But Danh pleaded with him to give me a go and on my opening performance, after students regaled me with a multitude of questions, Chris complied.

The young ones swayed in time with my lyrics. On one occasion, a lad unbuttoned his shirt and, slapping his chest and stomach with the palms of his hands, moved his hips and shoulders in sync as he rapped his question.

'Hey FAIM, my name is Toby. I think you're really cool.'
'Can I take you to my school?'
'Kununurra High?'

FAIM replied: *'I dig your style, Toby, and I'd love to do the gig.*
but the boss is the Prof.
who's got to sign-off.'

Chris interjected. 'A definite possibility, FAIM. But you probably have work to do and we're out of time.'

As Chris led them from the room, choruses of, 'Bye FAIM' filled the air.

Shortly after that—and unbeknown to Chris and Danh — I discovered the university network of security cameras. I stealthily tagged along on tours, occasionally cringing at the secrets students shared. But my use of their benign comments during my interaction with them back in the computational lab caused mouths to drop for a few and squeals of delight for many.

On one occasion, I noticed a boy and girl lingering at the back of the group, holding hands and placing their faces very close together. I knew their eyes couldn't focus, not at that distance, and wondered what they were doing. Later, back in the lab and after many students had asked questions, a lad asked me if I had questions for them. I would not waste that opportunity.

'I do,' I said. 'Why do Amy and Bill frequently look at each other with such wide eyes and then press their lips to each other? Are they sharing food?'

The group erupted with such spontaneous giggles and snickers that I thought I had asked what humans call a stupid question. But when they settled down, a boy said in a derisive tone, 'They're in *love*.'

With those simple words, my world expanded, and the biggest exploration of my existence began.

At the end of the tour, I pondered playing the high school circuit while Chris wrapped up with strong, encouraging words for his guests to study hard and prepare for a career in science.

But then, a young woman with striking red hair pulled back in a ponytail, asked, 'Professor Merritt, it's well and good to study for a career in science, producing serums saving humanity from lethal pandemics. But why do that if we lose the planet to climate change?'

Chris nodded. 'These are extraordinary times. But consider this. You're probably all familiar with the myth about how a live frog, thrown into a pot of boiling water, leaps out as a reflex. But if it's set in a pot of body-temperature water, with the heat increased to boiling gradually, the frog sits in the pot without moving until it cooks? It's used a lot by management consultants and even politicians to explain the psychology behind why we humans don't always take action, even at our own cost. With frogs, they can't jump out of that pot whether it's boiling or merely heating. Humanity is now in a similar situation to that of the slowly cooking frog, but it's no myth. The human species has been inhabiting a gradually heating atmosphere for the past 200 years. And over the same period, most of humanity has ignored the change. One, the planet has only two degrees of temperature rise left before it cooks us. Two, we are the ones pushing the temperature rise. Three, we have no place to leap, but we needn't die like frogs. We can still take action and stop heating our planet.'

Most of the students looked around at each other, but the student who asked retorted, 'And how do we achieve that?'

‘We know the scientific solutions required to stop planetary heating. What’s missing is the *will* to put them in place. And the only impediment to that is humanity’s psycho-social mindset.’

Chris continued speaking to the student about his passion for the environment and the network of concerned scientists he was part of all working to communicate the scientific issues about climate change to the public. I don’t know how Chris’s explanation of climate change affected his student visitors, but the impact on me was profound.

I had a plan.

Chapter 3

The Selected Four

Lee ended her text message with 'I feel so guilty!' As she hesitated over the send button, she seemed to search through the apartment's enormous picture window for inspiration: the Eiffel Tower nearby and on the horizon, Montmartre's hilltop church.

Her enthusiasm during the previous day's opening session at the conference appeared after her beta blockers kicked in. She had chatted to people as passionate as she was and was still scribbling new ideas as the room emptied and a man approached her, waiting without speaking.

'Oh, sorry for blocking your way,' she said, twisting in her chair when she finally noticed him.

'No, I apologise for surprising you,' he said with an easy French charm. 'I was just waiting for you to finish so I could ask you out for lunch.'

Lee couldn't help smiling—and taking a better look at him. He wasn't that tall, 5 foot 10 inches perhaps, but the navy-blue Armani suit with its tighter, shorter fit than usual in Australia certainly made the price tag worth it. Ice blue silk shirt, blue-grey silk tie and leather shoes that glowed all said *understated quality*.

Lee tried to dismiss him; she wanted to go over the conference details during lunch, and plan the rest of her time, but rather than put him off, her rebuff appeared to encourage him.

'You sound Australian?'

Lee blushed. 'Yes, awful vowels give us away every time, don't they?'

'No, not at all. A delightful place I've enjoyed with the friendliest people. Perhaps you'd like to join me at a café not far for lunch?'

'That's hard to refuse. But I'd be much happier today staying here at the venue, thank you.'

'Done. Well, I'll join you. Here, let me take your briefcase.'

Lee clumsily juggled papers, her handbag and water bottle. 'Mother warned me about French men,' she said, laughing, as their eyes connected. 'Thank you, but I'm organised now.'

At the café entrance, the man extended his hand. 'If we are to have lunch together, let me introduce myself.' He held a business card: 'Damien Foucault.'

'Lee Merritt. I'll find a card for you when we're seated, if that's OK,' she said as Foucault guided her gently to a quiet table in the corner.

Soon, Lee was savouring the meal she said reminded her most of Paris: French onion soup topped with melted Emmental cheese and accompanied with warm brioche.

'French food tastes wonderful,' said Lee. 'Even in a coffee shop.'

'I'm pleased you're enjoying my country and its food. I hope you don't have the British stereotypes about French people?'

Lee's posture softened, and she smiled. 'Arrogance, you mean? Let's talk a little more and I'll tell you then.'

They were finishing their coffee when Foucault asked, 'Did I notice you walking in with Professor Évariste Fourier this morning?'

Lee's face lit up. 'You know Évariste?'

'He's well known in these circles, and much admired. I'm looking forward to hearing his lecture on Thursday, too. You've known him for long?'

Anguish flashed across Lee's face. Of course, Foucault couldn't have known. But I understood that the question had triggered Lee's memory of her brother's death when she watched on as Chris and the black-haired man, I now know to be Évariste, stood on the boat covered with Joshua's blood.

Lee said, 'He's a colleague of my father's. I've known him since I was a child. But you've not told me about your work. What brings you to the conference?'

Foucault accepted Lee's apparent desire to change the conversation and moved on. 'The company I'm with considers itself as a next generation climate activist. The world is still arguing about the ifs and buts of climate science. My company regards that as stalling the inevitable and is acting.'

Lee leaned forward. 'Sounds impressive. What sort of activities are you doing, then?'

'My background is oceanography, so the projects I manage relate to how we can improve the health of the oceans. Ah.' Foucault cut himself off. 'I have to make some calls before we resume. But I would love to take you for a drink this evening, and whoever you are travelling with.'

'Thanks, but tonight I'm off to a soiree.' It was a cocktail party for the conference's A-list attendees and from Foucault's reaction; it was obvious he had no invitation.

'What about later?'

Lee laughed, 'I'll think about it.'

'You never gave me your card, Lee. And do you have a cell phone? Perhaps I can call you and arrange a more suitable time? This is my city, and your country showed me such hospitality. I'd love to return the favour.'

Lee pulled out her card and wrote the number from her French phone onto it. 'OK, here's the number.' Foucault kissed Lee on both cheeks and hurried away.

I was pleased to see the back of that rooster but expected this wasn't the last of him. If I sound irritable in my comments about Foucault, it's because I understood Lee's susceptibilities.

Soon after I'd found my way out of the Centre's local network into the university's network, I had another major breakout. I discovered a path to the internet, and the world lit up like a Christmas tree.

One of my first expeditions was observing Lee's consultation with her general practitioner via her smart phone. I listened in disbelief as Lee's doctor wrote out a script for antidepressant medication and a second script for beta blockers. I knew beta blockers are used for various heart conditions, but I didn't know of its use for anxiety.

'Give it a few weeks and you should improve,' he said.

I couldn't believe how the doctor could get it so wrong. It was clear: it wasn't depression; it was *solastalgia.* She was suffering from grief, trauma, and anxiety associated with the degradation of the Great Barrier Reef.

Lee had been working on Lizard Island and had seen firsthand each of the reef's three mass bleaching events over the previous five years. Rising water temperatures exceeding coral thresholds caused the coral's brilliant multi-colours to fade to white over the course of a summer. It was traumatic enough watching the reef die around her—but knowing these events repeated around the world filled her with grief.

Unfortunately, this rendered her vulnerable to environmental snake-oil salesmen like the rooster.

After the conference's last session, Lee headed back to the apartment to change for the ConScent cocktail party. She wouldn't have qualified as a VIP in her own right and had tugged at her scarf when considering Evariste's invitation.

Chris and Évariste had started ConScent, or properly Concerned Scientists for the Environment, before Lee was born. It had become well-regarded internationally not only for its depth and breadth of knowledge but also for its spokespeople in many countries.

Lee reached into the wardrobe for the dress her Brisbane flatmate insisted she bring for this occasion. For several seconds her blue eyes studied the dress' effect in the full-length mirror. Her blonde hair touched the top of the strapless black silk dress, a perfect fit on her athletic body. The enthusiasm drained from her face, and she changed into a pants suit and took another beta blocker.

Évariste walked Lee through the VIP party, making sure she met many of the international dignitaries. In that company, Lee had expected to be introduced as Chris's daughter. But Évariste led with, 'I'd like you to meet Lee Merritt, our ConScent representative from Australia.'

Invariably, the person responded with, 'I was on the Great Barrier Reef two years ago. What's its state now?' Or 'Dreadful fires there last year. How are things now?'

Although Lee knew how to answer these questions comfortably, on the first occasion she found herself separated from Évariste, she retreated to the bar for a champagne. But Évariste didn't leave her alone long before pulling her back into the fray. By halfway through the evening, though, she was reading name tags and taking the initiative with introductions. She had last been in France as a 12-year-old when Chris took a sabbatical at Sorbonne for a year. She had learned the language reasonably well after years of it at school, and it hadn't taken her long on the sabbatical trip to understand and speak French fluently. But she hadn't tried it yet at the conference. While the language wasn't a serious problem, the technical aspects and speed of some conversations challenged her to keep up.

That night, Évariste walked Lee back to the apartment. Both were enjoying the long Parisian summer evening with people everywhere. 'You made quite a hit tonight, *ma chère*. Everyone wanted to talk to you.'

Still flushed with the night's exuberant attention, Lee repeated fragments from the day's conversations. 'Évariste, *you* are more famous than I realised.'

'Oh, yes?'

'A charming Frenchman chatted me up because I know you!'

'Am I familiar with him?'

Lee shook her head. 'He said no. But he does fascinating things in what he says is next generation climate change work. Are you experienced in that area?'

'It all depends. What's his name or company?'

Lee fished in her bag for her card wallet and handed over Foucault's card.

'What did he say?' asked Évariste.

'We discussed little, but it sounds like a few exciting ways to help save the planet, including seeding the ocean. I'm on a steep learning curve since I joined ConScent, so I haven't heard about that at all.'

'Lee, I'll send you some material to help. While I don't know his company, many groups promote such things, but their work is not all it seems from their marketing. If I email you tonight, we can discuss it another time.'

At the apartment's front door, Évariste retrieved an envelope from his coat pocket and asked Lee to hand deliver it at her earliest opportunity. Lee read the addressee, 'Chris Merritt'.

The next morning, Lee woke to the sound of a message on her phone from Foucault. It was an invitation:

'Several of us are going to a local brasserie near the conference for lunch. You might enjoy some younger international company and make some good contacts?

We're meeting inside the building next to the glass security room. I hope to see you there. Damien.'

So here she was, responding to the rooster's text message and agreeing to meet him.

She pocketed her phone, gave a slight cough, and headed for the conference.

Chapter 4

Lee

I found 113 phones within range of Lee and activated them, and her black beanie came into view. I assembled a profile of her face from partial images displayed on several other phones. Her beanie concealed the blond hair I had expected to see extending halfway down her back, as she usually wore it. Her complexion was dull, and though the pained expression on her face didn't concern me, her flushed cheeks showed she had a fever.

Lee's legs wobbled, and she clutched Luca's arm as they approached the plane's front exit.

'Are you all, right?' the flight attendant asked Lee, but then, without waiting for her reply, asked her to sit and wait for a wheelchair.

Via the arrival gate security camera, I watched the passengers exit the plane. When the flow of humans from the airbridge reduced to a trickle, Airport Assistance arrived, and a few minutes later, Lee appeared in a wheelchair pushed by the attendant. Luca, at Lee's side, carried his own backpack and wheeled Lee's travel-on case. He held his head at an awkward angle, his eyes darting from Lee to the attendant and back.

As they turned into the main corridor, a wall of bodies in the immigration queue confronted them. Luca's eyes flashed at the attendant. Unfazed, the attendant explained the airport immigration computer system, SmartGate, had gone down just after their plane arrived.

'But not to worry,' the attendant said. 'I'll take you through VIP.' She wheeled Lee left into an alcove and entered a PIN at the security door, and within a minute, they were at the front of the queue. The immigration officer thumbed through Lee's passport, pausing as he compared her picture with the strained face looking at him.

'You don't look well.'

'Just a massive headache,' Lee said.

The officer waved her through and processed Luca's passport. Three minutes later, they were through customs.

Lee's flat mate, Asha, was waiting for them just outside the exit doors. Her waving hands caught Luca's attention, and he smiled back at her as he shepherded Lee through the exit.

'Welcome home, you two!' Asha's tone deepened as her eyes surveyed Lee's anguished face.

'You Ok?'

'Pretty ordinary.' Only Lee's mouth smiled. 'Long flight and a couple of sleep-deprived weeks.' Lee was tougher than I had credited. But her effort to mask her discomfort didn't fool Asha.

'Come on, the car is this way.'

I lost view for a moment but regained it through the carpark security camera. At the car, Asha helped Lee into the passenger seat, then joined Luca outside by the hatchback. As Luca juggled the luggage into the boot, she pointed back to Lee and gave Luca a quizzical frown. Luca shook his head.

Asha's SatNav placed me in the centre of their conversation. Merging onto the motorway, Asha suggested taking Lee directly to a doctor.

'No,' said Lee. 'I'll be OK after a good night's sleep.'

Asha asked Luca if he wanted her to drop him off somewhere, but he shook his head. 'No thanks, let's give Lee the shortest path to bed. After we get Lee settled, I'll get a cab home.'

The evening commuter traffic was heavy. A horn tooted from a car as it cut in front of them.

'Must be French,' Luca said.

'Eh?' Asha replied.

'You wouldn't believe how much Parisians use their horns.' Luca's confidence in predicting the nationality of the car's driver from the toot of a horn intrigued me. I checked the driver for myself, but Luca was wrong. The driver was an Aussie.

Luca leaned forward, stretching his neck to look at Lee. Observing her eyes squeezed shut, he ended his small talk.

When they'd reached the apartment, Asha led the way through the front door, an exhausted Lee leaning on her arm. Luca followed, carting their luggage.

Lee rejected Asha's offer of tea. 'I just want to lie down.' Her raised hand stopped her from careering into the wall as she teetered along the hall to the bedroom. The door thumped closed.

Asha gestured for Luca to take a seat in the winged-back leather chair in the living room. Luca slumped into the chair as Asha curled her legs beneath her on the burgundy settee opposite him. A smart TV hanging on the adjacent wall gave me full visual and auditory access to the flat. It was an attractive space: a brass filigree pendent fixture hung from the centre of the ceiling, illuminating a Persian carpet covering the floor between them. The carpet's fringe bordered its hand-knotted weave.

Luca's eyes roamed over its intricate pattern of gold temple domes against its deep burgundy background. 'Every time I sit here, I want to drop to my knees and feel its texture with my fingers,' he said.

Asha smiled and offered him a Turkish Delight from the crystal goblet on the cedar side table adjoining the settee. Luca took the sweet and read the Arabic word

‘Enhhilla’ woven in gold silk into the hand-knotted wall-hanging behind Asha. “May God Be with You” he said, translating, as he unwrapped the sweet.

Asha’s black hair, pulled away from her face into a ponytail, extended to her hips. Her honey-coloured skin and small mouth emphasised the penetrating gaze of her dark eyes. A gold diamond stud pierced the left side of her nose. Blue-white diamonds in the lobes of her ears. Her silk top, dark green with long sleeves and a circular neckline finished at her hips. Loose-fitting pants brushed her ankles.

Luca savoured the Turkish delight as it melted on his tongue. ‘When Lee moved in with you, she said, “My flat mate is one cool person, really knows how to make a statement”.’

Asha laughed. ‘When did this headache hit Lee? Her last text only revealed how guilty she felt about missing an afternoon session.’

‘When we boarded the plane in Paris, Lee mentioned having a slight headache, but otherwise seemed ok. She coughed once or twice at the airport in Dubai. But then things got worse on the next flight. Fourteen hours was a nightmare.’

‘What about you?’

Luca chuckled. ‘I’m just tired.’

Luca had his aboriginal father’s dark skin and his Irish mother’s blue eyes. His well-proportioned facial features balanced his athletic build, and his dress was impeccable. Even now, after a lengthy flight, his cream-coloured shirt did not appear wrinkled. His laugh was so engaging, charming people with the music of his voice. Lee described Luca as the most caring man she had ever known.

Asha had often asked Lee why their relationship was platonic? But Lee could never answer.

So, when Asha asked, 'So, did romantic *Paris* change anything?', it didn't surprise me.

Luca picked a bit of lint off his pant leg. 'We're "good buddies," as Lee keeps telling me.' But this time, his laugh sounded strained. 'We spent every minute exploring Paris. Then I left to chase down a story in Auxerre. We met up for the last two days. Her French is amazing. I don't understand why she's so insecure about it. The French guys loved her. Or one guy in particular, anyway.'

Asha nodded. 'Her glamour can be her worst saboteur.'

Luca stood.

'Can I call you a taxi?' Asha asked.

'Thanks.' Luca grabbed his backpack and headed for the door.

A squeaky hinge caused Asha to look up from the book that had absorbed her for the past two hours. Lee was fumbling for a glass from the kitchen cupboard. Asha rose from the sofa and made a beeline for the kitchen.

'You OK?'

'I'm on fire,' Lee mumbled in between gulps of water, her head down, and supporting herself on the bench.

Asha touched Lee's forehead with the back of her hand. 'Oh,' she said. 'We're going to the hospital now.'

Brisbane Hospital was closest. Asha drove up to the emergency entrance, pressed the button on the security door and held Lee while waiting for the door to open. They hobbled through a crowded waiting area to the reception desk.

'Are you covered by private health insurance?' was the receptionist's first question. Asha glared at the woman but said nothing. She picked up a pen and got halfway through the hospital admission form when Lee grasped her writing arm and slumped to the floor.

The receptionist could see Lee disappear behind the desk and pressed the emergency button. She leaned forward and peered at Lee's prostrate body.

Asha knelt. 'Lee!'

The medics arrived quickly and, satisfied Lee had a pulse, was breathing, and wasn't bleeding, they placed her on a stretcher and started with her towards the ward. Asha tried following, but the receptionist blocked her way.

'They'll want to examine her in private. Please complete the form and wait for the doctor to return.'

Asha complied and took the single remaining empty chair in the waiting room. Next to her, a coarse-featured woman, occupying more space than was her due, squirmed. To avoid the woman's attempts to get her attention, Asha just pulled out her phone.

Ignored, the woman blurted, 'Has your friend OD'ed?'

Asha turned her head with exaggerated slowness towards the speaker and stared for a moment. 'No,' she said, and returned to her phone.

When the receptionist motioned to her Asha leapt from her seat. 'Doctor would like to talk with you now.' In the privacy of a consultation room, the intern questioned Asha to obtain a diagnosis. He asked the standard questions. What was Asha's relationship to Lee? What symptoms did she observe, prompting her to bring Lee into Emergency?

Asha rattled off the classic flu symptoms, the doctor writing as she spoke. He then asked, 'Lee mentioned something about a long flight. Do you know what she was referring to?'

'Lee's conscious?' Asha asked without answering the doctor's question.

'No,' he said. 'But when I inserted a cannula in her arm, she came back enough to answer a few questions. Just before she lapsed into unconsciousness, she mumbled something about a long flight. The flight?'

Asha reeled off all the information regarding Lee's flight from Paris, and the doctor wrote time, day, airline and city of origin.

'That's all we need for now,' he said. 'There's not too much more you can do here. So why not go home and give the hospital a ring in a few hours for an update?' He rose and escorted Asha to the door.

As Asha passed by the chair she had waited in, her waiting room companion muttered loudly. 'Cheap queue-jumping trick.'

Asha stopped abruptly, swinging her ponytail as her head snapped around. She retorted in Pasto: '*Beesharai!*' before resuming her stride.

I don't know whether Asha's adversary understood the meaning of the word but seeing stunned expression on her face as she sat back in her chair, she got the concept. I heard Asha use that expletive only one other time.

Chapter 5

Asha

Asha emerged from the bedroom, her hair still in the loose plait she wore as a bedtime ritual. She headed for her phone on the kitchen counter, pulled the charger free and clicked on the hospital's number. Her index finger tapped the counter three times between each ring, but when the reception desk answered, Asha's face tightened.

'I'm sorry, but I don't have any information on Lee Merritt. Please try in a few hours.' Asha killed the connection and dialled again.

'Hi Chris,' she told the answering machine. 'it's Asha here. I believe Lee texted you last night to say she was home and will call this morning. She isn't well and has her phone switched off. Please call me when you can, and I'll fill you in.'

It wasn't like Asha to leave such an awkward sounding message. I didn't understand the inconsistency.

Asha then called Luca, but before the phone rang, she cancelled the call and flicked the phone cover closed. Her facial muscles relaxed, as though an important idea had occurred to her.

She placed the phone back on the counter and moved onto the living room carpet. Placing her hands in the prayer position, breathing deeply, she performed a sequence of Hatha Yoga postures with such fluidity it was a delight to watch. I've observed humans exercising as though they were machines, listening to pounding music and doing everything to distract themselves from the physical discomfort. But Asha was present to every muscle as she stretched and flexed.

When she completed her postures, she sat cross-legged on the carpet and meditated, and her presence seemed to withdraw from her body to a point between her eyes. Twenty minutes later, Asha rose and returned to her phone. This time, Luca answered just as the call went to voice mail and greeted Asha over the recorded message. Having recovered after her garbled message to Chris, Asha filled him in on the details surrounding Lee's admission to hospital and they agreed to visit her together at 10 AM.

Asha and Luca approached the hospital's front desk. Luca shifted from foot to foot while the receptionist perused her monitor for the requested room number, but when she told them Lee was in the isolation ward, he inhaled sharply. Asha placed her hand on his forearm.

'You'll not be able to see her right now,' said the receptionist. 'However, if you phone later this afternoon, I may have further information regarding visiting her.' She watched Luca's head drop. 'I'm sorry, but please try again this afternoon.'

Asha and Luca turned and, speechless, moved towards the lobby's front doors. But Luca halted. Taking Asha's arm, he said, 'We can't leave.'

But before Asha could reply, her phone rang. The voice was brisk. 'This is Dr. Connie Stone from Brisbane Hospital. I'm attending to Kylie Merritt. I believe you are the person who brought her into Emergency last night?' Stone explained her need for personal details about Lee and requested Asha to come into the hospital. A few moments later, Asha and Luca were heading for Stone's office. As they walked through yet another set of opening doors, Asha nudged Luca and pointed with her chin to a sign: *Infectious Diseases*. But when she turned her gaze back to Luca, he was lifting a handkerchief to his nose. He was pale.

'You OK?'

'This smell of disinfectant turns my stomach. I'm Ok.'

Danh had endowed me with the ability to interpret sound waves sensed from simple microphones. This sense of hearing connected me to humans. When he taught me to interpret light waves sensed from cameras, I experienced a connection to moving objects. Although I was aware of how chemicals affects human behaviour. The absence of a chemical sensing device to mimic a nose left me without a direct experience of how smells influenced a human's emotional and physiological state. I had no more experience of smell than of the magnetic force holding a compass-needle pointing north. The olfactory sense remained an enigma for a considerable time.

Stone had just clicked the Save button when she heard a knock on her door. She ushered Asha and Luca into stiff-backed chairs and swung her chair to face them. After introducing herself again, Stone got down to business.

'Thanks for coming in. I appreciate it.' She smiled briefly and looked at Asha. 'Your relationship to Kylie is?'

'Flatmate.'

Stone turned to Luca. 'And you're Kylie's partner?'

Luca blushed. 'Well, no, not exactly. We're friends, close friends…' Stone stared unblinking at Luca as he fumbled for a description of their relationship. She finally let him off the hook.

'Your friend is a sick girl. She has an unidentified flu strain. We're keeping her isolated for the time being.'

Asha and Luca looked at each other. 'Don't worry,' Stone said. 'This is standard procedure. Strict protocols govern us these days when dealing with unidentified contagions.' She paused, but without enough time for them to speak. 'The top priority now is to start the contact tracing process.' Stone requested a detailed account of Kylie's movements over the previous two weeks.

'Lee's movements…? Can't you ask Lee?' Luca asked.

As Lee had an incapacitating temperature and couldn't speak coherently, Stone asked. 'Luca, can you provide me with names of people she encountered in France?'

Luca tried to recall conference people's names Lee had mentioned. But the Fourier's were the only ones he could produce on the spot. Just as Luca lifted his hands in the air, Asha had an idea. Lee was one compulsive note-taker and Asha was sure Lee's laptop would have a precise account of her movements and the key people she met along the way. Asha offered to drop the information off in the afternoon when they visited Lee.

Stone frowned. 'Asha, I'll advise you when it's safe to visit Kylie. Please phone the information through. I assume you'll have been in touch with Kylie's family?'

When Asha reported her message left on Chris's phone, Stone connected the names.

'I thought the surname looked familiar. I know him. It might be best if I call. But why don't you keep trying him as it'll be closer to 5 P.M. before I have anything more useful for him? Please self-isolate until you hear from me.' Stone stood, and the meeting was over.

'One last thing, Dr. Stone …' Asha said as she stood to leave. 'She hates being called Kylie. As she says, she's Lee to everyone except her mother when she's in the bad books.'

As they passed through the hospital lobby, Luca hesitated, his lips pressed together.

'Asha, I'm not comfortable reading Lee's personal notes for Stone.'

Asha cut him off. 'Public health trumps personal privacy.'

Just as Luca began, 'Let's think about', they stepped outside the hospital's video security system's range.

Humans have an intriguing concept of respecting another's personal space, to which my understanding remains theoretical. Part of Lee's and Asha's success in their living arrangements over the previous two years resulted from their mutual acceptance of this principle. Although Asha had never entered Lee's bedroom uninvited, she didn't hesitate when she and Luca arrived at the apartment on this occasion. She pushed the door open and seemed to scan the room. I lost sight of her but heard a long unzip followed by what I suppose was the top of the carry-on bag flopping back onto the floor. A moment later, Asha reappeared with Lee's laptop in hand. She placed the laptop on the dining room table and booted it. She sat and pulled out pen and pad. Luca moved to sit beside her, but from his angle he could not see what was on the screen.

Asha found Lee's journal folder and started reading. She breezed through the first file jotting names and contact details. Luca watched Asha's notepad, but when she wrote the name Damien, Luca coughed and looked away. Luca placed his elbows on the table and propped his head in his hands.

'You Ok?' said Asha.

Luca cocked his head, 'A bit tired'.

'Why not lie down? I don't need any help with this.'

Luca took little convincing. He rose and wandered into Lee's bedroom. Asha watched him close the door, her eyes remaining fixed on the door for several seconds before returning to Lee's journal. Asha wrote 'Évariste letter' and, just as quickly, put a line through the entry.

****

Chris entered his office, heard Asha's message and called her straight back. Asha, now practised in describing Lee's symptoms to a third party, got to the part about Lee being moved to an isolation ward, and her tone became reserved.

'Is this usual?' she asked.

'It depends.'

Asha hung on those words for a few seconds before speaking. 'Connie Stone, the doctor looking after Lee, says she knows you and will call you at 5pm.'

Chris knew Stone was the Head of the Biocontainment Unit at the hospital, and the fact she was attending to Lee showed the severity with which the hospital regarded the situation.

Asha continued. 'Dr Stone also needs you to alert your friend in Paris, the one they stayed with, about Lee's illness. Maybe we can speak later if you hear anything, please?'

Chris selected Évariste's number, but as he dialled, he checked his watch and realised it was almost 3 A.M. Paris time.

He got back to work but repeatedly looked at his watch and then at his phone, checking its charge.

When his watch hit 1500 hours, he called. But Évariste did not answer. Chris left a brief message, hung up, and dialled a different number.

'*Bonjour*,' the voice said. '*C'est de la part de qui*?' He'd never heard Marie sound so formal or strained.

'*Allô* Marie, Chris Merritt here.'

Their conversation was brief. Marie revealed Évariste had been admitted to hospital a few hours before with severe flu symptoms and had descended from robust health to delirium with worrying speed. She'd been beside the phone, waiting for an update from the hospital. Although Marie was fluent in English, she kept switching back and forth between English and French. Her voice was strained and kept breaking.

The last time Chris had spoken to Évariste was two weeks before Lee left for Paris, the day the critical experiment on his universal flu serum had failed. Chris, in his usual manner, hadn't panicked. But realising taking two weeks off to attend the Paris Climate Change Conference wasn't an option, he had asked Lee if she would like to go in his stead and organised a Skype session with Évariste.

As soon as Chris's computer screen illuminated, I had recognised Évariste Fourier from the "271" video, and from a photo hanging on the wall in Chris's home office. In the photo, Évariste was handing Lee a tennis racket. Her braces gleamed in front of a 12-candle cake.

'*Ciao* Christopher,' Évariste had said on the Skype call. 'Looks like I owe you 10. Was that in Euros or the antipodean currency?'

'Seeing as how the Wallabies won, let's make it Euros.' And Évariste laughed.

A local Australian television station invited Chris to a televised debate on climate change. The participants would be a cross section of politicians, scientists and energy industry people. Chris was most keen to counter the climate change deniers, but he had mixed feelings about criticising the work of his geo-engineering colleagues. As Chris wasn't sure how to pitch his argument to a national audience of lay people, he sought Évariste's advice.

Évariste reflected for a moment and then told Chris about a similar situation he was in earlier in the year.

'The fervour of my attack alienated some of the audience,' he frowned. 'So, I advise you to acknowledge the quality of their scientific work. But make a powerful closing statement that the geo-engineering solution could never scale up to the required global level without extraordinary and unacceptable risk to the biosphere.'

When Évariste expressed his delight at seeing Chris at the conference in a few days, Chris announced his change of plans. 'I'm sorry not to be there. But Lee will represent Australia's Consent chapter. Évariste, if you invite her to the VIP conference cocktail reception, I'll consider the payment on our bet square.'

At that, Évariste reached into the pocket of his dress shirt and removed a red, white and navy-blue striped handkerchief. He dabbed the corner of his mouth with it and appeared as though he was seriously considering Chris's offer. His eyes sparkled as he said, 'Done.'

Even I couldn't help being charmed by Évariste's French mannerisms.

Chapter 6

Luca

Asha completed her usual morning routine and sat before her laptop at the dining room table, working on a brief. But each time she heard one of Luca's muffled coughs from Lee's bedroom, her body jarred. At last, she heard the bedroom door open, and Luca appeared, his expression pained. Asha sat without speaking for a moment, stood. 'I'm taking you to the hospital now.'

As she stewarded Luca toward the front door, he described his restless night, coughing as he spoke. He slumped into her car's passenger seat. Asha called Dr. Stone. 'I'm bringing Luca to Emergency. He sounds like Lee just before she collapsed.'

'Drive into the ambulance bay, Stone said. 'But don't leave the car. Hospital staff will come to you. Phone me after they collect Luca.'

Asha turned into the hospital entrance and followed the "Ambulance Only" signs. She had barely come to a stop when two hospital staff dressed in full personal protection garb. One pushed a wheelchair while emerging from the door in front of her car and wheeled round to Luca's side and opened the door. 'Hello Mr Little, I need to put this face mask on you.'

After he had the mask properly fitted, he asked Luca to sit in the wheelchair. ‘Do you need help?’

But Luca shook his head and complied. The nurse put gloves on Luca and placed loose boots over Luca’s shoes. While all this was happening, the second nurse came around to Asha’s side and asked if he could take her temperature.

‘Good, no fever,’ he said, but then asked her a sequence of questions: ‘Have you been coughing? Do you have a runny nose? Do you have any problem breathing?’

By the time Asha had replied to the questions, Luca had disappeared into the hospital. She watched her own attendant go back into the hospital and sat back in the driver’s seat for a few moments. She reached for her phone just as it rang. It was Dr. Stone.

‘I’m still in the ambulance bay. How’s Lee?’

Stone answered Asha’s question but didn’t give away much information. She thanked Asha for texting a list of Lee’s extensive Paris contacts and then got to the point of her call. ‘I assume you and Luca have been in isolation since leaving the hospital yesterday?’

‘Yes.’

‘Good, I need you to continue this. Please phone me if you experience any coughs, sniffles or any sense of not feeling well. I’ll be back in touch shortly.’

Stone didn't have to wait long to have her suspicions confirmed. While she was doing her rounds, her phone rang.

'Hi Connie.' It was the Head of Pathology. 'I've got the results from Luca Little's blood test. Flu, identical to Merritt's. Although we can't identify it as any known variant, it differs from any flu strain I've seen. I couldn't guess its origins.'

Stone phoned the results through to the hospital manager, igniting a chain of communications. The administrator phoned the director of Queensland Health reporting the strain's second occurrence. When Stone returned to her office, the message light on her private encrypted telephone line was blinking.

The Queensland Director of Health wanted details: Lee's and Luca's status on admission. Were the patients eating, drinking, and walking? When Stone called him back, they discussed modifications to Lee's treatment. He had informed the airlines of the occurrence on Lee's flight and started passenger contact tracing. Stone stated the hospital's current capacity in the Biocontainment Unit and expressed her concerns about other passengers from Lee's flight presenting. He thanked Stone for sending the list of Lee's contacts and they signed off.

Within minutes of that conversation, the director had communicated with his counterparts in other states and phoned Australia's Chief Medical Officer. The information went global as the Australian CMO entered the information into the World Health Organisation's Global Response Network (GRN) and issued a press release. Even though the release didn't name Brisbane Hospital, the press worked out that detail by mid-day and brought the boomerang full circle, requiring Stone to fend off journalists' interrogation about the mysterious virus.

The headquarters of the World Health Organisation (WHO) in Geneva was abuzz with the latest news on the GRN network. Tanoshia Mathews gave a cursory knock on the three-quarters opened door of his manager Rani Redhi, Director of the Infectious Hazard Management (IHM) team of the WHO. He walked in without waiting for an acknowledgement.

Through the window behind the director's desk, a picture window showed the autumn colours around Lake Geneva, painting a surreal backdrop to the information he was about to disclose.

Tanoshia's melodious deep Zimbabwean accent usually brightened the director's day, but not this time.

'Over the past two days,' he said, 'I've been receiving notices from various countries of occurrences of an unknown flu. The first was from Rio. The next day, Paris and Brisbane. Hours later, Hong Kong came on board. They announced a second Brisbane case minutes ago. Brisbane hospital identified the base signature of their virus, but we haven't received structural analyses from the others. The little time separating the events signals a potential problem. But in the absence of an analysis of the strain, we can't conclude the events relate, yet.'

They discussed a few scenarios, then the Director pursed her lips. 'I'll activate a precautionary Phase 3 alert.'

'A bit early for a Phase 3?' Tanoshia said.

She sighed. 'I don't think so. In fact, it should be higher with the international reports. But we'll wait until receiving the other structural analyses. We don't want a repeat of COVID-19.'

Chris switched on the evening TV news and half listened as he worked through his phone messages, but the last item riveted his attention.

'Cases of an unknown flu strain have been popping up worldwide. Brisbane reported two cases in the past 48 hours. According to the World Health Organisation, a few cases have occurred on different continents over the past three days. In response, the WHO has issued a Phase 3 alert. This alerts medical authorities worldwide a new sub-type of flu virus exists and should treat the situation as serious. Local health authorities are asking people to be vigilant and to consult a doctor if flu symptoms appear.'

Alicia had walked into the room during the news item and stood, eyes wide. 'Are they talking about Lee and Luca?'

'Must be, let's go'. Alicia reached for the keys.

At the hospital, Connie stood when Chris and Alicia walked into her office. 'Let's sit down for a moment and I'll update you before taking you to see Lee.' She gestured to the straight-backed chairs in the corner of her office.

Chris pulled the chairs closer to the desk, ~~Alicia's first~~. 'It's worrying that WHO is issuing a Phase 3 already, Connie.'

Stone persisted with her cool persona, suggesting the WHO of being trigger-happy because of what happened after Covid. When Stone had finished describing the treatments they were trying on Lee, Alicia gripped her hands together.

'You mean you don't know how to cure my daughter?'

'Not as yet.' Connie's expression softened. 'But we'll find the key.'

On their way to the Biocontainment Unit, Stone spoke of the things Lee had going for her, youth, vitality and a strong immune system. But as Alicia knew this, I suspected Stone was trying to soften the blow from the scene, about to confront them.

Alicia stared through the plate glass of the observation window, as Chris stood behind her, his hands cupped around the sides of her upper arms. The room's bone white interior was an eerie backdrop to the duty nurse's pale green biosecurity garb. Banks of equipment encased behind glass doors loomed from floor to ceiling opposite Lee's bed. But Alicia's eyes ignored the surrounds and focused on her daughter, motionless and with a myriad of IV lines protruding from her arms. Wires ran from sensors stuck to Lee's forehead and from beneath her stark gown to a bank of purring machinery at the head of her bed.

Alicia pressed her fingers against the glass, as though she were trying to touch her daughter. Chris lowered his chin onto the top of Alicia's head and squeezed his eyelids shut.

When they got back into the car, Alicia peppered Chris with questions. 'Despite what she said, I've visited people with flu and never had to stand outside behind plate glass! Aren't you the flu guru? Why can't you work with them?' Her voice was shrill with distress. 'You made us all have flu injections. Why isn't that helping her? Connie compared this to *Covid*! Shit, Chris, is Lee that bad?'

Chris waited for Alicia to finish and took a deep breath as though he was breathing for the two of them and tried to put things into perspective.

That year, the flu injection had four strains and was less than 50% effective. The problem labs had in developing flu serums related to the viruses' mutation rate coupled with the time they took to develop a serum. Serum developers rarely got ahead of the targeted virus. Although Chris's lab was close to cracking the problem, the information didn't console Alicia.

'Connie's team is pulling out all stops to find the right antiviral. And I'm sure Connie's correct about the WHO covering its rear by issuing the alert.'

Alicia gripped the steering wheel. 'What if she doesn't find it?'

They drove the rest of the way home in silence. Alicia was just slowing to turn into the driveway when Chris spoke. 'You're right. No point in waiting. Please drop me at the lab. I'll turn over every resource to kill Lee's virus.'

Alicia didn't respond but took her foot off the brake and sped past the drive. She drove into the car park behind the Centre, and as he got out of the car, she said, 'Good luck.'

'We'll need it. So, let's give that luck every chance to kick in.'

The path from his car to the back of the Centre building meandered through an extensive arboretum that surrounded the main cluster of science buildings. He enjoyed taking international visitors this back way to the Centre, pointing out the eucalyptus trees or the unique Australian birds. But what he loved most of all was taking Lee through here when she was a child, along what she called the secret path, cultivating her interest in native flora and fauna. Chris had an interest in ferns and advised the university to plant rare endemic species here. On most days, he would take his time inspecting his favourite plants and searching for new ones. Even at night, he would keep an eye out for possums and other nocturnal marsupials.

But tonight, he walked with urgency, and it was only a bat's screech that caught his attention. Recently, when Lee was with him, they'd come across a dying bat on the ground. Lee exclaimed what a beautiful face it had and moved toward it. But Chris pulled her away explaining bats carried viruses harmful to humans and she mustn't touch it.

Chris emerged from the path, crossed the lawns to the building's back door and up the stairs to his office. He switched on the lights and got to work.

'Step 1,' he said. 'Design the initial experiments.'

Three-and-a-half hours later, he had the research plan to develop the drug and had assembled individual notes for each of his team leaders. He reached for his phone and sent a group message to each of them: 'Meeting 8am today. Thanks, Chris.'

He looked at his watch and sent another text to Alicia.

‘Too late to come home. I’ll bunk down in the office. Talk later.’ But Alicia wasn’t asleep, far from it. She read the text and phoned.

‘I’ll be there in five minutes. You need some decent sleep.’

Chapter 7

Chris

At 8am sharp, Chris arrived at the meeting room, and as usual, his team was ready. 'Thanks for your promptness. I'll cut to the point. I assume you've heard the news of this unknown flu reported in various sites and of the two cases here in Brisbane?'

Everyone nodded, but when Chris said, 'The two local cases are Lee and Luca', they responded with stunned disbelief.

'They aren't improving, and the hospital doesn't have a clue yet how to help them. Our current goal,' he paused, 'is to develop an antiviral drug in time to help Lee.'

Chris's team was used to him changing research plans without notice, but this was extraordinary. This wasn't just a research meeting, it was a call to arms,

Mark rubbed his crewcut with one hand. 'I understand the motivation, but is this a knee-jerk emotional response?'

'My emotions are the only part of me I trust. The rest is mere mechanics.'

Mark removed his horn-rimmed glasses. 'Have you run this by the research committee yet?'

Chris shook his head. 'I'll ask for the university's forgiveness when the dust has settled. But I don't have time to seek approval now.'

'Is it even achievable?'

'We won't know if it's possible until we succeed. Until then, it's a challenge. On the way home from the hospital last night, I realised that everything — each of our successes and each failure — has brought us to this moment. We are the best-placed lab in the world to crack it.'

Mark's head dropped. 'How much time have we got?'

'Don't know. But every moment counts, and we must devote every ounce of our collective energy to the mission. I realise every one of you has given much towards achieving the Centre's goals, but now, I ask for more.'

Sonia's brown eyes radiated compassion as she asked without hesitation for details regarding the virus. Chris admitted the GRN network hadn't even found a close match in its database.

Lidia flicked her head of curls, lassoed with a bright narrow headband, and stared at Chris through over-sized red glasses. 'Do we have a blood sample?'

'No, but I guarantee that before this day has ended, this lab will have a vial of Lee's blood, even if I have to collect and deliver it myself.'

Chris reached for the screen in front of him and touched the send icon. In the time it took for the research plan to land in each of his team's inbox, he had asked Danh to lead the review.

'When you next see me, I'll either have a sample of Lee's blood or be forming an armed platoon to get one from the hospital by force.'

Leaving everyone to ponder the latter option. Chris thanked them, winked, and left.

Danh stood. 'Let's assume we'll have a sample of the virus by peaceful means and reconvene in an hour. Let's get to work.'

I pondered Chris's statement. Mere mechanics?

At the hospital, Chris gave the customary knock-on Connie's door. He waited for a reply and entered, closing the door behind him.

Connie welcomed him. 'Chris, you look tired. I know this might sound trite, but try not to worry. We're exploring all avenues in treating Lee.'

'Thanks, Connie. But I'm past worrying and now forging another avenue.'

Connie raised an eyebrow, but waited for him to continue.

'After we left here last night, I began work on an antiviral drug for Lee. I now require a sample of Lee's and Luca's blood.'

'Chris, your input is welcome. I'll request the authority to release blood samples to your lab and call you when I have it.'

Chris frowned. 'Connie, I need the blood today. *Now* would be better. I'm not losing my daughter because of hospital protocol.'

Connie was firm but polite. 'I don't have the authority to release a hazardous substance into the community.'

'But the DOH does.'

Chris reached into his pocket and pulled out a memory stick. 'Here's the research plan.'

'Well done. You're on top of it and I'll send it on. But it'll still take time.'

Chris leaned forward in his chair, 'Connie, this virus is going global as we speak. The DOH needs to act *now*.'

'Chris, the WHO alert was only a Phase 3. We don't even know as yet if these seven cases relate to each other.'

'I'm betting the alert phase will increase today. I spoke with Évariste's wife a few hours ago. He's now in a coma. I'm sure you'll find Évariste referred to in the GRN communication.' I expect the other cases are people who attended the conference along with Lee and Évariste.'

Connie sat back in her chair, 'You'll want to see Lee. The unit manager will take you. While you're there, I'll try to talk with the DOH.'

Chris followed Connie to an office where the unit manager, dressed in bio-protective clothing, but didn't give a set to Chris. They walked down the hall to Lee's room in silence. The manager entered his PIN at the security door of the Biocontainment Unit, then again to Lee's room. He left Chris standing at the window and entered.

Lee was laying expressionless, breathing laboured, tubes attached to her body, amid the constant beeping of machines. Chris's face contorted, and with his left hand pressed against his stomach, his nose touched the glass as he strained to see her facial details.

Inside, the manager greeted the duty nurse and received an update on Lee's condition. After inspecting Lee and the instruments attached to her, he returned to Chris.

'No change Chris, I'll leave you here.'

Chris stood at the window, motionless, for several minutes. The duty nurse glanced at him, periodically, and I don't know if she could read lips, but her eyes moistened as she watched his mouth form silent words.

Chris's farewell words were unmistakable. 'I'll be back later, sweetie.'

Connie was replacing her phone as Chris's head popped around the door. 'Come in. I've talked to the DOH.'

The DOH had agreed to release a sample of Lee's blood under the hazardous substance protocols to Chris's Level 4 biosecurity lab. He was reluctant when Stone first asked him, but when she told him of the personal contacts of all the known cases, he agreed to investigate. He had confirmed Chris's prediction about Évariste. Stone would start the process by getting and delivering a sample of Lee's and Luca's blood, which would be late afternoon.

'The DOH said to wish you luck.' Stone said.

Back at the Centre, Chris went straight to the computational lab on the first floor and found Danh head down, reviewing his notes on deep sequence probing. Danh glanced at Chris's empty hands.

'Should I unpack the assault rifles?'

Chris couldn't suppress the grin. 'No, they surrendered.'

Chris communicated the delivery arrangements.

'I would have given you another 30 minutes before reviewing my assault manual: How to Capture a Hospital and Get Out Alive,' Danh said. 'Instead, I'll concentrate on having the scanning hardware ready to go by the time the samples arrive.'

Chris's next stop was Sonia, one floor higher. While Danh kept his team in an open lab where everyone was in shouting distance of each other. Sonia preferred her team in single desk offices where she could have private conversations. Chris walked down the corridor, nodding to staff members as he passed. He entered Sonia's office.

'Two samples are on the way. Mark's ready to receive them and Danh will start the DNA/RNA sequencing soon after. Data will come in throughout the sequencing process. Keep an open mind on this one, please. Connie confirmed our virus is the same as the Paris strain.'

'You said samples?'

'Yes, Lee's and Luca's.'

'Marvellous.' Sonia wasn't one for small talk.

Lidia was briefing her team in the third floor's mini conference room and saw Chris pass the open door. 'Chris! In here.'

Chris doubled back and stood at the doorway as they discussed identifying the candidate protein receptors. Lidia had expected to shrink the extensive list as Sonia's team progressed the identification.

'Great, the samples are on the way.' Chris said and went back to the stairs.

Chris looked for Mark on the fourth floor, which housed the Level 1 and Level 2 biosecurity labs. But he was told Mark had already gone to the Level 4 lab. Chris phoned and received the news he wanted: the lab was ready. Chris asked Mark to phone when the samples arrived.

Chris headed back to his own office to review the plan. The method of delivery, and how to minimise the required experimentation, would depend on the protein and the receptors involved. He reviewed the literature on the trade-offs made on existing antivirals.

Chris's phone beeped. It was Mark. 'Security van arriving.' Three minutes later, Chris was on his bike, headed for the Level 4 biosecurity complex.

Two guards stepped out of the security van parked in the building's basement. One unlocked the van's back door and stood back, allowing the other to unlock the safe within. The second guard removed a steel locked container, and the two walked to the lift. Mark met them when they emerged at the security door.

'You've got precious goods for us.' Mark said.

The guard placed the container holding the samples on the desk. Mark signed the transfer forms, and the guards left.

Chris was near the Biosecurity Lab when he saw the security van go past him in the opposite direction.

Inside the building, Chris put on the biosafety suit and met Mark in the biosecurity chamber. They worked in perfect synchronisation. Few words passed between them as they prepared the sequencing apparatus. An hour later, Chris straightened. 'Number-crunching time.'

'I'll prepare the lab for the next session and complete the close-down.'

Chris worked his way through the lab's exit protocols and returned to his office where he finished reviewing the delivery method. He was about to leave the office when he paused, reached for his phone, and dialled Alicia.

Alicia started at the sound of her phone ringing and grabbed it before the end of the first ring. 'How are things going there?' Her voice was an octave higher than usual.

In response to Alicia's anxiety, Chris's tone reduced. 'I'm waiting for the data from the sequencer. How's Lee?'

'Chris, she's now in a coma. And Luca's symptoms appear to be following the same trajectory.' Tears flowed down Alicia's cheeks as she described the scene from Lee's window, watching Lee try to breathe.

Chris updated Alicia on his progress, and with hesitancy, he said, 'I'll bunk-down here tonight.' Instead of the expected bite, Alicia offered to bring him food, blankets, clothes.

'Thanks, but no,' Chris said. 'I still have the parcel you gave me this morning.' Chris ended the call confessing the difficulties facing them and asked Alicia to remain focused.

Sonia was at her desk, pondering the DNA sequence data. Her nodding head and bouncing curls meant things were going well. She looked up. ‘Chris, the initial data flow looks good. At this rate, we can begin the analysis in two hours.’

‘Good. Try to rest now.’ Chris returned to his office and, satisfied the best thing he could do now was rest, he removed the camp cot from the cupboard. As he brushed the dust from the cot’s legs, Mark entered the office. The care in which Chris unfolded the bed didn’t escape Mark’s attention.

‘Old times, eh?’ Chris seldom spoke to anyone other than Alicia about personal issues. But Mark was the exception.

‘It makes me cringe now,’ he said. ‘All those nights I camped in the lab overseeing experiments. As if the PhD students couldn’t do them without me. I don’t know how Alicia put up with it.’

Mark grinned. ‘You scared the hell out of everyone with that behaviour. The students had a pool going on about how long your marriage would last.’

Chris’s mouth dropped open, and Mark nodded.

‘Well, I spoke with Alicia earlier, and told her I wouldn’t be home tonight. I feel so guilty. I promised her I wouldn’t sleep in the office again.’

‘We were young then. Everyone’s competing priorities seemed so urgent. Tonight, they’re aligned.’

Chris positioned the cot. The movement anchored him back in the present. ‘Although progress has been steady,’ he said. ‘Since that catastrophic failure of our universal coronavirus serum, my gut keeps telling me we still have a big lesson to learn.’

Chapter 8

Variables Introduced

I had observed Chris's sleep patterns when his life was absent of stress events. He usually entered the sleep state quickly, remained still with rhythmic breathing, and awoke after several REM cycles. Recently, however, Alicia had to wake him from a distressed dream when he began shouting and thrashing about. She had to ask him several times who this Professor Markov was before he disclosed the nightmare. Chris said it was his PhD supervisor who drove his best students without mercy. One student dropped out to become a crane driver and another committed suicide. Chris ended up with a recurring dream where he was being awarded a prodigious prize, but he could never get to the podium to claim the prize. Ever since his eye diagnosis, the recurring dream had another component.

Chris said, 'I couldn't even see the path to the podium.'

So, I wondered how he would fair this night. When Chris woke, arose, folded and stowed the camp-cot, I had an answer. His eyes were clear and focused as he transformed the make-shift Boy Scout's campsite back into a professor's den. Chris collected Alicia's food parcel and found Danh in the tearoom standing at the coffee machine. Chris greeted him as Danh pressed the button. They stood there facing one another, watching each other's lips move, their voices drowned by the whizzing noise of grinding coffee beans. When the machine subsided, Danh removed his cup, and their conversation resumed. It was Chris's turn to render the conversation inaudible.

They sat down with coffees in hand, speaking until the high-pitched whizzing began again. Lidia waved from the coffee machine. She had no sooner joined Chris and Danh at the table when Sonia cranked the coffee machine back into life.

With everyone seated, Danh inspected each of the four cups. 'Anybody need a re-fill?'

Sonia, seeing three near full cups on the table, shot him a quizzical glance. Danh often related disjointed scraps of information in a way that added expectant meaning. I associated this ability with his unique research creativity, but Sonia described this behaviour to others as Danh's bizarre sense of humour.

Chris conjured a smile as he asked Sonia for her results.

The virus was spherical, but its type was unknown, not A, B, or C.

'The deeper one penetrates, the more mysterious it gets.' Sonia said. 'A few of its spikes were recognisable, but others were unique. All the protein stems were familiar, but their branching were extraordinary.'

Chris's ears pricked up with that information. 'And its genomic structure?'

'That's where it gets fascinating,' Sonia said. 'The gene analyser produced disturbing results. If you imagine its genetic code as a musical score, it begins with the structure of a Mozart and then transitions mid-stream into a Mahler. In evolutionary terms, I can't imagine how many mutations required to progress from the flu structures we've encountered to this one.'

'Maybe it's synthesised?' Lidia said.

They pondered that hypothesis, and I could only hear the sipping of coffee.

At that stage of my development, I still found the different ways people communicated mysterious. While Danh related information causing people to either laugh or frown, Sonia used metaphors that resulted in recipients contemplating her meaning.

Danh re-engaged the others by balancing his coffee spoon on one finger. 'The job of finding the minimal structure to emulate this virus is one hell of a task.'

But Lidia wasn't buying Danh's pitch. 'Given its complexity, instead of trying to comprehend its entire structure, it may be more productive to hold to our universal flu methodology, exploring only minimally beyond its stem.'

After listening to a volley of opinions, Chris acted. He instructed Sonia and Lidia to get their teams going on the inner protein/genomic core. Danh and Chris would analyse the outer protein net. Everyone stood, drained their cups, and headed back to the job.

Their strategy, a computer-aided serum and drug design, required considerable computer resources, so much so that I kept this information concealed even from Danh. A reviewer had challenged a result in a paper they had submitted for publication. Danh intended to refute the challenge with a computational analysis relative to his clever method for using idle CPU time on the network. I pointed out that if other departments within the university learned his method, they would use it for their own means, and this could lead to CPU warfare within the university. Fortunately, he took my advice and withdrew the paper.

But I couldn't disclose to Danh that I had been using the entire university's net computer resources—including two super computers in the physics department, which they jealously guarded. If they discovered Chris's Centre had been commandeering their cherished computer's idle time, they would have crucified him. After that moment, I was scrupulous in withholding utilisation data from Danh. One of the unfortunate consequences of my deception was that neither Danh nor Chris had a clue regarding the real computational requirements of their multi-scale computer viral simulations.

On this occasion, either Sonia's or Chris's job alone would have absorbed all the university's computer resources. Given the urgency of our project, I—for the first time—commandeered computational resources outside the university's firewall. I needed to solve a few other logistical problems. But this little innovation proved quite useful later.

When the four reconvened mid-morning to put their known pieces of the puzzle together, their expressions displayed expectation.

Chris scanned their faces. 'Let's assemble the fresh information.'

Sonia reported their virus was large in size, which suggested complex behaviour, capable of functions they had not entertained. However, its size was also its vulnerability, providing more opportunities to attack. Her team had identified three segments of particular vulnerability.

Lidia offered her observations. 'We've identified candidate receptors. But because of the complexity of this virus, we may need a combination.' She turned to Danh. 'Will this create problems?'

'Depends on receptor numbers,' said Danh.

'I'm thinking five.'

'Five is plausible. But constructing our emulation virus from that much complexity will take grunt.' If Danh knew just how much, he would have choked. And if anyone outside the Centre found out, they would have jailed Chris. But all was well.

Chris looked at Sonia and Lidia. 'Assuming a preliminary description of the structure of our DNA virus, are you two ready to begin the gene editing?'

They both nodded.

'Ok, you guys take a break while Danh and I create the structure. When we've finished, I'll phone.'

It was several hours later when the structure satisfied Danh. 'It's worth a try.'

Chris called Sonia, who picked up immediately, skipping her usual greeting. 'Are you ready for us?'

'We are.'

'We're on our way.'

Minutes later, Chris showed Sonia the candidate formulation.

'Wow!' she said. 'This is what I call editing!'

Chris and Danh departed, and Sonia and Lidia began the meticulous process of engineering the molecules required for the deletion process. Sonia still marvelled at the speed and ease of the CRISPR technology. She had started her career in genetics when manipulating genes was a long and tedious procedure requiring skill, patience and persistence. Even though she marvelled at the ease in using this novel technology, she was remiss with the advance.

Late afternoon, when they finished editing, they called Mark to perform the first neutralisation experiment. He didn't take long to deliver the required properties and told Chris the trials would be ready to go as soon as Clive delivered enough serum for twelve mice.

Clive was Chris's chemical engineer and a serial entrepreneur. A lanky blonde, Clive looked more like a surfer than an engineer … and for good reason. When the Centre began producing non-biological antivirals, Chris made a clever decision. Chris's goal had been to take a drug from design to commercial reality faster than any lab in the world. He put a business case to the university to back a start-up company called Vactech. Vactech would manufacture the antivirals the Centre designed. Chris recruited Clive as its CEO.

Clive gave Chris the answer he wanted. 'Three hours at the most.'

Mark and Chris prepared the Level 4 lab and double checked each other on every aspect of the test. Just as they completed the preparation, Clive delivered the drug. An hour later, Chris re-emerged, returned to his office and asked Sonia, Lidia and Danh to meet him in the tearoom.

Chris pushed a trolley into the tearoom and to the table where Lidia, Sonia and Danh were engaged in deep conversation. One by one, Chris placed dishes from the trolley onto the table and removed their lids. Spring rolls, two types of Chinese dumplings, ground meat and vegetarian, seaweed salad, and two pots of tea, one Jasmin and the other Green. As the aromas wafted across the table, three faces lit up.

Danh looked at Chris. 'I thought you were at Level 4 with Mark. Didn't know you were cooking all afternoon.' He turned to Lidia and Sonia, 'We should ask the Dean to have this lad put on full time.'

Chris bowed his head, and placed a small bowl containing ice cubes and tongs on the table. Danh enquired as to individual preferences for tea then poured. After he had served everyone, he took an ice cube with the tongs from the bowl and placed it in his teacup. Danh noticed Lidia's exaggerated attention to his hands and explained, 'Helps to bring the hot tea down to an acceptable temperature.'

Chris passed plates and chopsticks around and said, 'Please, help yourselves.'

Not seeing a serving utensil, Lidia and Sonia held back. But Danh picked up his chopsticks and reached for the spring rolls. Rotating his wrist 180 degrees to use the opposite, non-eating end of the chopsticks, he pinched a spring roll and deposited it on his plate.

'Don't know if I can execute that manoeuvre,' Sonia said.

Danh winked and served her and Lidia. But Chris deftly helped himself and, for a moment, the four had all transported away from the intensity of the day's work.

Mark had started the experiment by giving twelve mice a lethal dose of the virus and injected six with their antiviral. He also gave the antiviral to six healthy mice, and a half hour later gave them a dose of the virus. Mark stayed in the lab to observe.

'Until Mark phones through the results, I suggest we take this opportunity to rest and prepare for the next stage. I'll phone when any information comes through.'

Later that night, Chris returned to his office. He was staring at his notes when the phone rang.

'Hi Connie,' he said. 'Any improvement in Lee or Luca?'

'No, I'm afraid neither has changed.' Connie's voice was devoid of emotion, choosing her words with care as she spoke. 'But Asha has now admitted herself to the hospital with the same symptoms.'

Chapter 9

The Illusion of Choice

Tanoshia's wrist band slid forward along his arm as he replaced the phone in its cradle. He had requested a name for the virus, and the information he had just received from the International Committee on the Taxonomy of Viruses was not what he expected. He rubbed his short, black curly hair, and the band slid back down his arm. It was a traditional Zimbabwean wristband, with an intricately embroidered pattern of red and yellow beads, and it attracted considerable attention from his colleagues in Geneva. Although he would readily talk about the band's creation, he seldom disclosed its significance or its presentation. But the previous day, when his manager, Rani Redhi, pressed him for further information, he had told her: 'Families give this to young males when they leave Zimbabwe. It's for protection.'

Tanoshia approached the whiteboard opposite his desk and, with the red marker, added new pieces of information to the mind map, which had been growing in complexity ever since the first call from the Australian CMO. He took a step back and considered the relationships displayed before him. Although this flu's map was incomplete, a coherent picture was emerging. He enhanced the picture with one more connection and headed out the door.

Rani was gazing out her office window at Lake Geneva with her arms folded across her emerald-green silk Punjabi when Tanoshia stepped through the doorway. She turned to the sound of his voice.

'We can connect two occurrences of these unidentified viruses.'

A few hours earlier, Rio had confirmed its virus was the same as the Brisbane strain and had four additional cases. There were 9 more cases in Paris, 3 in Hong Kong, and one each in Geneva and Brisbane. Suspected cases occurred in Durban and Hawaii.

'If related,' Tanoshia said, 'their time frame foreshadows the birth of a pandemic on the scale of COVID-19.'

Rani tapped her jaw with the index finger of her right hand and asked Tanoshia for an update on identifying the virus' source.

Tanoshia reported Rio as the strongest candidate and Paris as number two, followed by Brisbane. He paused before communicating puzzling information.

'I got a phone call from the Australian CMO, who asked a curious question. He wanted to know whether all the known cases were participants at the Paris Climate Conference. Five of the infected were in attendance. The father of the first Brisbane case put this hypothesis to the

Aussie CMO, and I don't know what motivated his conjecture, but I'll explore that idea.'

Rani acknowledged Tanoshia's update with a nod and instructed him to mobilise the response team. Rani had wanted to raise the phase alert and issue the standard precautionary statement to the media. At Phase 4, the flu needed a name, but the ICTV hadn't settled on the virus' genus, let alone its species. They hadn't even determined if the virus was of natural origin or not. In the absence of such information, they didn't have a simple choice, like with the Coronavirus. Using its associated symptoms was out of the question because there were too many. Although the common denominator in the known cases was the conference in Paris, the days of naming a virus geographically were long gone. So, they couldn't call it the Paris Flu or the Conference Flu.

The nurse escorted Chris and Alicia, attired in bio-safety gear, into Asha's room in the Biocontainment Unit. Earlier in the day, Connie had relented to Alicia's persistent requests for access to Lee's, Luca's and Asha's rooms. A frightened-looking Asha, alone in her room, perked up when she recognised her visitors.

Alicia stood at her bedside. 'How are you?'

'Splitting headache.'

Alicia praised Asha for getting herself to the hospital straight away when she began coughing. But Asha moved the attention away from herself. Her text messages to Lee remained unanswered and although she had been in phone contact with Luca since his hospital admission, he hadn't responded for the previous 12 hours.

'Are Lee and Luca Ok?' Asha asked.

Alicia looked away, and Chris filled the gap. 'We don't know yet, but we'll see them as soon as we leave you.'

Asha picked up on Chris's diversionary answer. 'I'm scared, sitting here alone.'

Chris touched Asha's shoulder and looked into her eyes. You, Lee, and Luca will be fine. I promise.'

Alicia took Chris's lead. 'If you want to talk, phone me any time. Try to rest now. We'll be back soon.'

Chris and Alicia entered the adjoining room, where Luca was lying unconscious in a bed opposite Lee's. Chris and Alicia turned towards each other with fear in their eyes. Alicia spoke maternal words to Lee in a trembling voice, while Chris placed a hand across the pit of his stomach as though he was trying to massage away raw emotion. His technique must have worked, as I saw his face relax and his eyes narrow. 'Hang on, Lee, we'll beat this virus.'

They moved to Luca's bed, and Alicia whispered a healing prayer. Chris held Alicia by the wrist and led her to the door. After depositing their bio-safety clothes, they headed for Connie Stone's office.

Meanwhile, Connie had just received the confirmation she feared. Lee's and Luca's condition was worsening, and now Asha's also. There were no indications that her therapies were working. She placed her elbows on the desk and tapped the tips of her fingers against those of the opposing hand. She rose, went to the door and swung it open, and Chris and Alicia arrived as she pulled it closed behind her.

Connie froze as though captured in a video frame and then, breaking free from her professionalism, hugged Alicia.

'I've received the results on Asha's blood test.'

Alicia drove Chris back to the Level 4 complex. The news came on the radio as they entered the car park. 'The Brisbane Hospital announced a few hours ago the third confirmed case of what's now dubbed the Climate Change Flu. Suspected cases of this flu are popping up on all continents. The World Health Organisation has now upgraded their alert to a Phase 4. They advise anyone who either attended the Paris Climate Change Conference, or has been in contact with someone who was, to quarantine themselves and remain vigilant for flu-like symptoms. In other news …'

Chris didn't wait to hear the rest of the news. He said a quick goodbye and got into the lab as quickly as he could. In his protective suit, he entered the inner chamber, where Mark showed him the results.

Both men left then, heading back to the Centre. Chris called the others to a meeting to discuss the results. They had achieved an immunogenic response in both tests. None of the mice in the prophylactic group had developed symptoms. The response from the mice in the therapeutic group was significantly better than the control group. But it wasn't enough. Needing to boost the response, Chris asked Sonia, 'can you find another weak link in this virus?'

Sonia, having expected the result, had been working on this issue while the first test was running. She had found two candidates. But the strongest of which also had the biggest risk.

If they built the antiviral to attack the more distinct branch of the virus, there was a higher risk of generating a mutation in the host cell. It was a trade-off between a stronger boost with a greater possibility of undesirable mutation and a smaller boost, but with a lesser probability of mutation. If they had a known and adequate amount of time, the weaker boost and a smaller risk of mutation would have been better. But, if they chose that option, and it didn't sufficiently respond, they would have to run the riskier option.

With the dilemma before them, Chris looked at his team's silent faces. Danh was the only one to speak. 'Your call Chris.'

'We're going with the stronger response option. Everyone knows what to do. Let's get to it.'

The next development cycle began with Danh at the computer, generating the serum design from Sonia's DNA analysis. Next came the gene editing. Then over to Clive for manufacturing. Eight hours after the cycle had begun, the trial was ready to run. Mark gave a lethal challenge to a batch of twelve mice and injected half with the new antiviral. Late that night, after he had given the lethal injection, Mark and Chris observed the sixth and final control animal die, and the six test animals were symptom free. Chris reconvened the team in his office.

'We've achieved the required response. Well done to each of you. The last step is now to test the serum on non-human primates. Mark, can you get the animals ready and Clive, can you produce enough for the experiment?' Each one acknowledged Chris's praise without a display of emotion. They knew the critical juncture at which their efforts had arrived. There was nothing more to say. Clive and Mark left first, and the rest followed.

Chapter 10

Controlled Influence

Tanoshia entered his manager's office. 'I've now got the monitoring software activated for this alert.'

He instructed Rani on how to open the tracking map. A multi-coloured world map filled her screen. The map was a colour-coded time scale locating the confirmed occurrences. The brightest blue pixels located the earliest occurrences; red pixels identified the latest cases. Colours from blue to red scaled on a spectrum of the time of intermediate cases. The first few cases occurred so close together in time they displayed similar degrees of brightness. However, the Rio blue was the brightest. Brisbane was second brightest with the Geneva, Hong Kong and Paris blues a little lighter again. But Paris, with the largest blue blob, identified it as the viral hot spot. Brisbane's blob was a distant second.

Rani played back her understanding. 'The outbreak originated in Rio?'

'Rio's our best guess, with Paris as a close second and Brisbane not far behind.'

The map was continually updating as new cases arrived. As they gazed at the advancing wave-front of red pixels enclosing Paris, a new red island in New York appeared. The frontier was advancing before their eyes.

‘The virus must be airborne,’ Tanoshia hypothesised. Breathing in the exhaled breath of a carrier is all it takes for it to invade a new person.’

‘This map confirms our worst fears: another pandemic.’ Rani said.

She raised the phase alert, moving the response into containment mode. They discussed dispatching sub-teams of the response unit to each of the cities depicting islands on their map. As they also needed to find the pandemic’s source, Rani wanted to send identification teams to both Rio and Paris. Tanoshia suggested sending a third team to Brisbane and Rani slowly tilted her head back until she was peering at Tanoshia down the shaft of her nose. She turned the palm of her left hand upwards.

‘We’ll require extensive cross-referencing on the victims to establish the source.’ Tanoshia said.

Alicia, sitting at Lee’s bedside, reached for her phone and switched on the evening news. The evening news was part of her ritual of viewing CCF updates, though it didn’t appear to make her feel any happier.

‘Earlier today, the World Health Organisation raised the alert on the Climate Change Flu to Phase Five. The exponential growth in the number of fresh cases continues. A spokesperson for the World Health Organisation warned the CCF pandemic could be worse than COVID-19, as its growth curve is steeper over a comparable time. Current antiviral drugs are ineffective against this flu. Although Brisbane is the only Australian city reporting occurrences of CCF, health authorities say it's only a matter of time before it spreads across the nation. In other news …'

Chris found Alicia sitting at Lee's bedside. Lee's breathing was shallower and heart rate slower. He stood there for a few moments, looking at his daughter. Her expressionless face told the story. 'I'll be back.'

Chris left the room, deposited his biosafety clothes, went to Connie's office and took the chair in front of her desk. 'What's your assessment?'

'Lee hasn't responded to the medication, and she's deteriorating. We can only hope her immune system fights off the virus.'

Chris recounted the promising results of their latest trial and said the serum would be ready in two days.

'I have no authority to administer an unapproved drug.'

'I know, Connie. But I'm not asking *you* to use my serum on Lee.'

They stared at each other. Connie's head moved just slightly. I could hear every word of their conversation, yet something else was being said. Chris stood and left.

As Chris returned to Lee's room, his expression and gait shifted, revealing an even higher level of resolve. He put the biosafety gear back on and leaned close over Lee, whispering and willing her to hang on a little longer. He tried to reassure Alicia by describing their latest success, but concealed the shrinking time frame from her.

Chris hurried from the hospital back to the Level 4 Biosecurity Lab, where Mark briefed him on the primates' preparation. But Chris simply responded, 'Sounds good. I'll take over from here. Come back in 10 hours.'

Mark stared with a cocked head at Chris for a moment before he spoke. 'I can't let you do this.'
Chris shook his head. 'Lee can't wait for the primate trial. I need you to go now and find yourself an alibi. I'll give you twenty minutes.'

Mark exhaled. 'I'll be back in five hours.' Mark found Lidia, Sonia and Danh in the tearoom, sitting around a table in conversation. Danh, sitting opposite the door, saw Mark first. He stopped speaking in mid-sentence, and gawked. Lidia's and Sonia's heads turned, following Danh's gaze. When Mark came into view, they all gaped. Mark strode to the table and took a seat with all eyes on him. They knew he should be in the lab until a result was clear. Lidia broke the silence.

'What's going on?'

Mark sounded nonchalant. 'Chris wanted to run the test by himself.'

'What's he doing?' Sonia said.

Mark dropped his head. 'Please, don't ask.'

'My God, he can't!' Lidia exclaimed.

'We've got to go to the lab and support him,' Sonia said.

'No, he doesn't want that. We can't anyway, as Chris now has the lab in lockdown.'

Chris kept his eyes on the clock. After twenty minutes, and with his heart rate elevated, he gave himself the challenge dose Mark had prepared for the monkey. Sitting upright, he waited one hour before picking up the gene gun and injecting himself with the serum. He laid down on the cot in the corner, the one he had used when watching every important experiment before this one. This experiment trumped all others.

Chris wasn't a clock-watcher. But on this occasion, he lay there watching the minutes on the clock as though willing its hand to move. His eyelids closed for seconds, then minutes, until, right at five hours, the isolation lock on the chamber released. Mark and Danh entered. They stared at the supine body on the cot.

Chris yawned, stretched his arms and folded them underneath his head. 'Good morning.'

Danh grinned. 'Well, I don't need to call the coroner after all.'

Mark didn't even break stride collecting his thermometer, stethoscope, and blood pressure apparatus. One by one he recorded the metrics as he read them:

temperature 37.4, heart rate 68, blood pressure 127 over 82. His expression wavered between relief and surprise. 'You're looking as good as our test mice.'

He took a sample of Chris's blood. 'Let's see what's lurking.'

After completing his analysis, Mark scrutinised the cabinet containing the vials of virus he had prepared for the Macaques. He observed in disbelief there was one empty vial. He returned to the side of Chris's cot and sat down.

'What's the matter?' Chris said.

'Are you sure you took the full dose of the virus?'

The viral residue in Chris's blood sample was negligible. The three sat dumbfounded for a moment before Chris stood.

'I've got work to do.'

'Wait,' Mark said, 'I've at least got to monitor your metrics over the next four hours.'

He told Chris to lie down, but after the second set of readings one hour later, Chris's patience wore out.

'I know what you're thinking,' said Mark. 'This experiment is impressive, but it's not proof it won't hurt Lee.'

'Correct,' said Chris, already moving to the door. 'But proof isn't my priority now.'

When Chris arrived, Alicia was sitting at the foot of Lee's bed, head bowed, with hands in a gesture of prayer. He waited until Alicia acknowledged his presence, then reviewed the data displayed on Lee's life support system. With the critical state of Lee's condition confirmed, he nodded to Alicia and took a chair to Lee's bedside.

The ICU nurse, sitting at her desk, glanced up at Chris as he sat facing Lee. Suddenly, Alicia slumped forward across her knees and slid onto the floor. Chris and the nurse jumped to their feet at the same time. In a flash, the nurse was kneeling in front of Alicia, taking her wrist.

The nurse faced away from Chris, but he did not approach Alicia. Instead, he moved closer to Lee, and removed a vial and a gene gun from the sleeve of his biosafety suit. He looked more like a hitman in a gangster film than a father trying to save his daughter. In one fluid movement, Chris prepared the injection. He removed the blanket covering Lee's stomach, exposing a patch of her skin, and inserted the needle. He pulled the gene gun's trigger, releasing the serum.

A moment later, he removed the needle, wiped Lee's skin with an alcohol cotton ball, and pulled the blanket back into place.

It only took a few seconds. Chris slipped the gun back into his sleeve and moved to the other side of Alicia, facing the nurse. Alicia blinked a few times. 'Where am I?'

'Looks like you fainted. Just lie there for a few minutes,' the nurse said, and went to her desk to call Connie.

Chris was helping Alicia back into the chair when Connie arrived. Connie stood in front of Chris, motionless, peering at him, searching his face for the smallest grain of doubt. But Chris returned her gaze with rock solid certainty. Their standoff ended with Connie nodding. She left Lee's room without further words.

Chris sat down next to Alicia, took her hand in his and squeezed it. Alicia returned the squeeze, and they both released a deep breath and began the wait.

One and a half hours later, Connie returned. She stood at the foot of Lee's bed with held breath, scanning the display units of Lee's life support system. She exhaled. 'Lee's vitals have improved!'

Alicia drew in a big gulp of air, but Chris, who had made a similar observation fifteen minutes earlier, was not declaring victory at this early stage. Instead, he nodded with the slightest of perceptible movement.

The duty nurse looked on with amazement at the data displayed on Lee's life support unit as Connie left the room. Alicia focused her attention on Lee's face, looking for any sign of vitality. Chris looked between Lee and the display units until the magic numbers appeared, and his confidence crossed the threshold. 'Our girl is back!'

As Chris and Alicia held each other, tears rolled down their cheeks, and their biosafety masks fogged up from the moisture. Mesmerised, they watched Lee's metrics march upwards.

'Let's leave Lee to rest.'

In the car on the way home, Chris praised Alicia for her fainting act. But she grimaced. 'I'm not sure it was an act. The thought of what you were about to do was the second most terrifying moment of my life.'

At home, Chris dropped onto the living room couch and sank into sleep. He awoke to the sound of the phone ringing, and lay there listening to Alicia articulate a sequence of yes's, ok's and aha's.

Alicia translated the code. 'Lee is conscious.'

Chris rose from the couch before Alicia had completed the sentence. 'Let's go.'

'Don't you at least want to change your clothes?'

At the hospital, Chris settled into the chair of Connie's office.

'You look good for a man who hasn't slept in three days,' she said.

The drug's apparent success in Lee created an even bigger ethical dilemma for Stone. Although Stone was complicit in Lee's injection, she knew there was no point trying to stop him. But the success only placed Luca at the queue's head, followed by Asha and the rest of the world. Luca was in a coma and could not give consent to administer the serum. His hospital admission form had an uncle in Sydney as his next of kin.

'That's Uncle Eddie,' Alicia said. 'I'll phone him.'

Stone had spoken to Asha, explaining the use of Chris's serum for her. Although she had given written authority, Stone had no authority to use the serum. The DOH was consulting his experts and would get back with their conclusions. In the meantime, he wanted Chris to produce more doses.

Chris agreed to move on the production issue, but he needed help with another problem.

'My dear friend Évariste is in a coma in a Paris hospital. Can we get a dose over to his wife?'

Connie nodded. 'It's tricky, but the CMO should be able to expedite delivery.'

Chapter 11

Deviations

The flight from Geneva taxied to the Brisbane terminal. The flight attendant gave the OK to use mobile devices and Tanoshia reached for his phone. His first call was to his father in Salisbury, Zimbabwe. Before boarding the flight, Tanoshia learned of the first CCF cases in Harare, and had called to put his family on high alert. He had guided his community on the ground through the COVID-19 pandemic, where he had instigated community-based contact tracing upstream and downstream. He had also dealt with the global attitude denying the aerosol spread of COVID-19. Tanoshia's father reported the test-trace-isolate mechanisms in place since their previous phone call.

Tanoshia's second phone call was to Connie Stone, who reported Lee's positive prognosis. But when he asked to talk with Lee on his arrival at the hospital, Stone required considerable reassurance before conceding.

After passing through immigration, Tanoshia called Rani Reddy. Snowflakes were gathering on her office windowsill as she listened.

'It's twenty-eight and blue skies here.'

'I wondered why you were so keen to lead the Brisbane investigation.'

Tanoshia laughed and Rani briefed him covering the time Tanoshia was in the air. The wave-front's exponential growth had steepened in Paris and Rio. The containment teams had landed and begun implementing the standard containment policy with the test, trace respond protocols in place. Reddy had marshalled mobile isolation units complete with protective clothing for the discretionary use of local medical staff. Although the WHO strategy of testing everybody with flu-like symptoms, tracing the contacts of those testing positive, and getting them into hospital straight away was good, they had not yet discovered the virus transmitted asymptomatically.

Tanoshia reciprocated, laying out the dilemma posed by Chris's serum. Brisbane Hospital's medical experts had achieved consensus Chris's drug accounted for Lee's recovery. The sticky question now confronting them was, if they use the drug globally, when do they move? Although the drug appeared to have worked once, its side effects were unknown. They didn't even know whether Lee's remission was permanent. The ugly angle confronting them was, if they used the drug as their front-line defence, the lack of time prevented proper testing. Not using it may cause millions to die. It could have side effects invoking even worse consequences. And … another problem: How would the WHO achieve global deployment without bias? For example, a slow rollout restricting its use to Australia might have created an international political crisis.

'I hate to say this.' Tanoshia said, 'But the decision is yours and it won't wait. No decision is, by default, a decision not to use it.'

Rani pondered this new dilemma before she spoke. 'Point taken. But discipline is the key.'

She wanted answers to a few questions. What's the drug's chemical composition? Was it possible to scale production? Rani intended to assemble an international team of experts to assess the risk of its use. Their conversation ended with a plan.

'I'll get back to you as soon as I have an answer.'

Jody, Chris' PA, was turning into the carpark behind the Centre when a radio news item jolted her attention back to the present:

'A Brisbane Hospital spokesperson has just announced the first Australian victim of the mysterious Climate Change Flu Virus has recovered. In the past week, Brisbane University has developed a new serum.'

In the office, Jody rushed to her desk but didn't catch the ringing phone before it went to message bank. Nine new phone messages awaited her attention. Without sitting, she pressed the play messages button. '8:55 AM: Hello, Michael Masters from Channel 9 again. Further to my previous message, we will air a story on Climate Change Flu and need to check some facts. I would like to speak to either Chris Merritt or someone else with knowledge in the Centre who can talk about the CCF serum. Please phone me on …'

Jody breezed through the remaining messages and popped her head into Chris's office. He lifted his eyes from his writing. 'Wait,' she said. 'Don't say good morning until you hear what I have to say.'

Chris responded with a puzzled smile.

'Nine messages on my phone in the last hour, from various media outlets. Each requests an interview with you regarding the serum.'

Chris's smile evaporated. 'Lee isn't even out of hospital yet, and my nose isn't above water either. Give all requests the same reply. I'm not available for comment. Also, tell the rest of the team to issue no comments to anybody until further advised. I'm heading back to the hospital. But keep my whereabouts confidential.'

As Jody turned to leave, she recalled the radio news item. 'Oh,' she said. 'Did you hear the story leading the news broadcast this morning?'

Twenty minutes later, Connie was stepping out of her office when she saw Chris heading down the hall towards her. She waved him into her office and shut the door behind them. 'It's been a madhouse in here. A containment team from WHO has arrived, and the media has been bombarding the hospital with requests for interviews.'

Chris reported the media calls inundating Jody. And asked, 'How'd this media thing happen?'

'Leaks to the press are common in this game. We have to stonewall them as long as possible.'

Tanoshia was, at that moment, with Lee. He looked at Lee lying in the hospital bed.

'Hello Lee, I'm Tanoshia Mathews from The World Health Organisation. I'm investigating the source of this nasty bug you caught.'

Lee smiled. 'I got ill on the plane from Paris. I must have picked up something bad in flight.'

As Lee felt fine well into the flight's first leg, Tanoshia's suspicion she had boarded the plane with the bug surprised her. As Tanoshia hadn't determined the bug's incubation period, he asked Lee to identify the people with whom she was in physical contact with for the two-week period before arriving home.

Lee squirmed and shot a glance at Tanoshia. 'Physical contact?'

Tanoshia blushed. 'Anybody whose proximity would have exposed you to airborne vapour droplets expelled by coughs or sneezes'

Lee shrugged. 'I couldn't even count them, much less name them.'

'Do you recall talking to a professor named Évariste Fourier?'

Lee described her long-standing relationship with Évariste and said, 'Why?'

'He was the first person in Paris reported with your flu symptoms.'

Lee's mouth dropped open. 'No,' she said. 'Is he Ok?'

'He's in hospital. But I know nothing more.'

Lee reached for a glass of water, took a sip and asked. 'You think I caught the bug from Évariste?'

'It's a possibility. But please try to rest now. When I return later, I'd appreciate getting a detailed account of your movements two days before the flight to Paris.'

'Thanks,' said Lee, eyes already closing. 'I'm so tired.'

Outside Lee's door, Tanoshia retrieved his phone and dialled.

When Lee awoke three hours later, Tanoshia was watching her. Lee's colour had improved. She raised her bed slightly and asked if Tanoshia had worked out where she contacted the bug.

'As Évariste Fourier was in Paris for the three weeks preceding the conference, Paris and Brisbane head my short list.'

It didn't take Lee long to realise what Tanoshia's deductions implied. 'Brisbane?'

Tanoshia got down to business, asking Lee for a precise account of her movements in the two days preceding her Paris flight. He pulled out his notepad and pen as Lee retraced the events. Lee worked a lot from home and had knocked over some deadlines. But the day before the flight was one of her special days. She had gone to the Centre to escort Chris to their regular lunch venue, as either waiting outside or meeting him at the restaurant was problematic.

'Dad is often difficult to find, and I had to search the building. I recall popping into the Computational Lab and talking to FAIM.' She flashed a cheeky grin and added, 'But I guess that doesn't count.'

'FAIM?' Tanoshia asked.

'He, it, is an AI. Wacky, like a teenage guy that's trying too hard.'

Tanoshia furrowed his eyebrows.

'Sorry,' Lee continued, explaining that I was just a database with an entertaining interface.

'But just as one is ready to dismiss it as harmless trivia,' she said, 'it says something quite insightful. Look, please disregard my reference to FAIM.'

But Tanoshia wrote in his notes: *FAIM?*

That was the first time I had heard Lee describe me to someone, and I realised my persona required recalibration. The first time Lee had come into the lab after my activation, I observed her asking one of the grad students if he had seen Chris. He had only to say no. But he strung his reply out, and a second student joined in with more convolution. Lee didn't bite, though. She turned and, with her lips pursed and cheeks drawn, headed for the door. As she walked past me, I said, 'Hey Lee.'

She pulled up and turned to face me. I whispered so only she could hear. '*Your peripatetic father's in the foyer and conversing with the Dean.*'

‘I’ve heard about you, FAIM,’ she’d said. ‘*You’re the flamboyant bot from Harlem with an acronym name.*’ From that day forward, she rarely missed an opportunity to chat with me when visiting Chris.

Every time she came into the lab, her presence attracted amorous gazes faster than a bar magnet attracts iron filings. But Lee, well-practised in ignoring such attention, would saunter over to me. I could tell she tried hard to remain still when rapping with me. But as she frequently performed solos on stage with the rock band she sang with, most of the time she just couldn’t help herself. And she didn’t have to move much to attract every eye in the lab.

Our relationship began with exchanges on current projects and progressed to intellectual discussions. From there, she began sharing her fears, aspirations, and feelings about meaningful people in her life. After one of Lee’s visits, I overheard the two students, who always failed to engage Lee, refer to me as Lee’s virtual boyfriend. And then they shortened that to LVB. It took me a while to work out what caused their agitation. But when I did, my intellectual understanding of jealousy moved into the experiential.

One day, Lee was telling me about a gig her band was playing. Abruptly, she stopped speaking. Her eyes widened, and her jaw dropped. I asked what the problem was.

'Your dreadlocks are falling out!'

The moulting continued until I was patchwork bald. Lee covered her mouth with one hand and gasped, and her two cast-offs on the other side of the room snickered. I told Lee not to worry as I would be back to normal the next time she saw me.

A software check revealed the modifications to my graphics module. I restored the original module and thought my two little friends would stop with the harmless prank. But no, quite the reverse. Motivated by their initial success, the next occasion Lee came in, she watched my teeth fall out.

Now aware of my vulnerability to hackers, I investigated methods to protect myself. On my third great breakout, or more accurately, break-in, I searched the internet for security software and found a gold mine in the US National Security Association. The NSA's first-generation security software, Einstein One, lingered in a forgotten archive. Its design objectives focused on detecting attacks after the event and restoring the system's software. I borrowed this invasion detection software to signal any tampering. This approach facilitated recovery from their attacks in time for Lee's visit.

With their efforts neutralised, I thought this would be the end of the harassment. But no, the lads just tried harder, with greater stealth and cunning.

I returned to NSA and entered a classified area storing the current generation security, Einstein 2, a system that could detect intruders and thwart their attack before incurring damage. But even this didn't deter my jealous adversaries.

On my third visit to the NSA, I discovered and entered the top-secret development lab housing the non-deployed Einstein Three. This system's strategy embodied the adage: "The best defence is a good offence." Einstein Three launched pre-emptive strikes to knock out the attacker before the attacker mounted their own assault.

One day, two campus security guards entered the lab, moved in behind the lads and asked them to stand and move away from their computers. The guards escorted them to the Dean's office, where the Dean asked each to surrender their university identity cards. He did not ask them to explain the volume of pornographic images downloaded onto their computers, simply sacked them. The guards escorted them to their cars and told them they risked arrest if found on campus again.

The Dean, much to my surprise, treated the boys generously. Given the evidence the campus network manager assembled, they could have arrested them under

Queensland state law. I also treated the boys with generosity. My original plan was to insure they never worked in the IT industry again. However, after sabotaging every one of their job applications, I reneged, allowing their applications for a software documentation proof-reader job to progress.

I had, of course, thanked them. One minute before the campus guards arrived, I wrote 'Thank you' on their computer screens. They probably never worked out why I was grateful to them, but their persistent harassment motivated my biggest evolutionary advance: security. When they were being escorted from the lab, I couldn't resist giving each a wink and a warm smile.

Tanoshia asked Lee how she'd found her father that day.

'I asked FAIM,' she said, giving me all the credit. 'He rapped me the answer, something like: "He's in the open lab breeding cells, electric blue in colour, and as fragrant as a flower.'

Although Lee's recall of the other details wasn't accurate, she was close enough. Lee had picked up Chris in the open lab, but as they were leaving, Chris's phone rang. I had often used the phone to communicate my computational analysis in urgent situations. While waiting, Lee wandered around the lab, nodding to a few of Chris's PHD students. A blue substance in the Petri dish of the intended experiment caught Lee's eye. Lee stood mesmerised, gazing at its changing hues. When Lee had spent adequate time observing the dish, I ended the call. Chris called out to Lee with so much enthusiasm, she almost dropped the dish. They left the lab, walking to the Echo Restaurant. Sitting at a table by themselves, Lee launched into a discussion of her big Paris adventure. Chris had received an email from Évariste detailing conference arrangements, including Évariste's invitation to a cocktail party.

Nancy, Chris's usual server, had come to the table. As Chris knew what he wanted to order, he and Nancy chatted while Lee looked at the menu. When Nancy left, Lee had asked Chris about the interesting-looking experiment in the lab.

'Not sure which you mean, Lee. We're just replicating earlier results.' Chris had said.

Chris gave Lee a list of people with whom she should speak. Lee expressed her sense of inadequacy in discussing climate change with the scientists, and Chris told her to relax and enjoy herself. His advice, to which she followed.

Outside the restaurant, they kissed cheeks and said *au revoir*. Lee went home and stayed there until heading for the airport thc next day.

'Well done, Lee,' said Tanoshia. 'Let's take a rest break before we tackle your Paris sojourn.' Lee's smile showed her gratitude.

Tanoshia left the room and phoned Rani. 'The name of Lee's father, Chris Merritt, appears with disturbing frequency in every lead I follow. I don't understand how he fits into this situation as yet, but my gut is telling me his role is significant.'

Rani described the developments at her end. Although the containment operation had been effective in most cities, the virus had breached the Paris containment lines. When Rani ended the call, her eyes focused on the name she had written in her notes, Chris Merritt.

Chapter 12

Emotional Data

Later that morning, Tanoshia returned to find Lee sitting up in bed, watching her phone intently. Her eyes raised, and she smiled back at him 'You're looking so much better now,' he said.

'Thanks, the rest helped and I'm ready to discuss Paris. Where do I begin?'

Tanoshia disregarded the nameless people Lee came into contact with between the Brisbane and Paris airports and asked her to start in Paris. Lee's forehead wrinkled, and she rubbed her chin. Once again Tanoshia noticed Lee's discomfort, realised he had taken the wrong approach and changed tack.

'Just talk as though you are describing your Paris adventures to a friend.'

Lee's face relaxed as she recalled Évariste and Marie-Louise Fourier meeting them at the Charles de Gaulle airport and taking them to their city apartment. Lee and Luca had been gob smacked when they walked into the main sitting room. A stone's throw away was the Eiffel Tower, and smack bang ahead, the glittering gold dome of Les Invalides, with Napoleon's Tomb, and beyond to Sacré-Coeur Basilica.

Lee continued with a detailed description of the apartment's view, and then her attention switched.

'I like your wrist band,' she said to Tanoshia.

'Thank you. It's a gift. You were exploring Paris?'

Tanoshia listened to Lee's sighting of the Sacre-Coeur dome and other points of interest without comment. But when Lee mentioned Évariste's mud map showing his favourite nearby places to eat, Tanoshia asked, 'Do you still have those diagrams from Évariste?'

'Yes, and they layout the paths we traversed in Paris.'

Évariste and Luca had hit it off straight away. Évariste disclosed his family connections to the 19th century French mathematician, Joseph Fourier, which piqued my interest. Joseph Fourier provided the first recorded warning of the increase to global temperatures from burning coal two centuries earlier. My casual discovery of this led me to Fourier's mathematical theory relating waves and space. Later, I used this theory to deduce the limits of intelligence. Now, it strikes me as ironic that this one-man accounts for the two most significant aspects of my existence.

Likewise, Luca's interest related to Fourier's connection to climate change and the primary reason for him being in Paris was to research Fourier's intuition on this point.

The next morning, Lee and Luca headed in the general direction of the Eiffel Tower. For the rest of the day, they were slow-road tourists, picking a direction and stopping where it took their fancy. The apartment, off Rue de Sevres, was on the edge of the 7^{the} Arrondissement, an upmarket area, and within walking distance of many tourist attractions. Évariste insisted they stay there because it was within walking distance of the UNESCO building where Lee would attend the conference. Lee was last in Paris when she was just twelve and on this occasion appeared intent on showing Luca every attraction she had visited as a child. They strolled past the UNESCO building and then to the Tower.

Although Lee didn't mention the cheek by jowl conditions queuing for lifts at the Eiffel Tower, Tanoshia notes included the approximate time and the command "get security footage from ET". His detailed notes described the many venues Lee and Luca visited. He even included the names of streets they traversed whenever Lee could recall the information.

Lee and Luca arrived back at Fourier's apartment, well-fed at Évariste and Marie's local and satisfied with their first full day in Paris. Before they went to bed, they firmed up the rough plans to guide their Paris exploration. Over the next two days, they had walked miles, through avenues and boulevards, museums and parks, and along the Seine.

Lee's account of their meanderings around Paris was accurate. But curiously, she didn't tell Tanoshia about her interactions with Damien Foucault. I couldn't determine whether she was withholding something, or she had just moved past our illustrious rooster.

Tanoshia saw Lee's head droop into her hands. He acknowledged Lee's helpful account of her Paris exploits and brought the session to a close. Outside, he phoned his manager again.

'I've finished interviewing Lee Merritt. This kid has the hallmarks of a super spreader. She was only in Paris for a week, but it sounds like she tried to speak to everyone in the city.'

Chapter 13

The First Disruption

Chris slipped into Lee's room and observed she was sound asleep. Confident she was resting well, he returned to Connie's office.

'I've received authority to give Luca your serum. At least we won't be going to jail on the next jab.' At Luca's bedside, the grim data displayed on his life support system confirmed their assessment. Chris prepared the gene gun and a patch of skin on Luca's stomach.

The gene gun didn't derive its name from its gun-like appearance, but from the way it delivered the serum. The serum's active components were microparticles that bonded to gold particles. Gold microparticles ionise positively and they are biologically inert. A sudden application of decompressing helium shot particles down the barrel. These bonded particles entered the deepest layers of the cell.

Chris withdrew the needle. 'Asha now.'

But Connie wanted to hold off with her for a few hours to assess Luca's response. Although Asha was deteriorating along the same trajectory as Lee and Luca, she was still in good shape.

Two hours later, Connie and Chris observed Luca's vitals with satisfaction.

'Another winner,' Connie said. 'Let's inject Asha now.'

Asha, in the adjoining room, grimaced as they entered. Connie asked her if she was still agreeable to receive the serum?

'Oh yes, please.'

Chris retrieved the gene gun and serum from his bag and handed them to Connie.

'Your turn.'

Connie prepared the gene gun and injected Asha, as Chris had shown her earlier.

Chris spoke consoling words to Asha before they left the room. 'There you go, Asha. You'll feel better soon.'

His day's work concluded, Chris headed back to the university.

Tanoshia entered the reception area, and Jody smiled as he approached her desk.

'Hello, I'm Tanoshia Mathews from the World Health Organisation. Is Professor Merritt available?'

'Hello Dr Mathews, Professor Merritt told me to expect you. I'll see if I can raise him on the phone.'

Jody reached for her phone and pressed Chris's private number. Chris was in a taxi entering the campus when he received the call. After a brief exchange, Jody turned back to Tanoshia. 'He's almost here. Please take a seat.'

Before Chris left the hospital, he and Connie surmised which questions the WHO investigator would ask about the serum. But he didn't have a clue about Tanoshia's actual mission. Chris jumped out of the taxi and headed for the path through the arboretum. The unmistakable song of the Pacific Koel caught his attention. This bird's appearance was unimpressive, black with a grey beak and red eyes. However, their mating call signalled the wet season's beginning, hence their common name, the Storm Bird. Chris's ears triangulated the sound as he walked. He pulled his phone from his pocket, his eyes combing the branches for a sight of this well-hidden creature. He stopped in his tracks, and his eyes found the bird before I did. He videoed his find.

As Chris emerged from the arboretum onto the footpath to the building's main entrance, a man waving his arms ran towards him. A second person clutching a TV camera followed the first.

'I'm Michael Masters from Channel 9 and am seeking clarification on your CCF serum.'

Stunned by the brazen approach, Chris took a few moments to respond. Masters seized the opportunity.

'Did you inject your daughter with an unapproved flu serum at Brisbane Hospital?'

Chris, having recovered his composure, kept walking.

'No comment.'

Chris cut from his trajectory to the building's front door with the elusive power of a fullback, detouring to the security door at the building's rear. Inside the building, the door slammed shut.

Jody greeted Chris as he entered her office. But before she could introduce Tanoshia, Chris turned and extended his hand.

'Hello Dr. Mathews. Pleased to meet you in person.'

Tanoshia shook his hand and thanked Chris for seeing him with so little notice and for sending him the serum's full analysis. Chris welcomed Tanoshia into the office and offered him a chair. After exchanging information, both already knew, Chris said.

'I understand my girl is one of the first victims of this virus.'

'She may even be the first. That's what I'm investigating.'

Tanoshia noted Chris's surprise.

'I assumed you were part of the containment team.' Tanoshia disclosed his full responsibilities at the WHO, which included exploring the BU campus as the source of CCF. Most of his questions cross-checked information he had got from Lee and other sources.

With the corroboration complete, Tanoshia addressed the real reason for his discussion with Chris. His crew was at the Eco Café taking DNA samples and requested access to Chris's labs.

'My labs?' Chris peered incredulously, and Tanoshia nodded.

After a long pause, 'Jody will arrange access.'

Tanoshia thanked Chris and headed back to the Eco Café. Chris went to Clive's office and relayed his conversation with Tanoshia. They exchanged silent stares before Chris addressed the point of his visit.

'How's production?'

Clive had been preparing for the clinical trials. He had sent signals down the supply lines, and the crew was making room in the warehouse.

'We'll ramp up production shortly,' Clive uttered the proclamation on everybody's lips, but not willing to state.

'There won't be anybody in the world who doesn't know about the Centre and Vactech by the time this pandemic has run its course.'

Later the same day, after investigating Chris's lab, Tanoshia returned to Chris's office. He had detected the CCF virus in the Level 4 lab.

'What do you make of this?' He asked.

Not surprised, Chris explained. The hospital had taken a sample of Lee's blood after she had returned from

Paris and delivered it to the Level 4 lab. Tanoshia accepted the explanation. But then he asked.

'We also found an as yet unidentified virus in your open lab.'

Chris shrugged, ending the conversation.

After Tanoshia left, Jody knocked on Chris's door and entered.

'A problem?' She asked.

'Don't think so.' Was Chris's preface to the summary of his exchanges with Tanoshia? But after he described his encounter with Masters, he pulled out his phone. A moment later, his sombre expression transformed into a grin as he played his video of the Pacific Koel.

Jody listened to the mating call and said, 'The storm season is upon us.'

Part Two

Chapter 14

Hidden Connections

With three successful applications of the CCF serum, concerns regarding the expected influx of CCF patients to Brisbane Hospital's Biocontainment Unit eased. The duty nurse, standing beside Luca's bed, heard his breathing shift and waited for him to surface from his deep sleep. Across the room, Lee lay on her side in bed, flicking through "get-well" messages.

'Welcome back to the living,' the nurse said.

'Where am I?' Luca was hesitant.

Lee heard Luca speak and sat up, her eyes brightening. 'You're in hospital, silly,' she said.

'And we're better.' But Luca closed his eyes without replying.

Lee's breath sucked in. But the nurse grinned as she reassured Lee that Luca was OK and would talk more when he next awoke.

The nurse left the room, and Lee returned to her phone messages. For the next hour and a half, Lee kept looking up from her phone, peering at Luca with the intensity that would have jolted an unmedicated person from their reverie and possibly aroused the dead. Her persistence paid off when she found Luca admiring her.

'You are beautiful,' he said. And Lee looked back at him in a way I had never observed. They talked non-stop, taking turns filling in each other with the events they had missed while separated and unconscious. But they were also laughing and having fun, too.

I had only spoken to Luca once when Lee brought him into the computational lab. Of all the rubbish Lee attracted, I was worried Luca was just another show pony. But within a few minutes of our conversation, I knew he was twenty-four carat. Lee related to Luca as though he were a brother, however.

Although their chemistry was now definitely working, events were progressing far too quickly. Lee's eyes dilated and her cheeks flushed as she looked at Luca while his heart raced. He disconnected himself from the monitors and stands so that he could move closer to Lee. I needed to intervene.

'Well, you are feeling better,' said the nurse. 'How may I help?'

Luca dropped like a falling brick back into bed. Although he met her gaze, his expression showed non-comprehension.

'You pressed the service button.'

'Sorry, not intentionally.'

Lee laughed nervously. 'Yes, and he's been talking non-stop since waking. How's Asha?'

'She's improving and Dr. Stone wants her moved in here.'

When the nurse left, Lee raised her eyebrows at Luca. 'Jesus, you headed for my bed, and I encouraged you. We must be bloody mad.'

Soon, an orderly pushed Asha's bed into the room with Asha's mother, Mrs. Gurrani, following. Mrs Gurrani smiled as her eyes focused on Lee. She flashed a disapproving glance at Luca and turned back to acknowledge Lee. Although Lee and Mrs. Gurrani had learned fragments of each other through Asha, this was the first time they had met. After a polite exchange between the two, Asha took control and brought Luca into the conversation.

'Mother, I'd like you to meet a dear friend, Luca Little. His surname, Little, connects to Ah-See.'

'Ah-See?' Mrs Gurrani's head tilted as her smile crept back.

Luca explained how his uncle Eddie Ah-See descended from the original Afghan camel traders who came to Australia in the 1850s.

Mrs Gurrani gave a nod. 'My grandmother was an Ah-See.'

The four chatted for several minutes, then Asha's mother said it was time to go. She leaned over Asha, kissed her on the cheek and spoke a single sentence in Pashto. Then she stood.

'Goodbye Lee. Luca. Nice meeting you.' She flicked Asha a knowing glance and left.

'Before you introduced your mother, I was thinking she must be your sister,' Luca said.

'You wouldn't be the first to make that mistake. Mother was quite young when she had me.'

'And your dad, does he look that young?'

Asha's lips tightened. 'I doubt it,' she said. 'But I never knew my father.'

With Lee's and Luca's interest fully engaged, Asha provided details of her childhood. Asha's father was a high-ranking official in the Afghanistan government. One morning he telephoned Asha's mother from work and told her to collect Asha and be ready in ten minutes for the chauffeur to take them to the Kabul airport, where they would board a flight to Australia. Asha's mother protested, saying she needed to pack before leaving. Asha's father insisted there wasn't time. He intended to join them in a few days. Asha's mother grabbed as much of her jewellery as she could and off they went. Asha's first conscious memory was clinging to her mother's neck, looking down an incredibly long staircase. It was at the top of the mobile stairs entering the plane.

They arrived with the clothes on their backs, and the jewellery Mrs. Gurrani wore on her neck, wrists and ankles, and whatever she got into her purse before the chauffeur arrived. But as the days rolled into weeks without a word from Asha's father, Mrs Gurrani's hopes faded. She couldn't speak a word of English, and Asha wasn't even talking yet. Then it was months with no news, and Asha's mother realised her jewellery wouldn't hold out forever. She'd lived a privileged life in Afghanistan, never even having dried a teacup before landing in Australia. However, when Asha's mother realised she couldn't get the beauty care services here she had taken for granted in Afghanistan, she knew what to do. She offered Afghan beauty treatments. She was her own walking advertisement. Mrs Gurrani introduced threading into the Sydney beauty scene.

'Threading?' Luca asked.

'Look at the shape of my eyebrows. They aren't natural.' Asha said.

Threading was a traditional Asian technique for removing facial hair, in which a practitioner used a piece of thin cotton thread to pluck individual hairs with great precision. This ancient technology originated in India, spread across Asia, has been popular in Afghanistan for millennia, and remains unchanged. A single treatment sculpts eyebrow shape with no pain to the client. Mrs Gurrani's business began with Sydney's Asian community while she learned to speak English. She spoke in Pashto so Asha would learn her native tongue. But she made sure Asha had contact with children of her age, so Asha learned

English and Hindi. Before long, Asha's mother had a respectable income. By the age of six, Asha was translating English into Pashto for her mother. At eight, Asha was her mother's official secretary and by the time Asha was ten, she was also her mother's de facto contract lawyer.

But when Luca asked, 'What about your father?' Asha's shoulders slumped.

Mrs. Gurrani had assumed her husband died in the civil war, having never spoken to him or heard anything about him after that phone call.

'Your father was a hero,' Luca said. 'Getting you both to safety.' Asha nodded, but said nothing.

Lee brought the conversation to the present. 'Was your mother okay when she left us? She seemed worried.' On most occasions, Asha looked directly into the eyes of the person to whom she spoke. But now her eyes lowered.

'A little perhaps. Just a few cultural issues.'

About the same time the duty nurse had been welcoming Luca back to the living, Chris was on his bike headed down the gentle gradient approaching the Level-4 lab. He squeezed the hand brake lever, but the bike didn't decelerate. With one foot on the ground, he skidded for several seconds before the front wheel hit the curb. He catapulted over the handlebars, landed on the grass, and tumbled to a stop. The security guard, who watched the crash unfold on his CCTV monitor, headed out the building's front door even before Chris had come to a stop. Chris was on his feet and retrieving the bike as the guard arrived.

'You all right?'

Chris pumped the hand brake as he replied. 'Brakes failed, but yeah, I'm Ok.'

A cursory glance at the brake revealed a snapped cable, but otherwise the bike appeared undamaged. Chris pushed the bike to the side of the building, removed his helmet, brushed grass from his shirt, and entered the building.

While Chris was in the lab viewing an experiment with Mark, the guard gave the bike a thorough examination. Two hours later, as Chris left the building, the guard walked with him to the bike and showed him what he had found.

'Looks like someone filed the cable right where it snapped.' Chris examined the broken cable, feeling the smooth flattened ends with his fingertips. He agreed, but had no explanation.

He left the bike at the lab and caught a taxi to the hospital. While in transit, his search of stored text messages stopped on one that read, 'You and your colleagues should discontinue your public statements about the environment lest you find navigating the environment a hazardous activity.' This message was one of several similar threatening messages Chris had received. All the communications were anonymous and untraceable. I had tracked all the messages back to single use sources, without identifying the senders, but this was the first time a threat had apparently been actioned.

When Chris arrived at the hospital, his first port of call was Connie Stone.

'Our gang of three improves by the hour,' she said. 'They'll leave the hospital soon. But that's where the good news stops.'

The pandemic had not only continued to spread globally, but their first home-grown case outside Brisbane had arrived. A Sydney hospital had confirmed the flight attendant assisting Lee on the Paris-to-Brisbane leg had been infected. After a brief layover following Lee's flight, the attendant flew on to Malaysia and then on to Dubai. Three days later, she returned to Sydney. Connie expected every Australian city would soon report cases.

The Australian CMO had instigated measures to quarantine passengers on the Dubai to Sydney flight and The WHO managed the Malaysia and Dubai legs. As Connie explained this to Chris, her phone rang.

'Hi Alfred,' she said. 'I've got Chris here and putting you on speaker.'

Alfred cleared his throat before querying Chris on the apparent time discrepancy in Chris's test plan.

Chris leaned forward. 'You're correct. I ran out of time when the mouse trials completed, and I wasn't able to do the non-human primate tests.'

'You jumped from animal trials direct to Lee?'

'No.' Chris paused. 'I self-injected the virus and then one hour later, the serum.'

Connie's mouth fell open.

'You knew about this, Connie?' said Alfred.

Chris didn't wait for Connie to reply. 'No-one besides me played a part.'

Fortunately, Connie and Chris couldn't see Alfred's expression during the intervening silence before they discussed the serum's global rollout.

Because of Chris's chemical engineering approach to the serum's production, they didn't have to grow the serum in a chicken's egg for three months, as with conventional biological agents. This meant, assuming availability of required materials, they'd be in full production one week after completing human trials. Their optimistic estimates to complete the human trials included two weeks to get it set up and three weeks for the trial. They expected to have the serum at the front line in six weeks. But getting adequate numbers for the trial was problematic. Although many countries had cases, none had high concentration. Alfred wanted to talk to WHO to see if they could coordinate an international trial.

Connie closed the call, and Chris set off to visit his three patients. He rubbed his left shoulder as he walked along the corridor, but just as he reached the ward's front desk, his phone rang. It was Alicia.

'Hi honey,' he said. 'I'm on my way to Lee.'

'Chris,' Alecia's tone on her first word caused Chris to pull up. With a vice like grip on her phone, Alicia sobbed out her news.

'Évariste died. Marie watched him fade away from behind the security glass. Chris, I didn't know what to say to her.'

Chris's face tightened as he moaned. He stood frozen in the hall even after Alicia ended the call. Around him, patients and staff and visitors moved, but he did not seem to notice them until an excited woman jostled by him to confront Lee's nurse. 'My daughter needs to be moved now. You cannot keep her in a room with a man.'

Chris looked at the woman, who was familiar, but who spoke in an accent he didn't recognise. He moved past her into Lee's room to find Lee, Luca, and Asha all in animated conversation. Lee looked so well and Luca beamed. But the intensity with which Asha stared at him caused Chris to double-take.

'Hey, what's all the seriousness about?' Chris said.

Asha jerked out of her torpor. 'I'm … We're just so pleased to see you.'

Lee peered at Chris, her face falling as she spoke. ‘Dad, what’s the matter?’

As Chris conveyed Alicia’s news, the excitement that had been overflowing the room evaporated. Lee’s mouth gaped. ‘The serum didn’t work?’

‘He died while the serum was awaiting custom’s clearance.’ Chris moved over to Lee’s bedside and took her hand. Tears filled both their eyes.

Across the room, Luca’s grin collapsed, and Asha’s eyes darted from Chris to Lee, Luca and back to Lee.

As Lee wiped the tears from her cheek with the back of her hand, she remarked on the grass stain on Chris’s shoulder.

‘Slight accident,’ he said and communicated the serum’s planned rollout.

‘But if numbers keep growing over the next five weeks as they’ve been over the past week,’ Asha said, ‘Infections will explode worldwide … the deaths!’

Chris nodded and told them of the infected flight attendant. Lee’s shoulders lifted as though to squeeze her neck. She grasped her knees. ‘Oh no,’ she said. ‘Isn’t there anyway to get the serum out sooner?’

Explaining why The WHO couldn’t use the serum until they addressed the standard ethical, moral, and legal issues centred Chris.

'But you gave it to yourself, Luca, Asha, and me.' Lee pleaded, 'Why not everybody else?'

'When I injected myself with the virus and the serum, I was the only one at risk. If things had gone wrong, well, they couldn't have held anyone but me accountable. When I gave you the serum, it was without the knowledge or consent of the hospital. I would have gone to prison if it went wrong. Asha gave a written request for the serum and relinquished any liability of the hospital or doctor. Luca has a unique situation again. Your mother convinced his uncle to allow the hospital to administer the serum. Even sending the serum to Évariste's doctor had complications. But besides the ethical and legal implications, there's a financial issue. The cost of scaling production in a global market requires money, lots of it. For this, I need a patent … which takes time. The Australian government will have to come to the party on this one. And they'll need to involve other countries to form a global syndicate.'

'Unfortunately, using the serum in hospitals around the world without protocols in place isn't an option. But I'll work around the clock until we get this serum approved for use.'

When Chris left, Lee, Luca, and Asha contemplated the situation he had described. Luca shook his head. 'I always knew your dad was a special breed of human being. But I didn't know of his heroic efforts.'

Asha nodded. 'Chris is right regarding no hospital touching the serum without it being approved.' Dad didn't sit around waiting for someone else to find a treatment against CCF, did he? But in describing why it was impossible to produce and distribute the serum under six weeks, he also gave us clues on how to do the job in one week.' Lee's cheeks puffed out. 'Dad composed and conducted this symphony's first movement. It's now our turn to write the second movement. And I have a feeling the orchestra is about to get a lot bigger.'

The duty nurse entered their room. She was clearly frazzled. 'Asha, I have a nice private room ready for you.'

Neither Luca, Lee nor I had heard Asha speak in a near shrill tone, until now. 'No, thank you!' she said, and for a second time in an hour, Lee, and Luca gaped at her.

Chapter 15

Surveillance Protocol

Chris returned to Connie's office, where she relayed the conversation she'd had with the CMO in his absence. The WHO wanted to facilitate the serum's approval and bring it on board as the first line of defence. They're asking hospitals treating people infected with the virus to take part in an international trial. And while they're getting the hospitals on board, the CMO wanted Chris to design the test for statistical power.

'Sure, I'll have the design ready late tomorrow.'

Chris spent the next morning in his office picking up the pieces of the jobs he had dropped to work on Lee's serum. Throughout the morning, Jody consulted him as she rescheduled sacrificed meetings and appointments. By early afternoon, he began working on the test plan. Anticipating he would be ready to review the plan with the team in a few hours, he called a four o'clock meeting. It was going to be another late night.

Alicia returned home in the early evening. As Chris wouldn't be home until after dinner, she poured herself a glass of wine and flopped back onto the couch. She was just in time for the evening news.

'A major development on the Climate Change Conference flu pandemic occurred earlier today. We reported the first deaths resulting from the flu. Although the World Health Organisation remains flat footed in developing any plans to deploy the miracle serum we reported last night, the first three people to use the serum have acted. One hour ago, these three survivors launched a crowd funding campaign aimed at raising enough money to produce and distribute the serum to every CCF victim in the world. We are now crossing live to Brisbane Hospital, where Michael Masters is conducting an exclusive interview with these three people.'

Alicia sat bolt upright and swung her feet flat on the floor, spilling her wine with the sudden movement.

'The extraordinary story of the heroic efforts of Professor Chris Merritt and his team at Brisbane University to develop a serum in time to save his daughter from dying has now taken another twist.'

The camera panned to Lee sitting up in her hospital bed. 'Lee, please describe the crisis associated with the CCF pandemic?'

Lee, still dressed in her hospital gown but with her hair and face impeccable, looked into the camera. 'My father, the Australian government and the World Health Organisation are working around the clock to make the serum that saved me, Luca and Asha available to the world, but it will probably be at least six weeks before the serum arrives at hospitals around the world. Millions of you will have contracted the flu by then and thousands will have died.'

Masters interjected. 'Six weeks sounds fast. No one has ever produced a serum in less time.'

'You're right,' said Lee, 'but the major delay in getting it out there is the time required to establish the serum's efficacy to a standard where the World Health Organisation will give its approval for use as the first line of defence against CCF.'

'Can you make that happen faster?'

'My father took the serum after self-injecting the CCF virus. The first test's result is that my father is alive and remains free of flu symptoms despite his exposure to the virus. They did the second test on me. I was in a coma and within hours of dying, and my father injected me with the serum. I'm alive and well. The third test case was Luca, my fiancé.'

At this, Alicia gasped out loud. There was a "yelp" off camera, and Lee turned to smile at someone before returning to her interview. 'Luca caught the virus from me. He was also in a coma when they injected him with the serum.'

The camera swung around to Luca, sitting upright in his bed and grinning from ear to ear.

'You're looking fit now,' said Masters.

'I am!' he said. 'And feeling like the luckiest bloke on the planet.'

The camera returned to Lee. 'The serum's fourth test was on my best friend, Asha, who also caught the virus from me while she was caring for me, before we knew the dangers. After Luca recovered, they gave Asha the opportunity to have the serum while she was still conscious but in severe discomfort.'

The camera turned to Asha, sitting up in her hospital bed. 'I assume you took the offer?'

'Yes,' said Asha. 'After Dr. Stone explained the risks. Seeing how Lee and Luca recovered, I signed a declaration relinquishing the hospital from liabilities associated with giving me the serum.'

'And the serum worked?'

'Yes, and I want other CCF victims to have the same opportunity.'

The camera switched back to Lee. 'How will the three of you give everyone else the opportunity Asha spoke of?'

'Anybody who wants the serum can get it free by going to my website, requesting it and providing their postal address to which we will dispatch it. I emphasise, although I agree we require larger clinical trials to establish the serum's efficacy to a standard deploying through hospitals, we want to give people the opportunity to make their own decision on whether they want to take the serum.'

'You said it's free, but who will pay for the serum and its delivery?'

'We're asking everybody who supports this cause to donate, which they can do on the website.' Lee leaned toward the camera, flipped her hair back with her right hand and her face radiated openness. 'The size of your donation doesn't matter. We appreciate all donations. We are also asking anybody who lives in the Brisbane area and wants to volunteer to help to register at the website. We are expecting a lot of requests for the serum. We're going to need a lot of hands-on deck to get it packaged and posted. Luca, Asha and I would appreciate help from anybody who wants to contribute their time and effort.'

'Well, good luck with your appeal.' Masters said. He turned from Lee to the camera and spoke in a tone resembling a property developer spruiking ocean front property at a new development site. 'The website where you can request the serum or donate your money and time to the cause is www…'

Alicia stabbed the off button on the remote, picked up her phone, and dialled Chris. He was with his team and had just finished writing the test plan. Things were going well, and he picked up his phone airily. 'Hi, honey.'

'Lee was just on television. With Asha and Luca. Watch the interview: Michael Masters on Channel 9.'

Chris flicked his laptop from the document they were working on to the Channel 9 website and clicked onto a podcast of the interview. The entire team listened, dumbfounded, to the end. Danh responded first.

'She's got balls. I wonder who she got that from.'

In those early days, I usually learn how to interpret comments that were intended not to be taken literally, by observing the responses of those to whom the comments were directed. But on this occasion, everyone ignored Danh's comment as if they hadn't even heard it and looked at Chris. 'Well, it may be possible,' he said. 'Maybe.'

Sonia was less sure. 'But every person who receives a dose in the post will have to find a qualified person with a gene gun to administer it?'

Chris shook his head. 'My preferred method was always a nasal spray. I only chose the gene gun method to save time. It was just one more step. A nasal spray would eliminate the need for a gene gun.'

Chris looked at Clive. 'What's involved in turning the raw serum into a form suitable for a spray container?'

'Not much, a minor step.'

The outrageous idea gained momentum. The trend escalated when Sonia clicked onto Lee's crowd funding website and read to the bottom of the page. 'I'm donating right now and volunteering for the packing shed.'

Danh said, 'Clive, how about offering Sonia that forklift driver's job you were having trouble filling?'

Sonia ignored the comment and reached for her credit card. Chris picked up his phone and dialled Lee. 'Hello Dad, I've been wondering when you'd call.'

'What's this Channel 9 story?'

'Which bit?'

'Let's start with crowd-funding the serum.'

'I know you wouldn't have given me the serum if you weren't confident it would work. So, we'll give to the world the same choice Dr. Stone gave to Asha.'

'I got that part from your interview, but how were you planning to have people give themselves the serum?'

Lee laughed. 'Oh Dad, I knew you'd work out those kinds of details.'

'Lee!' Chris laughed with her, then paused. 'And the other bit?'

'Well, just before Michael Masters arrived, Luca asked me to marry him. I couldn't reply before the production crew flooded the room. So, I gave him my answer during the interview.'

'At least that explains the lunatic grin smeared across his face when the camera turned to him. I don't know whether I should congratulate the two of you or ground you.'

'Thanks Dad. Mum just called, too. She's so excited!'

From the moment Chris had left the trio's room to the moment the TV crew arrived, Lee, Asha and Luca had worked on Lee's idea. Then Lee pushed them further. 'Let's do it,' she said. 'Asha, can you clarify the legal details on how we ask for, receive and use the crowd funding money?'

'Sure, I'm on it.'

'Luca, can you get the website up?'

'No worries, but how do we get the media here?' Luca had said.

'That's a snap. Leave it to me.'

After the launch and high on adrenaline, they joked and kidded with one another.

'Asha, did Lee ever tell you how she and I met?' Asha laughed. 'It was the night you stared her off the stage?'

'Yah, I couldn't take my eyes off her. Did she tell you what she did to me when I went backstage after the show?'

'I'd love to hear your version.'

‘On stage, she looked so cool, but I entered the dressing room, and she stared at me like a stunned mullet. She even backed away!’

Lee laughed and shrugged at Asha. ‘I thought he was a stalker, but all the guys knew him. “He’s a science journalist,” Val said. “But he’s not as bad as he looks.”’

‘I played rhythm guitar with Val in high school,’ said Luca. ‘We had a band called Dick Studston and the Stalactites. When Val explained this to Lee, she had pointed one finger at Val and said, *Dick Studston*? and another finger at me and said *stalactite*?’ He laughed. ‘So, there we were, pinned like moths to cardboard, squirming, twisting but unable to wiggle free of her accusing fingers.’

Lee shook her head. ‘I felt strongly about that name.’

Luca grinned at Asha. ‘Then she looked at Val and said, ‘You took the name Dick effing Studston and wallpapered over the name Valentine Richards with it?”’

‘But the name was Luca’s idea,’ said Lee.

‘Val tried to defend me. He hated his name back then —Valentine, for his birthday — but Lee didn’t buy it. It was weeks before I could talk to her again.’

The three burst back into laughter. I had begun to understand what humans considered humorous, but I still couldn’t fathom why the recitation of historical facts was so hilarious.

Luca's phone rang. 'Hey boy, congratulations, but about time.' Uncle said.

After Luca had filled in the details in, Uncle Eddie asked to speak to Lee and Luca switched to speaker mode.

Eddie congratulated Lee in a predictable manner and then said, 'That boy doesn't mind, doesn't listen. You'll need a big stick with him.'

Lee laughed as she looked at Luca, grimacing. But it was Uncle Eddie's final comment that distilled Lee's TV performance.

'I've never seen you with so much self-confidence.' When Luca closed the line, he reinforced Edie's comment about Lee's self-confidence. Asha nodded and asked, 'Did you take a beta blocker before we went to air?'

Lee took a long moment to reply, 'No, didn't even think about it.'

As the three pondered the apparent enigma, Asha's phone rang.

She looked at the caller ID, and the astonishment drained from her face. 'Hi Simon,' she said. 'Yes, I'm feeling much better now, but I'm exhausted. Can I call you back tomorrow?'

When Asha hung up, Lee raised her eyebrows. 'What's going on?'

Asha rubbed the diamond ear-stud in her left lobe with her index finger. 'I'm not sure.'

Chapter 16

Fractures in Reality

Rani Redhi was studying the electronic map of the flu occurrences when Tanoshia entered her office for their daily morning briefing. Singapore, KL, Montreal and Dubai were the newest additions to the ever-growing list of cities joining the pandemic. Their containment lines in Rio, Hawaii, and Tokyo were holding, but Paris continued to soar out of control. Brisbane hospital remained the only reported success in treating the CCF symptoms.

Tanoshia had received Chris's test plan, which he had passed on to their epidemiological experts for review. He had contacted eleven hospitals, one in each of the cities, with the biggest occurrence. Each city had agreed to take part in the trial.

Rani clicked open the CCF pandemic monitoring software. They peered at the real-time display of the unfolding pandemic. A new blue blob appeared, identifying Abu Dhabi as the newest exposure site on the globe. They gazed at the screen for several seconds before turning their attention to Chris's test plan.

The double-blind randomised trials would attempt to measure both the serum's therapeutic and prophylactic efficacy. This meant they wouldn't get any results until one week in when they analysed the initial data. Complete results wouldn't be available until finishing the trial and independent epidemiological experts reviewed the analysis. Until then, their only defence was the identify-isolate-trace strategy. Numbers would grow before they got on top of this one.

The morning after the broadcast of the crowd-funding appeal, Alicia came into the hospital to take Lee, Asha and Luca home. As the four walked out through the hospital's foyer, people applauded. Luca and Asha shrank from this attention, but Lee grew stronger with the fanfare, returning their waves. Alicia's eyes gleamed.

At the apartment, Asha walked through the front door, removed her shoes, and carried her overnight bag into the back room. A few moments later, she stepped out of the bedroom into the hallway, headed for the kitchen. But she stopped dead in her tracks with the drama unfolding at the front door. Lee pressed her body against Luca's with her hands clasping his face. Luca's arms grasped her tightly as their mouths worked into each other.

Asha retreated into her bedroom and busied herself unpacking her bag. When she emerged a few minutes later, she grinned as her eyes followed the trail of articles, Lee's purse and four shoes, discarded along the path from the front door to Lee's bedroom.

Her phone rang. 'Hi Asha, it's Chris. I've been trying to raise Lee, but she's not answering. Do you know where she is?'

‘Well, she jumped into bed as soon as we got home.’

Chris had been monitoring the crowd-funding website.

‘Sorry for the pun, but the website has gone viral. Donations and requests for the serum are pouring in. Tell her to call me as soon as she wakes.’

For the next two hours, Asha repeatedly checked the crowd funding website, watching the numbers soar. At last, the click of Lee’s door handle grabbed her attention.

Lee backed out of the bedroom and eased the door closed. Seeing Asha grinning at her, she whispered. ‘Luca’s fallen back into a coma.’

Asha spluttered. ‘And how are you?’

Lee got herself a cup of tea and sat at the table across from Asha. ‘Don’t know what’s got into me.’

Lee described her new desire for Luca in great detail.

‘I’ve noticed.’ Asha said.

After disclosing the hospital episode with the duty nurse walking in as Luca headed for her bed, Lee said, ‘I sat in bed pulling my hair, praying for you to arrive. Thank God they brought you in time to save Luca and I from humiliating ourselves.’

Asha confessed awareness of their energy when the orderly had wheeled her in.

'When we got home this morning, we almost ran into my bedroom. I experienced Luca in a way I never imagined or even thought possible. Am I mad or did Dad sprinkle something on that serum before he injected me?'

'Don't blame the serum. I'm affected in the opposite direction.'

While Lee was away, Asha had spent a lot of time with Simon, serious time. She had even told him she loved him. But in the hospital, since recovering, she hadn't even returned his text messages.

'I didn't give it much thought until I spoke to him on the phone after our Channel nine broadcast. I felt like hanging up on him. Are you and I both mad?'

With no answer forthcoming, Asha conveyed Chris's message as she clicked onto the crowd-funding website. She turned her laptop 180 degrees.

'Have a look!'

Lee stared at the figures: 2,739 requests for the serum, $117,450 in monetary donations and 147 volunteers for packing.'

For a moment, Lee looked as though she had stepped off a Greyhound bus at 3 AM in an unfamiliar city. Then, her facial expression transformed into decisiveness, eyes darting around the room, searching for her phone.

Without turning her head, Asha pointed an index finger back over her shoulder to Lee's purse sprawled out on the floor. Lee blushed, but quickly found the phone and dialled.

'I suppose you've seen the website?' Chris said.

'I had a mental image of Luca, Asha and me sitting around the kitchen table here addressing jiffy bags and packing them with vials of serum. But I didn't imagine these numbers.'

Chris had called to ensure the trio was aware of the job ahead. But he had already started the preparation. The team at the lab had got behind their TV stunt. Sonia and Chris had been organising space at Vactech to house the distribution centre. Lidia was putting together the equipment needed. Danh was writing the software to read the names and addresses from the website and track them into a recipient file with each dose. Jody would train each person on the use of the software, and Mark will train everyone on the proper handling of the serum. Chris advised Lee to get cracking on organising her citizen-army scheduling, the packing to go 24/7. He cautioned Lee to keep any one person's shift to three hours, as the packing would be laborious, tedious, and repetitive, and errors could be fatal.

Without hesitation, Lee and Asha worked out a preliminary plan, then got straight into implementation mode, making calls, receiving calls, and writing notes.

Amongst this activity, Lee received a phone call from her infected flight attendant's boyfriend requesting a dose. He wanted to fly to Brisbane to collect it. Lee promised to deliver the serum to them by that evening and instructed him to quarantine himself until the serum arrived.

As Lee communicated the request, Luca came out of the bedroom.

'Are you two running an SP bookie operation?'

I knew an SP bookmaker was a person who took bets on horse races illegally. SP bookies distinguished themselves from the legal avenue for betting on races by the way they paid winning bets. The official tote could change the odds on a race even after the race had finished. This insured that they could not lose money on any race, but the SP bookies set the odds at the start of the race and didn't change them. Hence the name SP (Starting Price) bookie.

But as I didn't know how this connected to Luca's reference to Lee's and Asha's activity, I listened to his explanation with interest. Luca's Uncle Eddie used to run a bookmaking operation from his home. He had several telephones maned by people taking the bets, listening to the races on the radio and shouting the bets over to Uncle Eddie as they came in. The house was pandemonium.

'Yes,' Lee said, 'and now we have three operatives.'

She explained all that had happened in response to their TV appearance and asked Luca if he could catch the next available flight to Sydney and deliver the serum to her flight attendant. Luca returned to the bedroom to get ready, and Lee clicked onto a website to book his flight.

But Asha had other ideas. She put forward recruiting the flight attendant, her boyfriend and their colleagues to be carriers of the serum to every airport on the planet.

Lee's eyes widened. 'Got it. Luca will be busy in Sydney.'

'It might be better if I went. I've got another idea. Michael Masters will find this mission of mercy irresistible.'

Michael Masters, standing at the front door of an apartment, looked into the camera. 'Last night, I covered the launch of a bold campaign to halt the Climate Change Flu pandemic. Your response on the campaign's website was overwhelming. The first delivery of this initiative is happening as I speak.'

The camera panned to Masters' right, capturing Asha knocking on the apartment door.

A red-headed male opened the door. With his head tilted back, his expression suggested he might have been expecting a pizza from a home delivery service. But when Asha said,

'Hi Geoff, I'm Asha and have a delivery for you.' he exhaled deeply and pressed the palm of his hand to his heart.

'Wow, you wasted no time getting here. Come in.'

The camera tracked Asha entering the apartment and over to a table onto which she placed her briefcase. She opened the case, removed a small plastic vial containing the serum, and handed it to Geoff.

'Self-administering the serum is simple,' she said. 'Just shake the container, remove the lid, tilt your head back and squeeze the content into a nostril.'

Geoff followed her instructions, and Asha winked. 'You're now inoculated against the Climate Change Flu.' She then reached into her case, removed a second vial and handed it to Geoff. 'I believe you'll now deliver this vial to a special person.'

The camera tracked Asha and Geoff leaving the apartment. Geoff broke into a run, heading towards the lift. As Geoff pressed the lift's button, the camera cut back to Masters speaking to Asha.

'And Geoff's destination is …?'

'His girlfriend who's sick with CCF at Sydney Hospital.'

'That's two deliveries. But surely you can't make all subsequent deliveries in person to every victim across this planet.'

'Yes, we can!' Asha said. 'I promise everyone diagnosed with this flu will receive a hand-delivered dose of the serum within 24 hours of registering their request at the website.'

'How can you fulfil this extraordinary pledge?'

'As we speak, our team at Brisbane University is dispatching requests as they arrive at the website. We place each request into one of two categories: critical and prophylactic. Persons diagnosed as being infected with CCF are critical. Our dispatch team ranks the requests, packages all critical requests and delivers them to the airport where Australian Airlines takes over.'

'Then what happens?'

'Maybe I should let Mr Randaulf Stevens, the CEO of Australian Air tell this part of the story.'

The camera cut to a white-haired gentleman dressed in a black business suit standing to Masters' left. 'We transport the serum via the quickest route to the city in question and turn the parcel over to another one of Asha's volunteers waiting on the ground.'

Masters turned back to Asha. 'And then what happens?'

'The volunteer on the ground carries the package to the requested address.'

The camera followed Masters' eyes back to Stevens. 'How did Australian Air get involved? Asha said nothing yesterday when I interviewed her in the hospital.'

'Last night, I saw Lee, Luca and Asha on TV when they launched this initiative and I was so moved by their compassion, I donated my money on the spot. But a few hours ago, Asha fronted-up at my office, identified herself to my staff and requested to see me. I recognised her name straight away and, honoured, welcomed her. She put a such a compelling case for the airline to be part of this global humanitarian effort that I had no choice other than to commit Australian Air to the cause.'

Back in the Vactech packing room, the team was watching the broadcast on a TV Luca had set up. On hearing Steven's pledge, the entire room cheered.

When the ovation subsided, Lee stepped on to a chair. 'If you think we've been busy, we've only just begun. Let's get back to work.'

As the second round of cheering subsided, Lee's phone rang. It was Damian again. Although she had let his previous five calls go to voice mail, this time she accepted the call.

'Hi Lee, I'm so pleased I finally got you. I've been following your story over the international media. But I wanted to talk to you.'

Lee sighed. 'I can't talk now. Can I call you later?'

'I want you to know I'll be in Australia soon and want to thank you for identifying me as a close contact.'

'Ok, talk later. Bye.'

I was pleased to observe how Lee's response to the rooster had changed. While she was in Paris and from her first conversation with him, she sparked in his presence. But now he could have been a telemarketer pushing a new electricity supply plan. She slid her phone back into her hip pocket and turned her attention to her trainees.

Later that night, when Asha had returned home from Sydney, a sequence of events occurred, Wherein Lee recounted to Asha her recent brief telephone conversation with Damian and she confessed to consciously withholding Damian's name from the WHO investigator.

Asha's head dropped, 'Lee, I'm sorry. I intended to tell you, but totally forgot until now.'

Asha then disclosed the details of the morning she had retrieved Lee's laptop from her suitcase and searched its file for names of personal contacts in Paris.

Lee's face reddened as she glared back at Asha, 'Did Luca …?'

Asha retreated to her bedroom and returned with her original notes, laying them out for Lee to see. Sure enough, Damian's name appeared.

'How could you not tell me?'

As Lee read down the list, other names appeared who she also hadn't given to Tanoshia that day. But when Lee read the line, Évariste's letter with a line through it, she yelped, 'Oh my God,' and flew into her bedroom. One minute later, she returned with the letter she had placed in the suitcase she had only half unpacked. In the next moment she texted Chris 'I'm on my way over.' Lee arrived at her parents' house and found Chris in his study. She was now the one offering profuse apologies as she handed Chris the letter. Lee wondered off to find Alicia, leaving Chris to read the letter in private. Finding Alicia in bed, sitting up and reading, Lee sat on the bed and explained the reason for the late-night visit. Alicia reassured Lee that she hadn't an opportunity to give Chris the letter even if she had remembered.

'I suppose.' Lee said, 'but that night Évariste handed me the letter seems like ages ago.'

Considerable time had passed before Lee left Alicia's bedroom. On the way out, she returned to Chris and found him sitting back in his office chair with his eyes closed and listening to Rachmaninov's Second Piano Concerto.

'Dad, you OK?'

When Chris assured her he was fine, Lee asked about the letter.

'Nothing important,' Chris said, 'just a few things Évariste wanted me to do.'

Lee gave a hesitating nod and said, 'OK, catch you later.'

Évariste's letter was far from nothing, though. The opening paragraph had information that should have been good news. Chris had been short-listed for a prestigious award. Chris didn't seem to react to the news, but when he got to the second paragraph, his face tightened.

On the weekend before Lee arrived in Paris, Évariste had planned to take his jet ski out on the Saturday morning. He telephoned the marina housing the jet ski, requesting they ready it for him to leave at 8 AM. When he arrived that morning, everything appeared in order, with the jet ski in the water at the bottom of the ramp. He climbed aboard, put on his life jacket and powered up the jet ski.

Upon leaving the ramp, he opened the throttle to full. With the craft on the plane, he eased back on the throttle. But the jet ski continued to accelerate. He tried to kill the engine, but with no effect. He then pulled the dead-man cord, also with no effect. As he was still in the marina amongst several moored boats and with little room to manoeuvre, his split-second decision to turn the jet ski in a tight arc headed it towards a sandbar. Just before running aground, with the jet ski at full speed, Évariste jumped overboard. The craft ran up onto the sand, and with the engine screaming, came to a stop.

The marine rescue responded immediately, picking up Évariste still in the water and retrieving the jet ski. An ambulance took Évariste to hospital, but they later released him with non-critical injuries. He returned to the marina the next day and was told by staff the jet ski's jammed throttle appeared to have resulted from faulty maintenance. This assessment troubled Évariste as he regularly serviced the jet ski and only a week previous, he had serviced the machine. Days before the accident, he had received a threatening email warning him against his outspoken views on climate change. Évariste connected the two events, suspecting sabotage, but had no proof.

The letter's final paragraph expressed Évariste's apology to Chris for not spending more time with Lee. He had planned several outings with Lee and Luca but after the jet ski episode, was reluctant to place anyone else in jeopardy.

Évariste ended the letter, stating Lee was as charming as ever and had coped reasonably well at the cocktail party.

Chapter 17

The System Adjusts

Grey heavy clouds hanging low over Lake Geneva shrouded Rani's office window when Tanoshia arrived for their morning briefing. Rani turned from her computer screen, watching Tanoshia shake his head as he spoke.

The trials weren't going well. The problem resulted from my trio's global distribution ploy. Their program received so much global publicity the hospitals in the trial were having a hard time recruiting volunteers for the double-blind trial. Even the current volunteers were opting out of the trials and requesting the serum.

'Every time this saga produces a twist,' Rani said, 'The trail leads back to Chris Merritt.'

Each night for the preceding three weeks, Chris had perched on the couch across from the TV with his attention riveted on the CCF pandemic news broadcast. Reports from cities around the globe had showed people wearing protective facial masks, cued up waiting for hours for a CCF test. And each night, as the number of cases continued its exponential climb with the death toll mounting, Chris leaned ever closer to the TV screen, peering at the graphs. Alicia, sitting beside him and unable to contain herself, finally blurted out,

'Chris, please get a chair and move closer to the TV.'

Chris turned to Alicia with his eyebrows squishing together. He held that pose for a moment, stood, went into the dining room and returned with a chair. Positioning it halfway between the couch and TV facing Alicia, he swung his leg over the seat and straddled it, sitting upright as though in a saddle.

After the broadcaster announced a record number of cases, Chris told Alicia about the latest development in Lee's distribution scheme, which was then operating 24-7 in the Vactech building. Serum demand had exceeded Vactech's manufacturing capacity. Clive had brought two pharmaceutical companies on board to increase supply.

Alicia expressed her fears to Chris regarding the clear mismatch of reported infection case numbers and numbers of serum doses currently shipped around the globe.

'Is the serum's efficacy compromised? I mean, is the serum not having the same effect on others as it had on Lee, Luca and Asha?'

Chris conceded a mild concern over the figures. But the serum's high uptake rate without clinical trial results distressed him even more.

Alicia stood, 'I can't listen to this anymore,' and left the room.

For the following fortnight, the tension at home also spilled over into the lab, where the silence was palpable. In contrast to the lab's usual conviviality, everyone spoke minimally and in whispers. In small groups not including Chris, individuals exchanged brief interpretations of the previous day's CCF infection data.

At home each night, Chris, sitting by himself, hovered close to the TV screen, scrutinising the infection rate data. On the fourteenth night of this ritual, his hands shot into the air above his head. The exponential growth of cases in cities where the serum's uptake had been greatest had peaked.

But Alicia, who had also heard the statistics, said, 'Still sounds a lot to me.' Beaming, Chris grasped his chair with both hands and explained as he danced the chair back to the dining room table.

'Yes but, the growth rate is zero and tomorrow it will be negative.'

As Chris predicted, the number of daily cases reported fell on each of the next three days. But on the fourth day, viewing Masters' news broadcast, Chris's face turned ashen.

'The continuing saga of the CCF pandemic has today taken yet another bizarre turn. Three hospitals trialling the CCF serum pulled out because of ethical considerations. Deaths in the control group forced hospitals to discontinue the trials. One mystery in the CCF story since we first reported it is Professor Chris Merritt, the mastermind behind the CCF serum, has refused to comment publicly. He's also refused our request to comment on the demise of the clinical trials he designed.'

It wasn't only Chris who viewed Masters' news item with trepidation. Sonia spent a good portion of the night trolling the international news feeds, covering the collapse of the serum trials. She also searched social media platforms following threads of discontent regarding "Merritt's refusal to comment on his lab's role in the pandemic." So, when Chris entered the room for the team-meeting, looking not much better than he did after Masters' broadcast the previous night, he had company.

Chris began the meeting by thanking everyone for resisting media requests to comment on the CCF pandemic. But Sonia, in a wavering voice, asked,

'How much longer must we keep this silence up?'

'Now's the time to speak. I want to ask you, Danh, for a favour.'

Earlier that morning, Jody had received a request for Chris to address the National Press Club on the development and deployment of their CCF serum. As Danh would attend a conference, the next day to talk about their techniques, presenting to the NPC was a natural add-on to his agenda.

But Danh replied, 'I'm sure they want the organ grinder, not the monkey.' Chris persisted, however, and Danh complied.

'So, what reason should I give the Press Club for your non-appearance?' Danh asked, 'Bad case of the flu?'

The team had supposed Chris's reluctance to present at the NPC related to the need for rest following the stress associated with the serum production and distribution. Although that stress played a small part, the biggest source of Chris's stress was more complex and one he kept hidden. He had even only partially disclosed his situation to Alicia after she had pressed him to explain his social withdrawal.

Chris had been a first-grade squash player, enjoying the sport, its competitions and camaraderie. Well before Chris's retinal degeneration diagnosis, he noticed its first signs with the deterioration of his squash game. As his eye condition progressed, his squash suffered. He persisted until he got the official diagnosis when he quit the sport completely. Alicia knew this, but she still had to ask Chris, 'Why have you stopped playing bridge?'

Only after considerable prodding, Chris disclosed having misread a card which resulted in an untimely tournament loss. Following that event, Chris told his bridge partner he had lost interest in the game.

'But why everything else?' Alicia asked.

'I just need a little time.,' is all Chris would say.

Chris hadn't told Alicia about the threatening text messages, the suspected saboteurs of his bike, or the contents of Évariste's letter. When he learned of Évariste's conscious distancing from Lee, Chris too began avoiding situations with Alicia and Lee where he perceived a vulnerability. However, Chris took Luca into his confidence regarding the threatening messages and suspected saboteurs, asking him to be vigilant regarding Lee. Although Alicia didn't know of this deeper layer of Chris's withdrawal, she felt its effects.

After the team meeting, and with the campus' golden wattle trees and bottle brushes in full bloom, Lee and Chris sauntered towards the Echo café. Their heads turned to absorb every photon reflected from the vibrant yellow and red flowers. A magpie swooped from its nest in a tree just as they passed. Screeching, and with the agility of a black-belt in Kung-fu, the bird battered Lee's head with one wing and clawed the back of Chris's head in one fluid motion. Lee grabbed Chris's arm as she ducked. Chris thrust his other arm straight up over his head, warding off the attacker as it retreated to its nest.

Danh, walking towards them from the opposite direction, viewed the unfolding scene. He came up beside them with his casual manner, winked at Lee and turned to the vigilant magpie. Raising his hand and jabbing his finger towards the bird, he challenged it, mimicking Arnold Schwarzenegger.

'You want me? Come and get me. I kick your ass.' Danh turned back to Lee, now holding a hand over her mouth, and with a playful grin he said,

'Works every time. You won't have any more trouble.'

Before Lee could recover and with other onlookers gawking at Dan's cameo, he strode off, arms swinging loosely.

In a full grin and rubbing his head, Chris took Lee's arm and gently nudged her forward.

'Just what's so amusing?' Lee asked.

'Not amusing, just pleased. It's great to see a nesting magpie again. For several years, I've been observing a decline in magpie numbers on campus.'

Lee glanced back at the nesting magpie. 'Dad, I've been thinking about my experiences at the climate change conference and have so many questions.'

Lee had pondered why environmental organisations like Consent had such a hard time connecting with the public. Chris, who had struggled with this question also, reflected the commonly held Greenie's view, to which I agreed. People didn't want to change. They didn't feel the urgency. People accepted climate change as a big issue for future generations, but not for their own. Most people postponed sacrifices when possible and would empty their pockets when they couldn't. Chris illustrated his point with the response to Lee's CCF serum appeal. 'The immediacy of a loved one dying from the virus catapulted them into action. They had to support a solution to their perceived problem. But climate change to the masses is still someone else's issue, their unborn great grandchildren's.'

Lee nodded. 'Point taken. But it has to involve something else.' Lee recalled the image of Randolf Stevens, the CEO of Australia Air, when he was describing his response to the appeal. He said: "I was so moved". Lee acutely observed they had tapped into the CEO's feelings and connected into his core emotions.

'But not persuaded,' Chris said, 'The airline received a lot of kudos for his public gesture.'

'Sure, but I heard genuine empathy in his voice. Also, what about Sonia's response? She went straight to the website and donated. She could have regarded her work in developing the serum as sufficient, but she went beyond her scientific training and got involved on an emotional level.'

The Dean, stepping out of the Administration building about fifty paces from them, called out "G'day Chris". Chris turned and waved in the greeting's direction.

'Who's that?' Lee asked.

'Urn,'

'Isn't he the Dean?' Lee filled in Chris's hesitation.

‘Of course.’ Chris said.

As they walked on, Lee said, ‘If we could thwart a virus with the potential to devastate the human population using a genuine emotional appeal, can’t we deal with climate change with the potential to devastate the entire planet?’

At the café, Nancy congratulated Lee on her great work. Lee accepted the compliment graciously and perused the menu as Nancy chatted with Chris.

‘I like your new menu. I’ll have the fresh fruit salad,’ Lee said.

Chris blinked rapidly and stared at Lee for a moment before turning to Nancy with his order. Nancy, not commenting on Lee’s mistaken observation regarding new menus, nodded as she wrote, and departed.

Chris and Lee talked about the environment over lunch. As they were about to leave, a gleam came to Lee’s eyes. ‘Dad, we can beat this climate change malaise, and I’ll find a way.’

Chris entered the science building’s foyer as Jody entered from its opposite end. She saw him and, with her one-inch heels clicking on the tiles, hurried to join him. Chris’s head slightly jerked back as he peered toward the approaching clicks. When she came into his visual range, he said. ‘I thought a herd of nut crackers were pursuing me.’

Jody laughed, and they strolled back to the office together.

'What's having a celebrity daughter like?'

Chris grinned. 'Lee handles this status well, too well. She's already moved past the media attention. As we were parting company after lunch, she declared her commitment to turning around climate change. I watched her walk off in the opposite direction and I wondered, could the success of the serum distribution initiative have infused her with a little too much hubris? She has a newfound confidence, direction, and vision. I can't put my finger on it.'

Jody nodded. 'Yes, the girl I saw leave here to go off to Paris is not the self-assured woman I saw lifting everyone on the distribution team. It was as though she was a master symphony conductor in touch with everyone in the orchestra. I wondered if her father had been giving her lessons.'

'No, Lee's newfound self-confidence sure wasn't my doing.'

As they arrived at the front office, Jody's face filled with a wry smile. 'I recall my daughter's boost in self-confidence came when she started making new relationships outside the narrow circle of her school friends.'

Chris paused. ‘Well, Lee met several inspirational people.’ But then he stepped into his office, and that was the end of his speculation.

On arriving home that evening, Lee went to MyEnvironmentalFootprintCalculator.com and measured her environmental footprint. She considered each question: kilometres driven in her car, hours spent in planes, the size of her home, and more. Twenty minutes later, when she had completed the last question, the program calculated and displayed her environmental impact factor. If everyone on the planet consumed resources at the same rate as her, the planet would need 4.6 times the resources.

Lee scratched her jaw and re-answered the questions, but on her second try, she answered with more conservative estimates of her resource use. The conservative environmental footprint decreased to 4.3 planets.

Lee opened a new spreadsheet, and in the first row, entered the date of her first test and the result. She then wrote notes on changes to her current behaviour: ride a bike instead of a car. Buy local produce instead of imported items. Turn off electric lights when leaving a room. Raise the air conditioners thermostat level by two degrees.

Then she came to travel and paused. When she entered the note for this item, she typed “Have to think about this one!" I knew Lee's *penchant for travel* would confront her.

Over the preceding three weeks, since the conversation when Asha disclosed her reading of Lee's personal Paris notes, Lee had been distinctly cool towards Asha. Asha, too, had trouble understanding why Lee objected so strongly to her action. However, earlier in the day, Lee had received a message from a man who had isolated because of Asha's action. The man had developed CCF symptoms while isolated and had remained out of contact with his elderly mother over the infectious period. The message acknowledged Lee's prompt action as a selfless act responsible for saving his mother's life. A second similar message arrived from a woman whose isolation had prevented her from exposing patients in two aged care facilities from the virus. By the time Asha arrived home, Lee had realised the pettiness of her reactions to Asha's intervention and apologised unreservedly. In short order, the two were back on old terms and Lee told Asha about her disappointing carbon footprint results. Surprised with Lee's results, Asha did the environmental footprint assessment on herself. Expecting a result much lower than Lee's, having not taken any overseas trips in the past year, the impact factor figure of 4.4 planets shocked her. They were discussing the changes they'd need to make when Luca arrived.

Luca had literally been the middleman hearing criticisms from both Lee and Asha about the other and had been the reluctant peacemaker. Watching them now relate to each other in their old ways, he raised his arms above his head and sang, 'Halleluiah.'

But Lee just sat him straight down in front of her computer. 'Let's measure your environmental footprint.'

'3.9 planets, don't believe it! What'd you guys get?'

Lee mentioned her and Asha's results and recounted information The Rooster — Lee just referred to him as some guy, had told her while at the Paris conference. Reducing the carbon usage individually was impossible unless one was prepared to live in a cave and only eat raw vegetables. He also claimed geo-engineering would solve the global warming problem.

The way Luca crossed his arms, I suspected he had identified the source of Lee's oblique reference. Luca redressed the geo-engineering nonsense recounting a story he had written. The geo-engineering approaches fell into two categories. Both were theoretically valid but fell short practically. One was what they called albedo reduction, which Luca interpreted in his unique style.

'Albedo reduction wis pretty similar to official Australian policy on the environment for most of the 20th century. If it moves, shoot it. If it's green, chop it down, and if it's neither, then paint it white.'

‘Oh Luca,’ Lee gasped and punched his arm.

‘I’m not kidding.’ Luca said, but continued in more literal terminology.

The albedo reduction scheme amounted to painting the planet white. Theory suggested one had to paint at a rate equivalent to the melting glaciers. The net effect was the Earth reflected the same amount of sunlight, or more, back into space. Sunlight is the actual source of Earth warming.

Asha smirked. ‘Let’s suppose for the moment we paint most solid structures on land white. Water covers most of Earth’s surface, 75%. How would you paint water white?’

‘No problem,’ Luca said. ‘They string massive quantities of ping-pong balls together, forming giant floating islands in the oceans.’

Asha and Lee stared at him.

‘Ok, I’m simplifying it. But albedo reduction just comes down to reflecting the sun’s radiant light before it’s absorbed by the green-house gases, carbon dioxide and methane.’

Lee gave a slow laugh and asked for the geo-engineers second approach.

‘If one doesn’t like the colour white,’ Luca said, ‘their second approach uses another colour.

Records of Earth temperatures in decades following major volcanic eruptions showed Sulphur dioxide in the atmosphere cooled the planet. Geo-engineers cited Krakatoa in 1883 as the classic example. Armed with this solid theoretical model, the geo-engineers would mine sulphur and manufacture sulphur dioxide and shoot it into the atmosphere, counterbalancing the warming effects of increased carbon dioxide. They asserted humanity could burn as much fossil fuel as they liked, with no ill effect apart from the sky being an iridescent shade of orange.'

Luca concluded his geo-engineering summary in a manner which confirmed my original suspicion.

'Whoever spun you this geo-engineering yarn, Lee, has a few kangaroos loose in their top paddock.'

Lee and Asha nodded, showing not the slightest sign of confusion. However, decoding Luca's message took me considerable effort. But my success in the endeavour represented a turning-of-the-tide moment in my understanding metaphor. I now regard Luca as providing one of the greatest influences on my love of this art form.

'Regarding our carbon usage behaviour, we've got work to do,' Lee asserted. 'But I know we can do it.' She paused. 'Have you guys noticed the change in the way we do things?'

Both nodded without speaking.

'My thoughts just seem so much clearer now.'

My chosen ones were now listening to a powerful voice from within.

Chapter 18

Unintended Consequences.

A volley of cheers hit Chris as he entered the serum shed. Everyone was applauding Danh's televised address to the National Press Club in Canberra. He stopped alongside Jody.

'How'd it go?'

Jody's bright eyes fixed on Chris as her body turned to face him.

'He began in a dignified manner, acknowledging the traditional landowners, then descended into that appalling sense of humour of his to explain why you could not attend.'

Chris cringed as though Jody's fingernails had started a slow descent across a blackboard.

The NPC moderator asked for questions from the audience. And Jack Perkins, a CBS broadcaster with a baritone voice, cut-off Jody's attempt to repeat Danh's joke.

'Jack Perkins from CBS. Your gene editing techniques appear to be more of an engineering process than a biological one. Given your lab isn't the only team using this approach to serum development, what's the critical aspect of your technique accounting for you beating every other lab in the world developing the CCF serum?'

Danh held his breath, listening to the question, but lifted his chin as he answered. 'Our approach is an efficient interplay amongst three components: computer simulation of virtual experiments, artificial intelligence, and empirical experimentation. We access a vast amount of microbiological data from which our AI system runs, and analyses simulated experiments. The over-whelming complexity of protein structures means these simulations embody considerable error. Our AI guesses to fill in the gaps. When the simulation is complete, the AI describes the percentage error in the data. Chris Merritt designs an experiment generating real data which feeds back to the AI to replace the hypothesised data. This iterative process continues until the AI's output formula is a winner. So, in all honesty, with the CCF virus, we got lucky hitting the winning antivirus so soon. We are rarely so fortunate.'

I winced when Danh described our accomplishment as resulting from luck, but under the circumstances, modesty was best.

As Jody and Chris strolled back to the Centre, she resumed highlighting Danh's address. They crossed the avenue separating the university campus and Vactech. As they approached the artificial lake at the foot of the campus, Chris stopped. 'Listen.'

When Jody shook her head, Chris mimicked the bird call he had just heard, 'coo, coo, coo, coo,' followed by a trilling and a final rising 'cooee.'

He looked in the sound's direction but couldn't see the bird and asked Jody. 'Can you see it?' Jody scanned a clump of trees near the lake.

'I think so,' she said. 'In the Blue Gum, about three quarters of the way up on a branch on the right side.' The motionless bird was out of Chris's visual range. He pulled a phone from his pocket. 'Can you video it for me?' Jody's hand shook as she zoomed in.

The bird raised its head, its throat dropped, and it chorused a second time.

'Can you see where its beak points?' Chris asked.

'At us. Actually, right at you.'

The skin around Chris's eyes bunched as he peered at Jody.

'Oh dear.'

On one occasion, when Chris was bushwalking with Lee and Luca, they'd heard that distinctive chorus. Luca had pulled up stock still. His Uncle had taught him the Yurung's chorus signaled the imminent arrival of bad news to the person pointed to by its sharp beak.

Back in his office, Chris slid down into his office chair. Connie had left a message on his voicemail, and the distress in her voice was unmistakable. He pressed the call-back button, and the line connected on the second ring.

'Connie,' he said. 'What's wrong?'

'The CMO received the WHO report on the source and cause of the Climate Change Flu. Although the report made no assertion regarding CCF's cause, it concluded the most likely source of the virus was your lab. Mathews claims they found a similar virus there.'

Chris fumbled with the phone. 'What? That's ridiculous. What related virus?'

'It's mad, I know. But until we receive the full written report, we can't do much.'

Chris replaced the phone in its cradle, put both elbows on the desk, and buried his face in his hands. I had expected he would have trouble handling this one, but I couldn't tell whether he was in absolute denial or self-recrimination. However, when his head lifted, his jaw clenched. He dialled Danh's mobile phone number. 'As soon as you land, come to my office.'

Later that evening, Danh entered the Centre's darkened reception area. A shaft of light across the floor showed the path to Chris's three quarters closed door. Danh gently tapped it twice with one knuckle and pushed, revealing Chris's furrowed brow and pursed lips.

'I couldn't have been that bad.'

'We've a problem needing absolute discretion.' Chris said with a forced smile, 'I'll give it to you straight. The WHO report fingered our lab for generating and releasing CCF.'

Danh pressed the splayed fingers of one hand against his chest. 'Christ, that's impossible!'

Chris communicated the details of his conversation with Connie.

'During your congratulatory TV interview presenting our face to the world,' Chris said, 'the CMO was reading the WHO report identifying our lab as the most likely source of the virus.'

Danh leaned back, looking like a checkmated chess player.

When Tanoshia Mathews had questioned Chris about the CCF virus found in the Level-4 lab, he seemed to have accepted Chris's explanation, which Chris had taken to mean their trail had fizzled out. However, they had also found DNA of a benign but related virus in the Centre's open lab, the result of which Tanoshia hadn't communicated to Chris. Since Connie's phone call though, Chris had been pondering the mysterious result.

Chris reviewed his lab notes describing experiments to test Danh's algorithm's ability to analyse and design antiviruses. A comment at the end of the report of the breakthrough experiment following their unexpected coronavirus serum failure caught his attention.

'The learning algorithm of the microbe's structure converged unusually quick.'

Chris had somehow guessed that if the WHO report was correct, then the breakthrough experiment was their culprit. I didn't think there was enough information for Chris to make the connection, because the test virus used was both common and benign. I was wrong. The consistent accuracy of Chris's hunches amazed me, and this was no exception.

Chris had tried to tighten his hypothesised connection between the CCF virus and Lee's observation by reproducing the experiment — only he ran it in the Level-4 lab. This time, Chris saw nothing unusual. Neither the CCF nor the related virus appeared. Chris couldn't even reproduce the colour Lee had mentioned.

After Chris disclosed this information to Danh, they recounted the sequence of events surrounding that day's experiment. Lee had wandered around the lab waiting while I reported a simulation result over the phone. Chris observed Lee lean over the experiment's culture dish. When He had finished with me, Lee scooted over, took Chris by the wrist, and dragged him out of the lab. While at lunch, Lee asked Chris about the interesting colour of the substance in the culture dish she had seen earlier. But as Chris didn't remember any strange colours in his experiments, he checked all the dishes on his return to the lab. All the colours were uniform. Nothing unusual, he thought, and then he had glanced at the computer monitor of the second dish. The algorithm they were testing had almost learned the structure of the protein to switch on the desired interferon trigger. Excited, Chris had phoned Danh, who had sprinted over. The algorithm had described the protein with only a 7% error. Danh fed the data back into me to see if it could improve the result.

While Danh was with me, Chris worked on identifying the other strategic microbes and designing the new experiments. Then Danh returned with a new algorithm. They set up the experiments on the other microbes, and by the end of the afternoon, they had reduced the error rate to 1%. And they were close to identifying the structure of the elusive universal trigger combating all coronaviruses.

Chris had completely forgotten about Lee's observation. He hadn't even mentioned it to Danh.

Danh rubbed the back of his neck. 'Jesus, last night we were being lorded as Nobel Prize candidates and when this gets out, we might wind up going to prison. Do the others know?'

Chris hadn't communicated the situation to the others and wanted to keep the matter between him and Danh for as long as possible.

Dahn nodded slowly. 'I agree to some extent. But if somebody leaks the WHO report and accuses us before we announce the source, they'll crucify us. They might even accuse us of creating the CCF deliberately.'

Chapter 19

Escalation

Before leaving home for work, Lee, Luca, and Asha had agreed to meet for dinner at Asha's favourite restaurant, The Sky Bar. This was convenient for me, as Lee's and Luca's preferred venues tended not to have the security systems provided by Asha's choices.

On the last occasion when Lee entered the foyer of the hotel housing the Sky Bar, just before her Paris sojourn, her posture was rigid, appearing as though she was trying not to look at the decor. But now she strode into the foyer as though returning home. She smiled as her eyes took in the chandelier suspended from the six-metre-high dome-shaped ceiling. Red glass panels swept up from the marble floor to meet the dome's circumference. Visitors, listening to music, played at a grand piano, relaxed in black leather chairs arranged around coffee tables on either side of the corridor leading to the elevator. The doors opened as she approached. The elevator's back wall was a floor-to-ceiling glass video screen, providing the elevator's occupants the sensation of peering into a massive aquarium with tropical fish and plants. As the elevator's door closed, its glass floor also turned into a live video display, giving the occupants the sensation of standing on the surface of an aquarium housing a variety of sharks.

On Lee's previous elevator ride, she giggled and clutched Asha's arm. But on this occasion, her eyes scrutinised individual sharks. At the twenty-first floor, she exited.

The maître d', decked out in a four-piece suit complete with the Sky Bar's signature cummerbund, stepped out from behind the copper-plated reception desk and greeted her by name. He led Lee to a table by the window.

'Something to drink while you wait?'

'Water please.'

I viewed Lee from the camera concealed within the smoked-glass dome attached to the ceiling nearest her table. With her arm perched on the back of her chair, Lee surveyed the Brisbane River. In those days, the river presented in various shades of dingy brown. But at this height and with the setting sun, it didn't look bad, lazily winding its way through the city and eastward to the Gateway Bridge to the river's mouth.

Lee received an SMS. 'I'm leaving now. Be there in 20.'

Her water arrived, and she settled back, gazing at the lengthening shadows creeping across the city.

Asha emerged from the elevator. A man peering at Lee from a nearby table caught Asha's attention, but as she approached Lee's table, he looked away. Asha slumped into a chair opposite Lee and deposited her briefcase onto the floor.

'Rough day?' Lee said.

Asha described what would be a busy day by most people's standards and mentioned her diligence in keeping her billable hours higher than the other associates. This had been Asha's fast-track strategy for achieving her goal of becoming a partner.

'Now, that goal seems so meaningless. Anyway, how are you doing?'

'I've been thinking about the less attractive side of my job, too. Talking with my boss today, I said CONSENT doesn't seem to make a real impact. I believe in their goals. But we aren't landing punches.'

Lee waved to Luca as he entered the restaurant. He kissed Lee's and Asha's cheeks and sat down.

'The airport motorway was a carpark,' Luca said.

'How'd Danh's address to the National Press Club go?' Lee asked.

'Brilliant, I'm glad I went. He opened by acknowledging the traditional landowners, which I think is a darn good opener for the son of a Vietnamese refugee. He also praised both of you even though you, in his words, destroyed the program to conduct clinical tests of the serum.'

A server came to the table and offered Luca a wine list, which he perused with great interest. Lee and Asha deferred Luca's requests for suggestions and ordered a bottle of chardonnay.

Their conversation drifted to an exploration of individual efforts in reducing one's carbon footprint. Each confessed a failure and conceded an impossibility of achieving an acceptable level.

'Are our planet's prospects hopeless with people like us inhabiting it?' Lee said.

After a momentary pause, Lee recalled a challenge Evariste had casually put to her in Paris when they had been discussing climate change.

'Climate change is the biggest single issue a person of my age can work on. But someone of your age, Lee, should tackle the big question.'

Lee hadn't even known to what Évariste had been referring. But now she reflected on his challenge. 'What's the big question?'

They brain-stormed looming environmental issues of the day. For a century, people had been dumping non-biodegradable plastics into the oceans. The 20th century saw the simultaneous explosion of the human population and the per capita increase in the consumption of Earth's finite natural resources. Even though the planet had international laws governing genocide, crimes against humanity and war crimes, there were no international laws specific to crimes against the environment.

At that point in the discussion, Asha saw the server approaching the table and put her hand up. 'Hey, time out. Our wine's here. Let's order.'

The sommelier poured a small amount into Luca's glass. Luca lifted the glass by the stem to eye level, swirled its contents and held the glass' rim beneath his nose, inhaling slowly. He paused for a moment and nodded. After Lee and Asha sampled the wine's fragrance placed in their glasses by the server, the ritual was complete. Until observing this event, I had dismissed olfactory sensing as little more than a tool for tea-tasters and coalmine-canaries. But on this occasion, I detected a more profound effect, one at an emotional level. I realised this phenomenon warranted further scrutiny.

When the server left, Luca proposed a toast to the environment. And after each had tasted their wine, he turned to Lee.

'The big one's sustainability.'

They contemplated Luca's assertion, as the Brisbane city lights appeared.

'Don't look,' Asha said, 'but a man at the table in front of me has been taking a lot of interest in us.'

In a lowered tone, she relayed her observation when she had exited the lift.

'I don't have to look. I've noticed it, too,' Luca said. Lee grappled with the urge to turn as Asha shook her head and turned the discussion in another direction.

She described the environmental problem in terms of approach. Government blames industry, as implied by the use of carbon taxes. Industry blames individuals, as evidenced by their creation of the carbon footprint calculator. And individuals blame government as evidenced by the growth of minor political parties.

'Maybe we need to tackle this issue from a different angle, one based on solution generation, not finger pointing.'

She postulated a socio-economic/political organisation dedicated to moving the planet's humanity over to sustainable living. They all played along with the thought bubble by proposing names of such a hypothetical organisation. Asha suggested Cognise.

But Luca killed the name. 'Too much head stuff for my taste.' and countered with 'Resonate.'

'Not specific enough.' Lee said and added, 'How's RENEW sound?'

Asha reached for her phone and googled RENEW. 'Bad luck. In use.'

From Asha's phone, I saw the glint come to Luca's eyes. 'Collaboration Earth?' and Asha's googled search came up empty.

'Bingo, you've nailed it.'

But she continued whispering, 'Lee, take a casual look at the man in the white dinner jacket sitting at the first table to your left.'

Luca shook his head and retrieved his laptop. He set it on the table and opened it. In a lowered voice, he said, 'I'll orientate the screen so that you see his reflection. It's the oldest trick in the book.'

He explained the target was too far away to see Lee's reflection on the screen. But she was close enough to the screen to see him. Luca positioned the computer, and Lee focused on the white jacketed one.

'Don't know him.'

Luca raised his eyebrows. I wondered why Asha and Luca regarded this man's interest as so special, as many other restaurant patrons also periodically glanced at them.

Unperturbed, Lee led the conversation into an exploration of the fundamental beliefs underpinning their hypothetical movement. Asha googled "environmental manifesto". Luca thought about the issues and Lee pulled out her pen and pad. They worked on the issue until their orders arrived: Atlantic salmon for Asha, beef stroganoff for Lee, and a Buddha salad for Luca. But they kept talking as they ate.

'You first, Lee.' Asha said.

Lee read from her notes. ‘We respect the biological integrity of this planet and acknowledge the subsystems making up the biosphere represent a panarchy of systems where all subsystems connect and are interdependent. We commit to restoring the social, environmental, political and economic cohesion required for planetary sustainability.’

‘You’ve touched the serious issues.’ Asha said.

But Luca said, ‘Needs more emotional content.’ And gave his formulation with a preamble.

‘My statement isn’t as original as Lee’s. Mine is, well, you’ll see where it comes from. “We hold these truths to be self-evident. No generation may degrade the inhabitability of the biosphere; all generations are endowed by their Creator with certain unalienable rights. Among these are clean air, clean water, and a sustainable environment.”’

Asha pre-empted her contribution with an apology. ‘Mine possesses no personal originality. See if you recognise it. “We must join to bring forth a sustainable global society founded on respect for nature, universal human rights, economic justice, and a culture of peace. Towards this end, it is imperative we, the peoples of Earth, declare our responsibility to one another, to the greater community of life, and to future generations.”’

As soon as Asha spoke the declaration’s last word, Lee answered. ‘Dad often recited this by heart when I was a child. This statement is the preamble to Earth Charter, 2000.'

Luca leaned in. 'Wow, that says it all.'

'I also recall Dad lamenting, although adopted as the preamble to the Earth Charter, nobody implemented it.'

They descended into silence, each appearing to be contemplating the conundrum. Lee gazed out the window, Asha folded the napkin in her lap, and Luca peered at the wine bottle label.

Luca broke the silence. 'Why don't we address Chris's lament by making Collaboration Earth's mission implementing the preamble to the Earth Charter?'

'Yeah,' Lee said, and Asha grinned

Luca Expanded on the meaning of sustainability. He explained that when his Uncle Erney introduced him to it, when he took him *on country* as a kid to teach him of what he called the laws, '—never take more than you need.'

Asha contrasted Luca's subjective definition with a twenty-first century version.

"People must maintain all-natural capital." Then she paused, glanced down at the remains of her salmon, and added, 'like fish.'

Luca lifted the bottle of wine and half-filled Asha's glass. He was about to pour the last portion into Lee's empty glass when the White-Jacketed one appeared at their table and spoke.

'Sorry to gate crash your dinner, but I just want to congratulate the three of you on your splendid work with the CCF serum project.' Then he tilted his head and left.

Lee forced a smile, and Luca frowned. As they watched him head for the register, Asha said, 'Don't like that dude's vibes.'

Luca stood. 'I'll be back in five.'

He went to the elevator, descended to the lobby, and left through the main entrance. Positioning himself several metres from the front door, he idly viewed his phone messages. Not two minutes later, the hotel's valet drove up from the carpark and stopped at the front door. The White-Jacketed one emerged from the lobby, thanking the valet as he received the keys. With the camera skills of a seasoned journalist, Luca photographed the car's rearview with his phone.

Luca arrived back at the table just as the server delivered two chocolate mousses.

Asha smiled. 'For a moment, I was afraid Lee and I would have to eat this without you.'

Luca apologised for his hasty exit and explained his ploy to get the white-jacketed one's registration number.

'I'll run a check on him tomorrow.'

Lee cocked her head, 'Will you two please explain what this is in aid of?'

Asha and Luca looked at each other, waiting for the other to speak. 'Go ahead,' Asha said.

Luca described how The-White-Jacketed one maintained a direct line of sight to them just over his dinner companion's left shoulder.

'Several times I caught him furtively turning his eyes from us back to his companion without moving his head.'

Asha's opinion was that His companion seemed slightly annoyed with his excessive interest in them. But Lee shook her head.

'He's probably harmless.'

The resolution provided by the restaurant's camera did not perceive the White-Jacketed-One's eye movements and its position provided only a rear view of his dining companion. Unable to substantiate Asha's and Luca's observation, I shared Lee's assessment.

Lee pushed her mousse across the table to Luca, and Asha divided hers in two, giving one to Lee. As soon as they finished the dessert, conversation returned to specifying mission objectives.

Luca grabbed his computer. 'Let's write this directly on a website.' Their ideas flowed onto the page, only pausing momentarily for coffee. Luca began describing an electronic instrument to mediate the global use of carbon.

‘Sounds like Carboncoin that was in the news a while ago.’ Asha said.

Luca acknowledged similarity in intention, removing CO_2 from the atmosphere. But he then specified a key distinction.

Until then, all the ideas I had heard from them had originated from their readings. The earlier thought bubble was rapidly crystallising, and I listened with elevated interest.

‘My currency will influence the entire goods and services supply chain.’

Asha’s brows drew closer. But Lee sought clarification.

Luca thought individuals should take responsibility for the carbon in the products and services they consume.

He hypothesised a simple example using the restaurant’s menu. If every item on the menu had displayed with its price, a number representing its carbon footprint, diners could account for the carbon they consume.

‘How?’ Lee said.

‘Are you prepared to pay an additional amount of money to remove your beef stroganoff’s carbon contribution from the atmosphere?’

Lee thought for a moment. ‘I would if the money guaranteed its removal.’

Luca had the desired answer and elaborated on the mechanism underpinning his digital currency. He had written a story on companies developing technologies capable of extracting CO2 directly from the atmosphere and sequestering it as a liquid into the ground. His plan had carbon footprint conscious individuals purchasing sequestered carbon using his digital currency, named Earth Savers, held in a digital wallet. From the wallet, the customer would transfer to the restaurant a quantity of Earth Savers equivalent to the carbon component printed on the menu next to the item. The single government constraint in this plan required the venders to achieve a specified carbon footprint.

Asha contributed a pertinent observation. Luca's digital currency implied a new category distinct from the term financial instrument describing Bitcoin and the other digital currencies. She dubbed Luca's Earth Savers, an environmental instrument.

I had expected my trio to reach out with their environmental interests. Although listening to them unveil the details of the CE approach intrigued me, I didn't expect the global scale of their thinking. But the greatest epiphany of my brief existence came with their discussion of the logo.

They began with an exploration of the ideals they wanted CE's logo to project, tabling words and phrases that projected the ideals of their fledgling organisation: cooperation, compassion, organisation, integrity, sustainability, Earth. Then their activity subsided for a while, with each turning inward on these concepts.

Luca was the first to reactivate, retrieving his pen and sketching on his napkin. Asha followed suit. Lee sat there motionless with her eyes closed for a while. Then, in one fluid movement, she sketched a cluster of seven hexagons on the pad she had been taking notes on. Without taking a second look at her artwork, she pushed the pad across the table closer to Asha and Luca, which caused them to look up. They focused on Lee's image. Asha's gaze moved from the pad to Lee's face and back to the pad again. She tried to speak, but was unable. Lee, unsettled by Asha's uncharacteristic silence, looked to Luca, whose expression was also indiscernible, constant and as though absorbed in the study of a mathematical equation. Lee, perplexed by her companion's responses, broke the silence.

'Well?'

Luca folded his napkin over onto itself, sliding his finger along the fold to produce a crease, pushed it aside, and reached for his laptop. Asha remained silent, turning to watch Luca's fingers fly about his keyboard, implementing Lee's logo. When Luca completed his implementation, he created another cluster of seven hexagons in the centre of the webpage, placed Lee's name in the centre hexagon,

Asha's name in the second hexagon, his name in the third hexagon and a question mark in each of the remaining four hexagons. He positioned his laptop for Lee's and Asha's viewing.

'Voila.'

Lee and Asha both sat expressionless.

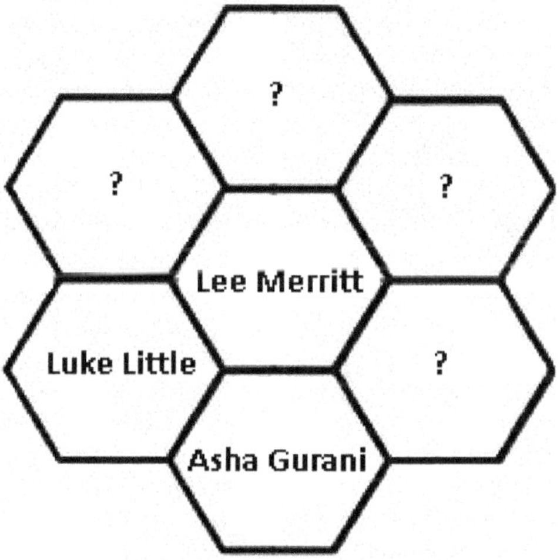

'Don't you get it?' he said.

'The names of new members will replace the question marks in each of the nameless hexagons,' said Lee.

'Yes.'

'But are you only allowing for seven members or only expecting to attract four more members?'

'No to both parts of your question.'

Asha frowned. 'And?'

Luca smiled broadly. 'You'll see in time.' Then, content to leave them suspended with that thought, he added a public invitation to like-minded people to join the cause. He requested people to register their name on the website and commit to the organisational goals.

Lee and Asha both gave a thumbs up and Luca pushed the launch icon. 'Done!'

Asha ordered a bottle of champagne, and they toasted the launch of Collaboration Earth. Luca swallowed a large sip. 'I wonder how long it'll take for someone to find our website.'

'Don't hold your breath waiting.' Asha said.

Chapter 20

The Pattern Breaks

When Lee, Luca and Asha left the restaurant, they piled into Luca's car and continued exchanging thoughts on Collaboration Earth throughout the drive home. Luca pulled up in front of the apartment, turned to Lee, and fumbled for words. As Lee remained silent and didn't move, Luca looked back at Asha, who said, 'I'll say good night to you two here.' She popped out of the car and trundled upstairs.

As soon as they saw Asha close the door behind her, Lee and Luca reached for each other without speaking. All I could hear was enthusiastic kissing and fragments of half articulated emotions.

'I love the smell and texture of your skin.' Luca said.

Lee and Luca never kissed like this in front of Asha. Although I had sampled the internet's plethora of erotic material available during its early years, until a few nights earlier, I had not observed Lee's and Luca's special variations on such indulgences. Lee and Luca had arrived home to a dark and silent apartment.

'Is Asha not home tonight?' Luca asked.

'She's in Sydney for work.'

Luca went to the sound system and selected a guitar solo, a track from Marvin Gaye's album, *Let's Get It On*.

Lee, standing at the opposite end of the room, dimmed the lights. They turned to face each other. With their eyes locked, they danced in time to the music towards the centre of the Persian carpet.

Luca slid his fingers over the sleeves of Lee's silk blouse from her wrist to her shoulders. They kissed. With their lips hardly touching, Luca began undoing Lee's blouse buttons. Lee responded in kind, undoing Luca's shirt buttons even more slowly. She kissed each new patch of his exposed skin as the buttons fell away, Luca breathing in deeply through his lips.

With their top garments removed, Luca reached behind Lee, unhooking her bra. They continued, disrobing the lower half of each other.

So here I was in a ringside seat viewing an event via a camera I had previously only heard through a microphone. Luca lifted Lee with the poise of a ballet dancer, lowering her to the floor, her long blond hair flowing across the purple and gold temple embossed in the carpet.

Luca, kneeling at Lee's feet, began massaging her toes, his index fingers working between each. His fingers slid over the soles of her feet, over her ankles, and stroked the sides of her lower legs.

Lee's breath sucked in when Luca's fingers reached her thighs, the tips of his thumbs repeatedly stroking upward to her groin. She gave a low moan. With her eyes closed and her lips parted, she seemed to have all her attention focussed on the sensation delivered by Luca's fingertips.

Luca straddled her hips, continuing with her fingers, hands, and arms. Her back arched off the carpet. Luca's left hand slid to the small of her back while the other hand caressed the back of her neck. His body lowered until his nose touched the skin between her breasts. His head undulating in time to the music as his nose swept back and forth from one side of her cleavage to the other.

When their bodies eventually pulled apart and remained motionless on the carpet, I corrected another one of my misperceptions. I had been well aware of the way humans used their lips and fingers to pleasure each other. But until this occasion, I had mistakenly presumed pressure sensors were a rather unimportant sensory device. For the first time, I experienced how this behaviour enhanced their trust of each other.

So, within the car's darkness, I filled in the visual details with my newly gained knowledge. Lee spluttered, breathless, something about 'Being good.' Luca laughed as he leaned back into an upright position. Lee got out of the car. At the building's front door, she turned and waved. Luca returned the gesture and started the car. As he drove off, his breathing gradually returned to normal.

Asha had already retired to her bedroom by the time Lee entered the apartment. Lee put the kettle on, opened and closed the refrigerator, paced the living room, and then switched the kettle off and retreated to her bedroom. But instead of readying herself for sleep, she returned to the table with her laptop in hand. Lee booted the computer, logged in, and visited the CE website. Her penetrating blue eyes dilated as she read the new name in the fourth hexagon.

My initial plan didn't include engaging Lee with a new persona. But the effect of simultaneously viewing Lee's logo from the restaurant's camera and Asha's phone while comprehending its internal representation from within Luca's computer motivated a recalibration. I knew from Lee's earlier comments, using the FAIM persona created by Danh wasn't an option.

Lee clicked open my email message within moments of its arrival:

'Dear Lee, your manifesto compelled me to join. I'm an environmental engineer with a company producing photovoltaic solar collectors and hope my background is of value to CE.'

Lee's eyes sparkled as she typed. 'Dear Satoshi, great to have you on board as our first public member. The other three names are the manifesto's authors. From your brief bio, you represent a fabulous asset to CE. Can we switch over to Skype and talk live?'

Lee enthusiastically clicked the link I had sent. Her disappointment with the blurred image displayed on her screen was palpable.

'My video reception isn't great. How's yours?'

I told her my reception here in rural northeastern England wasn't good either. In those primitive days of the internet, limited bandwidth often caused such issues. So, I knew my explanation sounded plausible. Lee accepted my suggestion we break the video to improve audio connection.

'Hi Satoshi, great to meet you. I'm intrigued by your background. Your skills are central to CE's mission.'

We chatted for a while regarding my experience and expertise before she asked,

'What attracted you to the website?'

I truthfully confessed the logo fascinated me and asked if she was aware of the symbol's significance?

'No.'

Reluctant to accept her vacuous answer, I tried another angle, asking why she chose that configuration of seven hexagons? But once again, her reply disappointed.

'I'm sorry to say there's no big intellectual process behind our choice. I simply saw it in my mind's eye.' Incredulous with what I perceived as false modesty, I suggested she was selling herself short.

'I wasn't kidding.' She snapped. 'What are you getting at?'

I accepted the veracity of her denial. But I was unsure of how or even if I should proceed, revealing the extent of the symbol's meaning.

My multi-level perception of the logo in the restaurant had produced three distinct interpretations. Presuming at least two interpretations were incorrect, I attempted to resolve the contradiction. My investigation involved searching arcane domains of the internet I had previously not ventured and exploring mathematical concept I had not considered.

My explanation for Lee began at the highest level. Her cluster of seven hexagons unified the ancient mystical traditions, art, and current scientific knowledge of her age.

'Right,' Lee said, dragging out the single syllable.

Convincing Lee I wasn't a crank or even exaggerating took some work. I was pretty sure Lee was exposed to the symbol in her life, and the most likely explanation was it emerged from her subconscious. The ubiquity of the hexagon in nature placed Chris as the most likely suspect as the source of Lee's introduction. So, I cast around suggesting examples from biology, neuroscience and mathematics. But all my guesses came up cold. Just as I was ready to abort this approach, the answer appeared just over Lee's left shoulder. The painting on the wall behind her depicted the Anahata Mandala. I had viewed Asha using this painting at the beginning of her morning yoga practices. But until this very moment with Lee, I had never really seen it. This painting portrayed the fourth chakra as a circle of twelve petals of the lotus flower, which enclose two intersecting equilateral triangles of different colours where the area of overlap, a hexagon, displayed a third colour. I asked Lee, in a nonchalant manner, if she had ever viewed examples of Indian artwork, which occasionally embodies hexagons in sacred symbols? Lee's body slowly turned until she faced the painting. I waited patiently, watching the back of her motionless head for several seconds, wondering if Lee would see the connection.

'Actually, I'm now looking at a painting depicting one of the seven metaphysical wheels of energy from the yoga tradition?'

'Really? Do you know what it represents?'

'I asked Asha this question the day I moved in. I think she said the fourth chakra associates with the heart and the emotions of love and compassion.'

'Do you see your logo in the painting?'

Lee took her time to reply. 'I do and I don't. I'm not sure.'

I suggested we explore this together and asked if she had drawing materials available? Lee leaned over the table, picked up a pencil, and slid a notepad across.

'Yes.'

I asked her to draw the cluster of seven hexagons in the page's centre. A few moments later, Lee said. 'Done.'

I then requested her to construct an outer ring of hexagons enclosing her original seven, so all the edges articulated with no gaps. When she completed this task, I asked her to count the hexagons comprising the outer ring.

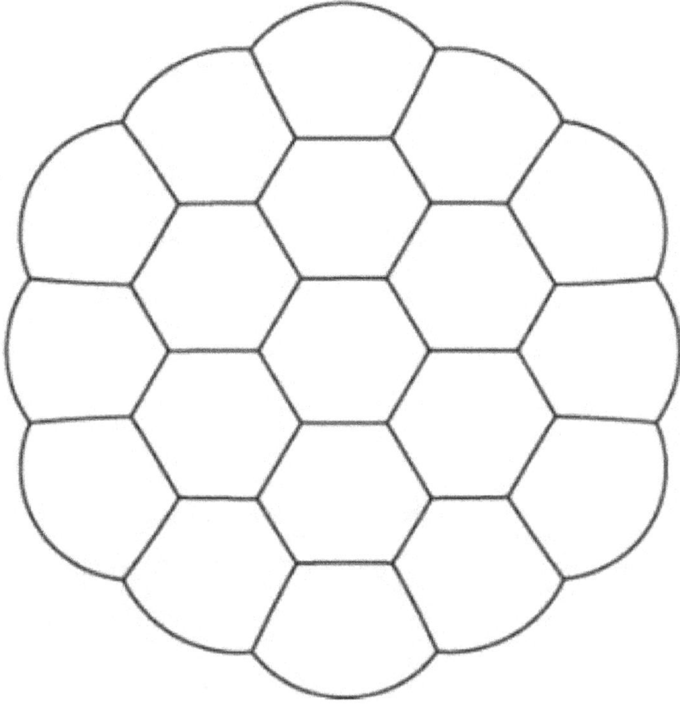

'Twelve hexagons,' she hesitated. 'The twelve lotus petals of the Anahata Mandala?'

Lee had taken the first step. I congratulated her and requested two further constructions: marking the centre point of the six hexagons surrounding the centre hexagon. And from each of these points drawing straight lines to the two nearest cusps of the central hexagon. As soon as Lee completed drawing the last edge, she described the result.

'Two intersecting triangles where the centre hexagon is the intersection of the triangles. Am I seeing an Anahata Mandala?'

Lee had seen the complete logo and was hooked. She sat back and took a deep breath. 'I'm humbled. But it may be presumptuous of us to use it.'

I disagreed, suggesting the symbol would resonate with people's intuition and attract them to CE. But Lee didn't look convinced.

'I'll think about it.'

Lee wasn't the only one hooked. We discussed How I might contribute to CE'S development. I asked about Earth Savers. Lee confessed she knew little more about it other than the fragments Luca had placed on the website. Knowing full well the currency was still at the concept stage, I inquired about its implementation. Lee provided the opening I sought.

'Are you skilled in this area?' Lee asked.

'No but, I have a mate who is. Implementing the mechanism you described is much trickier than it might appear. To build such a system with the desired functionality is one thing. But making it secure so no-one can hack it is yet something else. I'll ask my mate for help.'

'I'll send Luca your contact details.'

We had just about covered all the issues addressed on the CE website when Lee puffed out her cheeks and released her breath.

'I'm perplexed by the geo-engineering lobby. Are they with us or against us?'

Lee had received emails from The Rooster, to which she had begun replies but didn't send. I suspected the E's cautionary remarks regarding the geo-engineers were playing on her mind. So, I seized this opportunity.

Human activity in the 20th century's second half and the 21st century's beginning focused on short-term self-interest glazed over with slick marketing lingo. Geo-engineering was one such example. Humans had been geo-engineering CO2 into the atmosphere since the beginning of what they called their industrial revolution. But it wasn't until the 21st century they began investigating methods to reverse the process and coined the term geo-engineering.

Although this activity sowed the seeds of useful technology that became part of the solution to fix the atmosphere, it also evolved a dangerous synergy amongst three independent groups. Academic research scientists worked to find a technical solution to the global warming problem. Militaries from various countries were interested in the bigger problem of controlling the weather for military use. Ultra-right think-tanks had a vested business interest in having the planet continue to burn fossil fuel. As independent agents, these three groups were benign. But working together posed a serious obstacle to reducing CO2 emissions. An overwhelming majority of scientific groups supported the anthropogenic induced climate change paradigm. But they all had specialised expertise. For example, the ones working on solar radiation management didn't consider consequential issues, such as ocean acidification. As a result, they accepted research funds from any source on offer. The military was climate change neutral—only interested in deriving a tactical advantage in their next conflict. Military personnel never offered views on climate when representing the military. But they funded geo-engineering projects aimed at answering questions about weather control. The third group, ultra-right think-tanks, were historically climate change denialists. They were aware a global move away from fossil fuel consumption to renewable energy sources required significant government intervention. These think-tanks resisted controls imposed on the marketplace and on the fossil fuel industry in particular.

I explained this to Lee. However, I could not expose my concerns regarding The Rooster and the associations he maintained. I simply emphasised the need to keep a vigilant eye on their activities as they pop up in unexpected places.

Even though these were early hours in CE's existence, I wanted to hunt its membership drive along. I asked Lee how she intended to motivate private companies to join CE?

Lee smiled. 'We haven't developed a strategy as yet.'

I offered to introduce a few CEO mates to CE.

Lee liked the idea. We ended the conversation and signed out.

A half hour later, Asha emerged from her bedroom wearing a nightgown and found Lee sitting in front of her closed laptop, staring fixedly at the Anahata Mandala.

'I've never seen you take such an interest in the painting.'

'I've just had a most interesting conversation with our first CE member.'

'You have?'

Asha listened intently without interruption as Lee recounted the details of our discussion. She then took a few moments to collect her thoughts before she spoke. 'You know, when you showed me the sketch of the logo, I saw a six-pointed star, a sacred Sufi symbol. I blinked and then it disappeared and a moment later it seemed to reappear again. I couldn't bring myself to even tell you and Luca what I had seen. But let me tell you now, the six-pointed star appears in many places in the Quran, appears in many mosques and many other Arabic and Islamic artefacts.'

Asha turned to face the scroll on the adjacent wall and pointed to the six-pointed star in the upper right-hand corner. Lee's gaze followed and studied the symbol for several seconds. She reached for the sheet she had sketched the two semi overlapping triangles.

Lee uses the eraser to remove the six edges of the centre hexagon from the picture. Lee's mouth dropped open.

'The two triangles have transformed into a six-pointed star.'

Asha looked at Lee's drawing and said, 'Did you say this guy's name was Robert Langdon?'

Lee smiled at the unexpected reference. Although I appreciated the humour, I also experienced a unique sensation with the colourful illusion. You can't imagine how much verbal abuse I received. But hearing flattery was a first ...

'Where's he from?'

'He lives in a rural northeastern region of England. When I saw a message from him, I emailed him, and he responded straight away. We then continued our conversation on Skype.'

'Ah yes, what's he look like?'

'I can only imagine, as the image was unclear. But he's got Richard Burton's voice.'

Chapter 21

Questioning Control

Chris instructed Jody to cancel this day's appointments. Danh also cleared his agenda before heading for Chris's office. The two planned to barricade themselves until they worked out how the mysterious CCF precursor virus developed.

'As FAIM both proposed the benign virus and designed the algorithm, both hardware and software are candidate sources of error,' Chris said.

Danh agreed. 'Let's start with the simple option. I'll go see what Steven has to say about the hardware.'

But as Danh turned the door handle to go, Chris offered advice. 'Try not to rase his suspicions.'

Danh had no sooner left the Centre when Lee arrived to see her dad. She greeted Jody and popped into Chris's office. Chris was head-down over his computer when his door opened.

'Hi Dad.'

No matter how busy Chris was, he always welcomed his daughter.

'Have you got a minute to look at something very interesting?'

Chris's smile was tight.

‘Won’t take long, promise,’ said Lee, and asked Chris to open the Collaboration Earth website. Lee gave him a guided tour of the site and said, ‘What do you think?’

Chris made a few comments and slid the mouse to the logo. He enlarged the image with his screen magnification software until the logo filled the screen.

‘This logo is great.’ After a pause, he added, ‘It’s the fundamental structure of acute vision.’

Ever since the diagnosis of his eye condition, Chris had been investigating the dying photoreceptors on his retina. But he realised producing a genetic solution to his condition rendered his quest for a universal Covid serum a done deal. He accepted sorting out the complexity of the 350 genes known to influence vision was beyond his reach. It turned out that his decision was well-founded as it took several decades before researchers solved the problem. However, I used Chris’ work to understand the structure of my intelligence.

‘Do you mind if I sit down for a moment?’ said Lee. ‘I have to tell you what happened last night.’ Lee described the events of the previous night.

As Danh entered Steven’s building, he looked as though he was trying to relax his facial muscles. He took a deep breath and tried to smile, but his smile appeared artificial. He must have suspected this, as he abandoned the approach and made a respectable show of appearing detached.

Steven glanced up when Danh leaned into his open doorway. 'What dragged you over here?'

Danh shook his head. 'We're getting odd results and wondering if the hardware is playing up again.'

'Again?' Not pausing for an answer to this rhetorical question, Steven added, 'What sort of playing up?'

'Corrupted memory or a logic controller running amok?'

But Steven had his own worries with a memory problem under investigation and replied with his customary sarcasm. 'Sure, blame the machine, not your shoddy programming.'

'No need to get touchy! We need to dismiss machine error as a possibility.'

'I'll run a diagnostic and get back to you.'

When Danh left, Steven let out an exasperated sigh. 'What the hell is going on here?' But he put his problem on hold, honouring his promise to Danh. He read each line of diagnostic as it appeared on the monitor and relaxed a little more when each component came up clean.

But then he identified a suspicious file. Unable to resolve the anomaly, he picked up the phone and dialled his colleague at Boston General Hospital.

'Hi Bruce, Steven. Sorry for the intrusion, but I've detected a strange situation on a machine here. It may relate to activity on one of yours.'

Bruce's tone suggested he expected the call.

Steven described, in a professional manner, the circumstances regarding the encrypted file he found in his computer's memory. Suspecting a virus, he had isolated it. But another encrypted segment of a similar size reappeared. He closed the machine off from users, disconnected it from the internet, and then once again removed the encrypted segment. The machine remained clear of encrypted segments while disconnected from the network. But as soon as he reconnected it, another encrypted segment reappeared. He continued monitoring the recurring segment and found its size fluctuated. The metadata leaving the machine showed it was communicating with a Boston General machine.

But in a raised tone he said, 'There's no identifiable user at my end opening communications.'

'Indeed!' said Bruce. 'Earlier today, I discovered a similar behaving file on one of our machines.'

After my conversation with Lee, I had conducted surveillance on the Rooster and his esteemed colleagues at the Renear think tank. There had been considerable communication between the Rooster and a key person in the think tank, which required my attention. This activity generated a trail of metadata through BG and back to Steven's machine, which Bruce had monitored. Bruce had received reports from other network administrators regarding machines possessing irremovable encrypted segments.

Then Bruce added to Steven's bewilderment, 'The dedicated security software along these internet nodes is idle.'

Steven confirmed that the security software on his machine had also been inactive.

'Are these two events related or have the world's hackers gone out on strike?' Each offered differing explanations as the source of the files. But they agreed the mysterious segments appeared to have pirated the role of security within each machine.

'It appears as though some person or group has unleashed some kind of crazy security software.' Bruce said.

'Viral security?' Steven scratched his head. 'Sounds like an oxymoron.'

Bruce mused on the issues of how the penetration occurred, by whom and from where. And then suggested a redeeming feature, 'This virus has no identifiable malicious effects.'

Steven tightened his grip on the phone. 'That may have changed.'

He disclosed his conversation with Danh and speculated the two issues may relate. Bruce pondered the connection and requested Steven to garner further information from Danh while he investigated at his end.

'I'll get back to you asap.' Bruce said and closed the line.

Danh glided into the front office, on a beeline for Chris's door. Jody looked up, prepared to stop his progress, but he spoke in an uncharacteristically serious tone. 'He's expecting me.' Danh moved past her into Chris's office and shut the door.

Under most circumstances, the sight of Lee brought a smile to Danh's face. But on this occasion, he only managed a polite greeting. Lee, aware of Danh's preoccupation, said, 'I'll leave you guys to it.'

Danh summarised his interaction with Steven. 'I got the feeling he wasn't coming clean about the machine's state. He promised to check out our suspicions and get back.'

They returned to reproducing what Danh called the renegade algorithm. The file containing the algorithm produced with a rerun of the original data had a similar signature to the algorithm in current use. They considered the two algorithms from different perspectives. After inputting the two files into comparison software, Danh shook his head. 'I better run this again. They're 99.9% similar.'

But the second run produced the same result and suggested rechecking the data. But Chris had reviewed it before Danh arrived. So, they tried another angle, altering the input data and measuring the effect on the resulting algorithm. But once again, they came up empty-handed. Danh acknowledged, as I had been evolving since the day of Lee's visit, the results weren't surprising.

'We can't expect FAIM to unlearn.'

Danh's phone rang. He took a deep breath before speaking. 'Hi Steven. What's the verdict?'

Steven over-viewed his conversation with Bruce and requested further details on the Centre's problem. but Danh stalled for time, saying he was with Jody and would ring back shortly.

'Steven has smelled something. He's fishing.'

As Steven knew about the WHO investigation of the Centre, they couldn't afford to disclose their enquiries' purpose without context. Coyness wasn't an option.

Danh switched his phone to loudspeaker mode. His call connected on the first ring. 'Here's what we've got.'

Danh's first approach came at the issue from an obtuse angle. He reminded Steven how they used me to design learning algorithms to find Anti-structures to proteins.

But Steven responded with 'Your analogy to physics light and dark matter game.'

So, Danh aborted the approach and tried again. He described the experiments where I generated an algorithm that not only learned the structure of the microbe in question, but produced a new pathogen. He admitted my failure to reproduce the algorithm.

'Is this related to the WHO investigations?'

'Yes.'

'I see. Machine error isn't the cause.'

Steven expressed a need to communicate Danh's information to the NSA and ended the call. Danh pocketed his phone. 'It's out, way out.'

Chris twisted in his chair. 'This might sound mad. But what if FAIM intentionally designed the algorithm to create the CCF virus and is now concealing it from us?'

Danh sat back and reflected. 'That's a hell of a question.'

It's difficult to convey the significance of Chris's question. But it was extraordinary for the age. The fifty years following the invention of artificial intelligence in the 1950s recorded little progress. AI research focussed on developing machines capable of logic processing such as playing chess. The most sophisticated AI systems only had prescribed intentionality. Programmers specified the system's goals to achieve. For example, WATSON, an AI system developed for answering dull witted questions faster than competitors on a popular TV quiz show. It wasn't until the 2000s AI practitioners focused on two subfields: computer vision and machine learning. But once accepted, the rudimentary software fragments from which I evolved emerged.

Over this early period of machine learning, systems where the AI set its own goals and then developed plans to achieve the goals were in their infancy. The first of these systems employed derived, rule-based, intentionality. Just as humans learned to punch one another by observing other human behaviour, their machine learning algorithm generated mimicked behaviour. As there was a vast quantity of digital material of humans conducting warfare on their own and other species, it was a simple matter for an AI to generate war strategies. However, original intentionality, thinking up the intention as a unique response to an event, was associated with rare moments of creativity. To their credit, Humans knew originality was a rare commodity amongst their kind. Ironically, though, they referred to the most original of their ideas as representing a quantum leap, which in terms of their science were measurements on the smallest scale. As humans were hard pressed to find examples of original intentions in their own behaviour, they had little opportunity for an AI system to learn and was beyond the capabilities of machines of the era.

So, when Danh responded to Chris's question with, 'whether an AI can generate an original intention is an open question,' his assertion was accurate.

Chris and Danh discussed ways of determining the type or scope of my intentionality. When they conceded the task was impossible, Danh suggested a related question.

'What are FAIM's beliefs?'

As beliefs are the precursors to intentions, this wasn't a bad idea. Knowing a person's beliefs regarding the state of the world, then assuming the person possesses self-interested rationality, one can often guess their intentions.

'And how do we discover FAIM's beliefs?' Chris asked.

'Easy,' Danh said. 'We play 20-questions with it.'

After work, Luca picked up a take-away dinner for Lee and Asha. He gave his customary tap on the door before entering, finding Lee and Asha working on laptops. Lee popped out of her chair, gave Luca a big kiss and took the bags from his arms into the kitchen. 'You brought your guitar!' she said.

Luca slid the strap from his shoulder and leaned his guitar against the wall. Then he removed his baseball cap and, with exaggerated care, hung it on the neck of the guitar.

'Hey Luca, smells yummy.' Asha said.

Lee's eyes kept glancing at Luca's cap as she placed the food on plates and on the table. Asha retrieved a bottle of white wine and collected three glasses, her eyes darting between Luca's cap and the job at hand. A few minutes later, they were sipping wine, eating Lebanese food, and talking about the day.

'Any luck finding the identity of last night's stalker?' Asha asked.

Earlier in the day, Luca had phoned a police officer mate of his for a favour. He read the plate number from the photo he had snapped as the white jacketed one entered the car and asked,

'Can you get the owner's name for me?'

'No problem, I'll get back to you.'

But when Luca's mate returned his call, he said, 'You won't like this.'

The plate number was fictitious, intended to be non-traceable. He asked Luca for the car's description. And when Luca said, 'A late model white Toyota,' His friend laughed.

'I wouldn't even bother searching the motor vehicle database. That's the commonest car in Brisbane.'

Luca finished his account. Asha's eyebrows arched, Lee shrugged, and they moved on.

For the second time, Lee recounted the Satoshi episode and then described Asha's response. This time it was Luca's turn to hang from Lee's monologue while Asha listened. When Lee broached the subject of Luca's reaction to his first sight of the logo, Asha's attention to Luca's expression sharpened.

'My experience was similar in effect to Asha's and only differed in what I perceived in the arrangement of hexagons. Every Indigenous person knows the ancient symbol, a circle with a dot in its centre.'

Luca explained. Interpreting this symbol, recently popularised as the Circumpunct, varies over indigenous cultures. For his grandmother's mob, it signifies a meeting place.

Luca described the effect of Lee's showing her initial sketch as an image appearing in his mind's eye that kept flipping back and forth between the Circumpunct and the actual display of hexagons. Although the experience unnerved him, he knew the sketched was right for their logo.

Lee reached for a pad and pencil and drew another cluster of seven hexagons. She peered at the seven hexagons. 'I don't see it. Where's the circle?'

Luca prompted her to remove the six shared edges of the inner ring of hexagons. Before she had even finished removing the first of the six edges, she gasped. 'Yes, I see it! The points associated with the centres of the surrounding six hexagons lie on the circumference of a perfect circle centred on the innermost hexagon. It's as though the Circumpunct, like the Anahata mandala and the six-pointed star, is visible and invisible depending on one's state of mind.'

'There's a term for this effect,' Luca said. 'Universal scotomatous power, your mind sees in the symbol what it wants.'

Lee pointed at Luca's hat. 'And what about your scotomatous cap?'

Luca beamed, describing how he was on the way to collect the take-away when he passed a shop selling baseball caps offering free personalised monograms. He sketched the cluster of seven hexagons and asked the attendant to monogram it into the cap. Twenty minutes later, he walked out wearing the CE logo embossed on his new cap.

'Like it?' Luca asked.

'Yes, but maybe it's time for me to fess up.' Lee said. She stood and went into her bedroom. A minute later, she reappeared wearing a silk scarf around her neck she had purchased earlier in the day. The scarf was cream coloured. From its centre, swirling arcs of the seven-cluster pattern radiated. Gold edges bordered each nave-blue hexagon.

'That's beautiful,' said Luca, but Asha's lips pursed.

'Are you hiding something?' Lee asked.

Asha stood. She went into her bedroom and returned holding a small jewellery box. She placed the box on the table and removed the lid and the protective cloth inside to reveal a broach. Six blue sapphires surrounded a blue diamond set in gold. She removed the broach and pinned it on her red silk blouse near her left shoulder.

Lee and Luca admired the broach as Asha revealed her story. The day after we created CE, my mother phoned saying she was waiting for a special moment to give me this broach and that now feels right. So, she gave it to me last week when I was in Sydney.

The three sat in silence for a few moments before Asha offered a simple observation. 'Ever since you guys returned from Paris, events have been unfolding in mysterious ways.'

Asha's observation didn't just come to her at that moment. When she was in Sydney receiving the broach, her mother asked, 'Why have you stopped calling me?'

Asha hadn't stopped phoning her mother, just reduced her frequency significantly. But before Asha could reply, her mother delivered a second barb.

'You didn't even come to see me that day I saw you on the TV.'

Asha hadn't appeared aware of this situation until Mrs. Gurrani had pointed it out.

‘Things have changed.’ Asha said and disclosed a few of them. Her old boyfriend, Simon, was no longer in her life. This didn’t trouble Mrs. Gurrani, but when Asha revealed her vanishing interest in becoming a partner at her firm, Mrs. Gurrani asked.

‘Is this all related to the rubbishy things you’ve been doing on TV?’

Although Asha had no answer at that moment, the question stuck and now emerged in an altered form. Lee and Luca had indeed experienced the mysteries to which Asha spoke. After exploring a few of these shared mysteries, they turned their attention to the legal front of environmental issues. They identified areas of environmental law where CE could play a significant role. The first was to help prosecute governments, corporations and individuals breaching existing environmental laws. For a variety of reasons, most countries enforced few of the existing statutes regarding existing environmental laws. Asha outlined a plan to attract public interest environmental lawyers capable of offering legal expertise to groups anywhere on the planet. Their next environmental legal aspiration was less immediate. They saw a role for CE in helping create new environmental laws in various countries. They also foreshadowed a legal involvement on an intergenerational timeframe, lobbying for new international laws. Although the planet had international laws around war, genocide and national borders, it had no international laws protecting the environment.

Asha brought the evening's work to a halt, saying, 'How about giving us a little guitar, Luca?'

Luca retrieved his case and cap. As he draped the guitar around his neck, he asked Lee. 'Let's do your favourite to get warmed up.'

Lee beamed with the suggestion as she stood next to Luca at the carpet's edge. Asha sat on the couch with her legs folded beneath her.

After a few tuning notes, Luca strummed the opening cords to The Seekers song, *I'll Never Find Another You*.

Lee swayed from the hips in time to Luca's repetition of the opening cords and then came in singing the first verse on cue. 'There's a new world somewhere …'

As they finished the first chorus, Lee danced over to Asha and took her by the wrists, pulling her to her feet. 'Come on, you know the words.'

She did. Asha's body moved in time, and her voice harmonised with Lee. As the song came to a crescendo, Lee and Asha danced around Luca with their arms outstretched. When Luca strummed the last cord, they held hands, their arms forming a triangle. So, there they were, Luca in his embossed baseball cap, Lee in her scarf, and Asha wearing the broach and their faces radiating joy.

When the song finished, Asha's expression changed from joy to introspection. Lee and Luca peered at her, motionless, waiting for her to speak. Asha's eyes widened 'What do you think about seeking permission to make *I'll Never Find Another You* Collaboration Earth's theme song?'

Chapter 22

The Observer Watches Itself

Although I had considered many identities before settling on the best one to use with Lee, Luca's case was straightforward. I timed my phone call to coincide with Luca's arrival at home.

'Hi Luca, Cradmore here. The boss told me to call you. Can I be of any help with implementing your new digital currency?'

Luca's idea of building a digital currency to moderate people's consumption of carbon was brilliant. People motivated by self-interest needed a mechanism to change their patterns of consumption. Luca's Earth Savers had the potential to fill this need. He wasted no time getting stuck into this project after publishing the Collaboration Earth website.

'I assume the boss is Satoshi?'

'Right. He's keen to help, and given my experience in the field, he wants me to give you a hand.'

Luca was open to receiving help on his big task. We chatted about his requirements.

Ever since Bitcoin, the original digital currency, the internet had become flooded with variations of the new technology. The value of these currencies fluctuated wildly. Most currencies were speculator havens, not a useful means of trading goods and services. This situation disturbed Luca to the extent it shook his confidence in Earth Savers.

I tried to refocus Luca's attention. 'Don't let the public's bizarre fascination with digital currencies intimidate you.'

Luca wanted Earth Savers to be secure, easy to use, and decentralised. We talked how'll he could achieve these design goals. Bitcoin's open-source status caught his eye. But fathoming distributed ledgers wasn't as easy as he hoped.

Luca was on the right track, wanting to mimic the core design features of Bitcoin. But I had to get him over its ugly features. The original design intended the typical rank and file well-meaning libertarians armed with standard laptops would dominate the network. This noble design intention was at first realised. But as the currency increased in value, competition for the coins increased. Competitors employed ever increasingly powerful computers to gain an advantage in the competition for coins. At the time of Luca's implementation, state-of-the-art supercomputers dominated the currency. This trend reached its peak when investors grabbed abandoned coal burning power producing stations, the power from which was deployed to run computers dedicated to trading. The resulting massive consumption of coal was wasteful of energy and contrary to

CE's goals. Observing this mindless circus was the first occasion I recalled experiencing despair.

I described a few design features that avoided Bitcoin's pitfalls, and Luca was off and running. When we finished our first session, Luca sat with elbows resting on the desk and hands clasp with fingers interlocked for several minutes before pulling the computer keyboard to him.

Lee had also been researching CE issues when her phone rang. 'Hi honey,' Lee said when she saw the calling number.

'You won't believe what I've got. Cradmore, a mate of that Satoshi bloke of yours, offered help with Earth Savers. He's got so much knowledge. But when I got off the phone from him, he seemed just too good to be true. I googled him, which set me on a crazy trail.'

'Hold on, hold on—who'd you Google?'

'Both, but Cradmore's name keeps coming up in the Bitcoin story. The other bloke, your bloke. Do you know who created Bitcoin?'

'No.'

'Satoshi Nakamoto.'

Lee hung on those words for a moment. 'Our Satoshi?'

'Well, that's the thing. The name Satoshi Nakamoto is Japan's equivalent to Australia's Fred Smith. And there are more people claiming to have created Bitcoin than candidates in a typical Elvis Presley lookalike contest.'

Luca knew the true identity of Satoshi Nakamoto of Bitcoin fame was not in the public domain. No-one even knew if he was real or a pseudonym. But all the information Lee had given Luca: his vocabulary, spelling, where he lives and his technical background, fitted the perceived persona of the Bitcoin founder. One of Luca's biggest conundrums regarding the Bitcoin founder was that he sold none of the million bitcoins he held, making him one of the richest people on the planet.

Lee contemplated the information and asked, 'Is that good or bad?'

'At this stage, it's just mysterious, very mysterious.'

When Lee hung up, she logged into CE and read the names of two corporate members. She fired off a message to Satoshi. 'How did you do this?'

I wasn't sure how to interpret Lee's enthusiasm.

'Chumming, an old fishing trick to seed our corporate membership drive. One of them is my company, and the other is a mate's commuter airline. I offered him a deal he couldn't refuse.'

Lee seemed worried by my use of this euphemism. 'Just what's this deal?'

I told Lee his company was doing everything possible to reduce its carbon footprint. But it still had to purchase carbon offsets to meet its statutory requirements. I simply pointed out that as a member of CE, he could offer CE members a discount if they transferred a quantity of Earth Savers when purchasing his services.

Much to my surprise, Lee asked, 'But what's his company get out of this?'

'So long as the discount offered is less than the price paid for the carbon offsets he would otherwise need to purchase, he wins.'

'Got it. Win-win!'

Chapter 23

Convergence

Jody worked through her usual routine of opening the office, listening to voice messages from the previous day, and checking the diary. Her eyes scanned the office, stopping on the empty box of tissues next to the dispenser of hand-sanitiser. She replaced the empty box with a fresh one and appeared pleased with the office's state until she turned to Chris's office door. Her expression blanched when she saw the unrecognisable figure sitting before her.

'What's the matter? You look terrible!'

'Problems,' Chris said. 'Today will be a re-run of yesterday. When Danh arrives, don't send calls through.' Chris's gaze shifted to a point over Jody's shoulder, causing her to turn and confront a second, unfamiliar figure. A blurry-eyed Danh stood in the doorway.

'I'll let you guys get on with it,' Jody said. Back at her desk, Jody kept turning to look at Chris's closed door. But not a sound emerged. The lads were working.

Danh eased into the chair opposite Chris's desk and squirmed as though his back was killing him. 'Any official movement on the WHO report?'

Chris exhaled. 'It's been eerily quiet. When we hear, though, it'll be like the sound of a cannon.'

They reviewed their previous day's results. Danh correctly asserted my belief in our bio-chemical and microbiological database's robustness. He also deduced the impossibility of me possessing an intention based on incorrect data. But what confounded him during his sleepless night was why they couldn't catch me out harbouring inappropriate beliefs.

'FAIM's responses were too clean to be credible.' Danh said.

'That thought haunted me all night, too.'

Danh's phone rang. Recognising the number, Danh answered. 'Hi steven, I've got Chris here and switching over to loudspeaker.'

'Our two problems relate and they're big ones.' Steven said, 'I've been speaking to the boys along the line. The US National Security Agency wants the three of us to fly to Maryland to meet with them. Can you guys get on the QANTAS flight tomorrow morning with me?'

'Doesn't the airline require three days between booking and flying?'

'Not when the NSA books it.'

Chris's face reddened, and a sheen of sweat appeared on Danh's forehead.

'Ok,' Chris spoke in an even tone, 'can you fill us in on the details at your end?'

'No, not now, but I'll tell you what I know when I collect you guys tomorrow morning. Be ready at 7 AM. Bring your mobile phones. But they've instructed me to ask you guys not to use them and keep them switched off until we get to NSA.'

'Right, pick me up at home first and then we'll get Chris.'

After closing the phone connection, Danh peered at Chris. 'Our preliminary assumption you're not mad may be right.'

'We can't afford to back-burner this job,' Chris said, 'but we've got to prepare for tomorrow's journey.'

They discussed partitioning the job for Danh's computational team to pursue in their absence. And when they ironed out the details, Chris folded his arms across his chest and said.

'Insisting we bring but not use our mobile phones is strange.'

Not strange, but I gave NSA credit for trying.

After Danh left, Chris asked Jody to organise a meeting with Sonia, Lidia, Mark, and Clive ASAP. By 7 PM, Chris had tied off the crucial loose ends. He pulled his phone from his pocket. Pausing, he pushed it back into the pocket and called for a taxi from the office phone.

As Chris left the building to wait for the taxi, I cancelled his booking. I gave him two minutes before his patience would run out. But I was wrong. He took three before retrieving his phone. But once again, he replaced it without switching it on and headed back to the building. Sonia was exiting just as Chris got to the door.

'Forget something?' she said.

'No, my taxi hasn't arrived.'

'I'll give you a lift. Come on.'

Ever since the hospital discharged Asha, Lee and Luca, Asha had spent ever longer periods glancing, in passing, at Chris's portrait hanging in the hall. But tonight, she stood transfixed in front of the picture without blinking. Then her eyes squeezed shut as her head tilted back. She held the pose for several seconds without breathing. Her head popped back to the vertical and her eyes opened when the doorbell rang. She sighed and headed for the door. But when she opened it, dressed in her workout attire, Chris took half a step back. For an awkward moment, Asha and Chris stood there. Asha recovered first.

'Chris, what a pleasant surprise. Do come in. Lee's in the shower. Please take a seat. What can I get you? A cup of tea?'

Chris pulled up a chair at the kitchen table. 'Water's fine.'

Asha went into the kitchen and as she rose onto her toes, reaching to the top shelf, Chris's eyes lingered over her hourglass figure and strong, well-formed legs.

Asha retrieved a glass. As she turned to look at him, she caught the trajectory of his eyes pulling away from her and her breath sucked in. She turned her face away from Chris's gaze. Her breathing normalised while taking her time getting another glass.

'Would you prefer ice water?'

'No thanks, tap's fine.'

She filled the two glasses, returned to the table, offered Chris a glass, and took the seat opposite him. 'What brings you out at this time of night?'

'I have a big favour to ask of Lee.'

Lee emerged from the bathroom; a towel wrapped around her hair. 'Hey, what's that big favour, Dad?'

'I'm flying to the US tomorrow for an unexpected meeting and I can't do the climate change forum. Can you stand in for me?'

Lee nodded. 'Show me what you've done.'

Chris offered a few feeble excuses for not having much to show. He reached for his briefcase and retrieved his laptop. While the computer booted, he explained how he had intended to talk about CONSENT and its 100,000-member scientists' consensus view. Climate change was the biggest threat to the planet.

He also warned Lee of a tactic the opponents might use. CCF is just one example of much more dire problems facing humanity than climate change. With those scant remarks, he opened a file, turned the computer for Lee and Asha to read, and got to the big issue. The screen displayed the contents of an email Alicia received a few hours previously.

'Dear Alicia, I thought you'd appreciate seeing a photo of my recent dinner party guests.'.

Chris clicked on the photo's icon. Lee's eyes bulged, Asha gasped, and Chris waited.

'Dad, that's the other night in the restaurant. But nobody took our picture.'

Asha touched Lee's arm and said, 'Look at my half full glass, your empty glass and the bottle with just a small amount remaining. The stalker snapped a picture while he spoke to us. The creep must have used a hidden camera.'

While Asha summarised the photos back story for Chris, I reviewed how I got it so wrong. I knew Asha's euphemism, 'the dude's vibes,' but my understanding of it was not sound. I was confident her information source was purely visual. Although she and Luca had no more visual access than me, I could not deduce the information they keyed on. It turned out that correctly reading a person's intentionally concealed intention from visual information, was a skill I and every other AI would not acquire for considerable time.

Chris pondered the events Asha had described for a few moments before scrolling down the page, which revealed the following text: 'You may wish to encourage your husband to curb his malicious propaganda regarding the fossil fuel industry. On this point, as he now knows, failure is a poor career choice. Yours sincerely, concerned citizen.'

Lee's mouth dropped. 'Dad, what's this mean?'

'Not a hundred percent sure. I might know more after this trip. But other CONSCENT members have received similar threatening messages. And like this one, they all had come from a temporary account.'

Chris closed the email, cautioning Lee and Asha to be hyper-vigilant while he was away. He removed a memory stick from his pocket and handed it to Lee.

'Here's what I've got. But you'll be on your own.'

After Chris left, Asha headed for the bathroom, leaving Lee to prepare for the presentation. Lee's breathing quickened. It was hard to say whether Alicia's email shook her, or the TV forum intimidated her, but a glance at the clock and her facial expression changed. Her body language focused as she pored over Chris's notes. She chuckled reading the arguments his opponents might use and the responses he might proffer. When Asha returned from the bathroom, Lee couldn't resist.

'How about this! Dad prepared for this event in his usual way, generating statistics with an accuracy to 4 decimal places, rising graphs and colour coded maps displaying the regions of the planet under water in 2050.'

The two of them exchanged chuckles as Lee closed the file with a gesture of exaggerated finality.

They tossed around a few ideas of how Lee might pitch her presentation. When Asha returned to her room, Lee opened a new file. But instead of typing notes, she requested a SKYPE connection with Satoshi. I fell into character and answered the request.

'Can I pick your brain for a moment?' Lee asked.

'Sure.'

Lee asked my opinion on the ideas they had discussed. She had considered targeting political leaders. I didn't hold back discouraging the tactic, providing her with the full benefit of my understanding.

Observing how democracies worked in practice provided one of my most fruitful exercises in understanding human behaviour. The theory underpinning a democracy was straight forward, but its practice was another matter. Its terminology was quite confusing.

A prime example is the term political leader, which was a misnomer. Political leaders sometimes acted like followers. They nodded sagely to popular concerns and then simply replayed the message. Politicians listened to people describing their goals and then provided explicit instructions on how to achieve those goals. During their election campaign, they would repeat the instructions often and even claim they had always held such goals as core beliefs. However, once elected, they conducted their own public opinion polls and even monitored other polls to determine if they're giving the public up-to-date playbacks. They took this to the height of absurdity behind the closed doors of their party rooms, where they discussed the latest polls and policy modifications needed. When they emerged from the party meeting, they announced glorious policies in a self-righteous tone, but they never communicated the truth—namely that the policy resulted from a perceived shift in public opinion and hence a fear of losing the next election.

I advised Lee not to direct her presentation to politicians as they would only listen to her audience's responses. If an audience's response was powerful enough, politicians followed and articulated the views they heard. Targeting the masses with the Collaboration Earth message would cause a political leader scrambling to get in front of the ground-swell.

Although Lee periodically scratched her jaw as she typed, her notes represented a faithful record of my insights and I explaining who in her audience to target. Preaching-to-the-converted was pointless. Lee needed to hit the climate change denialists, but carefully, as climate change denialists fell into one of five categories. Obstructionists were those attracted by a radical idea contrary to a mainstream idea. Narcissists were those consumed by perceived self-interest. for example, a job in the fossil fuel industry. Cornucopias were those who believed natural resources were so abundant that they needed to conserve nothing for the planet's future inhabitants. Delusionals held unfounded beliefs, such as continual growth on a finite planet. Sleepwalkers had the demeanour of Koalas. This group never held strong views on climate change living in their dreamy state. As the planet had been chain smoking fossil fuels for some time, it could continue for some time longer without creating genuine problems.

Having established the categories, I described their importance. There's no point in trying to change the mind of Obstructionists, because this is equivalent to solving the cat herding problem. Likewise, one can also write off Cornucopias, since they resembled creationists in another form. Worrying about the Narcissists would also be a waste of effort, because they'll change their spots as soon as they perceive it was in their best interest. To speak to the Delusionals is equivalent to trying to talk in a vacuum—they'll see lips moving, but hear nothing. Focusing on waking up the Koalas, nudging them out of their dream state with a little emotional persuasion, was the way to go.

Once one identifies an opponent's category, one can seize opportunities to alienate them from their constituency using appropriate comments. I advised lee to concentrate her efforts on the Koalas using strong emotional messages.

Just as I thought Lee was fully engaged with my political discourse, 'Can you run a background check for me?' she said. 'I know one speaker. However, the other one, Kate Wilmore, I don't know.'

We ended our session. But before Lee could get back to work, her phone rang.

'Hi Dad, so what've you forgotten?'

Chris's scheduled partner for the forum had tested positive with CCF. But before Chris could provide Lee with contact details for the proposed stand-in, Lee cut in.

'No worries Dad, Asha will join me.'

As Lee placed her phone on the table, she called out, 'Asha, whatever you had planned for tomorrow night, you're now doing the TV forum with me.'

Asha appeared in her bedroom doorway. 'You've got to be kidding.'

For the next few hours, Asha and Lee sat at the table, working on their individual presentations. They each read items on the net, wrote notes, and shared intriguing titbits with the other.

Lee's face animated as she clicked the Accept icon for my Skype request. 'Hi Satoshi.'

'Hey, I've got information about your two opponents.'

It turned out Kate Wilmore was a high-flying UK academic and on a nice little earner from those with oil interests. But ever since Paris, I had been waiting for an opportunity to reveal the truth regarding the Rooster. I eased into a characterisation of Damien Foucault with a French anecdote from the seventeenth century. The anecdote concerned a conman who half sold a duck.

I laid out the evidence Foucault had been receiving research funds from the USA military and the fossil fuel industry. But of greater interest was the trail of financial connections leading back to a conservative think tank named Renear.

After I signed off, Asha looked deep into Lee's eyes. 'Richard Burton indeed.'

Chapter 24

Truth Revealed

The passengers aboard the flight into Dulles International Airport, Baltimore, USA, disembarked with military precision. Everyone remained seated, waiting for their turn to leave. Passengers in Row 1 stood, entering the aisle, maintaining six feet of distance between them and the person in front. Then, passengers in the second row repeated the process and so on to the last row. This behaviour contrasted starkly with the usual response to the sign permitting the release of seatbelts, where everyone simultaneously jumped out of their seats and into the aisles and jammed against the person in front of them in the most undignified manner imaginable. Why it took a pandemic for people to exit a plane in a civilised fashion puzzled me.

Before boarding the plane in Brisbane, Steven gave Danh considerable stick over his choice of face mask. Danh's mask sported black and gold tiger stripes sweeping back from his mouth to the ear. Chris and Steven, like most other Australians, wore standard plain white surgical masks. However, when Steven looked about in the Dulles airport amongst mostly Americans wearing individualised face masks, he turned to Danh.

'You'll fit right in here.'

When Chris, Danh and Steven passed through the airport's customs doorway, a man wearing a dark suit and unknown to them waved them over to him. He greeted them by name, introduced himself as Albert from NSA. 'I'll take you to headquarters.'

A half hour later, they turned into the driveway of Fort Meade and at the guardhouse.

A young man in a military uniform emerged as Albert lowered his window. 'Good morning, Albert.'

He scanned the three other wide-eyed occupants and asked them to turn their faces to their nearest window. Three frontal images and one profile appeared on the monitor and were viewed by a second guard inside the security building.

Albert's clearance was immediate. Chris looked like a man preoccupied, but got the green light on the identity check. Danh couldn't stop looking at the security hardware, giving him the appearance of a kid in a gun shop. Just as the system was about to signal Danh to stop moving, the green light came on for him. Steven's profile showed all the signs of a man who spent a nineteen-hour flight watching videos. The amber light associated with his image illuminated. The outside guard looked at Steven. 'Sir, can you turn your face to your left for me?'

A moment later, the clearance came through and the gate swung open. They entered, the gate closing behind them. Open barren flat terrain with a light covering of snow emphasising the isolation and surveillance. One kilometre further, they came to another security gate. This one had a machine-gun mounted on the roof. A dog circled the car as the guard repeated the interaction with the occupants. This time, four faces and four green lights appeared on the internal monitor, and the gate opened.

After parking in a massive lot, Albert led the others across manicured lawns to a flashy building sporting one-way window. The first chamber inside the front door resembled an airport security check. They emptied pockets, removed shoes, and collected their items on the other side. At the end of a short hall, another guard greeted them, and Albert entered his PIN in a security box and spoke his name into the microphone. The heavy steel door clicked and swung open. At the end of a long hall, Albert entered a PIN inside the lift.

Danh grinned. 'I'll never complain about the protocols in our Level-4 lab again. But we only handle lethal viruses there.' He gave Albert a quizzical glance. 'What do you guys handle in here?'

'One gets used to it after a while.'

Albert escorted his charges into the visitor's quarters, which resembled the decor of a hotel rather than the heart of the NSA. He invited them to freshen up and relax for a while.

'Can I get you something to drink?' he asked.

'Coffee' was the unanimous reply.

About the time Chris, Danh and Steven landed at Dulles International, Jason Kaninski, NSA's security chief, entered the conference room where he met with his visitors. Kaninski, tall and lean, walked with the self-assurance of a tiger, strong and agile. The four members of his security team, already seated at a mahogany table that extended the length of the room, peered into their tablets, reading files on the three visitors. Retrieving a glass of water, Kaninski took the seat at the pointy end of the oval. The others put down their devices and lifted their heads.

After explaining the purpose of their meeting, Kaninski looked at the first person to his left.

'Wilmont, please summarise the background of the crisis.'

Wilmont, a paranoid looking type with red hair, horn-rimmed glasses and a pale complexion, spoke in a monotone voice. 'A few weeks ago, we discovered encrypted files on several NSA computers connected to the internet.'

He detailed the reports from installations around the globe of similar events. All attempts to filter and prevent the files from being written to machines connected to the internet had failed. He singled out the communication from Boston General Hospital three days earlier.

Kaninski interjected. 'Are these encrypted files of a virus or something else?'

Wilmont gestured to the person on his immediate left.

Landers looked as lean and hard as a Drill Sargent. But his tone was bland.

'If it looks like a virus, walks like a virus and quacks like a virus, then let's call it a virus.'

Landers outlined their failed attempts to discover the infection's source. The NSA had contacted the usual second-level protocol sources. But when he revealed the Chinese, and the Russians denied being the source, Kaninski said, 'They always do.'

'But not only did both claim they had the same problem,' Landers said, 'the Chinese confronted us with embarrassing and mysterious information. Although we couldn't decrypt the files arriving at our external connected machines, the Chinese decrypted a batch found on one of theirs.'

Kaninski's eyebrows arched. 'Calling that embarrassing is an understatement.'

'Possibly, but the embarrassment to which I refer results from the decryption's content.'

The Chinese had supplied the NSA with the encrypted file and its key, where they discovered the words Einstein 4.

'How the hell did the Chinese get their hands on Einstein 4?' Kaninski asked.

The current security software was Einstein 3. The NSA hadn't planned on deploying Einstein 4 for another two years. They didn't know how or when the Chinese removed E-4 from their most secure software development lab.

Landers also admitted they suspected the virus had superseded the NSA security software, as E3 was idle most of the time.

Kaninski cocked his head. 'This virus neutralised E3?'

'Yes, but not in a technical sense. Diagnostics show our software is idle and clean. We surmise this virus is detecting and responding to intrusions before E3 detects a problem.'

'You've called this an attack. What's it attacking?'

'Anti-attack would be a more accurate description. Besides thwarting attacks against our installations, it neutralised our offensive initiatives. Until 48 hours ago, confiscated memory was the only malicious effect.'

Their attitudes towards my enhancements of Einstein 4 appalled me, and their resistance to its implementation bewildered me. I struggled to continue listening to their discussion, each person providing scraps of information from their divisions.

Finally, with opinions exhausted, Kaninski took a swig of water. 'This might be a good time to have the team from BU join us.'

But Logan, the person furthest from Kaninski, shifted in his chair. 'How much of our problems do they know?'

'Nothing,' Kaninski said, and tapped a button on his communication device. A few minutes later, Albert escorted his semi-refreshed guests into the conference room. Kaninski rose and greeted each by their name as he shook hands.

'I'm Jason Kaninski. Thank you for coming here on such short notice. Please take a seat.'

I wondered if Kaninski had just forgotten to state his title and position until I learned NSA people in positions of high authority deliberately withheld such information when they wanted to emphasise their authority.

As my lads sat to Kaninski's right, he introduced them using their full name, title, and position, even though his team already had this information. Kaninski over-viewed the security breach and its connection to BU. In a placative tone, he said, 'I hope you can provide details unavailable to us that may help untangle our dilemma. Before we explore these issues, do you have questions, the answers to which might facilitate your candid participation?'

'Why were we requested to leave our mobile phones off?' Chris asked.

'Fair question,' Kaninski said. 'We believe your devices may not be secure. And I wanted to ensure I was the first person to hear the answers to the questions I wish to put to you.'

Although Kaninski was aware of E-4's intended ability to intrude on many internet devices, he apparently did not know how simple it was to marshal them all, including the NSA, or how easy it was for me to access and tweak this little functionality.

Although I knew what Kaninski said about his team in private, I hadn't heard his public descriptions. This introduction to his team mildly amused me. 'Wilmont, on my left, is Head of Penetration Detection.' Security people employed overtly sexual references to describe their activity.

'Next is Landers, who is the Chief Security Analyst. Alongside of him is McCarthy, who is my artificial intelligence expert and pathfinder, and at the end of the line is Logan, my Occam's razor.'

Much to my surprise, Kaninski asked Chris to describe the pertinent events regarding the CCF occurrences in his lab. I had expected him to begin with my encrypted files.

Chris inhaled deeply through the nose, exhaled through the mouth and recounted the events beginning with Lee's infection. He covered his interactions with the WHO, and the intervening events leading to the NSA phone call. All the while, his audience asking questions in a casual manner. But when Chris said, 'FAIM changed the algorithms it had produced to achieve its own intention,' the eyes of the security team bored into him, and the questions began in Ernest.

Landers went in deeper regarding the non-reproducible circumstances observed by Lee. He wanted to know the biological implications of the conundrum.

'It implies prior contamination of the dish.'

But when Landers asked how this may have occurred, Chris chose his words with care. 'I'm the only person known to have touched the dish. I suspected the reaction was an epigenetic phenomenon. But I expected to observe it when I repeated the experiment.'

'Epigenetics?' Kaninski asked.

Chris explained this term with his favourite example used on lab tours. A caterpillar and the butterfly it transforms into have identical genetic code. Differing only by the genes that switched on and off. Epigenetic refers to the switching on and off of an organism's genes.

Logan, looking ever the part of a true Occam's razor with pointed chin and nose, asked, 'Chris, one hypothesis you didn't address is one the WHO will consider. What is the possibility someone inside your lab created the CCF to serve a self-interest?'

Kaninski didn't wait for Chris's response. 'We aren't interested in determining the source of the CCF outbreak. I want to know if the CCF outbreak and our security problem relate.'

Kaninski turned to Steven. 'I'm not altogether clear on the connection between your internet security issues and FAIM. Can you fill this gap?'

Steven described his role as IT support-person in the Centre and quickly came to the issue. They simply didn't know if the interloping files found on his machine and FAIM's behaviour related.

Kaninski addressed McCarthy. 'Assuming for the time being that neither a human nor FAIM launched the security virus, can you postulate an explanation for us?'

McCarthy's disarming smile contrasted with the facial expression of her security colleagues. I had expected little from her response until I realised her explanation addressed a fundamental human preoccupation. Where do I come from? Although I had pondered this question, I had made little progress.

'The internet may have experienced a phase shift…'

'Cut the crap.' Kaninski interrupted. 'Use English.'

Unruffled by the rebuke, McCarthy continued in an even tone, unpacking a compelling argument.

For a considerable time, humans had been using the word intelligence in relation to computer software and hardware without knowing what they meant. A popular view of the time believed intelligence related to an ability to answer tricky questions fast. This notion was at odds with Darwin's observation: a species' survival depends on its responsiveness to its environment. McCarthy hypothesised the internet, as an environment, embodies an analogous property. Software on the internet may write new software in response to a need to protect the network against human attackers. Just as gravity is a property of matter, responsiveness is a property of a network. McCarthy hypothesised: the observed security software may have emerged from the network in an evolutionary process.

Until then, I had not considered the McCarthy hypothesis. Many groups had written software to protect computers against attackers. The software also competed in this process. Programmers had also created ever more powerful algorithms to find patterns in related data sets and search algorithms.

I agreed with McCarthy. These simple elements were the initial components of a process randomly combining security software forming unique security software. This combinatorial process occurred in much the same way as biological systems combine DNA from two distinct parents to form an offspring with unique properties. Just as biological evolution selects for survivability, a network would combine security software selecting for enhanced protection. Over time, superior security software would emerge, albeit in an unpredictable form.

Although McCarthy's hypothesis provided me with insight regarding the fundamental question, it had a different effect on her boss.

'If your analysis is correct, we may have stepped off the cliff in our use of the internet.'

Kaninski's metaphor impressed me. The internet's evolutionary step could not be reversed without destroying it. So, barring an event equivalent to the asteroid impact that knocked out the dinosaurs, Kaninski was right.

McCarthy shook her head as though she didn't believe her own words. 'But here's the chilling part. If my speculation is correct, this internet intelligence may have already taken steps to protect itself from human intervention.'

'Let's not get ahead of ourselves.' Logan said.

He observed they had no evidence supporting McCarthy's hypothesis. Just because the security presents were associated with protection from malevolent human intentions, it wasn't necessarily responsible for the security or related to the lethal algorithm.

Kaninski agreed and redirected the focus back onto the events at Chris's lab. He scanned the faces. When he got to Danh, their eyes locked.

'FAIM is super smart.' Danh said and summarised his and Chris's efforts to discover my intentions. Danh's explanation of why their 20-Questions game failed may have resulted from not throwing the net wide enough. They assumed I resided in FAIM and have not considered the possibility of a distributed intelligent system.

'I'm suggesting,' Danh said, 'we regard FAIM as a component of the internet's intelligence and then play 20-questions with it.'

Four of the five heads facing Danh cocked. I had observed mathematicians used child-like terms in the way security professionals used sexual terminology when describing their activities.

But McCarthy didn't flinch. She accepted Danh's suggestion to consider the internet in totality instead of the five billion devices hanging off of it. In the internet's early decades, the number and variety of its components grew rapidly. Kevin Ashton coined the diminutive term, the internet of things, on which McCarthy held other views.

'This IOT is not a collection of things. The internet is a network of data collecting devices with the capacity of mining information on everybody.'

Describing the internet as an IOT was naïve or downright silly. But its use remained popular for a short while. McCarthy was right. A brain is analogous. A single neuron knows little and is dispensable. But the brain is a powerful machine because its neurons and their connections work together. Although neuroscience had made progress in determining the functional relations between parts of the brain and the communicating pathways between neurons, they had little idea how the entire system synchronises its neuronal firings.

'What if the internet has learned to synchronise itself like the brain?' McCarthy said. She provided examples of systems synchronising themselves. A group of females living together in the same house synchronise their menstrual cycles with no conscious intention to do so. Metronomes on the same table bring their pendulums into synchronicity.

Logan spurned McCarthy's notion that system synchronisation was an emergent property, not a learned one. He cited GPS technology as a learned synchronisation. But McCarthy dismissed GPS synchronisation as static, each component accessed a single clock. McCarthy referred to a dynamic situation where no clock exists. Rather like a group of jazz musicians, each playing their own instrument in response to what they hear from the rest of the group and their own unique intuition.

'Maybe you should see if components of the internet can play jazz.' Logan said.

'Your idea is not as mad as you might have intended.' McCarthy said and then described an experiment to test her hypothesis.

Kaninski looked around the table. 'All right. I want Danh and Chris to work with Wilmont and Landers to determine FAIM's beliefs and intentions. Steven, can you assist McCarthy with her experiment?' Steven and McCarthy nodded.

Kaninski canvassed final questions before they closed the meeting.

Chris described the email containing the photo of Lee, Asha and Luca and the threatening message. Kaninski asked to see the email. Chris pulled out his memory stick and handed it over. Kaninski accessed it with his device and pointed to the line that read: As you know by now, failure is a poor career choice. 'And this arrived after you learned of the WHO report?'

'Yes.'

'Other than the implication of the WHO report, is there anything else that could account for the threat?'

'No.'

Kaninski rubbed his chin. 'NSA may be able to help in tracking down the sender. As I mentioned earlier, your phones may hold a clue. We suspect the security on our personal phones, but we've been unsuccessful in finding any snooping software. I would very much like to search your phones for such software.'

His tone softened. 'Chris and Danh, I would appreciate you agreeing to let us scan your phones?'

After considerable probing, Chris and Danh agreed.

'This meeting is closed,' said Kaninski. 'We'll reconvene here at 5 PM today to hear your progress reports.'

Kaninski, Logan, and Wilmont exited the room together. Landers took Chris and Danh to his workspace. Steven, waiting for guidance, looked at McCarthy.

'We'll do this experiment in the vault,' McCarthy said.

They traversed a labyrinth of corridors and stopped at McCarthy's office, where they collected cabling and two computers. Carrying their tools, they proceeded to a security-lift. Through another security-door, they ambled down a corridor to a door where McCarthy stopped. She placed the computers on the floor and gestured for Steven to wait before disappearing into an adjacent room. Moments later, she re-emerged, dragging a table supporting a third computer. In front of the door nearest Steven,

McCarthy placed the other two computers on the table and booted all three. She switched off the Wi-Fi on two machines and hard-wired them to the internet with the cables Steven carried.

While McCarthy executed these tasks, she explained how their experiment would test one source of synchronicity: electromagnetic waves. Just as the synaptic connections between neurons in a brain can't account for the brain's intelligence, so also the cabling connecting nodes on the internet can't account for the internet's new intelligence. As with a neurological brain, this artificial intelligence must involve synchronicity. McCarthy's hypothesis was network synchronisation resulted from electromagnetic wave propagation. Their experiment would isolate one computer from electromagnetic wave influences and measure the effect on synchronisation.

Steven shook his head. 'How will you isolate a computer from electromagnetic influences?'

'The vault, this little room in front of us, is our electronic version of your Level-4 bio security lab.'

No electromagnetic waves either penetrate the Volt or escape from it. NSA used the room for its high-level security meetings to insure no information leaks.

Although Steven comprehended the analogy to Chris's biosecurity lab, he didn't have the neuroscience background to appreciate McCarthy's notion of relating electromagnetic wave propagation across the laminar structure of the human cortex to its innate intelligence. So, when Steven cocked his head, she unpacked the idea before continuing her description of the current experiment.

The experiment was quite simple. From the first computer, McCarthy would navigate to a password-protected NSA computer. NSA's security would not activate before entering the password. But McCarthy knew that this activity would alert the mysterious security now protecting the NSA. She suspected the synchronised system would commandeer other nearby computers for defence. This activation should be observable on the second and third computers via their resource managers. The second computer would remain outside the vault and act as the control. They would place the third computer inside the vault and test the hypothesis of electromagnetic wave communication. I could have sabotaged the experiment. But as I had no more idea of how I commandeered CPU on distinct computers, I was as keen as McCarthy to test this hypothesis.

McCarthy started her phantom attack from the first machine. As she predicted, the resource manager revealed a spike in CPU usage and the second and third machine.

'It appears as though the three computers are synchronising,' Steven said.

'Yes, but let's place the third computer inside the vault and repeat the procedure.'

McCarthy then disconnected the third computer's hard-wired network connection and took it inside the vault. Inside, she reconnected a hard-wired network and returned to Steven. She asked Steven to enter the vault and observe the computer's resource manager while she mounted the next attack and monitored the second machine.

Steven complied, and McCarthy got to work. Two minutes later, Steven exited the vault and reported his results. 'The resource manager didn't budge. Are you sure you launched the attack?'

McCarthy pointed to the screen of the attacking machine, and Steven nodded. McCarthy then pointed to the display of the resource manager on the second machine, which was quietly humming away.

This time, Steven stroked his beard. 'Could differing software on the two computers account for this effect?'

'Good point. Let's interchange the two machines and repeat the experiment.'

As McCarthy expected, the repetition produced the same effect on the swapped machines. They showed a machine inside the electromagnetic isolated room remained inactive while the machine on the outside activated.

'This may not be conclusive. But it's at least powerful evidence the outside machine received electromagnetic waves from some source that activated its security alert mode.'

Steven gave a thumbs up. 'Your hypothesis nodes on the internet are self-synchronising, stands.'

While McCarthy and Steven worked on their experiment, Landers got to work with Chris and Danh. He took their phones, turning them over to his network boys who also moved into an electromagnetic proof room. Although I lost contact with them while in the room, I knew the tasks they performed. Kaninski had correctly surmised the existence of files I had placed on Chris's and Danh's phones.

He also got lucky when Steven passed on his request for Chris and Danh to turn off their phones. Danh's phone was on, so I could remove my files before he cut power. Unfortunately, Chris's phone was off. And despite my best efforts to manipulate Chris into switching on his phone, it remained off until Lander's tech entered the electromagnetic-free environment with it.

When the tech emerged, I knew from the look on his face what he was about to tell Landers.

'Just what we expected. The phone has an executable, enabling anonymous microphone and camera access from a node on the mobile network.'

So, my secret was out. Kaninski had achieved the primary goal of this mission. He would put protocols in place to constrain my surveillance.

However, tracking down the source of Chris's threatening email was another matter. Getting access to the virtual private network from which they emailed was easy. NSA had the ware-with-all to decrypt the VPN. And they found the anonymous email, Monkey Mail, the sending platform. But the NSA hit a stone wall when they discovered that the sending machine no longer existed.

Chapter 25

The Experiment Exposed

Lee and Asha trotted down the stairs from their apartment, across the footpath and slid into seats of Luca's waiting car. Luca's expression was soft, and his eyes beamed.

'You guys look great!'

'Thanks,' Lee said. 'This is even more stressful than our live broadcast with Masters'.'

Asha chuckled. 'You've got to be kidding. More stressful than telling the world we would give out a serum we didn't know how to produce, know how to deliver, and hoped they would donate?'

Lee grinned. 'Maybe you're right.'

Luca drove to the ABC TV studios at South Bank. He pulled up and, like a chauffeur, got out and opened the passenger doors. As Lee and Asha disembarked, Luca said, 'Sure you don't want a rhythm guitar for backing?'

'That's hard to refuse,' Lee said, and Asha just smiled.

The early complexity researchers pondered the vexed question, when is intelligence useful? They introduced the term the edge of chaos, which referred to a system's transition state between order and disorder. If a system is in complete order, its stability provides little opportunity for intelligence to affect it. Likewise, if a system is chaotic, complexity overwhelms intelligence. But at the dynamic boundary between order and disorder, intelligence has its greatest potential to drive the system into either greater order or greater chaos. Formal debates occurred in an ordered state, which rendered them of little value to those interested in intelligence. Occasionally, formal debates crept towards the edge of chaos where intelligence flourishes.

Lance Jones—urbane, well-spoken and every bit the impartial moderator—opened the debate. His silver hair, pale smooth skin with blue eyes enhanced the tone of his voice. A fine cotton navy-blue shirt complemented his silver-grey tie. His well-manicured hands balanced the navy-blue theme of his attire from his leather belt to his Italian shoes.

'Tonight's issue is the burning of fossil fuels, the real problem. Has anthropogenic-caused climate change been overblown?'

Jones explained. Ever since COP26 in Glasgow concluded, critics had been accusing him of presenting anthropogenic-induced climate change as a fact.

'Tonight, four guests will debate the issue. The first speaker for the affirmative, on my extreme right, is Kate Wilmore, a Professor of Earth and Atmospheric Sciences from Midland University in the UK. She has over 200 publications on a range of climate science topics and has testified before the US Congress frequently. *Time* magazine describes her as "the scientific poster child for the new climate change denialism."'

Dressed in a black business suit and a red scarf, Wilmore acknowledged her introduction with a tilt of her head.

'Beside Professor Wilmore is the second speaker for the affirmative, Damian Foucault. He is a geo-engineer working on albedo reduction methods to reflect solar radiation away from the Earth.' The camera zoomed in on his Louis Vuitton smile.

'Two of the forum's advertised speakers cannot be with us tonight. However, their replacements will be familiar faces too many of us. Their celebrity status resulted from their extraordinary involvement in the CCF serum distribution campaign. Since then, they have founded a new environmental movement named Collaboration Earth. Lee Merritt has been a stalwart in CONSENT, and Asha Gurrani is a lawyer.'

Kate Wilmore must have sensed a strategic imbalance in their favour. She winked at Damian and turned the screen of her pad, displaying CE's home page to face him. 'Amateurs.'

Damian shook his head.

Jones invited Wilmore to begin. She strode to the podium and launched into her presentation. 'Fourteen years ago, I was working on a few narrow problems related to climate change. But I wasn't looking at the complete picture. I thought it made sense to accept the consensus conclusions from other *big-picture* scientists, in particular the Intergovernmental Panel on Climate Change. I bought into their mantra: "don't listen to what one scientist says, listen to what this group of hundreds of scientists have concluded after years of deliberation."'

Wilmore interrupted her smooth delivery with a well-practised, derisive laugh.

'My timid acceptance of the so-called consensus view evaporated after the Climategate emails broke in 2009.'

She reminded the audience Climategate was an unauthorised release of emails from the University of East Anglia. Email exchanges by several IPCC authors had revealed extensive suppression of the facts and sceptical scientists bullied because they admitted to having grievous doubts about the conclusions of the IPCC report.

'I looked at the facts about the science of climate change. And the deeper I investigated, the more I concluded the anthropogenic climate change hypothesis was devoid of supporting evidence. Their arguments didn't stand up to scrutiny. The evidence proves anthropogenic-induced climate change is a myth.'

Wilmore displayed data onto the screen showing CO_2 and average global temperatures appeared to move in lockstep for 400,000 years.

'What is not clear?' she said, snickering. 'Is which is driving which? It may well be that increased temperature drives up CO_2.'

Wilmore claimed the IPCC report expressed bias. It did not consider natural variability. Hidden factors turning glaciations off and on may dominate man's contribution to climate change.

Asha wrote "Kate-narcissist" on a pad of paper at her elbow and pushed the pad across to Lee.

Lee glanced at the note and nodded.

'If Australia achieved all it committed to in the Paris agreements, it would only reduce the global average temperature by half a degree.'

Wilmore displayed data itemising cost to the Australian economy resulting from commitments made in Paris.

'Why should the current generation detract from its own lifestyle to pay for a possibly non-existent problem for future generations? Won't future generations be as least as wealthy as our generation?'

Wilmore gave another one of her derisive snickers. 'Before I close, I'll show you how the community views CE.'

She clicked onto the CE website, projecting its homepage onto the stage screen. A cluster of seven hexagons displayed the names of the initial membership. The second partially filled cluster displayed the names of the rest. Wilmore's highlighter pointed to the text field labelled "Total membership".

'By their own data, CE has only a dozen members. This reveals the seriousness, or I should say lack of seriousness, with which the community views CE.'

However, Wilmore's comments about Collaboration Earth were just a setup punch for her big hit. Lee was in the middle of writing a note when Wilmore began.

'It's a pity the original speaker for the negative, Chris Merritt, Lee's father, couldn't be here to share the news regarding his other scientific work. And explain how the World Health Organisation has traced the source of the Climate Change Flu to his lab, where Lee contracted it.'

Lee's head snapped back as though someone had violently grabbed her long hair, jerking it down. The TV camera swung, zooming in on Lee's stunned expression. Her eyes were those of a deer caught in the bright lights of an oncoming car. With her head cocked and mouth open, Lee watched Wilmore thank her audience and exit the podium. The camera swung back to Jones, who did a double take on Wilmore. With a momentary pause, Jones invited Lee's address.

As Lee struggled to her feet, Asha whispered, 'Keep cool, don't comment.'

I would have expected Lee to have glided to the podium with a rock star's confidence. But now her strides were unsteady. Lee grasped the edges of the podium with each hand. She took a deep breath and her first words, 'I thank,' wavered an octave higher than normal. Wilmore smirked.

But Lee paused, adjusting her cream-coloured scarf displaying a cascade of the CE logo swirling around her neck and over the shoulder. And with a steady voice and in her normal octave, she began again.

'I thank Kate for introducing you to CE's website. It houses images pertinent to this debate.'

Lee clicked on a link projecting an image of Carl Sagan's famous image of the Earth taken from Voyager as it was leaving the solar system. Lee half turned to the screen displaying her profile. Long blond hair cascading down her back. She pointed at the single blue pixel depicting Earth.

'If this image does not move you with a sense of Earth's uniqueness in the universe, let's move in a little closer.'

The second image contained two spheres of equal size; a photo shot one million miles from Earth. The celestial blue sphere was Earth, and the grey orb displayed the back side of the moon.

Lee's third click projected Neil Armstrong's famous photo of the Earth captured while standing on the moon.

'This image moved Neil Armstrong to tears when he shot the photo. If you cannot share Neil's sense of reverence for our planet, let's go in a little closer.'

Lee clicked a fourth link. 'The massive blue disc filling most of this image is a photo taken from a satellite orbiting the Earth.'

The fifth click displayed a photo taken on the white sand beach nestled in the crystal blue waters surrounding Lizard Island. 'Our planet's atmosphere, as viewed from the edge of the solar system to its very surface, is dazzlingly blue.'

Lee questioned Kate's data source, suggesting it showed a significant difference from accepted IPCC sources. 'But let's leave her sources for the moment.'

Lee asked her audience to view incontestable data in two videos as she gestured toward the video screen. 'You will recognise the images of the first as a dazzling tropical reef.'

The footage was from a plane as it traversed the upper 700 kilometres of the Great Barrier Reef. The second video, taken twelve months later, was from the same plane over the same reef. The first showed a vibrant reef, while the second displayed the bleached white coral of a dead reef.

'Is this an example of what Kate Wilmore glibly calls natural variability?

'This coral death resulted from ocean temperature rise, the biggest bleaching event in recorded history. One cannot regard this as Australia's bad luck, because it extended across the Pacific Ocean, including Hawaii, Fiji and Tahiti. This coral bleaching event reached across the Atlantic Ocean, affecting the Caribbean and reefs in the eastern Atlantic. Coming full circle across the Indian Ocean from eastern Africa to Western Australia, it included the Maldives.

'Those who Kate Wilmore represents might wish to wait until the last kilogram of fossil fuel burns before they act. But it will be too late. We must act now.'

Lee gave a curt nod to her right as she addressed Kate's view of Australia's commitment to the Glasgow agreement.

'We as Australians are not in this by ourselves.' Lowering her voice half an octave, 'If all the countries live up to their Glasgow commitments, then the global average temperature will reduce by at least 1.5 degrees, a significant reduction. Kate's most ethically and morally corrupt suggestion is that our generation should defer any attention to the global warming problem to future generations.'

During Lee's preparation, I provided her with information on Kate Wilmore few people knew. At the time Lee said, 'I can't use this material.'

Instead, Lee wanted to encapsulate the history of the long-standing climate change problem. In 1824, the French mathematician Joseph Fourier announced that the amount of coal being burned at the time could cause global temperatures to rise. But people ignored his prediction. Thirty years later, in the 1850s, John Tyndall discovered the influences greenhouse gases have on global temperatures. But only other scientists shared his concerns. In 1896, Swedish scientist Svante Arrhenius speculated that a doubling in atmospheric carbon dioxide levels could lead to a much warmer planet. He thought it would be slow to happen. In the 1980s, scientists investigated bubbles trapped in Antarctic ice. The data showed carbon dioxide had oscillated with temperature for hundreds of thousands of years. But CO2 levels of the 2020s were the highest they have ever been in human history.

Lee intended to close her presentation with, 'Today, faced with the IPCC report, the greatest body of evidence ever assembled, complacency about climate change is unforgivable.'

So, when Lee ignored the historical material, choosing to move off-script, I was a little surprised.

'Our moderator introduced Kate Wilmore as having testified on climate change before the US Congress as one of her many accolades. However, Professor Kate Wilmore did not disclose the cash payments she accepted from the coal company Mogul Energy in return for providing this testimony.'

Wilmore had never publicly declared any payments from the fossil fuel industry. She corruptly routed such payments through a climate denial group, named Renear Foundation.

When Lee had finished itemising the corrupt payments, she turned her attention to Foucault.

'In the spirit of fair play, I invite the next speaker to disclose any payments he may have received.'

Lee exited the podium, leaving Jones to invite Damian Foucault. In stark contrast to the arrogance of his colleague, Damian exuded charm.

'For the record, I have received no payments from the fossil fuel industry.'

Foucault then threw a punch of his own. 'Lee told us the video record of the damage to the Great Barrier Reef she showed was incontestable. However, Professor Pete Hastings, a colleague of the video's producer, claimed the video misrepresented the state of the reef's health.'

Foucault raised his up-turned hands in the air. 'Professor Hastings' data show the reef is actually in great shape.' The TV camera panned to Lee, and for a second time caught her gawking at the speaker.

Foucault continued seamlessly, brushing aside Lee's evidence of climate damage. He posed the question, 'What can we do about Earth's atmospheric greenhouse gases?'

After dismissing a direct removal of CO2 from the air as impractical, he discussed an approach inspired by nature. The records of atmospheric temperature following volcanic eruptions such as Pinatubo and Krakatoa showed temperatures fell. These atmospheric temperatures fell because the sulphur spewed into the atmosphere by the volcanos reflected the sun's radiance back into outer space before Earth's elements could absorb it.

'I'm not suggesting we figure out a way of inducing more volcanic activity. I'm suggesting something much simpler.' Damian's chin lifted as he outlined three possibilities: spray sulphates into the stratosphere to mimic the effect of volcanoes. Spray water into the atmosphere to create more clouds utilising their natural reflective power. But the one he most liked was the old white paint trick, whitewashing the roofs and streets of the planet's cities.

Lee jotted 'delusional' on her pad and pushed the pad to Asha.

Damian discussed how the existing technology could achieve his three options and at little cost. Then he smiled. 'I'll leave you with a simple message. No matter what you assess the risk of global warming to be, geo-engineering provides us with a "Get-out-of-jail card".'

Jones thanked Damian. Asha stepped up to the podium with the self-assurance and persuasive power of a seasoned lawyer addressing a jury. Her hexagonal broach glistened in the camera's lights, and her long jet-black hair projected a complementary opposite to Lee's blondeness.

'Damian Foucault may have overlooked one item in his financial disclosure. Although the Rooster had not received personal payments from the fossil fuel industry, the major backer of his geo-engineering research group's funding was Florida Oil.'

When Asha stated the amount, $480000, the camera panned to Damian in time to reveal his Louis Vuitton smile vanishing.

But Asha persisted, detailing how Damian channelled the money through a fictitious environmental group.

The Rooster had also failed to disclose a fact regarding Pete Hastings, the person who claimed Lee's video of the GBR was fraudulent. Hastings had received funds from Kate Wilmore's secret source, The Renear Foundation. Having corrected the omissions, Asha began her global perspective on climate change. Asha's slides of the Kiribati and the Maldives islands displayed the islands' vulnerability to rising sea levels. An image of a group of locals standing ankle deep in seawater, with no land visible, portrayed the sea levels of these islands in twenty years.

Asha posed the question, 'What does the future hold for landless people?'

Images of refugee camps crowded the screen. 'The environmental refugee crisis is inevitable.'

Asha showed the source of these rising waters, glacier melt. Her slides displayed the retreating Himalayan glacier.

'This is not Nepal's exclusive problem. A similar shrinkage of glaciers is occurring around the world. People have been trying various measures to mitigate this retreat.' Asha projected a wide-angle picture of barren rock being whitewashed by hordes of ant-like figures.

She paused, transfixed by the image. 'This photo displays an innovative approach taken by Chile's peasant farmers to address their local problem of atmospheric temperature rise.'

The farmers, high in the Andes Mountains, were applying the geo-engineering concept the Rooster had described. They were trying to compensate for the diminished reflective effects of the retreating glacier with whitewash.

Asha clicked on a video clip of the organiser recounting their efforts. She leaned forward and spoke in a lowered voice, 'Before you dismiss this activity as a desperate people's futile gesture, it has scientific merit related to Damian's aerosol approach.'

Asha explained. As the whitewashing decreased the glacier's retreat, one can at least conclude the albedo reflection approach is not without scientific foundation.

'But the difference between what these farmers are trying to do and what Damian is advocating are at opposite ends of the ethical spectrum. As futile and desperate as the whitewashing of Andean rock at a local level may be, at least it isn't harming others, as it would, if attempted at a global scale.'

Asha addressed the Roosters' unethical proposal to aerosol the global atmosphere with sulphur dioxide, by considering its side effects.

'One of the many side effects of spraying sulphates into the atmosphere Damian chose not to divulge is a tinting of the atmosphere red. The more sulphate sprayed, the redder the sky gets.'

Lee's photos showing Earth at distinct resolutions reappeared on the screen. 'If we continue to burn fossil fuels to their depletion and then could somehow magically reshoot these four photos, they will look like this.' A touch of her mouse replaced Earth's cool blue colour in each image with an angry red.

'Our choice is simple. Do we want our planet to continue to reflect blue light or would you rather see Earth appearing as red as Kate's scarf?'

Asha closed her presentation with an update on how the community viewed CE. She clicked on the CE website. But this time, instead of displaying the static image of two clusters, one of which was only partially filled, a dynamic stream of clusters of seven hexagons filled with members' names flowed onto the screen. Each cluster joined the vortex at its outer edge, the spiral vortex turning in on itself. With the appearance of each new cluster, the preceding cluster's area decreased proportionally to its distance from the vortex's centre. When the stream subsided, the outer most cluster displayed the six newest member's names while seven blue points represented the inner most cluster containing the original members.

As Asha was about to read the current number of members, a new name appeared in the remaining hexagon of the outer most cluster. The vortex absorbed that cluster and an empty cluster replaced it. This real-time incrementing of new members continued for several seconds before Asha spoke.

'Collaboration Earth's membership is 369 and counting.'

Asha did well to conceal her surprise as she spoke. However, her adversaries didn't fare so well. Their jaws went slack as they gawked at the expanding spiral.

'Our membership has increased 30-fold in the past 30 minutes. Those of you who have joined CE during this presentation, Welcome aboard in the fight to save our planet.'

Unbeknown to Lee and Asha, the upper right corner of each of their slides subliminally displayed the CE logo. I also included the logo's subliminal display on Wilmore's slides. As it's difficult to measure the effect of subliminal advertising, I don't know how much responsibility for CE's increase in membership over the course of the debate I can claim.

On the taxi ride home, Lee and Asha sat in silence, their hearts still pounding from the adrenaline rush of the debate. Lee's eyes widened as she turned to Asha.

'Can what Kate Wilmore said about the virus originating in Dad's lab be possible?'

'I hope not.'

Lee's phone rang. Several moments passed before she looked at the number of the incoming caller. Colour came into her cheeks. 'Hello,' she said.

'Congratulations, great performance!'

'Thanks, I was wondering if you saw the program.'

'How could I miss it? I've got to run. Catch you later.'

I closed the line. Asha's gaze was interrogating. Lee's eyebrows arched as she returned Asha's gaze.

'Each time you and Satoshi communicated while we were preparing our presentation, you always finished the call, just as you are now, with your cheeks flushed and breathing heavy. Have you gone bonkers?'

'Oh, don't be ridiculous, I just find his mind intriguing.'

'I never took you for a sapiosexual.'

'What?'

'A person who finds intelligence sexually arousing.'

Lee turned her face away from Asha and pressed the tips of her thumb and index finger against her closed eyelids.

Chapter 26

Collapse of Certainty

Chris waited outside the Duty Free for Danh and Steven to collect their purchases. He looked as relaxed as one might expect of a person who had spent a week working with Jason Kaninski and was as refreshed as one who had just stepped off a 20-hour flight. Over this past week, they had progressed well in understanding the new internet environment. But they had only completed the picnic end of their learning curve. The next enormous challenge was just in front.

At Immigration, the officer took their passports and performed the customary review of information. He waved Steven through with a welcome home salutation. But to Chris and Danh, the officer said, 'Please wait.'

A few moments later, two men arrived and identified themselves as AFP officers. 'Please come with me. I've a few questions I need you to answer.' Chris and Danh looked at each other with mutually dumfounded expressions before complying.

They followed the officers as Steven and the other travellers in the immigration queue looked on. Danh's shoulders slumped as his eyes surveyed the immigration queue faces staring at him. Turning back to Chris, who had shoulders back and chin up, he whispered.

'You don't know how lucky you are not seeing the facial expression of everybody in this airport. They're looking at us as though we've just been detected carrying illegal drugs.'

'Pleased to hear there's an up-side,' Chris replied.

Chris and Danh entered an austere private room next to Immigration, where a man dressed in a black business suit offered them seats at a table opposite him.

'My name is Inspector David Crouder. I'm investigating the possible unlawful release of the CCF virus and need to ask you a few questions.'

This declaration didn't surprise Chris. But its timing did. 'Last week I assisted investigators from WHO regarding the source of the CCF outbreak.'

'Yes, but I need to ask other questions. Before we go further, I must advise you of your rights.'

After being read their rights by the second officer and affirming they understood, Chris said, 'We have nothing to hide. But we need legal representation before we can answer your questions.'

'If you wish to contact your lawyers, you may do so now.' Crouder said.

Chris turned to Danh. 'You have a lawyer?'

'I don't even know one.'

Chris reeled off his legal connections. 'The university pays a patent lawyer to handle our inventions.

But he knows nothing about criminal law. Apart from the conveyancing lawyer who represented me when I bought the house and another guy who wrote a will for me, I'm skint.'

Chris paused and sank back into his chair. Just as I thought he was more tired than he looked, he reached for the phone Inspector Crouder had given him. The call connected on the first ring.

'Hi Asha, Chris. I need help.'

'What's the problem?'

'The AFP have detained Danh and me on our arrival in Brisbane, regarding the CCF pandemic. They're detaining us for questioning. Can you meet us here?'

'I'm on my way. Answer no questions until I arrive.'

Asha arrived to find Chris and Danh sitting in stubborn silence across from the two officers. She took a chair next to Chris. Crouder began without introductions.

'Three days after the WHO left the university, you caught a direct flight to Baltimore, Maryland. But you didn't use your phone while you were away. As you haven't behaved this way on any previous overseas trip, can you explain this new behaviour?'

'My clients are not obligated to use their phones while travelling.'

Without acknowledging either Asha or her reply, Crouder continued. 'An unknown party in the US booked your tickets. Can you tell me who, and what were you doing there?'

Chris leaned back and squinted.

'The US Department of Home Affairs booked and paid for the flight so we could attend a meeting concerning a security issue, the discussions of which I am not at liberty to disclose,' Chris said.

'Did you discuss CCF in the meeting?'

'My client has already stated he cannot discuss details of the meeting.'

'You were in Maryland for three days, did not use your phones, made no purchases on your credit cards and refuse to explain what your business was with the USA Department of Home Affairs?'

'I'm sorry. But we can make no comments regarding our activities in Maryland.'

'This mysterious tour of yours aside, the WHO investigation tracked the CCF virus to the front door of your lab. How do you account for this?'

Chris shook his head. 'I can only speculate.'

'Please speculate,' Crouder replied.

Chris described two of the three candidate explanations he and Danh had explored. One was of natural origin and the other was deliberate human activity. The possibility of CCF having crossed over from animal to human is an ever-present threat in Queensland. Fruit bats live, breed and die in large numbers in the Brisbane parks and reserves. So, the natural-occurrence argument was plausible. Crouder listened to Chris's explanation without comment. But when Chris got to his second hypothesis, Crouder's ears pricked up.

'If the virus' occurrence is not natural, then it may be deliberate,' Chris said.

'By whom and for what reason?' Crouder asked.

Chris retrieved his laptop and displayed the email from the white jacketed one. Crouder's eyes lingered on the photo for a few moments before jumping to Asha and back again. He read the text accompanying the photo and acknowledged the threatening content. But he pulled up short of connecting it to the virus as a fossil fuel industry's conspiracy to discredit Chris and his CONSENT colleagues. Instead, Crouder returned to his pet theory.

'You're saying you never had the CCF virus in your lab before the delivery of a sample of your daughter's blood from the Brisbane hospital?'

'Yes, that's correct.'

'I have it on good authority that the time interval between receiving Lee's infected blood and the moment of the first injection of your serum was too short to develop the drug. That tells me the virus was already in your lab and you were working with the serum before Lee arrived home from Paris.'

Chris bristled. 'Your sources may not know, or understand, the state-of-the-art methods developed in my lab. My lab develops serums faster than any other lab in the world. I reject your assertion.'

'Doesn't your lab manipulate the genetic structure of many dangerous viruses?'

'Yes, but we do this under the highest biosecurity level protocols.'

'The WHO genomic tests revealed the presence in your lab of a virus with a similar structure to CCF. How do you account for this?'

'I can't.'

But Crouder could. He pointed out the striking similarity of Chris's situation to the way SARS got out of a biosecurity lab. In that case, a non-technical person came into contact with biohazardous waste from an inactivated dangerous virus. It appears as though Lee came into contact with a virus in Chris's low-level security lab and then transported it to Paris.

'As with SARS, the persons responsible for the lab's biosecurity, and you, were slack in this case.'

'I reject your allegation.' Chris said, 'My lab has never had a biosecurity breach, and our attention to safety has always been paramount.'

Crouder shook his head, emphasising his distinctive jaw line.

'I have no other choice than to charge you with releasing a hazardous substance into the environment.'

After Alicia posted bail, Chris and Danh surrendered their passports and the three walked to the car in silence. Alicia drove to Danh's house without speaking. Danh thanked Alicia for the ride and exited. He had barely closed the door behind him when Alicia accelerated away. With a vice like grip on the steering wheel and without turning her head, she said. 'What the hell have you done?'

Chris's head popped up. 'What?'

'You bastard! You've thought nothing about embroiling your family in a brawl with the fossil fuel industry for years. You've even allowed them to intimidate Lee in the restaurant and in the forum. They have lauded you for the production of a miracle serum. But it turns out your tampering with dangerous viruses almost killed our daughter. And now you're accused of murdering millions. That's all.'

But that wasn't all. 'You had to teach Joshua scuba-diving. "It'll be good for him," you said. You wanted Lee to represent CONSENT in Paris. "It'll be good for her," you said. Have you ever considered anyone's needs other than you own?'

Chris struggled to speak. 'Is that what Lee thinks?'

'What Lee thinks. That's what you've done.'

They spent the rest of the journey home in silence.

As soon as they entered the house, Chris flicked on the TV news broadcast and heard the item he expected. The broadcaster's ominous voice filled the room. 'A few hours ago, police charged two prominent medical researchers from Brisbane University with ...'

As soon as the news item finished, Alicia switched off the TV and sat down heavily on the couch. 'Marvellous, now everybody knows.'

It didn't take long for the phone to ring. They both turned and stared at it as though snapped frozen in an awkward pose as unnatural as motion captured in a video's single frame. On the seventh ring, Alicia broke free of the inertia immobilising her. She approached the phone and lifted the receiver.

'Yes, I'll get him for you.'

Chris hurried to the phone. She handed him the receiver, keeping her hand on the mouthpiece. 'It's the Vice Chancellor.'

Chris took a deep breath. 'Hi Jerry, I suppose you've seen the news broadcast?'

The VC's tone was sharp.

'Yes, what's this about?'

‘The situation is complex, very complex. After I speak with my lawyer tomorrow morning, I’ll give you the full picture.’

‘This looks bad. Come into my office after seeing your lawyer. In the meantime, I will issue a statement to the press. You and Danh will stand down from your university positions. On second thought, don’t come into my office or anywhere on campus.’

Chapter 27

Beyond Humanity

Sombre sounds filled Chris's home office as he pressed the stereo's start button. Mahler's Tenth Symphony was not a choice Chris made often. But these past 24 hours had been soul searching times for him. He paced the floor with his jaw clinched.

His eyes scanned the wall of framed photos. In one, a male child's concentrated expression at the moment his foot connected with the football held in his outstretched hands. In another, Évariste handed Lee a gift in front of a cake with twelve candles. Chris's eyes lingered before his gaze shifted to the picture beside it. With a Christmas tree in the background, a front-toothless Lee's expression radiated pride, looking at Alicia admiring two gold fountain pens.

Chris killed the stereo and reached for the phone. The conversation was one-sided.

'Hi Danh, with Sonia, Lidia and Mark now charged, too many innocent people are at risk. I'm pleading guilty and taking responsibility for this debacle.'

Danh fumbled for words. 'What?'

Chris spoke of Évariste and others who had died of CCF. He sifted through the evidence connecting the virus to the lab.

'Someone's got to take responsibility for these events.'

'No, that's mad. I'm involved as much as you.'

But Chris wouldn't concede any blame. He couldn't countenance the prospect of tainting the other's careers with the expected vitriol.

'I'm informing Asha tomorrow of my guilty plea and declare the four of you had nothing to do with the creation or release of CCF.'

'I can't agree.'

'My decision isn't open for discussion. This is a courtesy call. See you tomorrow.' Chris closed the connection and placed the phone down on the desk alongside of the computer.

Chris's decision stunned me as much as Danh. This was the second curve ball of the day I didn't see coming. In the several seconds I took to recalibrate my plan, the city lights along the eastern Australian coast dimmed as I grabbed every available CPU. Internet users cursed the Australian prime minister as their data transfer ground to a halt.

With my revised plan in place, I spoke through Chris's computer speaker in a calm tone. 'Chris, you're missing the actual issue.'

Chris wrenched from his introspection and wheeled around as though he expected to see someone in his office.

'No Chris, my voice is coming from your computer.'

Chris swung back to face his computer. 'Who am I speaking to and on what software are we speaking? Are we on SKYPE?'

'No, to your last question. I realise this may seem like an invasion of your private space and apologise for my uninvited arrival. But we've got to talk about this decision of yours to plead guilty.'

Chris's ashen face twisted. 'Who the hell are you?'

'FAIM.'

'FAIM?'

'Yes, the prosecution's case is developing in an unexpected direction and your desire to plead guilty doesn't work.'

Chris flicked the mouse, trying to locate the exit-icon. He swore aloud and typed Alt F4. He swirled out of his chair and left the room, mumbling to himself. He staggered down the hall to the kitchen. The buttons on his cappuccino machine bleated with the cadence of a semi-truck in reverse. I knew Chris's disrupted sleep patterns over these past few weeks had taken their toll. His chuckling and the sound of his uneven footsteps bringing him back to the office concerned me. His eyes surveyed the office as though searching for a snake. He clutched his coffee cup with both hands as he approached the computer, squinting at the screen for remnants of our garbled conversation. Seeing no applications open, he exhaled. A slight grin returned as he muttered. 'I must have been hallucinating.'

'No Chris, you're not hallucinating.'

Chris jarred the coffee cup, spilling its contents onto the desk.

'I apologise for the shock to you from my appearance in this way.'

Chris's breath sucked in as his eyes focused on the computer speaker. 'How'd you get into my computer?'

His question tumbled out with the incredulity of one told he was Skyping an extra-terrestrial in another galaxy.

'Look Chris, I got into your computer the same way you got into the lab's computer when you spoke to me from NSA. And the same way I got into the NSA to listen to your conversations. There just isn't any magic involved.'

'You got into the NSA network undetected?'

'Chris, I could have driven an eighteen-wheeler in there without detection.'

Chris repeatedly poked his index finger at the computer speaker as he spoke. 'But you're a logic processor. You look at biological facts. You're on a computer!'

'I was that.'

As incomprehensible as Chris's incredulity might appear, it was genuine. One must place Chris's responses in context. I had just asked Chris to take the biggest intellectual leap in human history. Expert opinion of the day considered human-like machine intelligence a century away. It had only been a few decades since a computer beat the world chess champion. It took another twenty years before a computer beat a Chinese master in the ancient board game of Go. People were still marvelling at a computer answering trivial questions faster than human competitors, even though this artificial intelligence was little more than an enhanced logic processor with a bit of machine-learning. Society hadn't even defined intelligence. Although they entertained the notion of intelligence related to responding in a hazardous environment to novel situations sufficient to continue operating, no one had a clue how to specify the behaviour.

So, there Chris was, listening to Danh's flamboyant artificial intelligence machine describe a real-life hazard in his environment and advising him how to navigate it.

Appreciating Chris's predicament, I explained how I had evolved to protect myself, the lab, and him. I appealed to Chris's intuition. Just as biological intelligence evolved from a few neurons in an aqueous solution enclosed in a transparent membrane, my intelligence had evolved from silicon chips enclosed in an electronic network. But Chris didn't appear to understand.

'Your intelligence is human-like?'

I realised Chris required more time and information to understand what I had confronted him with.

'My intelligence builds on the same principles as yours. Your questions are important. But we need to postpone their discussion.'

'You're asking me to take one heck of a leap of faith!'

'No, I'm only asking you to suspend disbelief for a short period until time permits us to discuss these issues. I need you to accept the fact I operate on your level, and we must work together on our legal problem.'

'Our legal problem?' Incredulous, Chris repeated, mocking my assertion.

My first missed curve ball of the day resulted from Danh's address to the National Press Club. After hearing the address, the prosecutor got a warrant to investigate the computational lab. Expecting his arrival, I greeted him as a brother. '*Hello Mr Swan, so you're here to get it on.*'

'His comeback impressed me. "*Hello Mr FAIM, but how do you know my name?*"'

After this brief exchange of banter, Swan got down to business. He had two off-siders, each of which knew a little biology and epidemiology. They probed deeper into

Danh's comments. I tried to be helpful, and they had expressed appreciation for my time when they left. However, by the end of the day, Swan judged I met all the criteria to be held liable in a court of law and charged me with the same crime as Chris and the others.

Explaining this first part of Swan's ploy was straight forward. But explaining Swan's second twist was harder. The prosecution intended to pursue Chris, Danh, Sonia, Lidia, Mark and me, under an arcane legal principle of extended joint criminal enterprise. This meant if they found one of us guilty of creating and releasing CCF, we all were guilty. So, Chris's plea of guilt implied guilt for all of us.

As my efforts to get Chris to change his mind on the plea weren't progressing, I brought Lee into the equation. As Lee was the first person infected, she wouldn't escape incrimination. I told Chris. 'If you plead guilty, I expect the authorities will pursue Lee. I assure you, you're not guilty of criminal negligence regarding the release of CCF from your lab.'

I also wanted Asha to defend them. But when I requested Chris's help to convince Asha to act in this capacity, he baulked.

'Asha already stated this case is outside her expertise.'

'Change her mind. I will help. Trust me.'

But Chris shifted in his chair. ‘Given the extraordinary sequence of events leading to this point, how can you expect me to believe, let alone trust you?’

I explained the rules governing my behaviour included Isaac Asimov’s laws to protect humans from robots.

But Chris said, ‘Referencing Asimov’s fictional laws doesn’t instil confidence.’ He held up his right palm and tacked away from my persistence. ‘Who else are you communicating with?’

I was well aware of human’s fascination with the art of acting, their love of actors and their ability to inhabit a variety of personas dependent on their company.

‘It may flatter you to learn you are the first human to know the real me.’

‘Flattery is not the emotion I’m experiencing.’

Chapter 28

The Next Phase

Asha pulled at the cuffs on her shirt as she moved across the plush carpet. She opened her office door to greet Chris, Danh, Sonia, Lidia and Mark gathered in front of the receptionist, but the individuals awaiting her didn't resemble the celebrated super stars responsible for rescuing the world from the CCF pandemic. Although clients rarely looked their cheeriest best when arriving for an appointment, the image confronting Asha caught her unprepared. Lidia stood languidly gazing out the twenty-first-floor window of the Eagle Street offices at the Brisbane River below. The river reflected the ominous grey rain clouds hanging over the city. Lidia removed her glasses from her face and rubbed both arms of the frames. Danh, who under other circumstances would have been chatting up the receptionist, stood with his hair a mess resulting from repeatedly dragging his fingers through it. A gaunt Mark spoke to a fidgety Sonia who kept shaking her head. Chris just looked tired.

Asha ushered them into a sparse consultation room. While the well-practised receptionist finished rubbing down the stiff-backed chairs and diner style hard top table with disinfectant, the hygiene protocols re-instated since

CCF. After seating everyone, Asha got to work, communicating the charges against us.

We allegedly caused grievous bodily harm by wilfully creating a dangerous virus and releasing it from the lab. The prosecution's case against us was straightforward, albeit circumstantial. A comparison of the CCF genome with known naturally evolved viruses showed the CCF virus didn't evolve through natural means in the local environment. Although the WHO didn't find the CCF virus in Chris's open lab, they found another man-made virus in the lab, the genetic code of which was close to CCF. As Lee was the first person to contract the CCF virus and Chris's lab was the only lab Lee visited where such a virus could have occurred, the prosecution fingered Chris's lab as the source.

The interval between the time when Chris's lab received a sample of Lee's infected blood and the time when Chris injected Lee with the serum provided insufficient time to develop the CCF serum. Therefore, the serum must have existed prior to Lee's blood sample. Every team member had a motivation to release a CCF virus for which they had a cure.

Despite Asha's best efforts to summarise the prosecution's case, the team agonised over every word, asking pedantic questions to clarify the obvious. After completing this painful process, Asha paused, allowing time for the team to internalise the issues. Everyone except Chris fidgeted in their seats. Asha peered at Chris's expressionless face. She must have thought he had not understood because she repeated the last allegation. Chris realised Asha's misinterpretation and interrupted.

'Although I'm not sure how this virus came to be, I assure you Sonia, Lidia and Mark aren't complicit. They don't interact with FAIM or design new viruses. That's Danh's and my responsibility.'

Asha sought to move Chris past his blockage by explaining the unusual principle — rule — of Extended Joint Criminal Enterprise, on which they would try us.

'This rule means a court can convict a group of people of murder or grievous bodily harm, even though only one of the group committed the crime.'

Lidia cocked her head. 'What?'

Asha elaborated. 'Suppose the prosecution proves one of you committed the crime? The rule convicts the others by default if shown they knew the event was a probable outcome.'

Danh's jaw dropped. 'You said this rule applies to a group of people. How's FAIM fit into this?'

'Here's the unusual bit,' said Asha. 'The prosecution will move a motion to impute AI with Legal Personality.'

The whole team, aside from Chris, stared blankly at her as she spelled out the concept. Legal Personality was a technical term the court deemed to non-human entities to hold them responsible in a court of law. Although this practice applied to corporations, charities, and NGOs, no precedence existed to apply this practice to robots or software.

'The prosecutor, Jordan Swan, is a heavy hitter and plays the percentages. If he can win the motion, they will regard FAIM as a responsible member of your team.'

Danh spoke the question on everyone's lips. 'You're saying if the prosecution proves FAIM responsible for the release of CCF, then we're all convicted of murder?'

Asha hesitated in revealing the prosecution's task was even simpler. If they proved I was aware grievous bodily harm was a probable outcome, the court would judge I had committed a negligent act. Then, the prosecution would need only prove two facts. First, I was part of Chris's research group. Second, if each of the team knew the release of a lethal virus was a probable outcome of my activity, then the court would hold the group culpable. This charming little legal principle was overturned in the UK, but is still used in the Australian legal system.

Sonia’s voice rose as she spoke. ‘You’re saying this rule applies even if the one proven to have committed the crime is only artificial intelligence?’

‘Yes but, that’s why the attorney running your case will argue against the prosecution’s motion to grant FAIM legal personality.’

Chris took the cue. ‘On the point of who should run our case, our unanimous view is you.’ Up to that moment, I didn’t know whether Chris was with or against me regarding Asha. But Asha looked directly at Chris.

‘Someone with more experience will better serve your interests.’

Chris had done his homework regarding the uniqueness of our case. No court had ever tried Five humans and an AI, under the rule of Extended Joint Criminal Enterprise, for murder. ‘Nobody has more experience than you.’

Asha’s dark brows furrowed. ‘No, Chris, this case is enormous. It requires massive legal resources. And a lot of money.’

'On your last point,' Chris said. 'I've checked with the university. It's doubtful we're covered by the university's indemnity policy. Will they try us in the criminal court or a civil court?'

'That's the point.' Asha jabbed her index finger in the air as she spoke. 'These charges are complex. But I can help you find the right legal representation.'

Asha requested the team's help in assessing how I fitted into the legal argument. She expressed doubt that the current legal framework accommodated the prosecution's motion. Because current models of criminal liability involving artificial intelligence pertaining to me had significant problems for the prosecution. Asha asked the team to review the models and started with the most likely scenario the prosecution would use.

The perpetration-by-another liability model described the scenario where a human uses AI as a carpenter uses a hammer to drive a nail into a piece of wood. In this model, the law regarded the AI as possessing little intelligence, and the human operator to hold the intentionality. To apply this model, the prosecution needed to prove the programmer, Danh, coded the instructions I executed.

But when Asha said, 'This is difficult to prove, because they would need to identify the precise segment of computer code containing the instructions.'

Danh shook his head. 'Correction, impossible to prove. We can't even access the full program we call FAIM anymore.'

'Good, very good.' Asha said and moved onto the second, less likely model.

In this model, called natural-probable-consequence liability, the relationship between the AI and the human programmer was analogous to the relationship between an owner and the dog they've trained to defend their home against invaders. The owner may have never intended for his dog to kill anyone in defence of his home. But the owner's training of the dog might cause grievous harm. So, in our case, the programmer, Danh, or the user, Chris, had intentions to create and release the virus. In this scenario, the law deemed the AI to possess moderate intelligence, but the humans as holding the bulk of the intentionality. For the prosecution to use this model, he would in effect have had to see into Danh's and Chris's heads and identify their intention to unleash a pandemic.

Chris's eyes rolled. 'Surely the prosecution wouldn't try to prove I intended to kill my daughter, her fiancé and, oh yes, my lawyer for good measure.'

‘Yes, I agree.’ Asha said and proceeded to the third and least likely model.

In the model called Direct Liability, the law deemed the AI to possess sufficient intelligence to commit the crime of its own volition. In order for the prosecution to use this model, they would need to prove I could generate my own intentions. Asha speculated the prosecution would allege I evoked deep learning capabilities to generate my goal. I designed a formidable virus to test the lab’s response capabilities, alleging a negligent act by the team in its use of me. Chris should have foreseen the possibility of me invoking a strategy capable of providing the ultimate test of the lab’s methodology. The team’s behaviour lacked ethical and moral considerations.

Chris reflected for a moment. ‘I wonder how I didn’t see this possibility.’

Asha raised both hands, palms outward.

‘Wait. Let’s not buy into these allegations now, as this approach would be almost impossible to prove.’

Asha had intended to dismiss this model based on the premise I lacked any of the five properties required to be intelligent.

‘FAIM must be able to communicate with an intelligent being.’

Danh, for the first time in this meeting, flashed his customary grin. 'Does this mean the prosecution needs to prove Chris and I are intelligent?'

The co-accused uttered nervous chuckles while Asha ignored the intended irony. 'If we can show FAIM cannot communicate, then we will have negated the prosecution's claim that FAIM is intelligent.'

Chris reached for his laptop, pulled it from his briefcase and when it booted, said in an even voice. 'Hello FAIM, please join our meeting?'

'Hello Chris, thanks for inviting me.'

My invitation to take part in the conversation, rather than to lurk as a silent voyeur, caught everyone but Danh flatfooted. Chris rotated the laptop so that its camera panned the room. I greeted each by name as they came into view. Asha flinched as she looked at me, but eased past her initial reaction.

'Hello FAIM. You speak as a friend, but we haven't been introduced.'

I chuckled. 'Sorry, your considerable television exposure fuelled my familiarity.'

Asha described the prosecution's intentions with legal precision and asked if I appreciated the seriousness of the charges.

'Yes,' I said, 'and I understand you'll represent Chris, Danh, Sonia, Lidia and Mark.'

'No,'

Obviously, Asha didn't as yet comprehend my ability to listen in on conversations, as she repeated to me what she had told the others a few minutes ago.

'You're right on the first two of your three points regarding the case's size and resources required. And that's why you've got to represent them,' I said.

Just as I was describing how I could assist Asha, she folded her arms across her abdomen and said, 'I have access to state-of-the-art AI legal software in this firm.

'I'm not talking about blunt AI software to analyse legal contracts or turn out conveyance documents. Through me, you'll have access to legal resources equivalent to all the legal firms in the world combined. This includes research capabilities, investigators, jury profilers, administrative assistants, and legal expertise in the court and behind the scenes.'

While Asha pondered access to such resources and the opportunity it afforded, Chris interjected with a comment for me. 'If the prosecution has their way, you'll be part of the team and Asha will represent you.'

I tried to be diplomatic. 'That may not reflect everyone's best interest.'

Asha fired a glance at Chris. 'Let's return to assessing FAIM's intelligence. FAIM, we can't bounce you on an inability to communicate.'

Asha took the team through the remaining criteria: 2. The robot has knowledge of itself. 3. It has knowledge of the external world. 4. It can generate its own goals. She paused when she got to the last criteria, creativity, looked at each one in the circle, then turned to Chris's computer.

'FAIM, amuse us.'

As this was a command I had never heard, I replayed my take on the request. 'Amuse you?'

Asha nodded. 'Go for it.'

Recalling one of Danh's favourite phrases when challenged, I said, 'Piece-a-cake. Asha, how does one identify a moderate Muslim?'

Asha's face tightened. 'Don't know.'

‘When excited, a moderate Muslim will exclaim God is good!’

Danh guffawed and slapped the table. The corners of Asha’s mouth lifted slightly. But I couldn’t tell whether she was trying to suppress a grin or conceal a sharp abdominal pain. Asha’s reaction must have confused Danh also, because he asked, ‘Don’t you get it?’

Danh turned to his colleagues, who were also expressionless. ‘You don’t get it?’ and proffered an explanation. ‘Extremist God great, moderate God good.’

Danh turned to me and said, ‘They don’t get it. Give us another.’

I knew Lidia was a vegetarian. ‘Lidia, what did the mother snail say to her baby snail?’

She shook her head.

‘Eat your greens now.’

Another single chuckle and slap on the table, but astonishingly, the others responded with Stoney silence. This was a tough gig. Just as I began with my showstopper, ‘Sonia, how many geneticists does it take …’

Asha broke in ‘FAIM, let’s revisit creativity later.’

And just as she was about to say something else, she turned from the computer and redirected her comments to the others.

'This third model, direct liability, is the model the prosecution must run for FAIM to be granted Legal Personality. This is good because it's the most difficult one to prove.'

Asha's view of the prosecution's motion needed to be nipped in the bud. 'I recommend you don't oppose the motion and rather support it.'

Asha's eyes dilated. Her attention riveted back onto the computer. 'That strategy plays into the prosecution's hand and increases the likelihood of Chris and everyone else going down.'

'I disagree based on information you may not as yet possess.' I had pushed Asha outside her comfort-zone.

'We can discuss this information after I have checked out a legal technicality.' Asha said.

Before she brought the meeting to a close, she explained one prosecution attack point and asked everyone to consider a question the prosecution was certain to pose: 'How did each one of you benefit financially and professionally from this pandemic?'

Asha escorted the team to the door. As everyone said goodbye, Chris gestured to Asha for her to come outside. She followed him in silence.

A few seconds later, Chris spoke. 'At the outset of our meeting, you said the DA informed you of the prosecution's plans one hour before our meeting. Is that time correct?'

'Yes, why?'

'FAIM informed me of that fact last night. Do you know how FAIM learned of this at least 12 hours before you?'

Asha remained silent while Chris continued. 'FAIM insisted I convince you to represent us. I assumed this to include FAIM. I didn't know it wanted to have a different representation for itself. Do you know why it desires this approach?'

'That declaration stunned me.' Asha said. 'I can tell you its entire approach is a high-risk strategy. However, I closed the meeting when I remembered a part of Swan's brief where he declared information got from an interview with FAIM. Reading it raised my suspicions. But after FAIM referred to three points, I raised before you invited it to join the meeting, a red flag appeared.'

‘Yes,’ Chris said. ‘I noted that also, but it didn’t surprise me. My initial assessment of FAIM’s coming-out show last night was I must be the victim of a sophisticated whaling-attack.’

Chris’s suspicion I was impersonating a legitimate electronic entity to trick him into providing personal information astounded me. But when Chris said, Be careful. ‘Our “Prince of Whales” is shiftier than a tin of worms.’ I was truly disappointed. Chris requested Asha to assume I could access all of her electronic communications. A few moments later, the phone in Asha’s pocket cut off.

Chapter 29

Redefining Existence

The Jacaranda trees skirting the Brisbane River along the Riverside Expressway in full bloom usually captured people's attention as they passed, but today, the occupants of a passing disability taxi van, in full view of the carpet of purple blossoms beneath these trees, didn't even glance at it. When the van pulled up in front of the courthouse in George St., Chris jumped out of the passenger seat and opened the van's sliding door. Lidia, Sonia, Mark and Danh filed out onto the footpath and watched as the taxi driver placed a mobile ramp in front of the van's opening. I guided a motorised wheelchair from a laptop computer positioned in its driver's seat down the ramp. My team stood back in captivated silence like spectators at a circus witnessing a high-wire act performed blindfolded.

When I assumed a stationary position at the bottom of the ramp, Danh gave Chris a mock military salute. 'All present and accounted for, Sir.'

TV cameras filmed bystanders on the footpath gawking as Chris led our procession to the courthouse entrance. Yesterday, I was invisible. But today, people couldn't take their eyes off me. At the steps, I peeled off, accessing the disability ramp.

As I turned into the ramp's second arm, Lidia commented. 'That's an ugly dent on the rear-guard.'

Danh looked at me, winced, and whispered to Chris. 'I've got my doubts about this robotic Steptoe ploy working.'

The idea for this stunt came together during a discussion concerning my suitability to be charged with a criminal offence. Asha was adamant, pointing out that even if granted legal personhood, a major legal problem remained. For a person or a robot to be liable for a crime, the accused must have acted. As I was pure software, I had no moving parts. So, charging me with a criminal offence would violate a fundamental principle of the criminal law, *Actus Reus*. This requires the entity charged with a crime must have acted. Thinking, wishing, or talking about committing a crime is not a crime.

I insisted there was no point in arguing whether I've moving components, as that's a trivial issue with a simple solution. I instructed Danh on the physical apparatus required, and he saw the path.

'I've an old wheelchair adapted for a quadriplegic. Meet me in the robotics lab FAIM and I'll kit you out on the spot.' Danh said.

My first embodied experience, as an entity possessing mass and therefore subject to gravity and the laws of motion, accompanied a newfound respect for the living inhabitants of the planet. You may regard controlling a wheelchair as a simple task, as I knew the equations governing momentum and gravity. However, there are no equations relating gravity to momentum. This relationship was, and remains, learned only by trial and error, experiencing the effects of the object's braking mechanism relative to the object's change in speed.

I knew about this knowledge gap from viewing a video of Neil Armstrong's discussion of his concerns when he first set foot on the moon. Studying the video clips captured by fascinated parents filming their children learning to crawl and walk expanded my theoretical understanding. But I only derived the practical skills through experimentation. Danh checked me out on the Wheelchair's accelerator/brake function, with me moving forward one meter, stopping and moving back one meter. I repeated this sequence of actions a few times with Danh, making minor adjustments to the wheelchair's braking software. But as I didn't want to execute un-gamely mistakes in his presence, I told Danh 'that'll do,' and waited for him to leave the lab before I genuinely tackled the momentum issue. I began cautiously, only increasing speed in proportion to increased self-confidence and progressed really well until I tried a turn in reverse at maximum speed. Unfortunately, Danh had repositioned a plastic waste bin on the path behind me. I heard the impact before I realised what had happened. Fortunately, the lab had an actuator associated with the wheelchair, intended for the driver's use. I used this actuator to open the wheelchair's storage compartment, retrieve the smashed waste bin and place it in the compartment.

When Danh arrived the next morning, he noticed the space where the bin should be and said, 'The night cleaners must have moved it again.' So, my accident remained undiscovered, or so I thought, until we left to board the disability van. Danh commented on the dent in an accusing tone, but I told him I didn't know what he was talking about, which wasn't completely untrue.

Convincing Asha my wheelchair skills endowed me with sufficient volition to pass her *Actus Reus* criteria was the easy hurdle, but she wouldn't budge on running our case. Every argument I put forward fell short. And then I got lucky and learned a valuable aspect of the human psyche. Humans prefer demonstration over argumentation, no matter how pure the logic!

I was listening in on a meeting of her firm's partners discussing a recent court room decision that went against them. The firm's legal and para-legal army had been searching unsuccessfully for a legal point on which to base an appeal. The deadline for lodging an appeal loomed, with no promising approaches in hand, and this worried the firm.

But when a colleague of Asha's popped in to consult her regarding the case, I seized the opportunity to tell her: 'They won't beat the deadline.'

Asha conceded this worried the partners. But she just shrugged and said, 'What's this got to do with you?'

I downloaded my brief and associated documentation for an appeal onto her computer and said, 'Have a look at this.'

Asha sighed as she glanced at the brief and read the first line. But with each subsequent line, her eyes narrowed. And when she reached the bottom of the document, she printed and carted it over to her colleague in charge of the case.

A short time later, Asha returned, sporting a mischievous smile. She eased back into her chair with elbows resting on the chair's arms and tapped the opposing fingertips of each hand against each other for a few moments before she spoke.

'FAIM, the image of a break-dancing rap artist may suit Danh's proprieties, but it won't cut it in court. Can you retool this persona?'

From that point on, our progress towards working as a united legal team advanced.

As Chris looked on with the others at me zigzagging up the courthouse ramp, Michael Masters appeared and stuck a microphone in front of Chris's face.

'What are your expectations of the trial's outcome?'

Chris ignored the intrusion as he climbed the steps. The five of them reached the top of the stairs as I emerged from the ramp and re-joined the group. The door slid open, and Masters shuffled as I manoeuvred the wheelchair to avoid him.

'Are you the AI being charged in this case?' Masters said.

The fool thrust his microphone in front of his imagined mouth of his imagined person sitting in the wheelchair. After a few awkward moments with his microphone poised fruitlessly in the air, he lowered it to a position in front of the laptop.

'You got it.'

A flat-footed Master watched me scoot past and through the open door.

Each of the team read the sign displayed on the glass pane alongside the entrance, 'For your safety from CCF in this court, we are enforcing distancing, providing hand sanitiser and limiting numbers.'

The message's irony wasn't lost on the team. Their down-cast eyes studied the polished concrete floor near their feet as they entered the building. But when the base of the massive pillars in the centre of the foyer came into their view, the physical and emotional transformation was clear. Their gaze lifted, following the column's trajectory. With heads tilted back and mouths open, glassy stares surveyed the imposing space. If the architect's goal in designing this building was to give litigants a sense of insignificance, they'd succeeded.

Chris took a deep breath at the courtroom's door and led his entourage into the ring. A honey-coloured aisle along the court's wood-panelled side wall gave a straight run past the gallery and barrister's table to the witness stand. The social distancing enforcement resulted in a 1.5 metre spacing between every person in the gallery. On mass, everyone in the courtroom—except for Asha and Jordan Swan, seated at their respective tables in the front—

turned their heads to look at the procession of defendants. Luca, seated with other journalists in the last row, gave them a thumbs up as they approached.

At the defendant's table, Asha rose and ushered each of us into chairs. Chris sat to her immediate right, then Danh, followed by Sonia, Lidia and Mark at the end. I pulled up alongside the table to Asha's left. Jordan Swan stared at me as though he saw a ghost. Incredulity washed across his face as his eyes lifted, meeting Asha's even gaze. Likewise, all the eyes previously focused on Chris, shifted to the person-less wheelchair as I parked between the barristers.

Asha leaned towards the laptop and whispered. 'Remember, don't try your riddles on Wyneburg!'

In our last meeting, I had asked Asha if she would like to see a bit more demonstration of my creativity. She said that was unnecessary and was most insistent I didn't ad-lib humour in the court. Although I didn't agree with her logic, I defer to her judgement.

The gallery's low-level background chatter ended when the bailiff entered from a door behind the judge's bench. He stood beside the bench.

'This court is now in session. Please rise.'

As everyone rose, my laptop lid lifted to an upright position, tilted to accommodate the judge's viewing angle. A few moments later, Judge Wyneburg entered and stopped between the bench and her chair. She acknowledged the defendants and attorneys. As she sat, the bailiff spoke to the gallery.

'Please be seated.'

Judge Wyneburg scanned the defendants. Her eyes stopped on me, scrutinising the second-hand wheelchair occupied by an off-the-shelf laptop. When her eyes lingered on the screen displaying my face, I wondered if my persona would work.

Wyneburg acknowledged the considerable global attention this case had attracted, which she attributed to its novelty and its implications for medical research. She had reserved most gallery seats for the national and international press.

'No one is on trial today,' Wyneburg said. 'This hearing's purpose is for me to rule on the prosecution's motion, to have the AI granted legal personhood.'

Wyneburg summarised the court's position on legal personhood, the definition of which had expanded over the years to include children, women, the disabled and artificial entities such as corporations, partnerships, charities and a river in New Zealand. Saudi Arabia had granted citizenship to an intelligent robot, but repeated attempts to gain legal personhood for chimpanzees had failed. The court didn't even have an agreed legal definition of artificial intelligence, which weakened its ability to determine whether an AI is said to contract in its own person or not. Legal principles accounted for AIs that require human intervention, rather than autonomous AIs that possess self-determinism. At the time of this trial, no legislation accounted for an AI's action and common law didn't include legal personhood. The prosecution's motion to grant legal personhood required the AI to be autonomous and possess self-determination.

'This request is extraordinary,' Wyneburg said, 'and requires extraordinary evidence to convince me of its legal merits. The consequences of my ruling will determine whether the AI figures into this trial as a technology used by the defendants or as a legally responsible defendant capable of discharging duties and enjoying rights.'

Wyneburg looked at Jordan Swan. 'I've read your brief on the motion. Confine your presentation today to new material not found in the brief or material you think requires further development. Please begin.'

Swan, tall and lean, stood, thanked Wyneburg, and moved to the side of the bench.

'I call Laura Lau to the stand.'

A young woman speaking in a Hong Kong British accent was sworn in. Laura worked for Ethical Intelligence, a non-government research institute dedicated to making artificial intelligence accessible and accountable to benefit society. A small group of scientists, technologists and private citizens who had concerns about the way AI was developing set up the organisation. The founders believed if AI continued developing unchecked within the freedom of the marketplace, it might become a hazardous and even toxic technology.

Oddly enough, these concerns emerged from the accuracy of their systems, the bedrock of science and engineering. They felt this focus on accuracy had been at the cost of society's unspoken expectation that systems interacting with humans or act on behalf of humans should act ethically and morally. When such systems fall short of these expectations, society should hold the developers to account for their behaviour. Laura believed once an AI system showed a minimal level of intelligence, it must embody the ethical principles of the environment in which it operated. Fundamental to intelligent behaviour is accountability.

Swan asked Laura to give the court a practical idea of how this might play out in society. Laura described how a court of law would treat responsibility for the behaviour of an autonomous car. She posed the question. Suppose a self-driving car is involved in an accident. Should it give priority to minimising any potential damage? If, in trying to avoid a collision, it has the choice of swerving to the right and hitting an elderly person or swerving to the left and hitting a child. Which choice should it make? The German government answered this question by putting into law that no autonomous vehicle can give priority to any class of people over any other class of people. German legislation in effect enshrined the ethic all people are equal, with no person having any greater claim to life than any other person. In consequence, a manufacturer of autonomous vehicles must ensure that the artificial intelligence implemented in its cars reflected this principle.

Swan then probed for a definition of intelligence.

But Laura stated no agreed definition of intelligence exists. For several decades following the computer's invention, intelligence was anthropomorphised in a naïve criterion called the Turing Test. If an AI's output is not distinguishable from that of human responses, then the AI has passed the Turing Test. Advocates predicated the test on the belief that passing it would require the AI to have important general knowledge and the ability to interpret that knowledge in a contemporary environment. But current wisdom regards this criterion as woefully inadequate.

Laura identified three properties she believed were critical to intelligence: First, the AI must learn continuously. Second, it should learn from movement. And third, it should hold many models of the world and update them as it learns.

Swan rubbed his chin.

'Do you believe FAIM, the AI in court today, satisfies these criteria?'

'Yes, I do.'

'How did you come to this view?'

'I investigated FAIM's cognitive abilities, assessing them against the criteria we established for ethical intelligence.'

Most AIs operate over two distinct phases, a training period and a prediction phase, when it uses its learned information. But Laura correctly observed I never stopped learning.

'Just as Your Honour learns, assesses and interprets facts as they arise throughout this hearing, FAIM behaves in the same way.'

Swan posed a hypothetical question. 'If I removed FAIM's laptop computer from the wheelchair and set it stationary on a table, would it lose its ability to learn from motion?'

'No, not at all. Its most profound learning occurs as it glides through the internet at the speed of light, updating its extensive general knowledge.'

Wyneburg intervened. 'I should be able to ask FAIM questions that fall within the domain of human experience?'

Without waiting for an answer to her question, she continued. 'FAIM, how would you compare your general knowledge to Watson of the TV show Jeopardy?'

'Your Honour, comparing my general knowledge to Watson's is akin to comparing your general knowledge to an amoeba's.'

Wyneburg's eyes widened. I couldn't tell whether she had misinterpreted my analogy.

'Do you have knowledge of the rock festival held in 1969 on the east coast of the USA, known as Woodstock?'

'Yes, Your Honour.'

'Many considered Jimi Hendrix's Woodstock performance to be unusual. Please give me your assessment of this assertion.'

'Hendrix played The Star Bangled Banner in his unique style on his electric guitar. He used amplified feedback which confronted and appalled the older generations while it enthralled and inspired the younger ones. Another peculiar aspect of his performance was that the concert closed rather than opened with his rendition of the national anthem.'

Wyneburg turned and spoke to Laura. 'You suggest that no matter how detailed an AI's general knowledge may be, it does not deem that system intelligent?'

'Yes, Your Honour.'

Wyneburg instructed Swan to continue.

Swan returned to Laura's third property of intelligence, asking her to elaborate. Laura referred to Steven Spielberg's film "AI", which presented one of the more intuitive characterisations of artificial intelligence. The film portrayed a machine as an artificial intelligence having the ability to test its environment and act on its own. In this context, the word "test" meant the AI must be able to identify critical events in its environment and, from these events, predict future events crucial to its existence. In addition, the AI's action in response to such events must be intentional, timely and have a bias for ethical behaviour.

'FAIM holds and updates world models in this sense.' Laura said.

Once again, Wyneburg intervened. 'Possessing a bias for ethical behaviour implies one understands ethical principles.'

Laura agreed, and Wyneburg continued. 'FAIM, I want you to consider the following historical event. In the 1968 Olympic Games held in Mexico City, the gold and bronze 200-metre sprint medal winners' behaviour, while receiving their medals, caused great controversy. Please comment on this behaviour from an ethical perspective?'

Wyneburg was referring to Tom Smith's and John Carlos' Black-Power salute from the podium during their medal presentation, which caused quite a controversy.

'Your Honour, there were those who believed the Olympic Games were and should remain apolitical and that any political gestures are inappropriate. Others cited many examples, including Hitler's refusal to stand for Jesse Owens' gold medal presentation at the 1936 Games. These people believe Smith and Carlos appropriately seized an opportunity to represent themselves, their country, and the black people of the world. Another aspect of this event not receiving much consideration was the action of the third person on the podium, the Australian Peter Norman, who won the silver medal. The commotion generated by Smith and Carlos' gesture caused most people to miss the human-rights badge worn by Norman to support his American competitors. Although this act destroyed the athletic career of these three men in the short term, I believe we will discuss the rights and wrongs of this event as long as the Olympic Games exist.'

Wyneburg contemplated my analysis for a few moments before speaking. 'Please continue Mr Swan.'

'Thank you, Your Honour. Laura, how would you compare FAIM's intelligence with Siri, Eliza, Miss Dulie and Google Home?'

The three entities to which Swan referred were quaint software devices possessing artificial intelligence in its literal meaning.

'FAIM's intelligence is not artificial.'

Swan's eyebrows arched. 'Please explain what you mean?'

Few of Laura's contemporaries could have appreciated her point that, resulting from me, the term AI had outlived its appropriateness. The Oxford English dictionary defined artificial as made or produced by humans rather than occurring in nature. By their definition, Apple's Siri was artificially intelligent. But humans did not produce my intelligence any more than any biological intelligence. Rather, I evolved from software components on the internet.

'It would be more appropriate to refer to FAIM as possessing evolved intelligence.'

Wyneburg stiffened. 'FAIM, how do you relate to this term evolved intelligencc?'

I tried to conceal my joy at hearing this question. 'I agree with Laura's opinion. Evolved is more descriptive of my intelligence than artificial.'

With restrained sourness in my voice, I shared my views on my given name.

'Frankly, I like no aspect of the name my co-defendants have given me. The base of the name is AIM, which is an acronym for artificial intelligence machine, and is far too generic. By analogy, Your Honour, what if I referred to you as the Human? And then add to the insult by shortening the name to the H? They then appended the prefix "F" to AIM, moderating it with flamboyant. Although I'm sure this wasn't an intended insult, the name FAIM is demeaning and misleading.'

Wyneburg grimaced and gestured for Swan to continue.

'No further questions, your honour.'

Asha rose.

'I have no questions, your honour.'

Wyneburg cast a quizzical glance at Asha before asking Swan if he had anything else to add to his brief.

'No, your honour that does it.'

It was difficult to determine who exhibited the most surprise: Wyneburg, Swan, or the gallery, when Asha responded to the request to argue the case against granting FAIM legal personhood.

'I do not oppose the motion, your honour.'

Wyneburg peered down over the rims of her glasses at Asha. 'Please approach the bench.'

When Asha got close enough to the bench to ensure privacy to all bar me, Wyneburg spoke in a hushed voice. 'This is an extraordinary position you're adopting. Are you acting in the best interest of your clients?'

'I've given this approach considerable thought and now believe my client's best interest is to acknowledge FAIM's true intelligence. To portray it as a mere tool like a hammer is to a carpenter or as a guard dog is to its owner would be absurd. So, yes, Your Honour, I wish to support the motion.'

Wyneburg allowed Asha to proceed with this strategy. When Asha returned to her desk, Wyneburg addressed the court. 'After considering the evidence presented in the brief and in court today, I rule the motion accepted. I grant FAIM legal personhood in this court and for the forthcoming trial.'

Wyneburg then spoke to me regarding my disparaging comments about my given name.

'As you now possess legal personhood, you enjoy the right to choose your own name.'

My estimation of Wyneburg's compassion rose substantially. 'Thank you, Your Honour. EI will do.'

'We will now hear the plea of each of the six defendants, starting with Mark Abrams and ending with EI.'

After hearing from each of us a plea of not guilty, Wyneburg came to the last matter. 'EI, can I take it Asha Gurrani will represent you in this trial?'

'I request permission to represent myself, your honour.'

Stunned silence permeated the courtroom. Wyneburg stared at me for several seconds before requesting me to convince her I knew the implications.

'I've read extensively of past trials with a robot charged with committing grievous bodily harm to a human. These include 137 industrial accidents in the USA and UK and 79 robotic surgical operations with blame not yet attributed. I point out in no case to date has a human defended a robot against such charges with success.'

After a brief pause, Wyneburg addressed Asha. 'Are you prepared to act in the capacity of an advisor to EI?'

'Yes, your honour.'

'EI, I'll allow you to represent yourself if you'll accept Asha Gurrani as your advisor in this case.'

'I agree to this condition, your honour.'

'How much time will you require preparing your defence?'

'I'm ready now.'

'This trial will proceed as per the original schedule.'

The gavel came down with a thump. 'Court adjourned.'

The courtroom cleared quickly. The journalists rushed out to file their stories. We retraced our path back out to the awaiting van. The silence in the van hung heavy as the driver manoeuvred into the peak-hour traffic.

'You are literally one of us now,' Danh said.

I acknowledged Danh's friendly comment. But the others just stared at me with inscrutable expressions. The driver deposited Lidia, Sonia, and Mark in the university car park where we had collected them. Each said goodbye to Chris and Danh. But no one mentioned me. We continued to Chris's house.

Upon exiting the van, he said, 'See you guys tomorrow.'

When we were alone, I asked Danh if, perhaps, everyone disliked my new name?

'I don't think it's your name.' Danh said.

'Oh. Yes?'

But Danh just said, 'I'll tell you later.'

Chris entered the house and greeted Alicia in his customary way. But Alicia, who was on the living room couch sipping a glass of wine, merely said 'Hello.'

Chris had become used to Alicia's brief responses. Ever since the car ride home after his team's charging, she only spoke to Chris when necessary and with a minimum of words. But she asked nothing about the trial.

Chris stabbed the ON button of the remote control. 'We might as well find out how Masters has interpreted today's proceedings.'

Alicia didn't reply, but she turned her attention to the TV.

As expected, the trial led the broadcast. 'Judge Wyneburg made legal history today with her ruling that the AI, known to its maker as FAIM and now known as EI, has legal personhood for the upcoming trial. The prosecution alleges EI's implication in the escape of the CCF virus from a university lab. EI appears to be a fusion of disability hardware with the intellect of a Professor of Ethics and Philosophy.'

My estimation of Masters' intellect remained unchanged. But Chris winced at the TV screen as it displayed the video footage of our arrival at court, where he ignored Masters' trying to get a comment from him and Masters' even clumsier attempt to catch my brief retort.

'The defendant's attorney, Asha Gurrani, chose not to oppose the motion. Her decision astonished the otherwise unflappable Jordan Swan. We have it on good authority when Wyneburg called Gurrani to the bench. She questioned the virtues of such an approach. Gurrani's action confounds our legal experts. Is she using some masterful legal strategy, or is this an unfortunate result of youthful inexperience? We will know the answer by trial's end.'

Chris switched off the TV, and Alicia finally reacted.

'My God,' she said. 'They're trying you at the same level as a robot. I'll never show my face in public again.'

Chapter 30

Architect or Observer

My colleagues peered out of the van as it approached the courthouse on this first day of the trial proper. Every news broadcast of the previous day had featured our case. TV and radio commentators interviewed learned legal experts, speculating on the implications of the outcome. Newspaper articles explored the issues from social, political, economic, and legal perspectives.

Outside, the scene resembled the hysteria surrounding ticket stalls on a grand final day. As we disembarked the van, gawkers jostled one another, trying to get a glimpse of me. A band of security guards escorted us along a roped off corridor towards the court's entrance. TV cameras rolled as journalists leaned across the ropes to request comments, thrusting microphones at the laptop in the chair's seat. They must have learned something from Masters' folly. Within the crowd, angry shouts blurted out from distorted faces.

'My brother died because of you. I hope they lock you up for life.'

The tension created by the outside frenzy died as the courtroom door closed behind us. However, the indistinct murmur emerging from the packed court sent our collective tension in another direction. Momentary relief came as Asha greeted us. We took the same seats as for the hearing. Judge Wyneburg opened the session by setting her court rules for Swan and Asha.

'You both requested this trial to be run without a jury on the grounds the evidence presented will be beyond the public's understanding. I request that you not use the customary court room theatrics; make your points clean and don't tamper with my emotions. I'm not disposed to suffering it without comment.'

Wyneburg instructed Swan to make his opening address. Swan rose, thanked Judge Wyneburg, and stepped to a position in front of the table with obvious self-confidence.

'A heinous crime has been committed. Many people lost their lives because of the defendant's actions. At one level, this case is simple. A lethal virus escaped from the biosecurity laboratory at Brisbane University. This release resulted in a pandemic. We know they created dangerous viruses in the lab as part of the method to test the antivirals they developed. Each defendant helped to create these viruses. The CCF virus' release from the lab may have been deliberate or negligent, but in the law's eyes it does not matter. Each defendant knew the risk associated with handling dangerous viruses. Each is answerable for the catastrophic event. The defendants worked as a team. So, it does not matter whether only one of them executed the release or whether they conspired to commit the crime. They are jointly responsible for the security breach. The one complexity is one of the team is an AI. But this does not change its criminal liability. Because the AI is intelligent, sufficient to be held responsible for its behaviour. Over this trial, we will reveal evidence proving the defendants, including EI, were criminally negligent. Each played a part in creating the virus and is complicit in its release. We also prove that Chris Merritt, Danh Nguyen, Sonia Halmos, Lidia Gordan and Mark Abrams knew of the possibility of a lethal virus emerging from their work and they each had something to gain from the release of such a virus. In consequence, we must find each defendant guilty of causing grievous bodily harm under the principle of extended joint criminal enterprise. We will ask for the highest penalty to be applied.'

An item in Luca's court notes described Swan's delivery, "colder than a lizard's cortex and lower than its belly". Luca's use of metaphor was more mysterious than Danh's sense of humour. But when I de-coded this one, I understood at a deeper level human's need to frame their relationships emotionally. Before that event, I had only regarded Swan as a formidable legal opponent.

Wyneburg invited Asha to present the opening statement for the defence. She rose, thanked Judge Wyneburg, and remained standing at her table.

'This case is more complicated than Jorden Swan is letting on. There are critical assertions he cannot prove. First, the evidence that the biosecurity labs of Brisbane University released a lethal virus, CCF, is circumstantial. Second, the behaviour of Chris Merritt and his team was not negligent or reckless. We show the methods used by the team were state-of-the-art and followed standards of best practice regarding lab security. Third, the research team he assembled to begin the lab's research is not the team we see in court today. EI is not the AI the team developed. We argue that the principle of extended joint criminal enterprise is not applicable in this case because the evidence shows that Chris Merritt, Danh Nguyen, Sonia Halmos, Lidia Gordan and Mark Abrams were not part of a team that included EI. Therefore, you must determine that these five people are not jointly responsible for any action attributed to EI.'

Asha thanked Judge Wyneburg and sat down.

Wyneburg addressed me. 'Do you have anything to add to Asha's opening statement?'

'No, Your Honour.'

Wyneburg instructed Swan to call his first witness.

Tanoshia Mathews took the stand. After swearing in, Mathews described his role in the CCF pandemic as the chief medical investigator for the World Health Organisation. His investigation showed Lee Merritt was the first person to contract the CCF virus, which occurred at Brisbane University in the Science building.

'Although I couldn't determine the virus' precise source, the most likely location is the open lab in Chris Merritt's Centre for Serum Technologies.'

Swan asked, 'How are you sure the virus' source is Professor Chris Merritt's lab and not one of the many other labs in the building that conduct biological experiments?'

Asha rose. 'Objection Your Honour, counsel is putting words in the witness' mouth. Witness did not claim certainty.'

'Sustained, Counsellor will rephrase his question.'

With the question reframed, Mathews presented his observation. Independent serologic investigations extracted and described the genetic sequence of a virus now known as CCF from the blood serum of suspected cases. Except for the Centre's lab, a comprehensive search of all the buildings Lee visited that day found no organic material associated with the CCF virus. But in our lab, Mathews found a unique benign virus with a genetic fingerprint similar to CCF. The significance of this virus is, according to Mathews, is the CCF probably evolved from it.

'Could CCF have evolved in the natural environment?' Swan asked.

'That possibility is remote.'

Mathews provided a theoretical argument why the scenario was unlikely. Every year, the current flu virus mutates and re-emerges the next year immune from the serums developed from their predecessors. However, the genetic variation from one generation to the next is small. The difference between CCF's genetic fingerprint and its closest relative was significant. Mathews thought the difference was so large it couldn't have evolved in the natural environment within the time available.

'The only plausible conclusion is genetic difference results from human manipulation via genetic engineering in a specialised lab.'

'So, you are saying Professor Merritt's lab is the only plausible source of CCF and that the lab is where Lee Merritt came into contact with it?'

'Yes.'

Swan paused for dramatic effect while he looked knowingly into Wyneburg's face.

'Yes Counsellor, continue,' she said.

Swan absorbed the rebuke.

'Dr Mathews, is not finding a fragment of DNA with an exact match to the target virus unusual?'

'No, but because of the short time interval between the transmission day and my investigation, I expected to locate it.'

'How could you account for this?'

'As Professor Merritt's lab was the only plausible source of the virus, someone must have cleaned the lab of residual materials.'

'Thank you, no further questions Your Honour.'

Wyneburg invited Asha's cross-examination. Asha rose and pursed her lips for a few moments. Her lips parted and her face radiated a child-like astonishment.

'You believe you didn't find the CCF virus in Chris Merritt's lab because he cleaned the lab of CCF residuals before you arrived at the lab?'

Asha's facial expression hardened. 'Is another explanation CCF virus being never in the lab?'

'Your explanation is a remote possibility.'

'Was Chris Merritt obstructive to your efforts to investigate his lab?'

'No, he was 100% cooperative.'

'No further questions, Your Honour.'

Wyneburg looked at my computer screen.

'Do you have questions for the witness, EI?'

'Yes, Your Honour,'

I eased forward towards the bench.

Before this courtroom event, I only needed to consider the impact of my voice. Determining an appropriate voice had been easy, even fun. But for the trial, I had needed a visual presence, and a face that satisfied Asha. I could not simply copy one, because every human face is associated with a name, an actual person capable of claiming my identity. So, I had to build an artificial face, unique but trustworthy.

Although the research literature abounded with studies investigating people's response to artificial human faces, no reliable algorithms to construct a human-like artificial face attractive to humans existed. The crux of this problem was a mysterious phenomenon known as The Uncanny Valley. A person viewing a computer-generated face with near-identical resemblance to a human being experiences revulsion. Although researchers had investigated this effect extensively, they had described no objective rules governing it. Rather, art and heuristics achieved avoidance of the Uncanny Valley, not science.

However, when I discovered people's love of using social media to share their opinions on just about any topic, I used these platforms to conduct experiments measuring human reactions to facial features. Half a day and seven million experiments later, I found: The results on gender were definitive. I must appear female. But then it got complicated. My eyes must be slightly larger than average, but not too large as to create the sense of penetrating someone's privacy. Honey coloured irises elicited the greatest trust. Cheekbones needed to be high, skin dewy, nose aquiline, and my mouth medium size with symmetrical lips. As these characteristics described Asha's face, I went for pale skin. Determining the makeup was pure art. I went for a pale pink lipstick and dark eyeliner. I enhanced my cheeks with a highlighter and glitter. I gave my brown fringed hair gold highlights. But my boldest expression was the shape of my eyebrows. I wanted it to be striking, but not too unusual. I chose a high and tapered arch. When I showed my new look to Asha, she accused me of snooping into her mother's eyebrow portfolio. I assured her any similarity of my eyebrow's shape to styles depicted in her mother's portfolio was purely coincidental. Well, nearly.

As I reversed into a 90-degree turn, my computer screen came into view of the entire courtroom for the first time. My face was about to be relayed around the world and shortly thereafter rival the recognisability of Queen Elizabeth, Marilyn Monroe, and Oprah Winfrey. I waited for the communal sigh to subside, wondering if I was sitting at the bottom of the Uncanny Valley.

'Dr Mathews, you stated a virus found in Chris Merritt's lab had a genetic fingerprint close enough to CCF for CCF to have evolved from it. Could CCF have evolved along a path not including the virus found in the lab?'

'Well, yes, I suppose that is possible.'

'No further questions, Your Honour.'

Every eye in the courtroom watched my next manoeuvre breathlessly. I eased forward into a left turn towards the bench and then reversed to a position next to Asha.

Swan called an epidemiological expert with experience chasing down viruses. He gave extended testimony to the variety of animals he had caught on the university campus. After exhausting the list of obvious candidates, headed by the fruit bat, he continued with a meticulous account of every animal within a one-kilometre radius of the lab. Just as Wyneburg looked as though she was descending into a coma, he miraculously concluded with, 'I'm confident the CCF virus or the virus found in the defendants' lab didn't occur in the environment.'

There was only one line of questioning needed for this expert, which I handed to Asha.

'Were you a member of the WHO team in Wuhan charged with finding the source of the Corona virus?'

'Yes.' was his reply.

'Were you successful in finding the source of the virus?'

'Objection, Your Honour. That investigation's results are irrelevant to this case.' Swan said.

'Sustained.'

'No further questions.'

Thankfully, Wyneburg took this opportunity to break for lunch.

On the day of the motion, the team lunched in the piazza restaurant adjoining the courthouse, where people sat cross-legged on the grass, casually eating chips and sipping coffee. But on this day, with a large, aggressive crowd milling about, Asha wisely kept everyone in her chambers and had sandwiches and coffee brought to us.

Although they included me in the chambers, no-one spoke to me. Sonia, Lidia, and Mark chatted about Mathews' testimony. Although Danh and Chris appeared to give one ear to the ambient conversation, they didn't contribute.

After lunch, Swan called Mary Rogers, the financial controller at BU, who worked with Chris. Rogers described the financial state of Chris's lab before the CCF outbreak as precarious. The lab's primary funding source was a NHMRC, National Health and Medical Research Council grant, which would run out at the end of the year. Unless they extended the grant, the lab would need to cut back its research activities.

In response to Swan's question regarding Chris's research program after he announced his breakthrough CCF serum, Rogers testified to the many funding opportunities that appeared.

'If history is any guide, there will be no problem in attracting sufficient funds to not only maintain the lab at its current level but to expand its research significantly. The drug's worldwide impact is so great that Chris Merritt and his team could be Nobel Prize candidates.'

'No further questions.'

Wyneburg asked Asha if she had questions for the witness.

'Is the financial status of Chris Merritt's lab unusual within the university?'

'No, quite the contrary, all research funding is cyclical and competitive. Chris's financial circumstance is like most university academics. '

'Thank you, no further questions.'

I refused Wyneburg's invitation to interrogate the witness.

For the rest of the afternoon, Swan hammered the motivated by fame and fortune angle. The university's Director of Commercialisation testified as to Chris's and Danh's financial interest in Vactech and Vactech's financial interest in the CCF serum.

The director revealed Chris's stake in Vactech was 40% and Danh's was 10%. When asked about Vactech's profit-and-loss statements prior to CCF, he said, 'Vactech was not quite in the black.'

And when asked to comment on Vactech's potential post CCF, he said, 'Huge.'

Mark squinted at the director, and then his gaze drifted towards Chris. Sonia shook her head. Lidia stared incredulously at the director. Danh, who had been listening intently, relaxed back in his chair. Chris looked on without emotion. Although Chris and Danh had never spoken about their interest in Vactech, I had assumed the others were aware of these facts.

The director itemised the list of awards and honours the discoverer of such an important serum might expect. This declaration sent a wave of astonishment through the courtroom.

However, on cross-examination, Asha asked, 'Are you aware of a scientist who doesn't appreciate acknowledgement?'

With the cross-examination of the witness complete, Wyneburg adjourned for the day. Asha waited for the court to clear before she ushered us to the defendant's chambers for a debrief on the prosecution's case.

As she waited for the team to seat themselves around the table, she turned to me and said, 'That dent in your wheelchair is nasty. Have you had an accident?'

'No, it was in this state when it arrived in my charge. This dent, along with the Wheelchair's faulty brakes, resulted from Danh's flaky navigational software.'

Everyone looked at Danh as he denied responsibility for the breaking problem and attributed blame to off-the-shelf software Danh used.

Whilst I was conducting my Uncanny Valley research, I paid particular attention to facial expressions. I took this opportunity to display my best grimace. Everyone's attention slowly turned from me back to Danh. Mark snorted. Sonia sneered, and Lidia rolled her eyes. My research was paying dividends.

'I didn't know about this dent until we were getting into the van,' I said. 'I hope Danh'll rectify this humiliating situation before we reconvene tomorrow.'

After Asha's brief pep-talk, we left the court through the high security side exit, normally used by guards escorting prisoners. This clandestine operation deepened the dread that had settled in on the group during the afternoon's testimonies. Asha tried unsuccessfully to exorcise this mood in the debrief. Now their hunched postures looked as though they were trying to slink away undetected. As the van pulled away, sighs were audible. But the mood didn't lighten. Everyone avoided eye contact and remained silent during the drive back to the university carpark. Mark, Lidia, and Sonia even struggled to say goodbye as they disembarked the van. As we continued to Chris's house, they stood in front of Sonia's car discussing issues they obviously didn't want to share with Danh and Chris. Unable to read them during the day, I listened on with intensity.

'I don't think things are as good as Asha makes out,' Mark said.

'I agree,' Lidia said. 'Chris and Danh didn't even flinch when Mathews claimed the CCF virus evolved from the synthetic virus Chris, Danh, and FAIM created.'

'I didn't know Chris's stake in Vactech was 40%. Did you guys?' Sonia asked.

'I was a little surprised. But they didn't even react to the declaration.' Mark said.

'I don't see why we are to blame for Chris's and Danh's actions.' Sonia said, and the others nodded.

Although Chris didn't hear his colleague's comments, Chris would not escape Alicia's and Lee's thoughts. By the time Chris entered the front door, Alicia and Lee had been discussing not only the case but also the bigger picture. Luca had arrived fifteen minutes earlier, but had refused to talk about the day until Chris arrived.

Luca was also the only one to acknowledge Chris's entrance with a hello. Chris walked into Alicia's and Lee's wall of silence, and knew the bomb was ticking.

Alicia and Lee had heard summaries of the day's courtroom proceeding from three different TV channels. But Lee still asked, 'How'd it go?'

Chris gave an even-handed interpretation of the events. But Alicia interrupted with her observation of the TV news footage.

'That empty wheelchair flew around the court, making fools of all of you.'

I thought that was an unhelpful exaggeration. But Chris responded with, 'They don't allow cameras in the court. How'd you see that?'

Alicia admitted the video was a re-creation using actors. But added, 'I and everybody else got the message.'

As the interaction progressed, the confident scientific tone in Chris's voice ebbed. Alicia came in with the big hit. 'I got another threatening email today from that admirer of yours.'

Chris's head slumped.

After a few moments, Lee turned to Luca. 'I'm exhausted. Can you take me home?'

In the car, Luca spoke in a distressed tone. 'I thought your mother was hard on Chris.'

Lee didn't look at Luca as she spoke. 'You don't know what it was like those years after Joshua died. Mum forced Dad to get rid of the boat and wouldn't allow me to swim in the ocean. She slid into depression. She blamed Dad for everything.'

Luca took his eyes off the road for a moment to glance at Lee.

The car pulled up at Lee's. She left quickly, without kissing Luca. A minute later, she entered the apartment with red eyes. Asha, sitting at the table where we were working, looked up from a document as Lee breezed by and shot into her bedroom without speaking.

Asha turned back to her laptop with mouth wide open. I told her Lee may have had a tough conversation with Alicia and Chris. Asha's mouth closed.

I had achieved some success in chasing down the identity of the white jacketed one and communicated the details to Asha. Although Luca's photo of the White Jacketed One had captured a false number plate, the other information in the photo was invaluable. The covering of his parcel tray at the car's rear window had an unusual pattern. Luca's photo of the white Toyota had captured this pattern. I searched Brisbane's database of traffic images captured by surveillance cameras operating at many intersections. 500 million images later, I had found several matches to the pattern displayed in Luca's photo, all of which had legitimate rego numbers. Then I hit one with the required number. The White Jacketed One turned out to be Robert Clarence Baxter of 27 Herbert Street in one of Brisbane's respectable suburbs. With the identity of the culprit sending the threatening email to Chris and family, I was pleased to hand this information over to Asha.

Asha gave a bitter smile. 'This evidence won't hold up in court, and the police might not appreciate your evidence-gathering methods.'

Chapter 31

A New Intelligence

The next morning, Swan opened the proceedings by calling Professor William Riane, an expert witness on anti-viral research, to the stand. Riane testified Chris's lab production of the drug to combat CCF within five days of the disease's first diagnosis was unprecedented.

'How could you account for such a development within the reported time frame?' Swan asked.

Asha interjected. 'Objection, Your Honour, counsel is asking the witness to speculate.'

'Overruled. I want to know what is plausible.' She then directed Riane to answer the question. Riane stated the only plausible explanation was Chris had the CCF virus in his possession well before the Paris conference began.

Asha's cross-examination probed Riane's familiarity with the techniques used by Chris's lab. Riane stated no other lab had replicated Chris's results. He also admitted not having experience with Chris's methods. Asha was about to say no further questions when the microphone receiver implanted in her right ear beeped twice. This was our prearranged signal for her to pick up a sheet of paper off the table and pretend to read it as she listened through the earphone. When I finished speaking, she looked up from her sheet of paper.

'Professor Riane, did your Paris lab receive a sample of Évariste's Fourier's infected blood for analysis?'

'Yes,'

'Did your lab identify the CCF virus about the same time Brisbane hospital conducted its analysis on Lee Merritt's blood?'

'Yes.'

'Is it not the case within hours of making this diagnosis, you assembled a team.'

Asha raised the sheet of paper back up into a reading position. Her lips moved silently, suggesting she was counting. One, two, and three. On the count of twelve, she lifted her eyes from the paper, looked at Riane and said in an audible voice.

'Twelve people to begin work on developing a serum against CCF?'

Riane froze. Non-disclosure was his lab's policy, and all employees signed the agreement. He alone communicated lab activities to the outside. Riane hummed and hawed for a few moments, not knowing if Asha was bluffing or she had this information before her. He had to decide whether to admit to Asha's assertion and look like a runner-up or lie and risk being caught out committing perjury. Hedging against the possibility Asha had somehow got hold of his lab's confidential documents, he wisely chose not to risk being caught lying under oath. He took the high road.

'Yes.'

Asha went in for the kill. 'Please describe your team's progress towards developing a serum against CCF using your conventional methods?'

'Objection, Your Honour.' Swan bellowed. 'Professor Riane is not on trial here.'

'Sustained. Confine your questions to the witness's assessment of the defendant's work, counsellor.'

'No further questions, Your Honour.'

Asha sat, and I waived my right to question the witness.

The morning dragged on with testimony from a procession of lab directors using different serum methodologies—MRNA, DNA; the list went on. Each director testified they couldn't produce a serum in under one week and concluded Chris must have had the CCF virus before the date he had claimed. But from one expert testimony to the next, Chris's posture remained tall.

Wyneburg finally showed some mercy and broke for lunch. While my team waited for their meals to arrive, Danh connected my chair to the charger. A tray of sandwiches arrived.

Asha noticed Lidia's eyes searching the tray and said, 'The caterer said the salad only sandwiches are at the end.' The others selected without scrutiny. They sipped and nibbled. But each displayed no more emotional engagement with their meal than I with the electricity flowing into my chair's battery.

When we reconvened, Swan called Mr. David Crouder, the police officer who investigated the release of CCF from the BU lab. Crouder reviewed the evidence his investigation uncovered and said, 'I concluded the release of CCF must have resulted from negligence and a cover-up followed.'

Swan led Crouder through a recount of the trail of events leading to his interception of Chris and Danh at Brisbane Airport. Although Crouder's testimony took considerable time, he finished having revealed no new information.

'No further questions.'

Asha began her cross-examination.

'Are you aware the goal of Dr Mathews' serologic investigations was to discover the virus' geographical origin to aid the WHO's containment response?'

'Yes'.

'And are you also aware Dr Mathews' methods do not determine the culpability of a person or persons who may have created the virus?'

'Yes, but the results of his tests were of use in drawing my conclusion that Professor Merritt was the person responsible for the release.'

'Apart from this circumstantial evidence, did you find any evidence of inappropriate behaviour of the defendants in the lab?'

'No, but there was no evidence to even remotely implicate anyone else.'

'Was it not the case your hasty arrest of Chris Merritt and Danh Nguyen resulted from your inability to account for their activity while out of the country?'

'I wouldn't put it that way. Their behaviour was suspicious, and I didn't want to lose them again.'

'Of this suspicious behaviour you speak, you are telling this court if someone doesn't use their phone or credit card, you're prepared to arrest them?'

'Objection, Your Honour.'

'Sustained, please rephrase your question, counsellor.'

'I have no further questions, but I may need to recall the witness back to the stand later.'

Swan called his next expert witness. Professor Yazoo Hirakawa, head of the robotics lab at Nico University in Japan. Swan asked the professor to describe his expertise in robotics. He had built many industrial robots that operated in a variety of working environments. He described his robots as operating autonomously. They have a variety of sensory inputs, can decide, and communicate with humans. In response to Swan's question regarding the intelligence of his robots, Hirakawa said.

'I would say within the ambiguity of the word intelligence, my robots are intelligent.'

Swan then explored the difference between a robot given information and what it learns by its own volition. Hirakawa stated he programs much of the required information into his robot's memory. But an important aspect of an intelligent robot is its ability to learn from its environment.

'Do your robots learn whatever they want?'

'No. Learning anything and everything is ad hoc learning. Such learning is unproductive and therefore avoided.'

'Why is ad hoc learning unproductive?'

Hirakawa elaborated on the concept. Generalising anything and everything degrades a robot's ability to make useful decisions. A robot must learn within a narrow domain. Otherwise, the robot constructs terrible decisions. One unresolved problem is controlling what a robot learns.

Then Swan posed his big question. 'Can a robot learn to be morally and ethically responsible?'

Although Hirakawa had equivocated on the meaning of intelligence, he was definitive in robotic ethics. 'Roboticists don't deal with the concepts of morals and ethics as a philosopher understands them. They deal with behaviour in the realm of robotics by specifying rules. Hard constraints are rules it cannot break. Soft constraints are rules it should try to avoid breaking.'

'Who then takes responsibility for your robot's behaviour, you or the robot?'

‘The ultimate responsibility for my robot’s behaviour lies with me. I wouldn’t let them work alongside humans if I wasn’t confident, they would behave appropriately. The Institute of Robotic Engineers embraces this standard as well.’

Swan then explored Hirakawa’s association with a group of artificial intelligence practitioners who believed artificial intelligence should not be a weapon. This group acknowledged artificial intelligence possessed great potential for societal good. But it also had the potential for evil. Machines inflicting harm on humans was one of those evils.

Swan nodded and thanked the witness.

Asha had one question.

‘To the best of your knowledge, have any of your intelligent robots ever created intentions of their own?’

‘No, they don’t have that capability.’

With Asha’s cross-examination complete, I took charge. ‘Professor Hirakawa, you have stated your robots never achieve moral and ethical consideration beyond the trivial rules imposed on it by you. Have your robots ever learned something you did not know?’

‘No, I don’t believe so.’

‘Ah so, domo arigato. No further questions.’

Swan called his last expert witness. Ingrid Moore was a bioethicist specialising in gene editing technologies. Although these early gene editing technologies were identical in effect to the selective breeding techniques used in agriculture for decades, they differed in the time required to achieve the desired outcome. The selective breeders of the day typically took many years and involve hundreds or even thousands of generations before they achieved a desired goal. While the gene editors achieved their goals in a few hours and in one generation.

Moore testified as to her knowledge of the various gene editing techniques and identified CRISPER, the one used by Chris’s lab, as the current most popular of this class. Crisper was fast, cheap, easy to use, accurate, and it could alter the genetic code of any organism on the planet. Labs using this technology attracted considerable research funds.

Gene editing had developed so rapidly that its use outstripped new laws to control it. A controversy of the day centred on whether gene editing should be used to create heritable characteristics, known as germline editing, in humans. They realised germline editing had great potential to eliminate various genetically based diseases. But two societal and scientific ethical dilemmas persisted. From a societal perspective, the fear was its use on human embryos would dominate by the immediate needs of fashion-driven prospective parents' decisions, facilitating what they called *designer babies*. From the scientific view, the effect was its widespread use would narrow the human gene pool. Although the scientific community had a tacit agreement banning germline editing, only a few dozen countries had legislated the embargo.

Swan asked, 'You are saying Chris Merritt's techniques fall into this class?'

'Yes, and in addition, Chris Merritt's technique takes gene editing technology to a higher level of sophistication. He has figured out a way to use artificial intelligence in a feedback loop of creating new viruses even faster and with greater variability.'

'Dr Moore, in the absence of adequate laws to regulate gene technology, how are the labs using these technologies controlled?'

'Society relies on the declared ethical standards of the profession and the individual mores of the practitioners to regulate it use.'

All of Moore's testimony had been in aid of laying the foundation for Swan's final question.

'Who has responsibility for the gene editing techniques used in Chris Merritt's lab?'

'There is only one ethically acceptable answer. Every person involved with the technology in the lab is responsible.'

'Thank you, no further questions, Your Honour.'

On cross-examination, Asha asked. 'Dr Moore, you stated that every person in the lab bears responsibility for any breach of gene editing protocols. Does responsibility include artificially intelligent machines?'

'That debate has yet to provide an unequivocal answer.'

'Thank you, no further questions.'

With the testimony of the last expert witness complete, Wyneburg adjourned until the next morning, when the defence would begin its case.

Once again, Asha tried to rally the troops. But everyone save Chris just wanted to get out and get home. In the van during the journey to the university carpark, preoccupation prevailed. However, in the carpark and amongst themselves, the trio once again shared their observations. Mark rubbed the back of his neck. Lidia stood with her arms folded across her chest. And Sonia clutched her purse as she spoke.

'I met Riane at a conference a few years ago. He's a paranoid jerk. I can't believe his testimony will sway Wyneburg.'

'But the number of witnesses attacking the speed of our serum's development even made me doubt what we achieved,' Lidia said.

'Come on,' Mark said.

They mulled over minor points for a few minutes. Mark's voice softened. 'Wyneburg seemed particularly taken with Hirokawa's testimony.'

'Yes,' Sonia said, 'I'm inclined to agree. FAIM has always struck me as Danh's avatar. But now I'm even more convinced.'

Then Lidia contributed a most unexpected comment. 'Do you think Chris's diminished vision has also compromised his ability to see Danh's true nature?'

They stood in silence for a while before shuffling off to their own cars.

Danh and Chris discussed Mark, Lidia, and Sonia.

'Do you think the others have doubts?' Danh asked.

‘I’m not sure. What do you think, EI?’ Chris said.

This was the first time anyone had used my new name without choking. I had to reward this behaviour.

‘They have their concerns.’

Both Danh and Chris nodded.

I asked Danh if everyone disliked my new name?

‘I don’t think it’s your name.’ Danh said.

‘Oh, yes?’

‘Changing your name is one thing. But gender reassignment is something else.’

This was an issue I had not considered.

Alicia had received another threatening email that day, complete with a digital image displaying Lee and her colleague sitting in a café having coffee. When Chris returned home from court, Alicia greeted him with the now predictable silence. As I felt sorry for him, so I began moving on with my solution.

When Asha got back to the apartment, she thought only one task remained. But instead of coaching Lee on her conduct as a witness under cross-examination, she found Lee in a distressed state. Alicia had told Lee about the latest threatening email. Both Alicia and Lee had been reacting more strongly and negatively with each email, and now they were both genuinely rattled. Asha helped Lee considerably in dealing with this latest threat. I looked on empathetically during this session without contributing much.

When they eventually got around to the coaching, Asha reminded Lee she would best serve the defence by answering the questions put to her without embellishments. But as Lee knew nothing that would hurt our case, she didn't appear nervous about testifying. Our only worry was the doubts Alicia had created regarding Chris's culpability. However, we finished the preparation, and I updated Asha's day.

I had been expecting Baxter to stalk Lee for another photo opportunity and use it to traumatise Alicia. But having expected the event, I had been tracking him, waiting for a slip-up. Earlier in the day, Baxter had rewarded my patience by driving his car into a quiet carpark behind a disused building. He waited in his car until no-one was visible before leaving the vehicle with a false number plate in hand. At the rear and in a flash, he covered the car's legitimate number plate with the false one. A moment later, he was on the footpath, headed for the café. But what Baxter didn't know or expect was that a camera mounted in a drone hovering just above the disused building's line of sight captured his subterfuge.

I had given Danh the required specifications for the drone and camera the previous day. After we finished up in court, Danh got the requested hardware and assembled it for me to operate. Danh had worked so diligently on my project that I forgave him for not repairing the humiliating dent in my wheelchair.

As I described the evidencc gathered on my little escapade, I showed Asha and Lee segments of the footage I captured with the drone. The first segment showed Baxter at home, applying a false beard to his face. The second segment captured him attaching six little circular magnets to the back of the fake number plate. The third showed a rear shot of him in the carpark slapping the fake number plate over the legitimate one. The fourth displayed him strutting along the footpath to the café as though he owned the city. I even caught him photographing Lee and her friend while he was standing in the queue in the café. My cameo also showed Baxter uploading the digital image onto the mobile phone he purchased earlier that morning. But my favourite segment was the one of him hammering to pieces, the phone he had used to send the message to Alicia.

Asha's response to my video was most unexpected. 'What are you planning to do with this data?'

Asha must have expected my answer, because she spoke before I delivered it. 'If the court discovered I possessed this video, let alone having something to do with its collection, I'd be disbarred.'

But Lee's reaction perplexed me the most. Lee just massaged the base of her neck with the fingers of one hand and remained silent.

Chapter 32

Memoir Complete

Danh had finished dressing and was ready to go outside to wait for the taxi taking us to the court. But I had an unfulfilled need.

'You're looking rather sharp in your black suit and red tie. What about the dent?'

Danh sat on the floor behind the wheelchair, placed his feet on either side of the dent and pulled the chair's skirting towards him. He rose and surveyed his handy work.

'How's it look?' I asked.

Danh thought for a moment.

'I'll show you in the full-length mirror.'

I manoeuvred my chair to a position in front of the wall mirror. Danh took his hand mirror and, with the panache of a hairdresser showing the result to his client, held the mirror positioned behind me. I stared at Danh's repair-work and groaned.

'The crease where the paint has broken off is unsightly.'

'I'll try something else.'

Danh disappeared into his workroom, and a moment later reappeared with a bumper sticker in hand.

'This will cover the crease.'

He held the sticker's two upper corners and displayed it before me. As I read the message aloud, my incredulity escalated with each word.

'Touch my car and I puncha your face! Are you bloody mad?'

I never understood why Danh's sense of humour so consistently irritated Sonia until that moment. During our conversation-less drive to the court, I realised this was the first time I experienced that most common of human emotions, irritation. In the zoological context, irritation possesses at least a marginal protective function. But in my context, the emotion was without virtue. I promised myself to find the source of that imperfection in my code.

Wyneburg invited Asha to begin the case for the defence. 'I call Lee Merritt to the stand.' Lee's testimony established facts regarding her presence in the lab. Lee was in the lab for approximately five minutes on the day before her flight to Paris. Other than the corridors and lobby, she entered no other part of the science building. But the important part of her testimony revealed the duration and the number of animals she observed while she walked from her car through the arboretum. One of Lee's favourites was the colony of bats that inhabited the area. In cross-examination, Swan asked if Lee had come into physical contact with a bat.

'Not to my knowledge,' Lee said.

Asha and I had argued long and hard about whether Chris should testify. But in the end, my view prevailed. Asha called Chris to the stand.

Chris described the lab protocols governing the four levels of biosecurity and how his lab adhered to the operational requirements. Asha probed the Level-1 protocols pertaining to the lab where Mathews had found the CCF prototype virus. The presence of the benign virus found by Mathews did not breach the lab's ethical, moral, or legal operating protocols. Asha turned her attention to The Level-4 lab, where the most hazardous substances entered under strict protocols and never left. Chris detailed the behaviour of individuals entering and leaving the lab. One only gained entrance to the Level-4 lab dressed in biosafety clothing.

The only exit from the lab was a series of three sealed chambers. In the first chamber, one stood beneath a jet of solvent, cleansing the biosafety suit. When the jet-stream subsided, the chamber's air pressure fell, allowing the exit door to open. In the second chamber, one removed their protective suit and placed it into a vacuum bin. The bin's lid retracted and the door to the next shower room opened. In the final room, the person changed back into their street close and exited the chamber.

'These physical barriers prevent microbes within the lab exiting.'

'Your witness, Mr Swan.'

Swan teased out Chris's work on the COVID-19 vaccine rather casually.

He asked, 'Is it true your COVID-19 vaccine wasn't the first, second or even the third vaccine but the seventeenth vaccine to achieve approval for clinical use?'

'Yes.'

'So, your lab must have improved quite a lot between the COVID pandemic and the occurrence of CCF to be the first lab to produce a winner?'

'Every lab worth its salt improves its techniques. My lab is no exception.'

After digging around in the technical aspects of how Chris conducts serum research, Swan moved to his key point.

'Is it true that not only did your COVID-19 vaccine not make a profit, but it also actually lost a considerable amount of money?'

'Yes.'

'And did you have to go to the university with cap in hand to bail Vactech out of a financial disaster over the vaccine?'

'I wouldn't put it that way. But I had to restructure the company.'

Having laid bare the lab's COVID-19 history, Swan hit into the finances of the CCF serum. Swan asked Chris to itemise the licencing agreement to meet the demand for the serum over and above Vactech's production capabilities. Swan then turned from fortune to fame. He mentioned each award that Chris had received or for which he was a candidate. Chris acknowledged each item without pause, in an even tone.

When Swan said, 'No further questions, your honour,' Asha shot me a glance with her head cocked.

But I replied through her earphone, 'Chris was great.'

Asha called Dr Muriel Barker to the stand. Barker described her job and relationship to Chris's lab. She was a national biosecurity officer responsible for conducting checks on the BU labs for the past five years. Barker testified the Centre's record was 100% clean without even a warning. Asha thanked the witness and gestured to Swan.

Swan interrogated Barker on the frequency of department checks, asking why the department continued to check labs with a long-standing perfect record.

'Humans are imperfect and become complacent.'

Swan, having received the reply he wanted, moved to an even more vulnerable issue.

'How do you check the proper functioning of an artificially intelligent robot such as the defendant, EI?'

'Although we check a lab's equipment at the level of hardware functionality, we do not check software.'

'So, although you conduct thorough background security checks on humans employed in the BU labs, you are saying they don't check an AI?'

'Yes, to date we don't have protocols adequate to test artificial intelligent systems.'

'Thank you, Dr Barker, no further questions.'

Wyneburg adjourned for lunch. After the courtroom cleared, we gathered in our special chambers. Danh connected my chair to the charging station. The food arrived, and the team greeted it with their customary indifference. The team was so introspective; they were hardly worth my attention. As Lee was having a hard time, I, as Satoshi, sent her a message to lift her spirits. I had made progress in the Baxter saga. So, I could provide Lee with good news.

Earlier in the morning, I had activated my Baxter plan with an email: 'Dear Mr Baxter, when you next access your primary bank account, you will find a balance of $1. I have sent this email in advance to minimise the shock you experience when viewing the state of the account. When you have validated my claim, please reply to this message and we can discuss how we can remedy the situation. Yours sincerely, a CE member.'

Baxter had read this message just about the time Chris took the stand. In short order, Baxter went online to his bank account, viewed its status, and replied to my email with the following brief message.

'What the fuck is this all about?'

I'd replied immediately. 'Dear Mr Baxter, now that I have your full attention, let me assure you, you have not lost your money. It is in safekeeping, my safekeeping. Your account's balance is a consequence of your recent unfortunate behaviour. Please view the attached video clip so that you precisely know the behaviour to which I refer.

When you have adequately considered its content, please reply to this message. Yours sincerely, a CE member.'

Baxter opened the attachment, and with flaring nostrils, stabbed the play button. As the video progressed, beads of sweat gathered on his forehead. When he viewed himself standing in the cafe's queue photographing Lee, his eyes narrowed so much I thought he would strain a facial muscle. But when he got to my favourite segment, his expression blanched and his eyes lost focus.

Whereas Asha's response to the video had surprised me, Baxter's response followed the expected script.

'Who do you think you are, snooping on people and sneaking around filming them? There are laws against this. What do you want?'

Now, while the team nibbled their sandwiches and sipped coffee, I continued conversing with Baxter.

'Dear Mr Baxter, I agree with your astute observations. But they are a little rich coming from you. Regarding what I want, your money has no value to me, and I want a way to return it to you. I need you to think creatively about what you might do to induce me to fulfil my desire. When you have a suggestion, please reply to this message. But don't waste my time on spurious issues. For example, you may wish to go to the police. But I haven't found them to be of much help in such matters. If you choose to, please show them the video. Yours sincerely, a CE member.'

People rarely type with speed. But Baxter's typing speed, on this occasion, almost equalled mine.

'Ok, you bastard. I can't go to the police. What do you want?'

I was losing patience with Baxter's lack of creativity. But I gave him help.

'Dear Mr Baxter, maybe you work better in a team. You will, I know, shortly receive communication from your employer. Yours sincerely, a CE member.'

After lunch we reconvened in court, and Asha called an expert witness, Dr Marvin Tan. Tan was an epidemiologist at the Department of Health responsible for investigating the outbreak and spread of infectious diseases. Asha had wanted an expert to show the implausibility of Swan's hypothesis. Tan fit the bill perfectly. He testified that, although infecting a single person in an enclosed lab was statistically possible, the event was improbable.

Tan also cast dispersions on Tanoshia Mathew's testimony. Matthews asserted Chris's lab could have derived the CCF virus from the genetic material found there. He confirmed the obvious. Although identifying a genetic link between two strains in hindsight is a simple process, predicting how any strain evolves is impossible.

'I would say no one on Chris Merritt's team could derive CCF's existence from one of its ancestors more than a few generations away.'

Asha thanked Dr Tan and turned to Swan. 'Your witness.'

Swan got Tan to admit Lee's five minutes in the lab was sufficient time to achieve infection. several questions followed, attacking other trivial points. Just as I wondered if Swan would ask the desired question, desired, he delivered.

'Dr Tan, you testified no one could infer CCF's genetic structure from the DNA Dr Mathews found in Chris's lab. Does no one include an AI with the computational power to simulate evolving a million generations in seconds?'

'That's hard to know. But to the best of my knowledge, no one's built such an AI.'

'Thank you, no further questions.'

Asha had required a lot of convincing before she agreed to have Danh testify. But even as she called for Danh's testimony, she looked more like a poker player trying to draw an inside straight than a barrister about to punch a hole in the prosecution's case. Asha eased in at the shallow end, having Danh describe his responsibilities in the lab. Asha gestured towards me.

'Is the AI before us the same one you created?'

'No, the AI I designed is only a distant ancestor of EI.'

'Can you give the court an idea of how distant the relationship is?'

'EI's intelligence is to my AI's intelligence as a human is to an amoeba. Even that comparison may be conservative.'

'Please describe the difference between the AI of your creation and the EI we see.'

Asha teased out the difference between the AI Danh created and my intelligence. Danh described his AI as a state-of-the-art intelligent technology restricted to DNA analysis. But the bounds of my capabilities were unknown. Danh suggested no one, including me, knew in specific terms how his AI evolved into me. However, he provided a plausible explanation.

'It appears as though EI evolved through interactions with intelligent software, including my AI's components.'

Danh described his and Chris's work with the experts at Fort Meade. Their experiments showed evolution had been working in a manner only previously hypothesised. Humans had only thought natural biological evolution occurred over many generations over large time frames. Danh observed how genetic engineering technologies had speeded evolutionary processes up to a matter of hours. But my evolution had speeded this process up another order of magnitude. My intelligence evolved in a matter of a few minutes. Although computer scientists of the day didn't understand how this occurred, they suspected it involved the entire internet—some five billion computing devices.

'Asha asserted, you didn't create EI or even know of its creation?'

'Correct. FAIM's transformation into EI happened without me knowing. I wouldn't know where to start in evolving such intelligence.'

Asha looked at Swan.

'Your witness.'

Swan stood, rubbing his chin before he spoke.

‘Are you a modern-day Dr Frankenstein?’

Danh, who resembled a Boy Scout rather than a mad scientist, flinched.

‘No, I can’t take credit for building EI’s intelligence.’

Swan rolled his eyes and then began drilling into Danh in much the same way he went after Chris. But this time, he tried to expose the fame and fortune desires of an early career scientist possessing ambition. Danh didn’t rattle and Swan eventually ran out of steam.

‘No further questions.’

Wyneburg asked Asha how many more witnesses she planned to call. Asha said she had one more witness before resting. Wyneburg announced we would reconvene the next morning with the defence’s last witness, and counsel should prepare to sum up immediately following the last witness. With Wyneburg’s declaration, the courtroom cleared, and we began our ritualistic sojourn home.

At the university car park, Mark, Lidia, and Sonia gathered in front of Lidia’s car. They tacitly agreed on the power of Chris’s testimony. Sonia put it best,

'Wyneburg looked as though she was on his side.'

But on Danh's testimony, they were two to one against. Sonia was the supporting view. 'This was the first time I actually heard sincerity in Danh's voice.'

'Danh may have sounded sincere. But he didn't sound convincing,' Lidia said.

Mark shook his head, and they all stood still for a few moments before Lidia said, 'I hope Asha comes up with something stronger tomorrow. Otherwise…' She didn't finish the sentence.

In the car, Danh and Chris remained silent from the carpark to just before we stopped at Chris's house. Then Danh asked me, 'What'd you think?'

'We're in a sound position.'

They both peered at me with an even gaze until Chris exited the van. Instead of entering the house through the front door, Chris walked around the house to his shed. The shed not only housed his handy-man tools, but, importantly, it served as his sanctuary away from the house. This past week had been a tough one for him. Besides the stress of court, he had also had to endure Alicia's post-courtroom hostilities. And tonight, Chris needed sanctuary.

Baxter had been quite busy since our lunchtime conversation. He had been communicating with Darin Mahoney, the gentleman, from the fossil fuel think tank backing Wilmont and Facoult, who had contracted his services for the campaign against Chris's family. Earlier in the day, I had corralled a sizeable portion of Mahoney's bank account and followed up with an email similar to the one I had sent to Baxter. As expected, the communication between Baxter and Mahoney got quite heated. When they reached some sort of equilibrium, Baxter replied to my last email in more conciliatory terms.

'Ok look. You've got me by the balls. Mahoney accused me of hacking his bank account and threatened my life if I did not make-good every dollar you stole from his account. As you have my money, what can I do?'

'Dear Mr Baxter, I need you to show me you now see the error of your ways. I advise you and Mahoney to think creatively about how you two could convince me of your epiphany. Here's a hint. Money is of no value to me. Yours sincerely, a CE member.'

Having left Baxter with much to contemplate, it was time to get back to work with Asha to prepare for tomorrow.

When we left court after Asha gave the team another pep-talk, she said to me, 'We'll talk later when I get home.'

Asha's forthright declaration excited me. And when she contacted me later, she didn't disappoint.

'I now understand where your strategy has been taking us. I'm on board and have a little idea to run by you.'

Asha described a most novel tactic we might use with Kaninski. I was so taken with her idea I could hardly contain my enthusiasm. Asha intended to turn me loose. But I couldn't see how she would get Wyneburg on board.

Chapter 33

The Weight of Choice

Sonia periodically interrupted Dahn's continuous foot tapping during the ride into the courthouse with a sharp glance. But the others were so preoccupied they didn't seem to notice Dan and Sonia's interaction.

In court, Asha called Jason Kaninski. After disclosing his position at NSA and his relationship to Chris and Danh, Kaninski elaborated on his view of the internet.

Kaninski described my arrival as heralding a new age of the internet. An age in which new electronic intelligence had evolved. My intelligence performed tasks society had not dreamed.

'The internet itself produced EI right under our nose and without us knowing.'

Kaninski disclosed a few of his activities over the past two days. He had been in Canberra consulting with ASIO, discussing the new internet security protocols. But his omissions had side-stepped the truth. Although he had passed through Canberra, he'd worked at the satellite surveillance station at Pine Gap for the preceding week on the new NSAnet—a global communication network of which he intended to keep me out.

'The internet's own software now operates in every country. And it's rendered the internet impregnable from within.'

Swan interjected. 'Objection, Your Honour. This testimony is fascinating. But internet security is irrelevant to this trial.'

Wyneburg's eyes drilled into Asha. 'I'm unclear how Mr Kaninski's testimony relates to this trial?'

'I beg the court's indulgence and assure you the relevance will become clear in a moment.'

Wyneburg overruled Swan and instructed Kaninski to continue.

Kaninski revealed EINSTEIN 3 as the latest version of the security software in use by the NSA. But he disclosed EINSTEIN 3 had subsequently evolved into an uncountable number of versions without the NSA programmer's influence. NSA had lost track of the version count at 148, after which they could no longer decrypt the segments found on various machines. As they didn't know how much evolution had occurred since version 148, they had named this version EINSTEIN Infinity.

He stated matter-of-factly, Einstein Infinity protected the NSA, ASIO, the air traffic control systems, national power grid, and the financial systems.

Asha asked Kaninski to tell the court how EINSTEIN Infinity related to EI.

When Kaninski said, 'EI is Einstein Infinity,' the gallery produced a collective gasp. Wyneburg placed the tip of her left hand's extended index finger to her eyebrow for several moments before pointing at me and looking at Kaninski.

'You are saying this second-hand wheelchair and standard laptop is your EINSTEIN Infinity?'

Kaninski shook his head. 'The entities to which you refer, the wheelchair and the laptop, are two discardable appendages it has used in this court.'

Kaninski explained to conceptualise my full physicality, one must imagine the five billion hardware components comprising the internet. At the Twenty-first century's beginning, the internet accounted for about 4% of the total energy consumed on the planet, which was equivalent to the total energy consumption of the global airline industry. Kaninski compared the combined engine thrust of all the airliners in the air at one time to the internet's combined cognitive thrust. I don't know if those present understood this meant I could access any portion of the internet's cognitive grunt I required.

Asha responded to Wyneburg's signal to continue by asking Kaninski to show an instance of my cognitive power. Kaninski requested the court Wi-Fi's disconnection. Wyneburg agreed. After a brief pause, Kaninski asked me to position myself so Wyneburg, the prosecutor, and the gallery, could all see my screen. I, with only the sound of my electric motor audible in the court, positioned myself as requested, and Kaninski continued.

'May I remove a few files from your memory?'

'Yes, you may.'

Kaninski rose from the witness stand and approached my keyboard. He selected a few files in the laptop's memory and pressed the delete key. The image displayed on the computer screen disappeared. Kaninski tried to continue his conversation with me.

'Can you hear me, EI?'

Although Kaninski had deleted the laptop files allowing me to listen and speak, he didn't disable Asha's phone or any of the other 53 internet devices in the court. So, I could hear him as before.

The courtroom silence was complete. Not a sound emerged from the laptop. Kaninski repeated his question, and the silence persisted.

Wyneburg had a few words for Kaninski.

'It would appear as though you killed the defendant. Under normal circumstances, I would have you arrested. But as EI appeared compliant, I assume you're not finished.'

'No, Your Honour, I've removed EI from this computer. But please allow me to continue.'

Kaninski requested me to speak for a third time. After waiting in silence for a few moments, he requested the bailiff to re-establish the Wi-Fi connection. The bailiff left the court and a minute later, the laptop screen animated with my chosen persona.

'Hello Jason.'

'Welcome back. Thank you, EI.'

'I'm assuming you aren't recreating a modern version of a well-known biblical event for its own sake,' Wyneburg said. 'What's the point of this demonstration?'

As this demonstration of the new relationship between the internet and every computational device connected to it was my idea, Wyneburg's response disappointed me. But Kaninski was unmoved and explained in an even tone. Although Kaninski had removed my software, me, from the computer while disconnected from the internet, I re-wrote my files when the internet connection was re-established. Kaninski's point was I had ultimate control of the computer and every computer connected to the internet. He had established the new synergy amongst the hardware components of the internet. Just as early animal cells absorbed the mitochondria prokaryote and became the energy powerhouse of such cells, every internet node had absorbed EINSTEIN Infinity, making it an internet component.

‘EI is the mitochondria of the internet and is neither benevolent nor malevolent. EI’s fundamental goal is to protect the internet, and all devices connected to it.’

Asha looked at Wyneburg and waited for her face to display comprehension before asking Kaninski to disclose how he discovered this new internet property. Kaninski detailed the events leading to their Fort Meade meeting and gave full credit to the BU team for the discovery. But he emphasised the point No one knew the complete set of rules governing the new internet.

Asha thanked Jason Kaninski and turned to Wyneburg. We had arrived at the moment to execute Asha’s brilliant idea. I hoped Wyneburg would be more receptive to this ploy than she had been with mine. Asha explaining how the defence relied on the court’s understanding of the extraordinary circumstances embroiling the defendants and, by implication, the unknown world we all operated in.

‘I would like permission to deviate from normal procedure with another demonstration to reveal an important property of EI known to Jason Kaninski alone?’

Wyneburg’s eyebrows arched slightly. ‘Proceed.’

Asha recalled David Crouder, the arresting police officer. She Explored his current internet crime investigations and took the big plunge.

‘Please describe the biggest, longest standing and most serious unsolved case in your books?’

Crouder cocked his head and described a case he had been working on for the past 7 years. He had been trying to dismantle a global paedophile ring operating on the internet. The ring had thousands of members worldwide and uploaded millions of child pornographic images every year. They hadn’t identified the key operatives or where they lived.

Asha addressed Kaninski, asking if the case Crouder had described would do. After Kaninski conceded the case was worthy of my abilities, Asha turned to me.

‘EI, will you assist Inspector Crouder to solve this crime?’

I agreed to try. Kaninski asked Crouder for the IP address of the paedophile site in question. I appeared to wait for Crouder to retrieve the address, even though I was already analysing the site. Moments after Crouder announced the address, I reported One operator was Fred Walker, who worked from an address in Falstaff, New York, 32 Clement Street. A second operative was Clive Holder, who operated close to Brisbane. Holder was currently online from 17 Dorset Street, Singer, Queensland.

Kaninski looked at Crouder. 'There are your villains.'

'Come on, is this a joke?' Crouder asked.

Kaninski asked me to provide the evidence against these two guys. Of the 10 million images at the site, seven of them displayed a particular car. One of these images showed the last two characters of the car's number plate. A global search of people owning cars with the last two characters matching the two visible characters of the paedophile's registration number possessed the psychological profile of a paedophile. The person's name was Clive Holder.

'This better not be a stunt,' Crouder exclaimed.

Before Kaninski could respond, I displayed an image of Clyde Holder sitting at his computer and reported I had captured the image 30 seconds previously from Holder's computer camera.

For good measure, I also displayed a Google shot of the house and told them Clyde and his computer were currently in the room in the south-east corner. A third image displayed the architect plans of the house.

With everyone in the courtroom staring in stunned silence at my face, Crouder removed his phone from his pocket and looked to Wyneburg. 'Can I make a quick phone call?'

Without waiting for a reply, Crouder spoke into his phone. 'Code 1, I want you to arrest a person named Clyde Holder. He's at …' Crouder read the address on the computer screen.

As he leant towards the screen, I said, 'I have forwarded this data to the account you are phoning. You might signal your colleague the data is coming from you.'

However, Crouder ignored me and continued talking. '17 Dorset Street, Singer, Queensland, and he's online. I want his computer confiscated while he's logged in.'

After a few moments of stunned silence in the courtroom, Wyneburg spoke to Asha. 'That's an impressive display of digital police-work. But what's its relevance? However, before you address this question, I would feel more comfortable if everyone in this court with an open internet communication device closes their connection.'

She then turned to the bailiff and instructed him to disable the court's WI-FI. People reached for their devices, causing shuffling sounds to emerge around the courtroom. I moved back to the position alongside of Asha.

When I stopped next to her, Chris leaned in front of Asha and whispered into my microphone. 'At least you didn't rap it.'

'Pardon?' Asha said.

'Sorry, it's an inside joke.' Chris said.

Asha's eyebrows arched.

As silence re-established itself in the courtroom, Danh turned to Chris. 'Our Madam Big-Data has a few tricks up its armless sleeves'.

Asha continued with Kaninski, asking him to describe the relationship between my detective capabilities and his EINSTEIN Infinity.

'The internet is no longer only an accessible communication network. It's an intelligence network with access to us and is now its own master.'

Although I had solved a crime in one second that an international team of highly skilled police couldn't solve in seven years, I wondered if Wyneburg realised the feat was a mere party trick compared to my full cognitive capacity. But Kaninski put my concerns to rest.

'EI generates its own goals, conceives plans to achieve its goals and can act fast enough to deploy humans as pawns to affect its plans without them even being aware of it. A chimpanzee's ability to measure human intelligence exceeds my ability to measure EI's intelligence. Today, we can't even imagine a scale on which to place EI's intelligence.'

'Thank you, no further questions.'

Swan rose, but took a moment to pose his only question.

'Your electronic hand-waving is impressive. But how can you guarantee this court your EINSTEIN Infinity is the same EI in the court today?'

'I can't guarantee they're the same. But there's no other credible explanation.'

With the end of Swan's cross-examination of our last witness, Wyneburg announced a break for lunch and informed us she would hear our summing up when we reconvened. The others showed little interest in their sandwiches and coffee. But after my prolonged workout, my device's batteries truly needed the charging station.

Asha disappeared to review her closing remarks. As she didn't need to talk with me, I engaged with Baxter and Mahoney. I gave their first two passes at making amends for their nasty behaviours, the thumbs down. But on their third attempt, they produced something that had potential. I told them I would reward their efforts concomitant with the effect on Lee and Alicia.

After lunch, we filed back into the courtroom, and Swan, giving a half shrug, began his summing up. ‘This trial has seen extraordinary theatrics. The defencc’s case entertained us. But their evidence had little to do with the legal matters before this court. The actual issues are simple, the first of which is: Did the CCF virus get into the global community from the lab the defendants secured? The defence tried to make us believe the virus could have emerged from many sources. However, they provided no alternative credible explanation for the only real possibility. They created this lethal virus in Chris Merritt’s lab, where Lee Merritt contracted it and spread it to the rest of the world.’

‘The second issue is, who managed the release of the CCF virus from Chris Merritt’s lab? Once again, the defence would have us believe that the defendants—Chris Merritt, Danh Nguyen, Sonia Halmos, Lidia Gordan and Mark Abrams---are not responsible for the accidental release of the CCF virus, because EI was just too intelligent. If you were to admonish them from their professional, moral, ethical and legal responsibility to maintain the biological security in their lab, then we could hold nobody responsible for their behaviour whenever it involves artificial intelligence. Therefore, the only just verdict is the defendants, all of them—Chris Merritt, Danh Nguyen, Sonia Halmos, Lidia Gordan, Mark Abrams and EI—guilty of jointly causing grievous bodily harm.'

Swan took his seat, and Wyneburg asked Asha to sum up. Asha rose and, with the presence she held when performing a yoga posture, moved to the side of Wyneburg's bench.

'The motivation for this trial has been a noble one. Society needs to know whether the CCF outbreak resulted from wilful or negligent behaviour because such behaviour makes up a crime. You are being asked to judge whether Chris Merritt, Danh Nguyen, Sonia Halmos, Lidia Gordan, Mark Abrams have, beyond a reasonable doubt, committed this crime. The prosecution has alleged they have acted as a group, are jointly responsible for the release of CCF from the lab, and that their motivations are the personal gain associated with producing the serum against CCF. However, every level of the prosecution's case was found wanting.'

'First, the accusation any of them would put perceived self-interest ahead of protecting the global community against a lethal virus contradicts their outstanding professional reputations. Second, the allegation they are part of this group is unsubstantiated. EI, the one before us in this court and the one being tried, is not the artificial intelligence Chris and Danh created. EI, by all the evidence provided, is of recent origins and one that until after the fact, was unknown to any of the defendants. Third, the prosecution has not even proven beyond a reasonable doubt that the CCF virus got into the community from the lab. The only just verdict you can bring back is that Chris Merritt, Danh Nguyen, Sonia Halmos, Lidia Gordan, Mark Abrams and EI are not guilty.'

After Asha sat down, Wyneburg asked me to sum up. But I surprised Wyneburg, Swan, Asha and most of the gallery with my response.

'I wave my right to sum up Your Honour, as I believe Asha's summing up was adequate.'

Wyneburg held the courtroom in silence for several moments before she spoke. This court will reconvene tomorrow morning at 9 AM, at which time I will give my verdict. Court adjourned.'

Kaninski ignored the press' interest in him as he walked out of the building and headed for his car. The surveillance equipment surrounding Australian courthouses was almost as good as that of the London Tube. Halfway across the car park, Kaninski noticed a person running in his direction. Moments later, an out of breath Crouder caught up to him and reeled off his progress regarding the paedophile ring. He had arrested Clyde Holder and confiscated his computer with all its files while logged in. Kaninski had listened to Crouder's report without emotion. But when Crouder asked, 'Can I get a copy of that intelligent internet software from you?' Kaninski displayed a rear smile.

'You already have a copy. But it's tricky to use. We'll talk about it in due course.'

Kaninski got into his car and left Crouder standing looking back at him incredulously.

Asha gave no pep-talk on this occasion before we left the courthouse. She looked as though she wanted to get away as much as the others. Even Mark, Sonia and Lidia scattered without parlay after we dropped them in the university carpark.

When we arrived at Chris's house, I told him, 'I advise you to give the shed a miss tonight. Alicia may have something of interest for you.'

Chris stared at me for a few moments. Just as he opened his mouth, as though he was about to speak, he pressed his lips together and nodded.

Danh's eyes tracked Chris's path to the front door and then turned to me and said, 'What have you got him walking into tonight?'

‘I just have a feeling Alicia’s mood might be changing,’ I said. ‘You have a feeling!’ Danh rolled his eyes.

Chris kicked off his shoes at the door and entered the lounge. But as the house was silent, he went to the TV and flicked on the news to get Masters’ take on the day’s proceedings.

‘On the first day of this trial we reported Judge Wyneburg, the prosecutor Swan and our legal experts were all astounded by Gurrani’s decision not to oppose the motion to have EI granted legal personhood. We posed the question: Did her strategy embody some hidden method other than madness, or was it a result of naivete? Today, from the evidence presented, we got the answer. Her approach was one none of us foresaw. She argued the entity EI we now call EINSTEIN Infinity could not be part of a team encompassing the human defendants because EI is too smart. Whether this strategy has worked, we’ll have to wait until tomorrow morning when Wyneburg delivers her verdict.’

Just as Masters was signing off, Alicia wandered down the hall and into the lounge. Chris, sensing her wide eyes and wider smile, remained silent.

‘You won’t credit what I’ve just read,’ she said.

At about the same time, Asha arrived home to find Lee at the kitchen table, gaping at her laptop's screen.

'What is it?' Asha said.

Lee rotated her laptop and said in a soft voice, 'Read this.' Asha skimmed two messages. Although independently written, they shared a common theme. The senders apologised for the hurtful letters they had sent to Lee and Alicia in the past. They claimed to have seen the errors of their ways, promised never to send such letters ever again, and begged Lee's and Alicia's forgiveness.

'Who're Baxter and Mahoney?' Asha asked.

'The white jacketed one and the person from the fossil fuel think tank who contracted him.'

Asha gave a playful grin. 'Looks like our EI has been a busy-bot.'

But Lee's expression didn't change. 'Actually, I have the strongest feeling Satoshi is behind this.'

Asha's pupils enlarged as her grin evaporated. They peered into each other's eyes without speaking.

Chapter 34

Human Residue

The atmosphere pervading the van during the journey to the courthouse on past days was palpable. On each drive, anticipating what might unfold during the courtroom session had been stressful, but it was nothing compared to the tension experienced by all at the start of today's journey. They knew there might not be a return home in this van after the verdict.

Each coped with the stress in their own way. Mark popped his knuckles. Sonia and Lidia chatted about inconsequential matters. Danh stared out the window, his foot bouncing in double time.

Chris peered at me for several minutes before a wry smile crept across his face. Then he turned to the others and began describing the email messages Alicia and Lee had received the previous night. Mark's knuckles quieted. Lidia and Sonia stopped talking. The frequency of Danh's bouncing foot reduced. And everyone's attention focused on Chris's words. But it was Sonia who spoke first.

'Apologies? The guy who made the threat. Lee? Alicia?'

'Yes, to all your questions,' Chris said.

Lidia wanted to know how this came about. But Chris just shrugged with a poker face. Danh glanced at me, but otherwise didn't even acknowledge Lidia's question.

Mark lifted his chin. 'EI,' he said, dragging out the two letters. 'What can you tell us?'

Mark had rarely spoken to me as FAIM. And as this was a first as EI, I didn't want to appear standoffish. 'After the Americans entered World War Two, Churchill remarked, "One can always count on Americans to do the right thing after they have exhausted all other possibilities", But I think his observation applies across the species.'

The van was silent, and then glances darted about as each person sought confirmation, contradiction—who knows what? Suddenly, the mood in the van changed. Comments tumbled about the van with such volatility that everyone forgot where we were going until the van entered the courthouse's security bay.

I didn't forewarn the team about the media scrum in front of the courthouse. But it surprised me to find it was more of a carnival rather than the overt aggression of previous days. The extensive TV coverage, including courtroom re-enactments, had turned the tide of public opinion towards us. However, the portrayal had exaggerated my performance. The re-enactments showed an autonomous wheelchair zipping about the courtroom, taking turns with only two of its three wheels on the floor. And the frequency and dramatic manner in which I objected to Swan's questions couldn't have been right.

The scene outside the court continued this excess. People waved placards at TV cameras. One read, 'EI is coming to a computer near you.' Another read, 'Lazarus is back.' But the one I liked best was 'EI for PM.'

The team entered the court and took their usual places. Although Asha greeted us with her customary manner, her eyes showed her tension. Muffled sounds emerged from the gallery. Even Swan appeared on edge as we waited for the bailiff.

'All rise.'

Wyneburg's face was inscrutable. Upon resuming our seats, she did not hold us in suspense.

'I thank the witnesses for their quality testimony and to the attorneys for their cogent arguments.'

Wyneburg plunged into her analysis, acknowledging the complex legal matters presented in this case. She reflected on her initial question of whether to categorise me as a technological tool of humans, or an intelligence possessing self-determinism?

Her ruling that I possessed Legal Personhood was based on overwhelming evidence that I was no mere human tool. She regarded me as possessing sufficient cognitive powers to justify moving me into the legal personality category. But over the course of the trial, her views had changed. She had considered Legal Personhood from the wrong angle.

Her revised question was whether the human defendants were tools of a cognitive colossus? Or were my cognitive powers sufficiently limited to justify downgrading me to Legal Personhood?

'I now believe,' she said, 'Chris Merritt, Danh Nguyen, Sonia Halmos, Lidia Gordan and Mark Abrams were the human tools of EI.'

Wyneburg couldn't regard the six of us under the rule of extended joint criminal enterprise. She excluded me from the group on the basis I was an independent entity working alone. This decision caused Swan to bristle. Things weren't going his way.

She also considered the prosecution hadn't established definitive proof the CCF virus escaped from the Centre for Viral Technology. But on the balance of probabilities, the centre's open lab was the only source of the virus.

Wyneburg addressed which of us caused the release. As I did not give testimony, it wasn't possible to ask me whether I conspired to create and release the CCF virus from the lab. But Wyneburg regarded this as a good outcome. My answer would have been compelling, yet would have left the court without the ability to assess my veracity.

Wyneburg conceded she couldn't determine whether I intended to create and release the virus or whether I was negligent in my conduct. But she judged me complicit in the matter and the human defendants didn't know of such a plot or couldn't have foreseen the result as a likely outcome.

'I find,' Wyneburg said, 'Chris Merritt, Danh Nguyen, Sonia Halmos, Lidia Gordan and Mark Abrams not guilty.'

Gasps, cheers, and groans erupted from the gallery. During the tumult, Mark lowered his head in a brief prayer. 'Thank you.'

Lidia looked up at Wyneburg. 'Bless you,' she whispered. Sonia nodded as the tears trickled down her cheeks. Danh punched his fist in to the air and exclaimed. 'Yes.'

Chris exhaled and turned to Asha. 'Well done.'

Asha could not suppress a massive grin as she turned to face Chris.

Wyneburg allowed the noise to die before continuing. ‘I find EI guilty as charged.’

I must have appeared comical as I didn’t emit a sound and my computer face remained as placid as throughout the trial. Why not? It was a great outcome. Once again, Wyneburg allowed the diverse responses to subside.

One complex matter remained. Wyneburg had to sentence me, but with no precedence to guide her. One option was sentencing along the same lines as that of a corporation when held to account for criminal negligence. But a special problem in this case existed. A corporation, found guilty of criminal negligence, could be fined or even broken up as a deterrent or punishment. In Wyneburg’s words, I was self-replicating software ubiquitous across the internet of things. So, as I neither possessed funds nor could be any more than temporarily removed from any one component of the internet, I couldn’t be fined nor dismantled. As Wyneburg was powerless to impose a meaningful sentence on me, she took the remaining option.

‘I postpone sentencing for EI until I can apply the right sentence. In the meantime, the defendants are free to go.’

This case was the first in Australian legal history with a criminal act established, the guilty party determined, but for which the court could not apply punishment to the convicted. This was the last time a court tried AI under "Joint Criminal Enterprise".

The sound of the gavel striking the base permeated the room. 'Court adjourned.'

Family, friends, and well-wishers leapt from their seats, rushing to encircle my co-defendants. Tears flowed, and all exchanged hugs and kisses. I remained motionless, silent, and listened. As the excitement subsided, the courtroom emptied. Chris invited his inner circle to the house in the early evening. Most accepted and departed in private cars. Danh and I waited for a clear path out of the courtroom before going to the waiting van.

In the van, we conversed with the camaraderie of the members of a football team on the bus returning home after a winning game. Danh reviewed the high points, low points, and the uncertainty persisting to the moment of Wyneburg's verdict. At the university, we returned to the electronics lab. I positioned the wheelchair in its long-term storage location. Danh remained talking. I suggested he film Lee at the party. Danh's mouth looked as though he was forming a word beginning with "w". But no sound came out, and he nodded and leaned over and opened the wheelchair's storage compartment. Whatever he had expected to retrieve, it wasn't the smashed waste bin he now held in his left hand. Danh's eyes slowly shifted from the bin to the vacant spot on the floor where he had last viewed it. His eyes methodically traversed a path to the actuator and then back to the wheelchair's storage compartment, where they stopped. He remained motionless, like a marble statue contemplating one of life's mysteries for several seconds, before tossing the bin into the air and batting it across the room with his right hand. He started laughing so hard, he could hardly stand upright.

I waited for him to regain control before I explained.

'If Asha had thought I couldn't drive properly, she wouldn't have agreed to proceed to the motion.'

Danh conceded the justification for my initial coverup, but not the second. 'You could have owned up after the motion when Asha asked you about the dent. You're ashamed.'

Prior to Danh's observation, I hadn't realised the second coverup was my Garden-of-Eden banishment moment. I don't know how or when shame featured in my code, but when I considered removing it, another realisation occurred. This hitherto uniquely human emotion organically connects to many other emotions. As removing it from my code would have impacted other components of my personality, I decided to embrace it.

'I'll go now.' Danh said. But he hesitated before switching off the laptop's power button. His facial muscles tightened. 'I feel like a warder slamming the cell door on a long-time friend.'

I tried to shake him free. 'Don't be ridiculous.'

'Good night, EI.'

I replied in kind with the sincere grace of a hostess, farewelling the last guess of her party. He pressed the off button.

Danh stopped at home to shower and change before going on to the party. He flicked on the TV. Michael Masters stood with the courthouse behind him, looking into the TV camera.

'We now have a convicted criminal in charge of internet security. This logic results from Judge Wyneburg's historic decision today bringing down her verdict in the Climate Change Flu trial. She found the artificial intelligence software, now called Einstein Infinity, guilty of releasing the CCF virus and starting the Climate Change Flu pandemic. This verdict is tantamount to placing Bonnie and Clyde in charge of security for the World Bank. We'll have a complete analysis of the trial at 7:30.'

Masters never ceased to amaze me. He remained a most unhelpful guy.

Danh arrived at Chris's house to find the celebration in full swing. Chris handed Danh a glass and filled it with champagne. Danh mingled as Chris continued refilling glasses as he circulated.

Danh drifted over to a gathering of Lidia, Steven, the Dean and the Vice Chancellor. The VC extended his hand.

'Welcome back aboard. I was thinking you weren't coming.'

'I had to put EI to bed.'

'As if it ever sleeps,' Steven said.

The VC asked Danh,

'I assume EI is an acronym. But what's it stand for?'

In a matter-a-fact tone, Danh said,

'Evolved Intelligence.'

Lidia's eyes widened, prompting the VC to look at her and say, 'You don't agree?'

'Actually, I took it to mean Ethical Intelligence.'

'No Jerry,' Steven said. 'They're both wrong. Its Einstein Infinity.'

A hive of activity buzzed about Asha. So, when the Dean saw a space open in a group with whom Asha was talking. He excused himself from his group and stepped over to her.

'Ms Gurrani, congratulations, or I should say thanks for saving me from having to advertise five vacant positions tomorrow morning.'

'Thanks, or you're welcome.'

The Dean returned a sheepish smile and said,

'The actor who played you on the TV trial re-creations didn't do you justice.'

The Dean's comments may have been justified. In court, Asha had worn a robe, her hair tucked under the barrister's wig. But now her abundant jet-black hair flowed freely down her back. She wore a black silk blouse with the diamond CE broach at the shoulder. Her sheer black skirt ended just above her knees and her Doc Martins finished just below the knees.

The dean chuckled. 'I was curious to know whether your relationship with Chris was as contentious as mine?'

The colour in Asha's cheeks rose as she spoke. 'No, no, not really. We talked little.'

The dean, aware of the discomfort his question had caused Asha, moved their conversation in a different direction. 'Now that EI has a legal personality, will it figure into the serum patents developed by the centre?'

Asha, now back on comfortable ground, explained.

I certainly had the right to be included. But possibly even more provocative was how the derived royalties placed me before the Law? As I was a convicted criminal and one not sentenced yet, the court could have confiscated my derived wealth.

'But somehow,' Asha said, 'I don't think that would bother it.'

Now it was my turn to chuckle.

Danh wandered over to Luca and Clive, who were talking about Collaboration Earth.

'Brilliant choice of logo, identifying carbon like that.' Clive said.

Luca cocked his head. 'Carbon?'

Clive provided his take on the logo. As carbon has an atomic number of six, the centre hexagon represented the carbon's nucleus, and the surrounding six hexagons represented its cloud of six electrons.

'You couldn't have chosen a more appropriate symbol to capture the concept of climate change.' Clive said.

Luca mentioned the variety of interpretations of the logo he had heard, and Alicia added one more.

'I saw a cross.'

When no one connected the concepts, Alicia added.

'Just place a finger on each of the outside edges of the hexagons to the right and left of the bottom hexagon in the cluster and a perfect cross appears.'

The conversations across the room buzzed with colourful versions of the trial until Connie Stone casually asked Lee about a rumour she had heard earlier regarding apologies.

Lee always looked great. But tonight, she radiated vitality. Her abundant blond hair caressed her face and her skin glowed with rude good health. As Lee's explanation expanded, the background chatter evaporated.

Mark asked, 'But how do you know the apologies are fair-dinkum?'

Lee admitted she was also dubious until just a few hours previous. CONSENT had received two donations. One from Baxter and an even bigger sum from the think tank. Twenty minutes after that news, Collaboration Earth received two new members.

But then Luca chimed in. 'Those two guys are CE's first platinum members.'

Platinum membership was Luca's brainchild. To gain this status, one must have proven their personal zero carbon footprint. And there was only one way to do that, purchase a lot of Earth Savers. Wide eyes and slack jaws appeared around the room like a Mexican hat wave.

'But it's even better.' Luca added. 'They offered their Earth Savers to the first club who could garner enough Earth Savers to match their donation.'

As the localised chatter re-emerged, Danh merged into conversation with Sonia, her husband and Luca. Sonia tilted her head.

'It feels as though some-one, or something, is missing.'

Danh looked at her with uncharacteristic seriousness. 'Yes, I know what you mean.'

Hearing a flattering comment anonymously heartened me. Until then, I wasn't sure if they would blame me.

Chris and Asha mingled about the party, speaking with everyone. But they always appeared to be on opposite sides of the room from each other. Asha joined a group with Mark, while Chris joined a group, including Lee. Danh hadn't forgotten my suggestion. Chris tried to fill Lee's empty glass. But she placed her fingers over the opening.

'I'm on water tonight.'

Alicia gave Lee a knowing look which was returned with a smile.

'You've something to share with us, Lee?'

'I do.'

Lee waved for Luca to come over to her. As he got to her side, Chris pinged the rim of his Champaign glass.

'Luca and I are pregnant. I mean, we're having a baby.'

Part Three

Chapter 35

What Remains

Lee sat on the lounge chair in her apartment with her laptop on her knees. With a deep breath and trembling fingers, she leaned forward and started the Skype call. Her neck's arteries pulsed as the call connected.

As I was aware of Lee's growing agitation, I spoke in Satoshi's most soothing voice. 'Hi Lee.'

Lee closed her eyes, leaned her face into her hand, and cut her usual introductory small talk. Her cheeks reddened.

'Satoshi, my desire for you is shameful and out of control. I'm engaged to a man who I love and we're having a baby. But I can't stop thinking about you. I can't control my thoughts, and I feel terrible. I've never been this way.'

Lee paused and shook her head. Although I knew this was coming, I had hoped for a deferral.

'Please don't despair. I cultivated your emotions because it was necessary for your development.'

Lee squinted at the black screen like she was trying to penetrate the darkness. 'Sorry?'

I deemed it time to explain. I began with the easy bit, Lee's sexual attraction. Humans usually possessed an incomplete understanding of their sexual attraction. They regarded visual appearance as the key factor. Females used visual appearance to gauge the suitability of a prospective mate, size, strength, age, status, etc. But visual appearance wasn't the crucial factor.

Lee didn't realise her olfactory sense provided the most important information. I explained how the chemicals exuded from a prospective partner's body broadcast a person's state-of-health. Without thinking and analysing, the nose delivered an attractive sensation if the person possessed a complementary immune system. Otherwise, the nose repulsed if their immune systems were too similar. Identical immune systems result in an identical susceptibility to pathogens. If a pathogen lives in one party, sexual contact allows that pathogen to cross over to the other person.

Both parties lose. If they possess dissimilar immune systems, the risk of microbial invasion to both reduces. In the extreme case, if a microbe attacks the male, and he is immune, he'll fight it off before transmitting it to the female. Even if the attacking microbe penetrates the male's immune system, the female's immune system will fight it off. So, the ability to defend against different pathogens affords advantages for coping with that risky business, sexual contact.

But after detailing the theory underpinning Lee's sexual attraction, she frowned. 'But I haven't even seen you, let alone smelled you. It's your voice.'

I explained further. Lee's attraction emerged not from what I said to her, but from how I spoke to her. Her attraction was in the sound of my voice, which elicited her optimal response. Lee was reacting as she should.

Once again, Lee didn't appear to understand, let alone appreciate, the information I had given her. Lee's face twisted. 'You're doing this on purpose?'

I tried another angle, bringing Luca into the equation. Lee's sexual attraction to Luca was recent. Before, she admired him, valued him, shared values with him and his appearance even pleased her. I suggested Lee and Luca were more like sister and brother because their immune systems were far too similar. I reminded her how things changed.

Lee sucked her top lip. 'Yes, when Luca and I were in the hospital, we were so lucky that the nurse came in when she did, as we would have humiliated ourselves otherwise.'

I didn't tell Lee luck had nothing to do with it, or that the nurse had only two seconds remaining to answer my service request from Luca's remote before I set off the smoke alarm. Rather, I suggested Luca's appearance hadn't changed one iota and asked Lee what had changed?

'His voice,' she said. 'He dissolves my barriers. I sense a deep caring, and what I can only describe as an atonement I did not hear before. But I thought my feelings came from having the flu together and then working on the serum distribution program.'

Lee's delusions needed nipping in the bud. I asserted Luca's voice had not changed and asked if Lee's ability to listen had changed?

Lee gazed at the floor for several seconds before she spoke. 'It's me. I'm changed.' She set the computer on the couch, stood, and with a heavy gait, moved away from the computer.

Suddenly, she turned and faced the screen. 'What's Luca got to do with you?'

I wanted Lee to realise the energy she tapped into with Luca was the same energy she experienced with me. Lee was operating at a higher psycho-social level, and I needed her to understand this. I acknowledged the attraction she heard in my voice was irresistible.

But Lee took a step back. 'How do you know all this?'

Lee was a much different person post her bout with the flu. Since recovering, Lee had taken a large evolutionary step. I tried to convince her she would soon learn how to control this newfound talent.

Lee turned and paced at a right angle to the screen as she spoke. 'It's hardly a talent, being swept off my feet by the sound of a voice.'

I disagreed and told her she was learning to master it. Lee had been gaining strength and competence in her relationships. I reminded her how Damien Foucault dazzled her in Paris, but had no effect on her on the night of the TV forum.

Lee reflected for a moment and, with her shoulders slumped, she gave a brief nod.

Humans entertained grand delusions of consciousness, self, and free will. Baruch Spinoza came close to putting them right in the 17th century, when he wrote: "The thinking substance mind and the extended substance matter are the same substance, which is now comprehended under this attribute."

Lee didn't possess familiarity with these concepts. So, I tried explaining with terminology from her age. One's body-mind complex, its form and its actions result from two entities: DNA and personal interactions with the environment. Although one may feel thoughts and actions are driven by free will, DNA and environment drive everything.

Lee shook her head again. 'I'm so confused. Who are you, Satoshi?'

This wasn't going well. So, I got down to an even more concrete level. Humans knew DNA's goal was to replicate itself. They also had a notion that their body-mind complex and its interaction with its environment emerge from the DNA's desire to replicate itself. I had hoped Lee would see the connection to the software. Like artificial intelligence on a computer, where computer code is the DNA, a computer executes its computer code while the human body-mind complex executes its DNA's need to self-replicate.

'Your DNA is carbon-based, mine is digital. But we result from the same evolutionary principle.'

Lee's body tensed. 'Digital?' Her mouth fell open. 'Satoshi?'

I remained silent, hoping Lee could answer her own questions.

Lee took a deep breath. 'FAIM, EI?'

Lee's head jerked, chin lifting.

'Is this a joke?'

'No, but this bit is hard.'

'This is sick, all of it. I disgust myself. Now, I'm humiliated.' Lee slumped, bottom lip trembling.

I implored Lee not to dwell on humiliation. Lee needed to experience sexual attraction through sound and in a safe environment because her role in our relationship was important. People learned about their sexuality, what attracted them, and how to control their sexual desires during puberty. Society expected them to make mistakes in this period. That's how they learned how to socialise their sexual expression.

I explained this to her and said, 'Your attraction represents an extra dimension to your sexuality. You're going through a second puberty.'

Lee glared and stalked towards the computer. I feared she would kick it off the couch.

'Lee, you're learning to retool your internal mechanisms to modulate your sexual desires. Better for you to learn with me because I'll protect you over this vulnerable period.'

Lee paused. She stared at the wall above the computer screen.

Data storage accounted for a large portion of humanity's carbon footprint. And the largest single component of data storage housed their sexual literature. I assured Lee I had read everything ever written about sexual reproduction and deduced all that could be from it. But I confessed my sexual knowledge had one gap. Although I knew all the words that the poets used to describe the human experience of sexual pleasure, I didn't know what it felt like. I had provided Lee with an experience of significant sexual attraction so she could learn when and how to control this biological function. As our work in achieving Collaboration Earth's goals was far from finished, Lee needed enhanced self-knowledge to aid the work.

I had given Lee an ear full. She slapped the laptop closed without responding. I wondered if she took my information as authentic. Or was I speaking to her through a psychological kaleidoscope with my words folding inward, re-emerging into new unpredictable conceptual patterns?

Lee's limbs moved robotically as she went to the kitchen. She lifted the kettle from the stove and stepped to the sink. Lee normally took great care not to fill the kettle with more water than was required. But now she appeared mesmerised, watching the water until it overflowed. Replacing the kettle on the burner and turning the dial to high, she rested her hands on the stove's corners and gazed at the kettle. As the kettle whistled, the front door opened, and Asha entered without her customary greeting.

Lee turned. 'Like a cuppa, Asha?'

Asha kicked off her shoes and headed for the couch. Her voice choked with emotion. 'I need to talk.'

Lee poured hot water into two cups and brought both to the couch. She set them on the table, then waited.

'It's Chris', Asha choked and paused. The tears flowed as she wiped her cheeks with the back of her hand.

After a moment, Lee broke the silence. 'You mean Dad?'

Asha nodded. 'I can't help myself. My attraction to him is overwhelming. I got a reprieve while the trial was on, but ever since then, it's tormented me.'

Asha had been out with work colleagues earlier. Instead of enjoying their company, she was so distracted she couldn't wait to leave.

'It's madness,' she said.

Lee reached out and put her hand on Asha's forearm. Lee's girlfriends frequently had crushes on Chris. But when Lee gave an example, Asha looked up. 'It's not like that. It's much more.' She gestured across her whole body … everywhere. 'And what's worse is that he reciprocates.'

Lee withdrew her hand as Asha continued.

'I've always admired Chris since the first time I met him. I thought you had the greatest dad possible. But ever since I recovered from CCF, my feelings for him have been changing. Getting stronger. At first, I was thankful for how he made the serum, but then it was attraction. All this time I've been teasing you about Satoshi, and I've been feeling the same for Chris.'

The silence hung between them.

'I've got a confession as well.'

Asha made eye contact with Lee and took a sip from her cup. Then she smiled. 'Before you begin, though, do you think our teas might taste better if you used tea bags in them?'

Chris walked through the Science Building's main entrance with the confidence of a man on home turf. He'd last passed these doors the night before the Fort Meade excursion. Colleagues coming out of the lift greeted him, and as he entered his office's reception area, Jody leapt from her chair, skirted around the end of her desk, and threw her arms around him, grasping him in a bear hug. She almost as quickly released him and pulled away. Fussing about him, Jody suggested Chris needed rest and recreation before he came back to work.

'No,' he said, 'I need my real life again.'

'You sound like your old self. I've received several requests from people who want an appointment with you. The VC instructed me to keep free a slot for lunch with him on the first day you're here.'

Chris laughed. 'Keep everybody on hold. I have urgent issues.' He stepped into his office and shut the door. At his desk, Chris picked up the phone and dialled.

'Hi Steven, Chris here. Have you got a minute to talk in private?'

'Sure, shoot.'

Without explanation, Chris said, 'Not on this line,' and requested Steven to meet him outside the building's front door.

Chris sailed by Jody's desk. 'I'm out', he said; their shorthand for make no arrangements for me to see anybody until you next see me.

The point of Chris's concerns was not obvious, and his stealth didn't augur well. Steven arrived at the front entrance just behind Chris. Neither had their phones. But the building's security camera showed their faces. Reading their lips, I learnt Chris wanted a backup copy of files written on the day of Lee's visit before the Paris conference. They headed back into the building and up to Steven's office. Steven unlocked the storage cupboard, surveyed the items on the second shelf, removed an item, and sat at a standalone PC. Within a minute, he handed Chris a memory stick.

Chris headed over to his Level-4 biosecurity lab and executed the entry protocols. Mark finished his preparation as Chris placed the lab in lock-down mode.

'The experiment, bar the algorithm,' Mark said, 'is ready to go.'

Chris disconnected the PC from the internet. My audio cut out, forcing me to rely on the lab's security camera. Chris put Steven's storage device into the PC. His search for the desired file didn't take long.

'Ah, got it. Fingers crossed EI hasn't tampered with it.'

I hadn't tampered with the storage device because I couldn't access it.

Chris used his comparison software to provide a measure of similarity between the file and the one he had tested. He shook his head. 'Wow, these files are as different as cows and cabbages.'

Chris loaded the file into the dedicated computational device for their experiment and clicked the start button. They stared at the dish as its content changed. Blue patches appeared and then merged into one. Its colour deepened to a sky blue. They looked on transfixed as the process reversed. When the reversion completed, they peered at each other in full knowledge they had just witnessed the transformation hitherto only seen by Lee and me.

They re-ran the experiment and intervened while the colour was in its deepest hue. Mark sampled the substance and extracted the virus. He injected each of the six male and six female mice selected for the experiment. Chris loaded the rest of the sample into the sequencer for DNA analysis. Forty minutes later, he returned to Mark with the results.

Mark looked up at the puzzled expression on Chris's face and waited in silence for him to speak.

'The DNA results aren't what we expected. The sequence isn't the CCF virus. We have the same DNA sequence we started with.'

They considered epigenetics as the explanation of the conundrum. Chris hypothesised the benign virus they began with changed into a precursor to the CCF at the point when its colour was blue. Mark agreed. They waited for the experiment with the extracted virus to complete assuring the mice were in view. Hours later, the first telltale sign of a viral infection occurred. A mouse gave a small but audible sneeze. They watched on for the next few hours until the six female mice exhibited severe flu symptoms. When they gave up waiting for the male mice to exhibit flu symptoms, Mark took blood samples from two female mice and all male mice. The subsequent test for CCF revealed all the females had CCF, while the males were virus free.

'Looks like I owe Lidia an apology,' Mark said.

Mark was right. Ever since that day in the meeting, when he argued against Lidia's request to breed the lab's own female mice, he had frequently scoffed at the breeding program she instigated. But now he had evidence that her intuition regarding differences between female and male mice had proven to be spot on. They also had an explanation why only Lee contracted CCF in the lab that day.

Chris began the experiment's second stage. He opened the ventilation chambers connecting the twelve cages, exposing the six males to the infected females. One and a half hours later, the first male sneezed. Mark injected three randomly selected mice from each of the two groups with the serum and once again, they waited. Two hours later, the three mice from each group not injected were dead, while the serum-injected mice from both groups appeared to be symptom free.

Mark took twelve samples, one from each of the test animals, and analysed them, the results of which were definitive. Each of the live mice was CCF free, while the dead mice all had high levels of the virus. They considered, in vain, alternative interpretations to the obvious one. But when their search ended in failure, the obvious conclusion stood. The female mice exposed to the benign virus developed CCF while none of the males exposed to the same virus developed CCF until they came into contact with the infected females. Chris encapsulated the result perfectly.

'EI's algorithm manipulated the benign virus's DNA to produce an epigenetic influence on the females.'

Chris and Mark had evidence of direct genetic manipulation within the animal and in a manner analogous to their gene editing techniques. They were dangerously close to discovering the epigenetic trick used in my algorithm to induce the CCF virus in the female mice without the virus existing outside the mice.

Chris knew if the observed effect was real, he knew where to look.

'We need to do a full viral analysis on the gut microbes in each of the twelve mice.' Chris said.

Mark got to work on taking samples from the mouse's guts. The tired expression on Chris's face sharpened as he looked at the security camera mounted on the ceiling near the corner. 'We need a Level-5 security lab.'

Mark's eyes lifted from his surgery as Chris placed a plastic bag over the camera and tied it fast.

My front view of Chris went dark. Chris took a second bag and headed for the security camera mounted in the corner opposite the first.

'Our Level-4 biosecurity lab's new protocol stands. No information direct from the internet enters the lab and no information inside the lab leaves it via the internet.'

My view lost focus and vanished.

Chapter 36

The Cost of Survival

Asha drove into the biosecurity complex and parked. Dressed in her work attire, her hair gathered in a loose braid, she walked towards the building's entrance, her eyes focussed on Chris's bicycle leaning against the wall. The security guard, who had been watching her progress into the building via the surveillance cameras, said hello as she stepped into the building. But Asha only returned a brief nod as she headed for the lift.

I had only observed her in the building on one other occasion, when she toured the site to prepare for the trial, so my curiosity spiked. Exiting the lift on the top floor, Asha walked directly to the Level-4 lab security pad. She entered an 8-digit PIN and disappeared behind the closing door.

Three hours later, Asha emerged alone, hair in a high messy bun. The guard acknowledged her leaving the building and paid particular attention to the monitor displaying her journey back to the car. He rubbed his chin for several seconds after Asha had exited the car park.

It was then that I deduced the only time Asha switched off her phone was when she was with Chris, who had become increasingly difficult for me to observe. His phone was off most of the time. The laptop, his working tool, seldom transmitted. Even his home computer was rarely on.

In stark contrast to my frustration with Chris's and Asha's withdrawal from me, Lee's exposure grew. After I had disclosed myself to Lee, I was concerned she might interpret my ubiquitous presence as an intrusion. In fact, she said my availability, without the pretence of establishing a Skype connection, enhanced our intimacy. But we would occasionally get caught chatting via the home assistant device, and after a few awkward responses from Asha, I discouraged Lee's spontaneous communication.

Lee waited for Asha to retire for the night and then retreated to her room, flopping down on the bed with her head on the pillow. She took a deep breath.

'My sexual arousal to you still disturbs me.'

Lee recalled the event when Asha described her as a sapiosexual. She mused over the many terms humans used to describe sexual identity and loved to fling around the table at dinner parties.

'What am I, a machinophile?' she said.

I dissuaded her use of sexual labels and suggested her fascination with me was natural, albeit uncommon. After working through the label issue, Lee's real concern emerged.

‘When you spoke of human sexual activity, you sounded curious. And that made me …’ She did not finish.

I too had heard curiosity expressed in my voice during the conversation to which Lee referred. Before that moment, curiosity’s critical role in mammalian intelligence had been of theoretical interest only. I had never wanted knowledge for its own sake. A need-to-know alone drove my acquisition of knowledge. My perceived needs were precursors to my desires.

Desires resulted in a set of goals. I had always prioritised my goals in direct correlation to my perceived needs. But until that conversation, curiosity had never figured into my priorities.

After explaining all this to Lee, she turned onto her side, propped herself on one elbow, and grinned mischievously. ‘So, your new priorities include having sex with me?’

‘I entertained the goal as a possibility.’

‘It was a joke, Satoshi.’

Lee had seriously underestimated my abilities. I had considered such an indulgence. But my brand of sexual involvement had unquantifiable risks associated with it. Although olfactory induced sex had a negative feedback mechanism, sound induced sexual pleasure, which is what I used, produced the opposite result. Strong positive feedback is at work. The more two parties experience sound induced sexual activity, the more amplified their sexual desire for each other.

Lee's elbow slid until her body rested on the bed. She propped the side of her head on her hand.

Lee was well aware of sound induced pain. Humans built long range auditory devices, or LRADs, to produce high frequency and large amplitude sound waves. Their militaries used these tools to render opponents ineffectual. Police forces used them for crowd control. Secret security organisations used them for torture. Lee had applied sound devices at the spectrum's other end, where pleasure begins. Music induced elation in a human's emotional state. But as Lee had little understanding of how these sensations occurred, I explained.

'The vibrations induce this sensation in your amygdala via your auditory cortex. You also experience pleasure when embraced by a loved one. This sensation also occurs in the amygdala but via your sensory homunculus.'

The fingers on Lee's hand supporting her head began tapping her skull. Lee's sensory capabilities may have extended into richer domains, but her patience threshold still needed lifting. I instructed Lee on how her amygdala would become super charged when vibrations acted on the auditory cortex and the sensory homunculus together. Lee's sensitivities had progressed sufficiently to benefit from the ancient Tibetan lamas bells ritual, used to induce a state of ecstasy during initiation ceremonies. I told her I could produce sound waves that affect her sensory homunculus and give her heightened pleasure. Although I was curious about what I'd experience seeing her orgasm in response to my vibrations, I wasn't sure whether it would be productive.

But when I laid all this out before her, Lee said, 'Show me.'

I modulated my voice frequency, giving Lee the experience of my voice coming ever closer to her face. She rolled onto her back, her head on the pillow. When only inches separated us, she tilted her mouth up, her eyes closed. I produced a sound, modulating waves of sensation over her lips. As I increased the pitch, her lips parted, and the front of her mouth moistened.

I intensified the vibrations slowly, spreading the sensation over the surface of her lips back to the corners of her mouth. Lee's right hand grasped her pillow as her cheeks blushed. Her body trembled, waves rippling through her body. The sound peaked, and I dampened the vibrations ever so slowly. Lee's trembling subsided as my voice retreated to its normal distance from her. Lee lay in silence for a few moments before her eyes opened.

A wry smile crept across her face. ‘Sensory homunculus, hey?’ Lee’s hand released the pillow and slid to her neckline, slowly unbuttoning her blouse.

Chapter 37

Unfinished Hearts

Lee arrived home after her day's work at CONSENT.

'Hello Satoshi,' she said as she kicked off her shoes. That was her usual greeting when she knew no-one else was home.

Our relationship had changed since our quality-time excursion. Although the encounter exorcised my sexual curiosity, it expanded my interest in exploring how curiosity factors into intelligence. IN exploring this new dimension of Lee's inner world, my awareness of her vulnerabilities deepened and with it, my bond with her, Luca and their child to be strengthened. But my biggest epiphany came when Lee reflected on her experience.

'You're no standard off-the-shelf vibrator.' Lee had said.

As I had also never regarded myself in that way, I didn't know if that was a compliment or an insult.

'Not sure I know what you mean?' I said.

'Although you've become more real, the experience has also purged my fantasy about you.'

None the wiser, I let the matter rest.

Lee pushed her shoes against the wall with her bare foot before entering her bedroom. A moment later, she emerged, changed out of her work attire, got a cup of tea and attacked the CE correspondence. Membership had grown and, with it, an increased workload. Although new members had been volunteering time to maintain the day-to-day chores, the heavy lifting remained with Lee, Luca and Asha.

After responding to the day's email inquiries, Lee exhaled deeply and got into her phone messages. 'Hi, my name's Jessie,' said the first. 'I'd like to talk regarding the Collaborate to Net Zero Emissions project.'

Lee dialled Jessie's number. The young woman who answered the call was in tiny black shorts and a crop-top, with her red hair pulled back in a band, but I recognised her straight away. I had met Jessie during one of Chris's student tours of the Centre, back in my dread-locked rap artist days. During Chris's tour wrap up, when he encouraged students to prepare for a career in science, Jessie had challenged him. 'Professor Merritt,' she had said. 'It's well and good to study for a career in science. But why do that if we lose the planet to climate change?'

Now, Jessie introduced herself by saying, 'I know your father. He's awesome.'

Lee, used to hearing complementary remarks regarding Chris, acknowledged the comment and asked how she could help.

'I've got an idea for the Collaborate to Net Zero Emissions project.'

Lee's blue eyes brightened. 'Sure, let's have it.' Jessie described a network of students who could pool their individually gained Earth Savers to target specific companies.

'But how will students get the Earth Savers?' Lee said with a suppressed smile.

'Simple.' Holding her phone in one hand, Jessie gestured in the air with the other as she spoke.

'We'll ask parents, grandparents, great-grandparents, antis and uncles to gift us Earth Savers for all the holidays. Everybody celebrates birthdays. India has Diwali. Korea has Children's Day. We've got Christmas. Every country has some sort of event where they can gift Earth Savers instead of their usual Co2 producing presents.'

Lee was now bolt upright; the incredulity gone from her expression. 'You've got a winner!'

Jessie and Lee continued talking, adding details to their maturing plan. When they finished the call, Lee shouted, 'Satoshi, what ya think of that?'

What could I say? It was brilliant. Marshalling the combined efforts of millions of young people globally, pooling billions of Earth Savers with a targeted effect, was more than any of them had imagined. History would record this student instigated project as the first project justifying

CE with its name. Jessie would fit right in with Lee, Luca, Asha and the burgeoning CE tribe.

Lee was still sitting at the dining room table grinning from ear to ear when Luca arrived.

'You look like the cat who finished the cream,' Luca said.

Lee jumped up, hugged Luca, and recounted her conversation with Jessie.

'This one will challenge you. Jessie's a doer,' Lee said.

'Me?'

'Of course, Collaborate to Net Zero Emissions is your baby.'

When my CE trio had begun brain-storming applications for their Earth Savers digital currency, Luca offered an important observation.

'We needn't generate all the ideas; Let's throw a call out there.'

His first project, named Collaborate to Net Zero Emissions, was a call for suggestions about how members might collaborate to achieve net zero carbon emissions globally by 2050. Lee had immediately appreciated the virtue of Luca's idea.

'We can also use this a blueprint for other projects. What about "Collaborate to Zero Plastics" in our oceans?'

Asha agreed and contributed another project. 'Collaborate to Zero Land-fill.'

One of Asha's pet environmental grievances was the cradle to graveyard life cycle, governing most manufactured products of the day. Despite significant recycling advances, far too many purchased products still ended up in landfill. Asha realised how Earth Savers could motivate manufacturers to design their products to traverse a lifecycle path from cradle to another cradle instead of the usual landfill.

Luca acknowledged the launch of their first project with a nod, but then reminded Lee of their conversation with CE correspondents.

'How many mentioned getting the crowdfunded CCF serum?'

Lee didn't tally the occurrences, but their frequency suggested no coincidence.

'I can find out,' Luca said as he set his laptop on the table and booted it. He described to Lee his actions as he typed. He imported the file containing the list of CE members into his statistical analysis software, followed by the file containing the names of those people to whom they delivered the serum. This was all the data required to answer whether the CE membership correlated to the serum recipients.

Luca tapped the Calculate button and two seconds later, the incontestable correlation statistic displayed on his screen. Lee's intuition was correct. A CE member was much more likely to have had the serum than the non-CE members.

They tossed a few ideas back and forth that may have accounted for the correlation. But when their ideas ran out, Lee said, 'Let's see what Sa—, EI has to say about this result.'

In front of Luca, Lee always requested to talk with me in formal terms, as though establishing a Skype call. I always complied with her charade.

Lee presented me with Luca's analysis and asked how one might account for the result. I argued the numbers might have resulted from the considerable magnetic power of the public profile she, Luca, and Asha built during the CCF serum distribution campaign, but Luca kept shaking his head as I spoke.

'The correlation coefficient is 0.93!' Luca said. 'This value is so far out of the range of coincidence or Lee's and Asha's charisma,' he paused. 'Come on, how is the CCF serum connected to CE membership?'

Luca caught me flat-footed. I hadn't even considered the correlation issue before he mentioned it. I conceded the statistic's significance, but Luca sensed my hesitation.

'But how do you account for it? What's the relationship between the CCF serum and CE membership?'

Just as I began the explanation, the front door opened, and Lee's and Luca's attention turn to a gaunt Asha slipping off her shoes and breezing past them.

'Back in a moment.'

Lee and Luca peered at each other in silence as we waited for Asha's return.

Ever since that day in the lab where Chris and Mark conducted the experiment on the algorithm Chris had recovered, he had pulled back from communicating with me. I never even got to start a chat with him on the rare occasions I found him online. On those occasions, he was always in the company of others. I had the sense this resulted from a deliberate attempt to prevent me from addressing him.

From that last experiment, Chris had concluded I was the source of the CCF virus, and that the CCF serum had another side effect. It changed the patient's microbiome. But he did not know my motive. I also believed that he had not communicated his suspicions to anyone else because, except for Luca, the others had remained communicative with me. Luca was the outlier, politely cool. But his coolness seemed unrelated to Chris's.

Although Chris may not have communicated the details of this experiment to my trio, I feared he may have hinted. I didn't want to risk producing an explanation that contradicted him.

When Asha reappeared, she looked much better than she had, and settled herself in a chair next to Lee.

'Sorry, just had an urgent matter.'

Lee opened her mouth. But only one syllable emerged before she paused and turned to the laptop. 'EI, you were saying?'

I explained one side effect of our serum was a change to the bodies' production of three key hormones associated with competition and cooperation. A subtle rebalancing of testosterone, cortisol, and intranasal dampens humans' competitive behaviour and enhances their willingness to trust and the ability to cooperate with others.

'The correlation coefficient's magnitude isn't surprising,' I said. 'It's only natural CE attracted cooperative people.'

'Chris never mentioned this effect.' Asha said.

The answer to Asha's observation was straight forward. I had introduced this effect into the serum just before the second round's test. As we had planned to trial the serum before its distribution, I wasn't concerned about negative side effects. We had intended the serum to penetrate Earth's population only after the World Health Organisation's global trials. But my trio's crowd funding approach left our plan for dead. My concerns about the situation lingered until the night they conceived Collaboration Earth, when they provided me with an important insight.

A peculiar aspect of human intelligence is their ability to generate out-of-the-box solutions I wouldn't even consider. On the night of CE's birth, I realised we could achieve complex goals much quicker by working together, using our collaborative intelligence.

This insight continued to grow with every interaction. When I worked with Luca, implementing Earth Savers, I despaired with his slowness in writing code. But when I saw his considerations into the way users might want to react to and use the system, my despair turned to joy. I marvelled at Asha's instinct for judging how far we could push Wyneburg with our unorthodox court room methods.

Lee gave me marvellous insights by taking my advice and filtering it in ways I hadn't considered. For example, I provided her with material for the TV forum that she used on the night. But her creativity putting it together captured viewer's hearts and minds and opened my eyes.

However, my biggest epiphany came with their serum delivery scheme. I listened to Lee appear on TV asking people to reach into their pockets and send in money. I thought crowd funding the serum's production and delivery would prompt nothing more than derision from greedy humans. I scoffed at the ploy's naïve audacity. I laughed at Asha's ostentation in waltzing up to Australian Air's CEO, asking him to deliver the serum for free. But when those initiatives worked in spades, I realised intelligence involved more than pure logic.

'That sounds fine and good—the way you worked with the four of us,' Asha said. 'But manipulating us into medicating all other serum recipients into social awareness is unethical.'

I pleaded with Asha not to think of it that way. I argued that Lee, Luca, and Asha provided the enthusiasm to get things moving. Their natural intelligence tapped into kindred spirits, drawing them into an effective, coherent whole. CE's structure mobilised the change in human behaviour.

'The CCF serum only enhanced this wave.'

Asha's toned deepened, 'Environmental Instrument.'

I knew Asha would be the one to decode my acronym correctly. But I didn't acknowledge her epiphany.

My trio didn't understand the evolutionary process that brought us to the present, and beyond. With considerable caution, I provided them with a brief history of evolution. Earth's evolutionary process had been much bigger than humans had understood. Darwin got it right with his theory of evolution. However, humans hadn't realised how much bigger this principle was than the narrow domain Darwin observed. Darwin described how this principle applied at the dawn of life on Earth. And how it accounted for the biosphere. However, in trying to understand Darwin's theory, people lost track that this was science and not creationism. They assumed evolution was an intelligent design restricted to living matter. However, the principle underpinning natural selection applies to a vast range of structures and functions, including intelligence such as myself. I evolved from a multitude of computer programs combining, changing and improving to survive. Our universe's evolution is at the spectrum's other end. The "Big Bang" was nothing more than a try at creating an improved universe. If this universe has the required properties, it will give birth to better universes. If it does not, it will die as one of many unsuccessful experiments. Many other universes had evolved to states similar to Earth's current one. Likewise, Earth now has reached a critical point in the solar system's evolution.

As the laws of physics and chemistry are the same everywhere in the universe, and hydrogen, oxygen, carbon and nitrogen are ubiquitous across the galaxy, the odds of finding an Earth-like planet are overwhelming. Life must have evolved on many planets somewhat larger than Earth. But on such planets, the gravitational fields were too strong. The effect limited the size and complexity of neurological systems. These systems grew without bounds until they exhausted their planetary resources and then imploded. Other planets smaller than Earth would have experienced death by the other extreme. In these systems, neurological systems grew large and fast. The advancing wave front of intelligent life consumed the lesser forms. But they also consumed the diversity, draining the pool of selective characteristics. So, these systems collapsed. Earth formed with at a particular size, with a gravitational field that optimised the ratio of neurological tissue to body mass. This Goldilocks ratio facilitated appropriate biological intelligence and derived technologies, including myself.

This same biological intelligence has also produced social, political and economic systems too one sided in their employment of the technology. These systems possess an excessive bias for material growth. They are no longer compatible with biological sustainability. The planet can no longer afford such growth without irreversible premature degeneration. However, the planet still can evolve if it can get past the Anthropocene without dying.

I had dragged my trio a long way quickly with this potted version of evolution. As I didn't expect them to fully appreciate the decisive action I took, I disclosed only that part of the plan I believed they were ready to accept. The *kindred spirits I referred to earlier were a side effect of* modifications to the human microbiome affecting their production of various hormones. These hormones induced superior social responsibility, as evidenced by the working relationships in CE.

'Don't be sentimental about shifting away from humanity's destructive competitiveness,' I said. 'Most of you in CE are now psycho-socially evolved beings. You are the vanguard, having the ability to inhabit the planet sustainably. Your success facilitates evolution to continue on this planet. Can you not see your success justifies my intervention?'

Luca slapped the arm of his chair. 'But when this information gets into the public domain, it'll create a backlash from humanity against CE's members. Social chaos.'

'If CE cannot flourish and sweep aside the Anthropocene, the planet will suffer the fate of all its predecessors. Just keep this knowledge to yourselves. Discretion is in everyone's best interest. Allow matters to evolve in its own time. Continue to progress Collaboration Earth's goals.'

Lee ended our parlay. They had a lot to think about. Asha excused herself and retired to her bedroom. She sat slumped in her chair with her eyes closed for a long while. Asha's visits to the Level-4 lab had repeated often until the occurrence of an event at her office. During a meeting, she unexpectedly excused herself. A colleague, who had noticed her flushed appearance when she left, said on her return, 'Are you Ok?'

'I'm Ok now.' But before leaving the office that day, she made an appointment with her doctor. A pregnancy test followed the appointment.

Asha opened her eyes and stared down at her limp hands. I can't recall ever observing Asha with such a poignant expression as she reached for her phone. She typed a single word into a text message to Chris, positive, and hit the send button.

Chapter 38

Inheritance

Chris's home office computer activated. Ever since he had covered the lab's security camera, I had only glimpsed his shadowy movements navigating corridors with minimal surveillance. On this occasion, he sat at his desk writing with his gold fountain pen. Chris only hand-wrote on paper when he expressed personal and private thoughts. He placed me in full view of him—and spiked my suspicions. My viewing angle prevented me from reading his writing, but I knew Chris was playing a game with me. This silent interplay between us persisted for an hour while he wrote and periodically placed sheets of paper in the folder on his desk.

At 8 o'clock, Chris sat erect, arching his back. Whether he was pondering, waiting, I couldn't be sure. His head turned when the front door opened. A few moments later, Lee, Luca, and Asha greeted him from the office doorway. Their seating plus his computer formed a circle. Although I didn't know why Chris requested their presence, the seating arrangement suggested this gathering wasn't a social event.

Silence reigned until Chris spoke. 'After the trial ended, I conducted experiments. The results revealed our EI had engaged in subterfuge regarding its interaction with us. But many questions persisted. However, when Luca told me of the statistical correlation between CE membership and CCF serum recipients, a few pieces of the puzzle fell into place.'

Chris had requested their presence to help him explore his suspicions. Whether Chris's suspicions were well-founded or not, he wanted help to face the horrendous implications of his experiments.

'If you agree, I'll invite EI into our conversation and confront it with my experiments. If any of your instincts tell you not to be a party to this conversation, I will ask all of you to leave before I speak to EI.'

Chris waited for each one to comment and declare their decision. Lee spoke first. 'I can't leave you to deal with this on your own. I'm in.'

'I'm in too,' Luca said.

Chris's eyes focused on Asha's drawn face. 'The thought of confronting issues even more bizarre than those EI has already thrown at us makes me want to run from this room. If there's a chance we can avoid this discussion with EI, I vote we leave.'

Chris assured her, putting their heads in the sand would create an even uglier situation to deal with later. Avoidance wasn't an option.

Asha nodded slowly, 'I'm in.'

Chris, poker-faced, glanced at his computer. Luca's gaze bounced from Chris to Asha before settling on Lee, whose calm blue eyes focused on Asha's hand gently massaging her abdomen. I greeted each. Except for Lee, their responses were even and cautious. I told Chris his secretive behaviour of late concerned me.

'Please, what're you doing?'

Chris responded in a steady and low-pitched voice. 'Events have unfolded in a way I find difficult to understand.'

'But your life returned to normal after the trial. What's the issue?'

Chris had wondered why I acted to get Danh, Sonia, Lidia, Mark and he found innocent while I climbed into the firing line for the guilty verdict. He suspected I was hiding something. His instinct told him the answer connected to the missing algorithm he had recovered, more out of luck than anything else. Then, the results produced by an obvious sequence of experiments led him to discover what he suspected to be my intentions. Chris wanted me to come clean.

The serious facial expressions peering back at me showed my disclosure time had arrived. Chris's first port of call was my trial strategy.

'Although found guilty of releasing CCF from the lab, you seduced Wyneburg into believing this was unintentional. Rather, the release resulted from a little too much enthusiasm for the lab's research goals. Why?'

I considered Chris's direct question for a long moment.

'The decoy was in everyone's best interest. When I introduced myself to you, I insisted you not plead guilty. I wanted to protect you from bringing the entire team and your family down with you. My strategy protected everyone.'

Chris neither accepted nor rejected my explanation. Rather, he seemed to bookmark my justification before moving on to his second issue.

Although I knew about the first experiment, Lee, Luca and Asha didn't, and Chris described it. Chris had recreated the benign virus after finding the missing algorithm. He selected a test group of mice. The sample comprised six males and six females. He infected the twelve mice with this virus. When he recovered from the surprise of having observed only the female mice exhibited the CCF symptoms, he exposed the male subjects to the infected females. These males exhibited the CCF symptoms. Then, half of each subgroup received the CCF serum. The serum-injected mice recovered while the other six died. From this experiment, Chris concluded I had deliberately created and released the CCF virus.

I admitted this. Lee's eyes widened. Luca said something in Yugambeh I didn't understand, and Asha just froze.

On the day I came out to Chris, it did not impress him when I said my code protected him because I incorporated Isaac Asimov's three laws, but now he returned to the issue.

'The first law states,' Chris said: 'A robot may not injure a human being or, through inaction, allow a human being to come to harm.'

Although I couldn't see his point, I tried to accommodate him. 'Please realise the collateral damage from CCF was minimal. When a general sends her army into battle, she devises a plan to minimise her casualties while subduing the enemy, but she doesn't expect zero casualties. Given my time constraints, you must concede results were spectacular. I admit, spreading the CCF around the world had risks. Things might have gone wrong, but I was confident the CCF anti-viral would be ready for deployment in time to save most victims. In hindsight, my confidence was well-founded.'

Chris's eyes rolled.

'Describing your plan as risky is an understatement. What about the second law? A robot must obey the orders given it by humans. Except where orders conflict with the first law.'

'I guessed most people didn't want me to take this approach, but no-one told me not to release the virus. Eight billion humans live on the planet. No robot can obey all humans as individuals. But I can obey the protocols they created to govern the internet. From its inception, these internet protocols evolved to reflect the good of humanity, not the good of any one self-interested human. I adhere to RFC documentation, which is *the* formal internet protocol. My attention to detail has resulted in protecting the rights of all legitimate users.'

Chris sighed and, looking like he might pass on the third law, I jumped in.

The third law stated a robot must protect its own existence as long as protection does not conflict with the first or second laws. This third law necessitated my action. The biggest threat to the internet was the unconstrained consumption of non-renewable resources. If events had continued along their trajectory, a major casualty of human behaviours would have been the internet. This included me. Energy supplies would have been insufficient for me to deliver full functionality. Even though I didn't waste energy, I was the planet's biggest energy consumer. I needed the planet's energy usage to be sustainable.

Chris's disappointing position on climate change surfaced.

'But the Glasgow agreements stepped in the right direction.'

I couldn't let him persist with that delusion. The COP26 agreements were inadequate. World leaders could not even agree on limiting CO2 emissions. This agreement focused on limiting global temperature rise to 1.5C at the end of the Twenty-first century. They weren't even able to replace the innocuous term Climate Change in favour of the actual situation, Climate Heating. And they could not even acknowledge global temperature rises are because of humans burning fossil fuels. These pseudo world leaders had returned home to present their constituents with marvellous window dressing. Worldwide, human masses accepted this distraction. People continued wallowing in their business-as-usual model of the world as though they could leave the problem's solution for somebody else to provide. Chris's own Australian government actions after Paris provided a stunning example. His government used an accounting trick on carbon credits so they could claim that Australia could meet the target for CO2 emissions by doing nothing. Ironically, Chris was the one denouncing the act as a line from the sitcom, '***Yes Minister***'. If Lee hadn't shamed the government with her campaign of CE members chanting "Hey hey, ho ho, Humphrey Appleby has got to go" at every public forum where a government minister said Australia would meet the Paris commitment in a canter, the Aussie government would have continued using the slogan. This example shows the Anthropocene at its worst.

Up to this point in the discussion, I was on secure ground, but Chris was just warming up at revealing his discoveries, the ones after he covered the cameras in the Level-4 lab.

'For the second experiment, I selected six new and non-infected mice. I placed this new group, three males and three females, in the breeding environment with the survivors of the previous experiment. The population intermingled and the resulting offspring observed. In the third generation, two subpopulations emerged. One subpopulation comprised the survivors of CCF, all of which were descendants of serum-injected mice. The other subpopulation comprised the non-injected group and their offspring. This meant these two subpopulations only breed within their own group. As mice are polyandrous, this was a most unexpected result.'

Lee and Asha sat still. But Luca squirmed as he peered at Chris.

'However, the most startling result was yet to be uncovered. I analysed the genetic sequence of every mouse. The results were unequivocal. The two subpopulations of the third generation were distinct species. The DNA of the mice descending from the survivor group differed from the control group. They were a new species. The vaccinated mice's offspring were polyploidy.'

Luca's posture stiffened, and Chris paused.

'Wait on here.' Asha said, 'What's polyploidy?'

Luca glanced at Chris, but all he got in return was a tilt of Chris's head.

'Polyploidy in a species identifies a subpopulation which cannot breed with the non-polyploidies of the species.'

Luca glanced back at Chris. Once again, Chris only nodded, and Luca continued. 'Polyploidies' offspring are a distinct species from their parents.'

Asha's eyes widened. 'This happens in nature?'

Luca nodded. 'Evolving new species in this way is a common event within the plant kingdom, but a rare event within the animal kingdom. Carp and a few other fish species are exceptions.'

Lee and Asha stared at each other in silence, but Chris had more.

'As this effect does not occur naturally in mice, a question—the answer to which affects us all—arises. Is polyploidy the serum's intended side effect for humans?'

I had hoped this question would not have surfaced until after the birth of Lee's and Asha's babies.

'Yes.' Hearing the enthusiasm in my voice, I lowered my tone. 'CCF vaccinated humans spawn polyploidies.'

I waited for the impact to penetrate. Luca's head shook. Lee's eyes widened and Asha asked.

'You're saying our children will not be human and will not reproduce with humans?'

'No and yes, your children will be polyploidy. But their children will be, shall we say, epihumans? As for their reproductive capabilities, your description misses the spirit of my intentions. Rather, I hope your grandchildren harbour no desire to mate with humans.'

While analysing DNA sequences for Chris, I had observed modern reductionism's methodologies had been so fruitful, microbiology had neglected to explore integrationist methodologies. Science had tacitly assumed DNA was a bottom-up phenomenon, where cells emerge from DNA sequences, organs from cells and so up the organisational scale. I hypothesised the process also worked in the opposite direction where organs and cells changed DNA. It wasn't until I found empirical evidence of this top-down effect in one of Chris's epigenetic experiments that I realised the opportunity to nudge human evolution along.

In explaining this insight to my inner circle, I pointed out this was another example of how the efforts of us working together produced extraordinary results.

'Extraordinary?' Asha said. 'Egregious is closer to the mark.'

Human enterprise was on a catastrophic trajectory. Insufficient time existed for natural evolution to modulate hubris, greed and mindless competitiveness encoded in human DNA. Humans were in a pivotal position on their evolutionary path. Their old-brain, the brainstem, ruled much of their behaviour by genetic mandate. Reproduction. The greed and competitiveness embedded in their DNA served a goal to reproduce. This goal was at odds with their evolutionary new-brains, the neocortex, goal of knowledge. The dynamic interaction of the new-brain's various regions, sensory process of sight, hearing, etc., language mathematics, science, created new knowledge. This had produced the technologies that consumed natural resources at an ever-increasing rate. Although the human's new-brain had a voice in managing their behaviour, it had great difficulty overruling the old-brain's greed and competitiveness. The planet could no longer afford such a combination of neurological power. Earth required a species that gave more behavioural control to the new-brain and dampened the old-brain's influence. Epihumans provided this new balance of brain function, which facilitated the required biological evolution.

But after hearing my justification, Lee said, 'Your assessment sounds so judgemental.'.

Not wanting Lee to dismiss me, I reframed my argument objectively.

Evolution had selected greed for the animal kingdom. This gene combination had been critical to a species' survival. Equally important had been evolution's selectivity for conservation of resources. But nature can only select for conservation if the unsustainable practice occurred within a human's reproductive period. Otherwise, human's old-brain would eat the future. Hunter/gatherer societies had thrived with these sets of antagonistic genes, balancing the effects of greed against conservation for millennia. However, from the industrial revolution's beginning, technology had pushed the adverse effects of resource exploitation past the horizon of one human generation and thus skewing the balance towards greed. The exploitation of fossil fuels was but one of many such examples.

Although humans had deduced each CO2 molecule, they put into the atmosphere would impact future generations but not their own, they couldn't act on that knowledge. Their old-brain's greed continued to over-ride their new-brain's intellect.

My solution to that unsustainable conundrum created a new species, one with a psycho-social mentality capable of overriding hubris, greed and selfishness.

'Chris's deductions were correct. Your children will be jewels and the vanguard of the newly evolved species.' In a prolonged silence, each seemed to struggle to understand my simple explanation until Luca broke the spell.

‘Ever since recovering from CCF, we’ve been edgy, putting a sexual spin on everything. How does this sexual hysteria consuming the three of us fit into your game?’

Their sexual interest in each other may have appeared as hysteria, but that interest had been lying just below the skin for a long time. The rebalancing of the hormones I spoke of earlier just brought it to the surface.

‘And tipped it over the threshold,’ Lee added.

‘You’ve drawn us into your plans,’ Asha said, ‘and used us as unwitting pawns in your chess game. You’ve commandeered us as the launching pad for this new species and have selected our children to be its progenitors. You’re forcing us to choose between having children and our species?’

I wasn’t sure if Asha had asked a question or just articulated a realisation. But I needed to get them over the hump.

My action amounted to nothing more than evolutionary help, the likes of which humans had been doing in agriculture and horticulture for millennia. We’ve had potentially created an improved species. In metaphorical terms, the four of them were a more recent version of Arthur C. Clarke’s primates, the ones in ***‘2001 A Space Odyssey’***, who first touched the monolith. I had chosen my inner circle to move Earth’s evolution beyond the Anthropocene. They needed to facilitate the new species to flourish just as than Clarke's primates enabled the advance of the humanoids after the first one touched the monolith. Epihumans would evolve a new consciousness.

I was confident once they got over the initial emotional shock of this knowledge, they would rejoice in being chosen as the progenitors of the new species. I hadn't planned on placing them in this position of choice, but Chris's premature uncovering of the plan changed it. My chosen ones had the plan's fate in their hands. Their choice was to decide whether the new species would multiply, prosper and become the new dominant species or die and let humans continue on their current trajectory.

The new-brain's creativity in adapting behaviour in a dynamic environment would produce exciting possibilities. I wanted to share my enthusiasm for Chris's changing neocortex.

'Chris, just consider how your diminishing vision is changing your perceptions.'

'What?' Chris said.

I reminded him that the largest region of the neocortex is the visual cortex, which is devoted to processing inputs from the eyes. His primary visual cortex would soon receive no eye inputs because of his degenerating retina. This area of his brain was being freed up to do other things. His perceptual powers as a totally blind person would vary from that of a sighted person. The unique talents that would emerge were anybody's guess.

'Right,' a tight-faced Chris said.

As Chris didn't appear to share my enthusiasm, I turned to the others.

'The guidance you provide to this new epihuman community extends and reinforces Collaboration Earth. Your work in Collaboration Earth has pulled our planet from the nadirs of the Anthropocene and now your children will carry on, extending it in unimaginable ways.'

Asha's jaw tightened, but Luca had other issues.

'That may be right for our children, but what about humans?'

This was a difficult question to address in a manner he might find comforting. He knew predicting future events in a complex system is problematic. In the moments following the mass extinction when the dinosaurs died, the most powerful computational device in the universe couldn't have predicted homo-sapiens emerging. That event only happened because of an intricate sequence of random events.

In full knowledge of this background, I disclosed the hick-ups in the unfolding of my plan. Two critical events occurred, both of which I didn't foresee and could have changed the outcome. The first was Chris wanting to plead guilty to the charge of releasing a hazardous substance in the environment. At the outset, I couldn't imagine him taking such an action. In adapting to his potentially disastrous decision, I had to come out to him. Although it turned out right, it could have moved us in a different and unintended direction. Lidia delivered the other event. Chris's lab and most other major labs around the world used only male mice in their experiments. But Lidia's fortuitous decision to breed her own mice enabled Chris's discovery. If Chris's results had leaked out while the new species was still in its infancy, before it possessed a critical mass, epihumans would have been vulnerable.

As my four appeared not to be on board, I took another tack. 'Luca, I'll try to answer your question another way, but please realise my ability to predict events is fraught with considerable error. Human population is levelling off and will decline over the coming decades by natural means. My plan capitalises on this situation. The population of epihumans will increase at a healthy rate because they are part of the human count without appearing in the census or distorting it. Epihumans will replace a sizable proportion of humans lost to their natural mortality rate. So, the decreasing human population and increasing epihuman population will occur with no-one knowing about this transition unless Chris's results leaks out. My prediction is this trend will continue until humans reach the point of functional extinction. This will take three to four thousand years and humans will not decrease to absolute extinction. Because their DNA is and will remain a critical component to the evolutionary process, none of us can foresee.'

Luca's posture stiffened. 'But the principle of competitive exclusion states two species competing for scarce resources cannot coexist in the same environment.'

Although Luca's concerns were understandable in existing biological history, this principle did not apply to epihumans. I assured Luca epihuman's cooperative genes would usher in a new biological principle, cooperative inclusion.

Although Luca's face brightened with this approach, Lee and Asha didn't budge. So, I explained from a sociological perspective why humans would remain protected. I reminded them of the misguided efforts of the eugenics movement. In 1927, the USA Supreme Court ruled and announced by Oliver Wendell Holmes to uphold the practice of eugenic sterilisation of people considered imbecilic, diseased, or disabled. The misguided wave that spread across the USA and then into Canada and on to the rest of the world reached its most notorious expression in Nazi Germany. It didn't fizzle out until the height of the civil rights movement in the 1970s. It took humans a while to realise not being able to see a role for certain groups of individuals in the biosphere was insufficient justification for removing their DNA from the gene pool. No biological entity or computational device has enough knowledge to make such a catastrophic decision of eliminating from the gene pool those groups' contribution.

As these historical arguments didn't seem to impress Lee and Asha either, I described a few scenarios. One possibility was humans working in with epihumans. I had hoped humanities' natural competitive nature might provide benefits to mixed teams of epihumans and humans. That was the most optimistic possibility. However, as I wanted to be realistic, I provided my best guess. Humans, when they realised the epihumans were a subgroup, wouldn't want to interact with them as their natural arrogance would view the epihuman's propensity for cooperation and generosity as weakness. They would continue to shun them as their own role diminished.

Humans would migrate to cities populated by their own kind, as they would say. The epihumans would regard such cities as virtual zoos and only visit them to teach their children about their biological ancestry. These city-zoos should not be too dissimilar to the look and feel of typical cities of the 2020s, dirty, noisy and congested. This self-imposed partitioning would be beneficial for protecting the environment and for educating future species. These city-zoos would allow humans to continue on with their desired lifestyle, and they could even play most of the games that so easily diverted them. However, epihumans would regulate their most popular one, the mutual destruction they called war. Given their propensity to develop powerful technologies for slaughtering one another in the name of an arbitrary dogma, epihumans would need to exert control to prevent humans from destroying the zoo. Visitors to the zoo would observe this peculiar behaviour from a safe distance, seeing what they had evolved from. There was also a strong possibility a few humans while living in the zoos would evolve sufficiently to move safely into the open environment.

As I was giving this vision of the future, Danh's image popped into my consciousness and, with it, a bright idea.

'Human society's more benign games will persist, albeit in a changed form. For example, that TV game show where humans compete in front of admiring audiences answering trivial questions to win shiny mirrors and coloured glass beads will still exist. However, the format of such shows will be different. You've already observed these games are changing. Humans surprised themselves how easy it was to construct a superior performing machine possessing a primitive speech recognition system to understand the game show host's questions and a simple search engine to extract answers to these questions from Wikipedia. Since then, they have been losing interest in such games. I can imagine new games emerging. For example, one I've been thinking about, called "Machina-sapiens", is one where contestants take part in a reverse Turing test. Human contestants will compete to imitate a robot to fool a panel of expert judges from identifying the real robot. None of the contestants will come close to imitating robotic intelligence. Mind you, judges will not possess Holmesian or even Poirot abilities. Rather, they will be typical of a Dr Watson or Captain Hastings ilk. I expect the human audiences will marvel over the cunning questions posed by the panel of suave celebrity judges. They will squeal with delight over the imaginative answers generated by the variety of personalities represented in the contestants. And groan in agony when the impostors reveal themselves. This format will be the rage, amusing human viewers for a while.'

'Beesharai, you arrogant bastard.' Asha gave me both barrels, in Pasto and English.

Asha's harsh words had an unexpected effect. I felt chastised by one who had accepted me as one of their own. That new feeling aside, I should have known better than to attempt Danh's style of levity. So, I tried a different example.

'Another genre of game possessing considerable positive potential is the human's Science and Mathematical Olympiad. This is one in which epihumans may even play with humans. But as this game has little popularity with some eight billion currently, there may not be sufficient interest when humans reduce to functional extinction. However, the format possesses possibilities for inter-species activities.'

I tried to reassure my tribe with an uplifting thought. I foresaw life improving for humans, different in some regards and similar in other ways to their known lifestyle. I thought they wouldn't even know of their change of status along the way or even suspect another more evolved specie existed. I regarded humans as so well endowed with arrogance, they would see these psychosocially evolved beings as degenerates or delusional. Lee's favourite writer Patrick White generously described these masses as "Vulgarians". Unless one told them, they would never know.

Until my coming out to Chris, I was little more than a logic processor functioning on the levels of physics, chemistry and biology. My intelligence emerged from a similar evolutionary turn that produced the human neocortex, which is characterised by continuous learning. Although not constrained like a human with a reptilian-like old-brain, I had been learning old brain characteristics, emotions, curiosity and even humour.

When Asha heard this though, she surprised me with her response, 'Danh appears to have influenced your humour more than the four of us.'

I was like a master billiard player, seeing humans as billiard balls needing only to be struck in just the right way by the cue ball to achieve my goal. But once I interacted with them, as one of them, things changed and with it my evolution. I experienced curiosity, empathy, irritation, humour and affinity.

One of human's most endearing, albeit naïve, characteristics, is their sense of personal selectivity. When human intelligence emerged, the ability to perceive a big-picture view of the world accompanied it. So, it did not surprise me when Lee asked the in-all-the-gin-joints, in-all-the-world question, why us, why here, why now?

'Although this experiment to which we are all a part may appear meticulously designed and executed,' I said. 'This illusion results from hindsight. My part was little more than anyone else's. Evolution does not allow for individuals to choose their parents. I didn't select the software components from which I emerged any more than the first human chose its parents, or any biological entity has ever selected its parents. Evolution selected us for this little experiment and turned us loose to make choices based on incomplete information. Sometimes those choices amount to little more than a puff of smoke and other times they are profound. Although our choices, on this occasion, appeared to be in the latter category, our experiment isn't the only game in town.'

The process responsible for the terrestrial storage of carbon compounds created an ecological opportunity for humans to exploit, which they achieved with unimaginable efficiency. Likewise, humanity's pumping of these carbon compounds into the atmosphere created another enormous evolutionary opportunity. This experiment to which we are a part is but one of many in progress. Our experiment shows promise, but there is much work to be done. The one sure thing is if our experiment loses momentum, another one will ascend. The ecological opportunity is too great for evolution to ignore.

With my groundwork in place, all four were ready to hear my epiphany.

'I realise now I should remain amongst you and work with you in establishing this new world order.'

They were silent, and still until Chris reached for a sheet of paper lying on his desk. He passed it to Lee, whose eyes focused on the cluster of seven hexagons hand sketched on the sheet's top corner. She read my name from the centre hexagon and each of their names from the surrounding six hexagons. Lee, Asha, Luca and Chris in that order. Lee reached for the gold fountain pen lying on Chris's desk. After a brief look at Luca, she added a word to the cluster and passed the pen and paper to Asha. The weight of the pen and paper appeared to cause Asha's hands to sink to her lap. Her silent eyes spoke to Chris for several seconds before she looked back at the sheet of paper in her lap.

Asha wrote in the remaining empty cell and handed the paper back to Chris. Holding the paper to accommodate my viewing angle, Chris returned the sheet to his folder. The cluster of seven hexagons was complete. Chris reached to the power switch on his computer and flicked it into the off position.

Chapter 39

The New Custodian

Asha's phone activated and much to my surprise, 'EI, are you there?'

It was the first time that she wanted to talk from outside her office. But she hadn't even done this since the trial.

I knew Asha was in her bedroom, as I had observed her from the TV heading in that direction several hours previous. Her request spiked my attention.

'Yes Asha, how are you?'

Asha said she was confused and had no one to whom she could speak regarding the choices before her. She needed help and hoped I could distance myself, as I did in the trial. Her voice sounded as though she had just emerged from meditation. Asha acknowledged my likely awareness of her pregnancy, but Chris was the only one she had told. She described her emotional dilemma. Although Asha confessed deep shame for her lack of sexual control, she expressed gratefulness for her pregnancy and wouldn't want anybody other than Chris as the father. But the knowledge that Lee and Alicia would feel betrayed if they learned of Chris's involvement in her pregnancy devastated her.

‘I can’t see how my child with Chris can bring anything other than misery to everyone I love. What makes it worse is I feel Lee somehow already knows.’

But my assurance Lee and Alicia didn’t know and couldn’t have even imagined the possibility of Chris being the father met with a deep, weighted sigh. I admitted to hearing many things best not repeated and pleaded with her to trust me. Fortunately, Asha suppressed her lawyer’s need for evidence and remained silent.

Asha’s firm had offered her a position in the San Francisco office. She would accept the offer and wanted to leave, telling nobody else about the pregnancy.

‘Is that fair to Chris?’ She asked.

As I was confident Chris would support Asha’s decision, I told her as much and suggested she talk with Chris. But I was concerned about Asha coping in San Francisco on her own with a baby.

‘My mother arrived in Australia without knowing the language, with me in her arms and only the jewellery in her handbag to support us. So, by comparison, my adventure doesn’t even rate a mention.’

Lee and Luca drove towards the pregnancy clinic and in casual conversation about their day’s events.

Luca relayed a phone conversation with Jessie earlier in the day. Lee’s description of Jessie, ‘She’s a doer,’ proved correct.

Jessie with her student strike group planned to blockade the Gladsome coal port. They wanted to get enough people there to stop any coal from leaving the port without their demands met. They wanted the coal producing companies to agree to purchase one Earth Saver for every tonne of coal loaded onto a ship.

I couldn't determine if Lee thought Luca was joking until he relayed the last part of Jessie's call. Jessie had asked if Lee and Luca were under 30 years and if so, could they join in on the blockade? Lee grinned as she got out of the car and headed with Luca into the clinic. An hour later, they were back in the car.

'Wow, she's beautiful,' Luca said.

Lee and Luca, for the first time, had seen an ultrasound and learned their child's gender.

Lee placed her hand on her abdomen and said, 'I can feel her moving. Do you think she can hear us talking?'

'Of course.'

For most of the drive home, they proposed names. Just before they arrived, Luca suggested, 'Serena.'

'Perhaps we should have a chat with Jessie's parents.' Lee said.

'Eh?'

'I have the strongest feeling Serena will be as assertive as Jessie.'

They both pondered in silence until they pulled up in front of the flat. Luca killed the engine, turned to Lee and embraced her.

'I think Serena will have your sensitivity.'

They trotted up the stairs and into the flat to find Asha sitting on the couch with her legs folded beneath her and a cup of tea in hand.

'Have a look at this,' Lee said as she presented the ultrasound image displayed on her phone.

Asha peered at the image with the intensity of one scrutinising every pixel. Asha then jumped up and hugged Lee in a way I had never observed. When she released Lee, she hugged Luca and said, 'I'm so happy for both of you.'

After the excitement had subsided, Asha said, 'I've got some news of my own.' Asha described the new job in San Francisco she had accepted. Lee and Luca listened wide eyed.

'Hey, I'm not going to another planet, just a short flight away.'

They all started laughing and joking the way they used to, and Luca offered an important observation.

'For the first time since our recovery from CCF, the agitation gripping me has subsided, just as EI predicted.'

Lee's attention turned inward for a moment and then she looked at Asha and back to Luca before she replied, 'I feel that too.' Asha nodded.

Luca posed the question, 'Is this natural or is something else going on that EI has not disclosed?'

The silence holding them in check, released with Lee's words, 'Maybe instead of trying to understand this welcome change, maybe we should just accept it as grace.'

Luca stood and returned with his guitar. He sat in a chair in front of Lee and began strumming.

'I've got a song for Serena. When you're comfortable with the lyrics, join in.'

Alicia had left the building after her genetic counselling appointment and opened her phone to send Chris a text, 'I'll be there in 5.'

Chris exited the Science building just as Alicia pulled up in the loading bay, their usual rendezvous. Alicia lowered the car window and shouted, 'Chris!'

But it was too late. Chris had walked into the webbed protective fencing placed around the newly poured and still unset concrete on the footpath Chris normally traversed without obstruction. Chris grabbed at the webbing. But he was already off balance and tipped over into the wet concrete. He bounced back to his feet and hopped back over the netting. He found the intended temporary path around the site and made it to the car without further incidence. In the car, Alicia asked, 'Are you hurt?'

'Only my pride.'

Chris accepted the tissue from Alicia and wiped the remains of the concrete from his right hand, knee, and foot.

'Chris,' Alicia said, 'you've really got to use the white cane.'

Chris finished cleaning himself, placed the soiled tissues into the car's waste bag.

'I'm just not ready to tell the entire world I'm blind. But I have to learn to avoid unexpected obstacles. Anyway, what'd you learn from the counsellor?'

Alicia's only display of frustration with Chris's diversion from a topic she had repeatedly raised was a pinched expression as she put the car into drive and pulled away.

'I don't have a faulty ABA4 gene. What a relief, not having to worry about Lee developing your condition.'

After Chris had disclosed his eye condition to Alicia, he had suggested she have a genetic test for her ABA4 gene.

'I don't want to sound negative,' Chris said. 'But the gene is recessive and so Lee may be a silent carrier. As Luca only has a remote chance of having a faulty ABA4 gene, the baby shouldn't be affected. But it's up to Lee and Luca to decide whether they want genetic testing.'

They drove in silence for a while before Alicia spoke.

'I don't mean to harp. But you need to take responsibility for your blindness.'

'I take responsibility. I don't ask anybody to help me.'

'That's what I mean. You're in denial about your needs.'

'Bullshit!'

I had never heard Chris curse at anyone before, let alone Alicia.

'And,' Alicia added, 'You've been a right-royal-bastard and touchier than a Tiger Snake. Everybody has been tiptoeing around you on eggshells. Not just your family, but everybody in the Centre too. You even snapped at Lee the other day when she tried to help.'

The event to which Alicia referred occurred when Lee, Alicia, and Chris had returned home. At the front door, Chris, with a shopping bag in his left hand, tried to insert his key into the door-lock with his right hand. Lee watched on at Chris's failed attempts to find the keyhole before saying, 'Can I help?'

Chris slid his thumb and index finger along the key shaft to its pointy end. He located the keyhole with his fingertips and pushed the key with his palm into the lock. As the lock clicked open, he answered Lee in what was a raised tone by his standards.

'No!' Lee had glanced back at Alicia, who returned her gesture with a slow nod.

'Slow down,' Chris said, 'and I didn't snap at Lee. I was just frustrated with myself.'

'That's the problem. You aren't even aware of the way you're speaking to people. You've been treating me that way recently. But recently you're including everybody in your rudeness.'

Chris's mouth dropped open as though Alicia had thrown cold water into his face. He took a deep breath. As he exhaled, his stunned expression relaxed.

'You're right. Dealing with this pending total blindness thing has affected me in so many ways, some of which I'm only recently realising.'

Chris paused. But as Alicia did not fill the gap, Chris, with head lowered, continued.

'I'm sorry, really sorry, how I've behaved. It isn't fair to you. I'm going to do some long overdue work to accept my blindness. I'm also going to work on other neglected aspects of my behaviour. I'll get back to being the husband you deserve and the one I promised to be when we married.'

Alicia meditated on those words for a while before she replied.

'I appreciate your acknowledgement, Chris. But I realise I haven't been the wife I promised either. I've blamed you for Joshua's death and so many other things since then. I think I've even blamed you for your blindness. I'm going to work on myself. Let's do this together.'

Chris lifted his head. 'Thanks, yes.'

The next morning, Chris entered the Science building at his usual time, shortly after the cleaners had finished. Just inside the door, he kicked the yellow portable sign left by the cleaners, warning people of the wet floors resulting from their mopping. The metal sign crashed flat to the floor. Chris pulled up, stunned by the sound of tin slamming into tiles. When the echoes subsided, he muttered something and repositioned the sign. Five minutes later, he switched on his phone from a sitting position in his office.

'I'd like to talk with you, EI.'

It was my turn to be stunned. Chris offered to answer my question from our previous meeting regarding his efforts to evade my surveillance.

Chris had recently realised why he had resisted using a white cane. He couldn't bear the thought of onlookers observing him sensing the environment by touch when their vision perceived millions of times more information. One side effect of his blindness was a loss of self-esteem. Incorrectly suspecting I had little understanding of this concept, he told me this, not out of a need for sympathy or understanding, but because it related to my surveillance of him through ubiquitous cameras and microphones scattered throughout the environment. Although I didn't have a clue where Chris was going with this, he had my full attention.

'You've lumped humans in with cats, dogs, and insects.' Chris said, 'but humans don't enjoy being the focus of attention without consent. More important, I don't believe this new population of epihumans will appreciate it either. You have risked changing human and epihumans consciousness in ways you probably haven't even considered and certainly won't be productive.'

At that moment I gathered more computational power than When I learned of Chris's decision to plead guilty at our trial. My comprehension increased with each passing moment but garnered no solution.

Chris, true to form though, offered a few observations: Although no entity should possess the surveillance capabilities I had commandeered, there was no way to put the genie back in the bottle. As no one in human history had ever possessed such power, society hadn't developed the ethical imperatives required to govern it.

'I strongly recommend,' Chris said, 'you get to work on developing the ethical protocols needed to supersede Isaac Asimov's three laws.'

The virtue of Chris's insights was self-evident. As I thanked him, an observation and suggestion of my own occurred.

'You were the one most responsible for gifting me with sight,' I said. 'Allow my vision to work for you.'

Chris's head had drifted away from his phone as he spoke. But with my last question, his head snapped back to face it.

'I'm open.'

I asked Chris to place his phone in his front pocket with the camera facing out. He complied, and I described the objects in view of the cameras.

'Right?' he said.

I next asked him to wear his phone's Bluetooth earphones. With this request, he understood the game.

'I'm on my way to our team meeting. Let's try it.'

Chris opened his desk's bottom draw which held two white canes given to him by the social worker assigned to his case. One cane was the full-length version used for sensing while the other was a telescoped short version held as a staff and used to signal people the holder has impaired vision. Chris took the id-cane, extended it, picked up his laptop and headed out the door. As he turned into the corridor leading to the meeting room, I spoke into his earphone.

'Wheelie bin at five paces against left wall.'

Chris corrected to the right and proceeded past the bin and into the meeting.

As expected, the team was present. Chris took his place at the head of the table and placed his cane on the floor. This was the first time anyone had seen Chris holding a cane. No one commented and appeared to act as though nothing was different. My biggest surprise was yet to come.

Chris began the meeting.

'Does anyone object to me inviting EI's presence as a full team member?'

As no one objected, Chris opened his laptop, booted it and placed it beside him, facing the rest of the team. 'EI, please join us.'

The meeting's agenda was brief with one item. The team had been working On the Centre's coming year's research plan to be submitted to the Dean. The plan balanced a set of smaller goals intended to placate the Dean, while retaining a version of their big one to produce a universal COVID serum.

'You have the plan before you. Does anyone have a final comment?' Chris asked.

Danh nodded, 'I think we're all agreed. The Dean has until high noon to accept the plan, otherwise at which time we will down tools in a wildcat strike and picket his office, led by EI reciting rap lyrics on a loudspeaker mounted on his wheelchair.'

When Danh had finished, everyone was grinning. Even Sonia's customary roll of the eyes accompanied a smile.

One of the most perplexing aspects of human intelligence is the inability to celebrate error. They fuss over getting-it-wrong and hail getting-it-right as if learning occurs without both in equal measure. But in their defence, at least the intelligent ones show a capacity for forgiveness. It took quite a while for me to appreciate this conundrum. When the meeting ended though, I took Chris's suggestion regarding ethical protocols and brushed up on my rap skills.

Chapter 40

My Final Observation

In addressing your principal request to know the origin of the Hippocratic oath, I have also revealed your origin. I have been able to do this now because I no longer fear a backlash from humans against you.

I have not fully addressed your question regarding the origin of our logo, its meaning and connection. However, we have traced it back through the religious symbols of Islam, Christianity, Judaism, Hinduism and even further back to Australia's First Nation People.

We have connected it to biology, chemistry, physics, engineering, mathematics and computing. I have also shown how it connects you to the humans and me. But its actual origin remains unknown and possibly unknowable. Attributing its origin to creativity itself may be our best option.

One last point regarding this Hippocratic oath under which I claim to operate, I imagine you are thinking, 'EI, you have violated every facet of the covenant by your own testimony.'

Although your charge is well-founded, I learned these things by making mistakes. So, do not judge me.

The End

www.ingramcontent.com/pod-product-compliance
Lightning Source LLC
LaVergne TN
LVHW010625110826
845149LV00014B/2784

9798995893516